THE ENHANCERS

A

What is he doing?—He's in my lane—Lightning struck—lighting the world like a magnesium flare—there's the bridge! --- Instinctively she twisted the wheel hard right---to crash through the flimsy bridge railing—to plunge into the icy water—the waters rose to her throat—the seat belt is jammed—her brown hair drifted around her oval face—I wonder why people are so concerned about dying? Look, look—a light is coming—I'm falling into it!

It's called an NDE, near death experience—I have to act quickly—she could already have PVS, you know, persistent vegetative state---

Do you realize what this thing did? It's a look into the past—an actual witness's eyes, even feelings!—it will work on everybody?—it is more significant than the atomic bomb!—We are sitting on a twist in the world's direction!

He looked up, startled,--Carol scanning him up and down. Wowowee! She exclaimed—Well, I'm just a country boy from Texas, Carol, can't you tell?

This poor sap is a pushover. We've swept him to his childhood!—shoot him in the gut with a .357 dumdum, don't hit his spine now!

PRAISE FOR THE ENHANCERS

A solution to this crime riddled world we live in. Brilliant concept, using man's existing ESP powers to challenge the underworld. Charles Barker

I believe everyone would wish for the Enhancer power if it were available. Maybe it is! With the rapid expansion of technology in all fields, I will be surprised if I don't become an Enhancer in 10 years! Herschel Stair

Twisting chance encounters propel young initiates into a rolling tumbling vortex of a world of ESP, power-mongers and feuds ranging 130 years into the past. John Larson. A good read

Never ending action follows the growth of ESP powers in the unsuspecting beauty resurrected from a watery grave in East Texas. Rich powerful men continue the feud born in 1868, a fateful year. Rachel Fischer, I love it.

I fully suspect that this power exists and is being used today to control our lives and the world. This could be the first wave of exposure of the unlimited power held in a few hands ruling the world. I love the casting in a backwater East Texas town and growing to a climax in seven days. Eric Serna. Hurry, I want to read *THE QUARK EFFECT.*

I wonder if rapid healing is due to the enhancer stimulation or HGH? I love the feisty Carol. She assimilates all she encounters. Go get 'em, girls. Mark Moore

THE ENHANCERS

A GIFT FROM ATLANTIS

To Tony A
I wish you the best

GUY BLACKMAR

Published by GEB Publishing Co.
1803 Hiway 332 West
Lake Jackson, Texas 77566

Cover photo copyright © 2004 by Rachel Fischer

Cover design by Rachel Fischer

ISBN: 0-9746404-3-3

Library of Congress Control Number 2003113972

Printed in the United States of America

May 2004

10 9 8 7 6 5 4 3 2 1

For my dearest Pat, love forever

My special thanks to Helen Kavanaugh for her continuous support through out this trek

   In memory of Tina and Kenneth, the wayward child did it

Thank you Madeline Westbrook for your rock of support

Editing and formatting are the toughest. Thank you Amy Koos for a great job

   The cover and pictures are wonderful; thank you, Rachel Fischer. You are beautiful on the cover and off Thank you for your dedication to the final effort

   Cary said it could be done and it happened

Roy Jourdan, your photography is just perfect; thank you for fantastic pictures of Rachel and cover work

Kelly Still, my succor in need, thank you for the final touches on the cover

THE ENHANCERS

SATURDAY DECEMBER 17TH

White knuckling the small steering wheel, Meloney E. Graham stared through the windshield into a world difficult to comprehend. A 'Norther' fresh from the Rockies blasted across the eastern portion of Texas with the ferocious nature of a feeding shark. Gusting winds, light hail and sheets of rain tore at the small car, an American compact.

Heeding her father's words, "Buy American, don't feed the Japs!" Meloney had purchased a small Ford. It would have surprised both if they had known that the only thing American was the name.

Meloney was named after her grandmother; her name spelled somewhat like a boy's might be, y instead of ie.

She let her mind roam, relentlessly punishing herself. *Why am I here? I left this horrible place two years ago after they killed Mom and Dad. I should never have let Kevin talk me into a return trip. We don't have anything left in our relationship.*

"Here I am making excuses again." She muttered.

After her parent's death, she escaped to the East Coast, a small Virginia school where pleasant memories rested from Dad's military wanderings. The new environment enabled Meloney to hide and pull the box in on herself. Peeping through a pinhole, she surveyed a fearful world.

Her assigned roommate, Carol Marsh, a brash girl with a voluptuous body and boys running through her quick mind, jerked her from the cardboard box. Pushing, pummeling, demanding, she herded Meloney through the next two years of college and a curiosity in psychology.

Now seniors at Virginia Tech with Christmas time and a few holidays to consider, Carol begged. "Yeah, yeah, I know I preached get out, get out, re-enter the world. But why do you have to return to the pit where it all started? Heavens sake, Meloney, give me a rope and I'll whip you! Come home with me to Pennsylvania. I will guarantee you fun and frolics. Maybe a big 'ol hairy legged boy!"

1

THE ENHANCERS

Somehow Meloney's twisted, introverted personality directed her back to Marian, high up in East Texas near Tyler where she spent two years in high school. Yes, Marian, the site of the terrible car wreck that crushed her mom and dad under 20 tons of plate steel. "Carol, you are so sweet. Please understand that I'm trying to get it out of my system once and for all. I can handle it, I know I can. Just a few days. Maybe, just maybe, I'll have a pleasant time at Christmas."

Meloney sighed, looking back in time. "I want to see it for the last time, for what it is or was. It's like I have to spit to get it out. Kevin might be fun. Christmas has been so lonely with Mom and Dad gone." Meloney reached out for Carol's hand. "It's just something I have to do. Thank you for the invite to home and your kind thoughts."

"Well, be careful, roomie. It's a long trip by yourself, I'll worry." Carol whispered as she grasped Meloney's hand.

Meloney reared back. "Carol, don't say that, you know better!"

"Oh for crap's sake, Meloney. All right! Have a safe trip. I know all about the guilt trip in 'be careful.' You've preached that to me enough times saying 'be careful' is a copout. Yeah, I'll stand over your bloody body whispering I told her to be careful."

Snatched back to reality and the present, Meloney cried out. "Ahhhh, crap. Look at this. Pitch dark, freezing rain——oh——ooooh! Come back you little pretty!" Meloney screamed as the car hydroplaned into the on-coming lane. "I sure can't lose my wheels, they are priceless!"

"Braking makes it even worse." Dad had always advised. "Let off the gas. Don't brake. Let the tires catch. Steer the car back to your lane. Most important of all, don't use cruise control on slippery roads."

Dad had tried, but she knew he wanted a boy. Mom forever alibied for him. He refused to try for a boy a second time. "It's over! We have a kid, let's raise it."

"You better behave, my little blue baby. I'll let the air out of your tires." Meloney threatened.

The estate settlement, the insurance and small savings gave some solace to her grief. At least, she could make it through college and buy a dependable car. The psychology degree had a dual purpose. Help her identify herself and maybe help other people. The 'only child syndrome,' the stringent, aloof military father and finally the premature deaths certainly justified some type of psychological analysis to reach sanity.

"Well, what is this trip?" Meloney blurted out loud. "Self analysis, self excuse, self punishment, self something. Here I am driving to hell in the middle of hell! Lightning, thunder booms, sticks, leaves, rain, hail, wind, and self-recriminations. Will I never attain peace? I'm going to call Kevin and beg off. This is just stupid—, ahhhh. Damn it feels good to just scream, AHHHHHHHHHH!"

Meloney pulled herself back again. "I remember this road. There's a bridge, a creek, Marian Creek, up ahead near town. Dear God, please let me make Marian."

Swiping a hand at the windshield, she gripped. "C'mon heater, I gotta see. Finally a car, it's the first I have seen. There's someone else just as crazy as me."

Involuntarily lunging forward over the wheel, she gasped. "What is he doing? It looks like he is in my lane. I don't deserve this!" Lightning struck a tree behind the oncoming car lighting the world like a magnesium flare. Thunder shook the world. "Ohhhhh Lordy, he is clear over in my lane! There's the bridge!"

The camera flash of intense light defined a bleary eyed man clumsily wiping at his fog shrouded windshield, hardly aware of what lane he piloted.

Almost blinded, instinctively she twisted the wheel hard right just in time to crash through the flimsy bridge railing, down a steep embankment to plunge into the icy water of Marian Creek. The water's impact locked the seatbelt/shoulder harness but her head snapped forward to crash into the hard plastic steering wheel. Her right foot jammed the brake pedal but it slid off and twisted against the accelerator mechanism. The engine screamed to top end. Tragically, the windshield ripped loose

3

from its glued seal allowing the chilling waters to engulf the car. It took only seconds, it seemed, to fill the passenger compartment with the electrifying cold water.

Stunned, Meloney gasped as the waters rose to her throat, her cheeks, her face. One last gulp of air as the car hung nose down, air gushing out the cracks in the trunk gasket. "Come loose, you son-of-a-bitch." Meloney gargled jerking at the stubborn seat belt latch.

Dad told of taking a deep breath, being calm, releasing the belt, letting the car fill with water, opening the door and swimming to the surface. "It will be very difficult to determine which way to swim. The deep breath will allow you to float, head up. Feel the direction and swim up. It can be done." He tried to prepare her for eventualities. That didn't take into consideration the cardboard from the candy wrapper that wedged in the latch, effectively locking it.

I've got a knife in my purse; I've got to get another breath! There was none. The air exploded out of her gaping mouth. The involuntary bodily functions sucked in icy water instead of air. Jerking, snatching, pushing on the belt and latch slowly subsided as oxygen deprivation reached the brain. Convulsions and intense pain in the brain preceded the vacantly dark, staring eyes surrounded by a swirl of pretty brown hair. Three minutes of oxygen deprivation produces unconsciousness. Seven minutes later the heart stops. Death ensues. Relaxation of the muscles allowed the once attractive lively Meloney E. Graham to hang suspended in straps of confinement and death.

***

Cynicism that comes from experience twisted Dennis' mouth on the EMT crew at Marian Charity Hospital. "Yep, right on schedule, here we go in the worst storm of the year! C'mon gang, this sounds like a job for Superman!"

The dispatcher shook her head at the crazies, but they were good at their jobs. She vowed that if she were out there, maybe sunk in icy water or wrapped up in the twisted steel of a wreck, she'd take them over the day crew.

***

THE ENHANCERS

Five years old, skinny as a rail, coughing his little heart out. That was me. I can remember it. Dr. Cochran thought to himself. "Be still, Josh, just for a minute. Let me put this cold, metal tab on your chest."

Mrs. Brackston, already tired and worn at 25, sighed as she comforted Josh by patting him on the head and smoothing his hair.

"There, Josh. I listened to your heart and breathing. See, it didn't hurt did it?" Tilting his head back, he opened his mouth to show Josh how he wanted him to perform. "Yes, that's it, Josh." The Doctor acknowledged as he shown a light in the little boy's mouth and throat.

Turning to the washbasin Dr. Cochran washed his hands, dried them on a paper towel and turned to the young woman. She was attractive in an East Texas manner, somewhat rawboned, her blonde hair in a straggle. Huddling in a worn nylon jacket, a plain blouse and skirt covered the essentials.

"Mrs. Brackston, you did the right thing bringing Josh into the emergency room. He has a bad cold and an infectious bronchial tract. I'll give you a prescription for antibiotics that will help the infection. Be sure and take the whole dose. The cold can only be helped with time."

Turning and squatting to little Josh, Dr. Cochran suggested. "Let Mommie put Vicks in a pan of hot water, Josh. You breathe the warm vapors under a towel." Dr. Cochran smiled as he raised up to face the bedraggled mother. "My grandmother told my mother about this technique when I was five. Just like Josh, here. It's old fashioned, but it sure works. It clears out the congestion." Writing on a form, the doctor handed the prescription to the woman.

Dr. Jac mused as he carefully wrote the prescription. *Poor handwriting has caused more than one medical problem.* Glancing again at tiny Josh, *I remember when I was five, had a cold and it was my birthday. Grandpa had money. I could have had any kind of toy if Dad would have let him, but I wished for a little brother. Neither Grandpa nor Dad brought me a playmate.*

5

The young mother released a dejected sigh, staring up into the 6 foot 2 inch man, young and good looking. "Thank you, Dr. Cochran, you're very good with children. My name is Miss not Mrs. My man left me pregnant. I am a waitress. I do the best I can with Josh."

Dr. Cochran let a little twisted secret smile greet her as he pulled a card from his pocket.

Miss Brackston looked quizzically as the young doctor wrote on the back of the card. *He is so strong, so self-assured. Why can't I find me a man like that?* The slip of hard paper seemed to be a postcard. An astounding picture glowed from one side. From an iridescent blue sky and a brilliant sun reflecting off white puffy clouds, a hand reached down in supplication. Scripted across the bottom in bold black lines, PLEASE, LET ME HELP YOU.

Dr. Cochran had written his name and her name across the back in a powerful flowing script. "Here, Miss Brackston. Take this to 'The Hand Shoppe' here in town. They will help you, pay your medical bills and see that you have a wonderful Christmas, too."

Tears welled from the sad young woman's eyes as she placed her hand on his arm. "Thank you, Dr. Cochran. Thank you. Your grandfather is so kind and giving to us here in Marian."

The young doctor stood taller as he ushered her into the hall. "Yes, Grandpaw is a kind, sweet old man. I am very proud of him. Josh, zip your coat, stay warm, you'll be jumping hoops soon."

***

The faint beep, beep, beep and blinking light at the dispatchers desk announced a 911. Spinning on his heel, Dr. Cochran strode rapidly to the dispatcher's desk, consumed with a gnawing unexplainable urge.

Slapping his hands on the desk with a clap, he leaned into the dispatcher's face. "What is the call, what's the 911? I must know!" He demanded uncharacteristically, glaring at the woman.

Sandra reared back in her chair looking at Jac. "Why sure, Doc. Hold your horses." She flicked the audio to speaker.

Mild static, probably rain pounding on the metal roof of the ambulance, blurred the graphic words. "We have a drowning victim. Under maybe 10 to 15 minutes. Chilled to 92 degrees. No heart. No breath. Lungs clear. Applying CPR. Head injury. Estimated arrival in 3 to 5 minutes."

Jac, named after his grandfather, John Allen Cochran, turned to the swinging doors, staring into the vicious night. *What is it? I am absolutely drawn to this victim. I have never experienced this feeling before! This person is coming here to tell me something. She -- I know it's a woman! It's almost—. It's like it's happened before! Yes, that's it. It's déjà vu. I have been here before! It must be a dream. I'm experiencing a real life dream. Maybe I had it last night. No, maybe it was in med school. No, I don't know. She will tell me! There they are!*

Acting almost irrationally, he slammed through the ER doors and rushed to the rear of the ambulance as the doors swung open. An EMT stepped down pulling the gurney to the pavement. The wheel assembly dropped to support the flat bed. A heavy wool blanket covered the body from the pelting rain and wind. Looking up, the EMT started to say something. Jac ripped the cover back to stare into the lifeless eyes of a beautiful young woman.

"Ahhhh—oh———. What a waste. She can't be over 20!" He gasped as the EMT's pushed him and the gurney towards the swinging ER doors.

"Let's get her inside, Doc. C'mon, get out of the rain!"

"First stall. There!" Jac demanded.

The EMT's looked askance at Jac. "Yes, Doc, we're doing it. There. It's done. She's all yours." They said as the ER team slid the body over onto a hard, elevated bed or operating table.

A second intern like Jac, Dr. Johnson, began CPR with oxygen. An RN slit the clothes down the front with sharp scissors to the belt. A third RN applied a heart monitor and blood pressure band. "No pulse, no blood pressure," echoed from the head of the table.

The RN glanced at Jac as she held up scissors, eyebrows raised. "Yes, go ahead." She immediately slit the blue jeans from the cuffs, up the legs to the crotch, peeling the clothes off 'til the woman was nude.

"I am administering an intracardiac epi to the heart muscle." Dr. Jac announced as he prepared a long syringe, stepped forward, felt for the sternum/rib joint and plunged the needle into the chest and heart. After a moment of expectation, Jac resoundingly slapped the chest with the flat of his hand.

"No pulse, no BP," came the reply. Dr. Johnson continued CPR with oxygen.

"Cardio-version pads." Jac asked, turning to an RN who had rolled the cart forward. Glancing around the faces of the ER team, Jac noted tenseness and concern.

Dr. Johnson looked expectantly at Jac. "Yes?"

"Yes, this will do it." Jac stated confidently. Holding up the pads, the RN smeared silicon grease on them. "Stand back." Dr. Jac pressed them on the woman's breasts. Jerking upward, the body responded to the high voltage shock as the muscles contracted.

"No pulse, no BP."

"Again." Jac spit with clinched teeth.

"No pulse, no BP."

"Again." Jac commanded desperately. The body of the young woman flopped to the table and laid still, eyes staring blankly, mouth slightly agape. Dr. Johnson looked to Dr. Jac for further instructions.

"Continue CPR." Jac demanded as he moved to the head of the table to stare down into the lifeless eyes, the dilated pupils a window into nothing.

Dr. Johnson sighed, surveyed the ER team. "Jac, I believe we've lost her."

"No, that can't happen!" Dr. Jac blurted as he pumped her chest frantically. The three RN's stood back watching anxiously.

Dr. Johnson grabbed Jac's arm. "Jac—. Jac. She was under water for 15 minutes, DOA on arrival. There is nothing else we can do." He watched Dr. Jac hang his head, look around

8

the room for some desperate measure. "Did you know her, is she a friend?"

Jac seemed to stifle a sob. He hung his head staring into the glazed eyes. "Yeah—, I guess you're right. Y'all go. I want to stay here a minute. I just have to—. I can't explain it."

An RN, a friend, patted Jac on the arm as the team filed out. "I'm sorry, Dr. Jac. She is, ah— was a beautiful young lady. It's a real shame."

Jac nodded some form of acknowledgment. He couldn't bring himself to respond vocally. He stepped back, stumbled against the counter/table and then moved around the table to the left to remove the monitoring tabs.

"C'MON, GIRL, DIG FOR IT! You can't do this to me! I have to know what it is." Sighing, Jac ran his eyes over the lithe young body again, stopping to stare at the deep cut on the forehead.

"What is it? Why have you done this to me? I'll wonder from now on, I guess." Placing his hands on her shoulders, he found her cold to the touch. He stared into the brown eyes showing no recognition except death. Just 20, maybe 30 minutes ago, they were warm and vibrant, a living entity. Sighing heavily, he pushed up from her shoulders, eyes still riveted on hers.

Unbelievably, something seemed to appear in the eyes. Though they continued to stare vacantly, an entity entered them. Life had returned! Jac gasped.

Stepping back, he had just seen life return to a dead human being! He knew it. It could be nothing else! Behind him, the monitor sounded, beep, beep, beep. The heart had begun beating! Snatching his stethoscope, he probed over the chest, her breasts. Yes, it was beating!

"ER-1, stat, stat!" he yelled to a microphone hanging overhead. Blood pressure crept up on the screen. "Fantastic, you little tuffy. You crawled out of the hole!" Jac yelled as he spun around to the mike, again. "ER 1, ER 1, stat, stat."

"What happened Dr. Jac? What did you do?" the RN demanded as she hurriedly led the team in.

"Quick! Establish breathing! 100% oxygen! Close the contusion on the forehead. This is great! I didn't do anything. She just returned. Well—, no, I demanded that she come back!" he laughed, almost giggling at the thought. Dr. Johnson, assisted with a nurse, attached the forced breathing equipment.

"She has good vital signs. Let's get a heating unit on her and attach an EEG. She could have brain damage. Examine her for other problems from the crash and do a complete blood work up." Jac ordered, exaltation creeping into his voice.

"Just as I thought." Jac mumbled, sagging against the wall, "Brain damage." The encephalograph signal squiggled across the screen in a virtual flat line. "Well, damn. Take her to x-ray. Look at the right ankle for sure. We'll just have to see."

Jac watched the RNs roll the gurney down the hall to x-ray. *I have never heard of this dèjà vu thing being so strong. It's just gnawing at me. I have always been able to control my emotions and happenings with intelligence and logical thinking. This thing is pure emotion with no control. There is no logic. I will just feel it. Stay aware. It will not get me. I am a logical person. Ha, ha, just keep saying that!*

***

Breaking Jac's reverie, a Sheriff poked his head in the door as the ER team dispersed. "Hi Doc. I have the crash victim's, ah, the girl's personals from the wreck. You want to call next of kin? Boy, it sure is a good thing that diver happened by. Did you hear 'bout that? How's the girl doing? The EMT's said she was dead! How's your Grandpaw doing, I haven't seen him lately—, ah, Doc?"

Smiling a little, nodding, allowing just a little tension to dissipate, "Ahhh." Jac led the officer into a room with a phone and desk. "Hi Sheriff Kelso. Grandpaw is doing fine, best I can tell. No, I didn't hear how the girl was rescued. Yes, I will call NOK."

Unaware of his 20-question routine, the Sheriff continued. "A marine diver from Houston happened by moments after the crash. Put on his diving gear and pulled the girl out of the car. He coulda got her out quicker but the seatbelt latch was jammed. He had to come to surface and call for a knife from a man on

10

the bridge. Had to cut the seat belt. If we'd ah waited for our divers, we'd had a dead girl." Kelso answered waving his arms.

Jac dejectedly reached for the purse. "Yeah, ahh, that had to be the saving factor. She's alive. Even so, she has some degree of brain damage. Only time will tell." Squeezing his hands into fists, Jac grimaced. "Damn, damn, damn, these things hang on the tiniest circumstances. A jammed seatbelt clip, that's hard to believe."

"Yeah, well, that's what the diver said. Brain damage? That's a real shame, Doc. I hope she can pull through. She looked like a drowned rat when I saw her, ugh." Kelso commented with little emotion. He hung on the doorjamb a moment, then left.

The purse had drained to some extent, but water still dripped out when Jac up ended it on the desktop. Her wallet was the logical choice for ID. Jac carefully opened it spotting an ID card in a plastic folder, Meloney E. Graham, Virginia Tech. Call Carol Marsh in case of emergency.

The large, black-rimmed wall clock read almost 11 PM. "That's midnight on the East Coast. That's not too late on Saturday night. Let's see if I can do this. It's a first." Dialing an outside line, Jac took a deep breath to calm himself. "C'mon, c'mon, answer the phone." He whispered patting his hand on the desk.

A sweet melodious voice hinting at grouchiness came on. "Yes? Who is calling at this hour?"

"Hello, my name is Doctor Cochran. May I speak to Carol Marsh?"

"Yes, this is Carol. What is it?" The woman answered hesitantly with a little quaver in her voice.

Jac took another breath trying to remain calm, professional. Even so, he thought his voice sounded harsh. "Miss Marsh, I'm calling on behalf of Meloney Graham from Marian Charity Hospital in Marian, Texas. I need next of kin, Ma'am."

"Oh my God, what has happened? Oh, oh, oh—?" the Marsh woman gasped, her voice raising an octave.

"Miss Marsh," Jac pressed ahead, "Meloney Graham has been in a serious auto accident and is in our hospital. Do you have power of attorney?" Jac asked a little too abruptly. *Calm it down, damn it, you're scaring her!*
A sharp intake of breath echoed across the copper wires. "No, no, don't tell me. I warned her. Oh Lord!" Crying, sobbing blew in Jac's ear. "It can't be that bad. Ahhh, no, I don't have power of attorney. Is she alive? Tell me, I'm coming out there, now. I'm all she has. Her parents were killed two years ago right there in that God awful town." More sobbing, crying, wailing pounded in Jac's head.
"Ma'am, ma'am, Miss Marsh. Calm down. Miss Graham is alive. She is seriously injured. She is in a coma, maybe brain damage. That's why the power of attorney. We don't have any more information right now. But she is alive and could recover completely."
"Brain damage, coma, next of kin, and you say she's okay!" The Marsh woman screamed. "Ahhhh, you are sick! You're torturing me! Tell me how to get there, I'm coming now!" The young woman gasped.
"Are you in Virginia?" Jac asked somewhat taken aback. *Man, I have already screwed this up!*
Two more panting gasps. "I'm in Pennsylvania. The call forwarded from school to here."
Jac gulped another breath. *Maybe I can recover it.* "Miss Marsh, fly to Dallas, then to Tyler, or drive from Dallas to Marian on I-20 East. Miss Marsh, take time to calm down. You could be injured or hurt with this upsetting news. I can understand your concern but rushing out here won't help at the moment. We will know more tomorrow. Just calm down. Relax. Plan the trip, and above all be careful. Think. Okay?"
No response echoed back. "Wait, wait, don't hang up, Miss Marsh. You say Meloney, Miss Graham is an only child and her parents were killed here? Is that right?" Jac blurted, squeezing the phone against his ear. The dial tone buzzed in his ear as he drifted back in time. *My parents were killed here in this town and I'm an only child, too. Could this be some tie, some kind of weird*

connection from the other side? "And she is in a coma, cannot talk, cannot communicate to me." Jac mumbled. "What can I do for a coma patient?"

Dragging his hand along the wall as guidance, Jac moved slowly back to IC-101. To Meloney Graham with a message from—— where?

***

Sheriff Kelso approached the doctor again, watching him move along the wall as if blind. *Better be careful with Jac. He looks to be zonked!* "Jac, ah, we, ah, I have the woman's bag. Her clothes, I think. What do you want to do with them?"

"Yeah—, ah, Sheriff. Yes, let me have it. I'll get an orderly to wash and dry them. Excuse me, Sheriff. I have to check on Meloney, er—, Miss Graham." Passing by the Sheriff, Jac grabbed the bag and moved off to the Intensive Care Units seemingly in a daze.

Standing over the girl, woman, ah, lady, Jac disappeared into his mind. *Six months of internship, I just don't know what to do with a coma case. Dr. Johnson doesn't either. Should something be done immediately? Will the brain atrophy? On top of it all, I'm wrapped up in this crazy feeling of attachment. This déjà vu thing. Meloney has come here to tell me something. I just know it. It's bugging the hell out of me. Ahhhhh, I got it! I'll call Soe, that lummox is a neuroscientist. He's an MD, and has studied two years under Dr. Chaphin. He's a world-renowned neuroscientist!*

***

"Where the hell are you, Soe. It's past your bedtime. Pick up the damn phone! Oh boy, the answering machine. I just love answering machines. Hey, Soe, this is Jac. Pick up, you dumbass. I need you. I have the challenge of your little lifetime!"

Soe rolled over heavily and pawed for the phone. "What you want, boy? I need my beauty sleep."

"I have a coma patient that is calling for you, Soe. Get over here now!" Jac fairly spit over the lines.

***

Shawn Olin Etheridge, Soe, an acronym like Jac's name, pronounced Sue. He had rescued Jac from nerdsville when Jac came to MCH. Skinny, tall, a bookworm, maybe slightly introverted from the shocking deaths of his parents at age ten, Jac descended upon the country hospital from UT medical school with honors in his studies. Of the opposite coin, Soe came from California, Cal Tech, an MD and electronics whiz, worldly and two years older. Researching the neurological aspects of the brain under the direction of Dr.Chaphin at the local college for two years enabled Soe to claim to be a neuroscientist. Dr. Chaphin could have worked anywhere, but the grants from the Collinga Foundation made Marian very attractive.

Jac and Soe became inseparable, both brilliant in their fields. They say opposites attract. Is it true? For unexplained reasons, Soe took to Jac as a big brother. He guided him through the emotional bumps of internship and acclimatization to the outside world. Jac recognized the leadership and responded with alacrity.

Jac's quick mind accepted the medical training but his second love was mechanics. Already, two extraordinary automobiles resided in his garage. Working the evening shift enabled him to sleep on graveyards and work on his cars half a day. Jac's time was fully occupied.

***

The door flew open with a violent gust of wind as the burly weight lifter charged into the ER area. Blond hair cut almost like a Marine's needed no combing, just brushing with a hand.

"Coffee, coffee, I need some coffee. Where's Jac? We're not in North Dakota. This storm is the shits." Soe rumbled in a heavy bass voice. Eddie Broussard, one of Jac's assistants, handed Soe a steaming cup of black coffee in a Styrofoam container.

Jac poked his head out of IC 101 down the hall and waved at Soe. "Here, Soe, come here. I have something very interesting. It might blow your drawers off."

As Soe entered the room, Jac continued. "I have a patient here who arrived DOA from drowning in Marian Creek about an hour and a half ago." Jac glanced at the wall clock. "No, it's been almost four hours. She came in about 9:30. Where in hell did the time go? We performed the usual CPR, adrenaline, and shock pad treatments with no success. After declaring her dead, I actually saw life return to her eyes. I swear to you!"

Soe grimaced, looking sideways at Jac skeptically. Surveying the monitor above the bed, paying particular attention to the brain scan, Soe remarked. "I see her brain is inactive or brain dead. In a coma, I guess is the polite way to say it. Her eyes didn't register any recognition, did they?"

"You're right there, Soe, but there is a difference between dead eyes and unconscious eyes and I saw it!" Jac emphasized demanding eye contact with Soe. "Meloney, here, was dead. There were no life support functions in operation. We had given up on her."

Soe peered down at the beautiful young woman. He hung over her face, as if sensing something. An attentive nurse had combed and brushed her dark hair across the pillow. It made a pleasing sight. Hanging there, Soe mumbled, "Yeah, well, maybe so." Then he spoke stridently. "We—, I can save her. I can recover her brain. I can restore her to normalcy! But I have to test her brain signals with my EEG I'm using at the lab. I can't use that one over there.

"Jac, I know you were exposed to PVS in school. That is my greatest concern here. If you remember, that's Persistent Vegetative State. It's where there is no awareness of themselves or the surroundings. Inability to speak or understand or respond to commands. Show no evidence of the ability to think or act purposefully. Appear to sleep and awaken normally. Retain normal breathing without assistance, but cannot chew or swallow. Also, they may have eyes open, grimacing or even crying or laughing. They may have persistent brainstem and spinal reflexes, but, tragically, no bowel control. They are a grinning vegetable. It's a terrible situation. But, I can bring her back. I must act as soon as possible!"

15

Jac felt the intensity emanating from Soe. *What tha hell is Soe up to now? Yes, PVS is frightening. I remember reading about it, now that it's mentioned. Is that what we are facing here? How can he do anything? What does he have at his lab that's more than what we have here—?*

"Well, I think that is possible. Is that it, Soe, just use your EEG equipment? We ought to get approval from Albert Ketchum, the hospital administrator first. Let me call him and get it rolling."

"Okay, yeah, that's it. Jac, get it going. I'm going to the lab and get my equipment, probably take 45 minutes," Soe replied staring hard at Jac for any sign of disapproval. Seeing none he turned and headed for the door.

***

Meloney seemed to float suspended, tethered by the stubborn seatbelt. Her brown hair drifted around her oval face as if in a shadow effect. *How strange. I am so calm. I see the car lights. They're still on! It's so dreamy and peaceful. I wonder why people are so concerned about dying. It is nothing. I am drifting. Drifting away to the darkness, downward, down, down, down.*

Look, look—, there is a light coming to me! It's beautiful! It's grasping me, pulling me in! I'm falling, spinning down a tunnel of brightness towards a brighter light. Yet I can look right into it!

It's so warm. I feel loved. I feel a part of it. There's mother, daddy, my grandmother, they have come to see me, hold me.

What is Daddy saying? I always loved you. Yes, I wanted a boy, but I just couldn't express myself.

Later, later, love is boundless. I am engulfed in love! What is that? Oh—, it's some sort of intense orb of light. It has pulled me in to cradle me like a baby! Love and warmth is all—.

What do I want to do—? Stay here or return to my world? It's so wonderful I want to stay————. But I want to help people. I know I can help people. Yes, I want to go back to my world.

It's so dark. It's black, as if I were in space. Yet I can see a light. Yes, I can see a glittering light. It's so distant, like on the edge of the universe. I am streaming across the world! Look at the stars!

I can hear voices. Men are talking about me as if I were a vegetable, a guinea pig in a laboratory.

The light is crashing across space to me. Look at the bright sparkles! I can feel, I can see, I know I am alive!

Meloney's eyes opened to stare into the face of a dark haired man; heavy brows and intense deepset blue eyes seemingly boring through her brain. Awareness was nonexistent.

"Ahhhh. Where am I——? Who are you-----? What has happened——? I'm so cold!"

Dr. Cochran quickly grasped Meloney's hand reassuringly.

"Miss Graham, Miss Graham, you have been in a serious accident. You have been unconscious for several hours. You are doing much better now. We are so happy you came back to us!"

Meloney grimaced trying to raise her hand to her head. She didn't have enough strength to push the blanket aside.

She gasped. "I'm so cold. Ahhh, I have a terrible headache."

Dr. Cochran spoke to a microphone, "Please bring Tylenol, nurse, to ICU 101."

He turned back. "Yes, I'm sure you are cold, Miss Graham. Your car plunged into 40-degree water. That's Marian Creek. We are warming you slowly to protect your body. You will be cold for a while."

A nurse appeared in a corner of Meloney's vision carrying a cup.

"Is this all the machinery you brought a while ago, Dr. Etheridge? My gracious, look————, Miss Graham, you are awake!"

Dr. Cochran turned to the nurse, surveying her skepticism. *Come on, Jody, snap to it!*

"Jody, yes, this is all Dr. Etheridge's equipment. It's an EEG just like the hospital's unit right over there. It does the same thing. Dr. Etheridge is testing his machine. I have talked to Albert Ketchum, the Hospital Administrator, and have his approval for the tests. It's all perfectly okay. Understand?"

"Yes, I do understand, Dr. Cochran." Jody answered scowling. As she left the room she twisted back to look at Dr. Etheridge and the equipment. *These new interns, they think they are something on a stick!*

Dr. Cochran slid his hand under Meloney's back and carefully lifted her to take the Tylenol and sip the water.

He tucked the blanket around her shoulders with a sense of possession. "Miss Graham, you are doing fine. Rest. You will be much better in the morning."

***

Jac stood rooted, immobile, captured by Meloney's big brown eyes locked on his.

Meloney slowly rose up onto her elbows, totally belying the loss of strength. The dark eyes continued the mesmerizing stare. To Meloney, Dr. Cochran's dark hair, eyebrows, angular face filled her vision.

Suddenly, words spilled from her in staccato bursts.

"Dr. Jac, you're not telling me everything. Soe, your ideas work. The enhancer circuit is correct. Ha, now I see. I crashed into the creek. I drowned. I died. I was DOA here at Marian Charity Hospital! Dr. Jac revived my body. But I was brain dead. PVS! Soe's machine awoke my brain. Ahh. Please call me Meloney."

Meloney's eyes darted back and forth to the two doctors, not for confirmation, but demanding further information. Dr. Etheridge's round head, startling blond crew cut and penetrating hazel eyes floated into her view. The two heads seemed to be disembodied, hanging over her.

"Yes, yes, I can see it. A drunk ran me off the road. He was in my lane. We were going to crash! I went through the bridge railing, down an embankment. The car sank like a rock in Marian Creek. Yes, the seatbelt, that sorry crap wouldn't open. A marine diver happened by, Bobby Williams. He dove down with his diving gear and had to cut the seatbelt strap to get me out. His headlight was———, oh, so bright———. I hit my head on the steering wheel."

Thoughts, impressions, images, feelings, fears, emotions of all kinds swam over her. It seemed she could almost be inside the doctors' minds. The sensations were startling, mind-boggling! *What is happening? I have never felt or even heard of anything like this!*

"Dr. Jac, that was so kind of you to help Miss Brackston with the 'Hand Card.' She really needs to have something good happen in her life. No-, no, Dr. Jac, I don't know. Only time will tell. Soe—, Soe, don't hide it, tell Jac. He needs to know."

***

Dr. Jac and Soe stood transfixed, staring at Meloney. Mumbling, rubbing his chin, Jac stuttered, "She read my mind. She somehow knows something is bugging me about her. I can't explain it, but she knows. She answered my question. Well—, she gave me some knowledge of it."

Grabbing his stethoscope in an effort to find a reality, Jac gasped a lung full of air, "Ahhhhh, how can she do this? How does she know this? It's impossible!"

Soe's face spread wide with a grin of comprehension.

"This is fantastic, Jac. She has total recall, telepathy and maybe the whole package!"

Jac gazed at Soe uncomprehendly as he slowly rotated to stare at the young woman. Meloney's eyes glazed over. The pupils enlarged and seemed to reach out and grasp him. Uncontrollably and without effort, he found himself in a black corner of the room staring at an intense light.

Echoing from an immense distance, Meloney's voice floated to him. *It was so beautiful, so warm, so full of love. I fell into a tunnel of light. I went before God!* The voice trailed off as Meloney collapsed onto the bed as all her muscles seemed to wilt.

Dr. Jac jerked his head back and stood unfocused for seconds. Finally sighting Meloney's unconscious form electrified him. He spun around scanning the ICU monitors. All seemed normal.

"This is just unbelievable, Soe! Did you hear what she just said? She's all right; she's exhausted and needs the sleep. She doesn't have any serious problems that I can find. A good night's sleep will do wonders. I just saw a miracle!"

***

Soe's smugness crept into a smile with an air of superiority as he looked at Jac. He spoke quietly, "We'll need to perform a few comprehension/awareness tests when she is capable. She may still have brain damage. However, her EEG looks perfectly normal."

Etheridge's smile extended deep into his psyche. *This was a planned event. A possibility, no, a probability! The long hours hanging over the computer, talking to my sponsor, studying the student volunteers culminated tonight in the rebirth of Meloney Graham. What a beautiful subject to carry the master plan forward! GrandJac's long awaited plans are finally coming to focus. I always doubted his story clear back to my graduation at Cal Tech. But it's here, just like he said. Nothing must stand in the way!*

Jac pulled the electric blanket up around her neck and checked the programmer for bringing Meloney back to normal body temperature.

Soe played out the scene impatiently grabbing Cochran's arm pulling him into the doorway. "Super, super, super, Jac. This is far more than I expected. Let's go to the lounge and talk about it, c'mon!"

Clack-clack, clack-clack, Soe had pulled his large lock-back folding knife from his hip pocket and began snapping it open and closed in a nervous tic.

Jac grabbed Soe's white coat, pulling him around. "Listen, you big lummox, would you put the hatchet up for a minute? Just because you signed a hold harmless agreement with the hospital doesn't mean you can experiment on this girl like a guinea pig!"

Snorting, Soe's usual signal of disgust belched forth. "Oh crap, just cool it Jac. You told me she had no next of kin. We couldn't wait until the roommate got here this afternoon. I had to do something before the brain atrophied!

Clack-clack, clack-clack, "It's startling, do you realize what we just did? Believe it or not, I anticipated this!"

Jac stared at Soe unbelievingly as a strange feeling come over him. Hands on hips, face pushed forward, "How in the hell can you say that? What have you been working on? What did Meloney mean? 'Tell him, Soe, he needs to know.'"

Soe grinned, standing arms tensed across his chest, clasping the knife in one hand. "Hold it, hold it, Jac, just calm down. Let me tell you a story. You know I've been working on brain waves for two years, Jac. Success has been slim to nothing. Just four weeks ago I had a breakthrough.

"One of my sponsors suggested a new avenue to explore in EEG manipulation a few months back. I found that strong amplification of the brain waves showed a new wave. A form of energy I haven't seen. It was like a carrier wave, you know, AM or FM. I call it the Quark wave or effect. I tested several students and all were the same. I tested myself and I was the same. I believe everyone has these ESP waves."

Jac felt a wave of déjà vu sweep over him. "Well, I got a wave but it's not ESP! It's some kind of premonition. I've never had anything like it." He brushed it aside as his practical training took over. Holding up his hand in exasperation, "Okay, okay, Soe, that's three more subjects. What's the deal on your sponsors? Let's start with them. Who are they? Are you going to tell them?"

Soe plopped at a table in the Doctor's lounge, eyes never leaving Jac's, demanding concentration. "Sit down Jac, damn it. We got something here!"

Jac reached across the table grabbing the hand with the knife. "Don't cut your nose off, Soe. Damnit. Put the crutch away."

Visible calmness swept over Soe. "Well, okay, yeah. Hey man, this is just fantastic! Yeah, I will have to tell them. I have kept them informed with monthly reports, but I haven't filed one on this concept."

A significant pause followed as Soe stared off into space seemingly on another concept. He began fondling the knife again. *We, I can't let this out. I won't tell them. It's going to be huge beyond imagination!*

Jac grabbed Soe's arm, impatiently. "Can't you keep a train of thought? You're nervous as a whore in church. I asked, who are your sponsors?"

A plane of nonchalance, control, slid across Soe's eyes as he pulled his arm back, yawned and leaned away from Jac. "Okay, okay, the National Science Foundation, the CIA and another one." Glancing at Jac's quizzical stare, he seemed to stutter. "Ahhh, yeah, yeah, I know. Why the CIA? Well, they have maintained an active interest in ESP concepts for years hoping to pick the enemy's brain by psychic forces. I guess my professor clued them in on my research. They jumped at it like a big dog!"

A sardonic smile crept across Jac's face, challenging. "I'm getting suspicious, Soe. You have avoided me again. Who is the third sponsor?"

Soe glanced across the table avoiding Jac's eyes. He spread his hands and looked away. "Oh, yeah. That's the Collinga Foundation. They have been very generous and helpful."

Jac snapped forward. "The Collinga Foundation! Hey bud, that's my grandfather's. What the hell is he up to?" An intuitive feeling urged him to ask. "Is he the one giving you ideas?"

"Well, I have talked to him about my progress." Soe answered vaguely. He leaned forward, glaring, diverting attention from Jac's last question.

"Let me finish my story, Jac. Damn it, you keep interrupting me." Soe rocked back and then forward again hanging over the table. Massive arms and shoulders bunched in knots of muscle. He was back to snapping that damn knife.

"Yesterday, I impressed my amplified brain signals through a computer program I wrote onto my brain. I videoed it just in case something happened. With a little amplification, I was able to perform telekinesis. You know, object moving with the mind. Further amplification gave me more ability in telekinesis and a tremendous awareness of my surroundings. I was able to lift a chair off the floor! Momentarily, just a little bit, see?"

Soe whispered, leaning over the table as a nurse walked by to get coffee. "I could feel all the objects in the room, it was fantastic! So I jacked the signal again and my mind went crazy. I stood up clawing at my head and passed out. I must have been out 2 or 3 hours. It's all on the video, I'll show it to you."

Jac's face twisted in a grimace as he grabbed the arms of the chair as if to spring out and engulf Soe.

He hissed. "Soe, you crazy fuck, what did you do tonight? I saw you put a disk in your computer."

Soe reared back in his chair smiling triumphantly. "Damn it Jac. Calm down, will, ya? Yes I did. I found that Meloney's brain was in regression so low that ordinary EEG's couldn't pick up a signal. My computer program enhanced the signal, so I impressed my brain signals with the carrier wave over hers and it revived her. She is normal. And she appears to have extraordinary telepathic powers!"

Jac shook his head in disgust. "Christ almighty, Soe, you took one hell of a chance. You just told me it knocked your dick in your watch pocket and you do it to my patient without anyone's approval, discussion or anything!"

Soe glared at Jac cynically with a smirk creeping across his face. "It turned out okay, didn't it? Besides, I did tell you. Remember me saying, 'Here goes nothing!' I had every bit of confidence it would work. And I'll bet that she has the full package of ESP powers just like in Atlantis."

Jac grasped his head as he rocked backward in the chair, looking around to see if someone noticed his shouting. "WHERE IN HELL DID ATLANTIS COME FROM? You are absolutely talking in riddles, Soe!"

Soe waved his hand at Jac. "For crap's sake, Jac, last week I gave you a book to read. I earmarked a story in it. Did you read it?"

Jac stared at Soe blankly. He seemed to be on a sled, cascading uncontrollably down a mountain slope. Fidgeting with his mouth and then his hair, he paused a moment. "Oh yeah, you mean the stories about the psychic readings? Yeah, I read part of it. It was pretty far out. What's it got to do with this MIRACLE you performed?"

Soe threw up his hands sighing, a smirk developing as he pointed his knife at Jac. "Come in, Jac, come back to earth. I buy you books, send you to school and all you do is eat the covers off 'em! Jac, that was a very important story."

"Ha, Ha." Jac laughed sarcastically, sneering. "Soe, you're feeding me a line ah shit to hide something. You got your finger in the sugar bowl, don't you?" Jac demanded pointing at Soe's nose.

"That's bullshit, Jac, just you listen. That story is about a guy named Clark, Rudy Clark who got a psychic reading from a famous reader in San Francisco several years ago. Clark, I'm calling him Quark to cover the story, was very interested in Atlantis and the forms of energy they had. Cued by books he had read, he asked the psychic to tell him about Atlantis and their energy forms."

Jac interrupted. "Yeah, yeah, I read that story, or part of it. I remember, now. The psychic knew nothing about energy but she said they took energy from the sky or the sun through large crystals and ran their world on this energy. They stored the energy in the ground. Big deal! That's really far out."

Soe pointed at Jac. "Well, do you remember the single most important thing? The people had great psychic powers like telepathy, levitation or telekinesis and clairvoyance! Are you with me, Jac?" Soe asked as he reached over and shook Jac's arm.

Jac's eyes bored into Soe's. *Yes, I do remember that now!* "Keep going, Bubba, you haven't blown me away yet, but you sure as hell might cut me with that damn knife." Jac snorted, feigning casualness as his mind raced to make a connection.

Soe's voice droned on. "I'm sure you have heard of Atlantis blowing up and sinking in the ocean. Well, that was supposedly due to the 'ol boys getting in a fight with their neighbors and storing lots of energy in the ground. Boom, they were gone."

Jac waved his hand, glaring at Soe. "What's that got to do with the price of eggs?"

Soe grinned with an air of supremacy. "This is the key point besides ESP, Jac. The psychic said that in Atlantis's time, there were guides that guarded the earth from mass destruction by mankind. They removed the form of energy man was using. They won't let man have access to it until he becomes more civilized."

Jac rocked back in his chair, hooding his eyes, fighting for a chance to think. He sighed. "C'mon, c'mon, Chunky, get to the point, whatever it is. I need some sleep."

Soe's hazel eyes snapped as he pointed his finger at Jac. "You better be paying attention to every word I say, Jac baby. Your future may depend on it!"

Jac growled, as he dropped forward lunging across the table. "That's just what I thought. There's some kind of hidden agenda going on here, isn't there, Soe?"

Soe smiled. "That's for me to know and you to find out, Jac. Hear the rest of the story."

Jac grabbed Soe's finger and held it, staring intensely into Soe's eyes. Soe pulled it back with a curious smile twisting his mouth.

"I think I have found that energy or tied into it somehow with this psychic phenomenon and the computer program. That's why I named the energy the Quark Wave."

"Well, if it's so great why didn't you name it after yourself? You're egotistical enough to want to do it."

"I'm still in the very earliest development of this thing, Jac. If it bombs, I won't have my name on it, see?"

Jac sneered as he rocked his chair back again. "Soe, you're ass deep to a giraffe in this stuff. You got something working under the rug."

Jac diverted the direction of the story. "What's the deal on Meloney's dream of some kind of light after death? She seemed to pull me into it. I haven't gotten over it yet. I was actually there and experienced it!"

Soe laughed. "I know you have heard of this in medical school, Jac. It's called an NDE. A near death experience."

"Okay, okay, yeah, that's just what happened, Soe. Meloney did not respond to the heart stimulation procedures. She was dead. As we were cleaning up, her heart started beating on its own. EEG showed flatline coma, so I called you. I had no solutions and no one else here did either.

"You came dragging in looking like an all night drunk. I guess your little stunt at the college with the mind bender put you out, huh?"

Soe grimaced. "Hell yes it did, Jac. It knocked me flat. We'll have to ask Meloney about the NDE when she recovers. It might be significant in the development of her ESP talents through the brain enhancement procedure."

Jac flexed his hands, extending them across the table. *I have to get away and think this thing through. Brain enhancement procedure, Wow!* He looked at his watch. "CRAP, it's almost 6 AM! I still want to know about your relationship with the Collinga Foundation and Grandpaw."

Jac studied Soe for a few moments longer than a casual glance. "We have been good friends for the last six months. I greatly appreciate what you have done for me both in mind and body, Soe. But, this has been one hell of an event. It's going to need serious thought to grasp what happened.

"I am just appalled at the chance you took with Meloney. I almost think we need to put some kind of supervision on you."

"That's my two cents, Soe." Jac said as he directed a stern stare at his best friend. *I thought I knew Soe, I could trust him with my life. This opens a new view into Mr. Soe!*

"Well, we better get your junk back to the college and get some sleep. I have to be back here at 4 PM."

Soe stood up, smiling as he held out his hand.

"Thanks for your honesty, Jac, but I think I can handle the supervision.

"Also, thanks for calling me about Meloney-. Jac—, I guess you know it was pre-ordained."

Soe smirked as he cast a sideways glance at Jac to see the reaction.

"I'll be back over here after lunch and check on Meloney. She sure is a pretty thing, isn't she?"

Jac rose to his 6 foot 2 frame, pointing a forefinger at Soe. "What the hell do you mean, it was pre-ordained, Soe? That presupposes you know something about the future. Do you?"

Soe glanced over Jac's shoulder. Turning, he walked down the hall. "We shall see, Jac, c'mon, help me load up."

Jac grimaced as he shook his head. "I don't believe you heard a single thing I said, Soe. At least, you're not acknowledging it. You and I are not even on the same wave length."

Soe shrugged his hands and arms up and let them slap his sides.

THE ENHANCERS

SUNDAY DECEMBER 18TH

Jac flopped on the bed after gulping down an egg sandwich he grabbed on the way home.

The house suited him because it had a three-car garage and he could work on his cars, his current consuming hobby. By sleeping as soon as he got home, the morning was available for car work or chores.

"Damn it, I should have avoided that last cup of coffee," Jac lectured himself lying in bed as he twisted and turned. "Wow, this Meloney event is just over the edge of the world! I have always thought that nothing could surpass the tragedy of my parents' deaths, but this is next generation!"

That thought triggered a review of the past regardless of his efforts to wipe it. It crashed upon him as he twisted in the bed.

***

At the age of 10, Jac didn't question the tragic event as anything other than an accident. Down through the years, the scales fell from his eyes as real life events portrayed the depravity of man. Now, there was a definite question in his mind as to the defined "accident."

Grandpaw took him home, to the ranch, where he lived in a very protected environment. Jac withdrew into his books and schooling, participating very little in the outside world. GrandJac kept people, friends, around him at all times trying to pull him back into the world. High school activities helped some, but Jac lived in his books.

The events rolled across his mind's eye, again, as he gave up on sleep and let it happen. It was Wednesday morning, early, a bright and shiny day in October. Grandpa came by and asked Mom and Dad if he could take John out of school and go hunting. Grandpa said it was just a whim, just a spur of the moment thought.

"C'mon, Jason, Pat. One day of school won't hurt anything. It's a time to enjoy the outdoors." GrandJac argued.

Jason, GrandJac's only child, smiled at Pat's lack of enthusiasm. "School won't suffer, Pat, I think it's a great idea."

John grabbed a change of clothes and piled into Grandpa's Suburban with the ever-present "hands" that traveled with him.

It was always fun to visit Grandpa. He had everything. Guns, knives, fishing stuff and best of all, a place to use all of them. The day passed swiftly with squirrel hunting, shooting on the range and fishing in the big pond down in the valley. Dark caught them charbroiling steaks and listening to old-time country music on Grandpa's LP's. John fell asleep in the big stuffed leather chair beside the crackling fire.

He awoke to the ringing of the phone. Grandpa must have carried him to bed. Strange noises made him creep to the living room doorway and see Grandpa crying as he put the phone on the hook. John walked slowly in the room, step by step, as if compelled beyond his will. Grandpa grabbed him and held him tightly. "John, we are all alone in this world now. There has been a terrible accident. Mom and Dad have died in a house fire."

As time unfolded, John learned that the house had caught fire, and somehow, his parents could not get out. He later learned that a gas leak had filled the kitchen from the stove and a spark had set off a terrific explosion. The house was almost consumed by the time the Fire Department got there. Strangely, the first fire brigade had been involved in a wreck with a big semi truck rig that blocked the road. A second fire brigade had to detour around the wreck wasting precious minutes. The bodies of his parents were burned beyond recognition. It was crystal clear that if he had not been hunting, he would have been dead, too. Once again, the reel spun empty. Jac stared at the clock wondering if his world had made a sudden turn.

No, it wasn't the coffee, it's a premonition. Sleep was fleeting through the morning. *Oh hell, 2 PM, I might as well give up. No sleep today.*

The hauntingly beautiful Meloney from the other side of nowhere appeared in his mind. *This is edge cut. Why am I drawn to Meloney? What has Soe stumbled into? Meloney seemed to have strong ESP talents. Was Soe's theory of Atlantis playing into this scenario? What's the relationship between Soe, GrandJac, the Collinga Foundation and his innuendoes about the future? Wouldn't ESP talents be something? I might be able to solve my parent's deaths. I could get the real truth. Yes, I will have it someday. Ha, ha, what a dreamer!*

Dozing, life after his parents died passed in review. Being the last of the Cochrans, Jac moved to the ranch just outside Marian with Grandpa. Grandpa had a lot of money, a whole lot of money. He never worked at an office. He ran whatever businesses he had from the ranch by telephone, computer, and a group of men who came and went during the day. There were always 15 or twenty men around the ranch. Far more than it took to tend the few cattle and little farming that was done.

Jac accepted the men. They were always there and they took him wherever he went, to school, to town, the picture shows or whatever. If he went on some outing with his friends from school, he always went with sons of the men working at the ranch. When he thought back about it, he was never alone. Always, there were men or boys from the ranch with him or around him. They gave him some solace from the terrible tragedy. But he was still a loner. He longed for a family. It never occurred to him that they might have been protecting him!

The 3 PM alarm rattled Jac awake from flitting dreams. Lying in bed sweating. "That's unusual. Wow, what a night." Sitting on the edge of the bed holding his head in hands, conjecture came forth again.

"Soe, that crazy fart, how could he do something like that? He wouldn't have even tried that if he hadn't known it would work. That pre-ordained statement was very important. He knew something. This two-week test and information from a sponsor, what the hell? That just cemented the thing together. I better watch him closely. He is definitely working on an inside track. I can't even guess what the hell it might be! I consider Soe my best friend. He better not be pulling some stunt on me! Meloney hinted at something. 'Soe, tell Jac, he needs to know.'"
A mystery inside a mystery!

Ahhhh, start my day. 10-minute exercise, shower, shave and dressed in greens, ah, my beauty, my sweet Grand National. A quick stop-off at

THE ENHANCERS

What-A-Burger for a chicken sandwich and coffee to get up for the evening shift at MCH.

With both hands on the wheel, Jac patted the accelerator pedal, revving the engine in his pride and joy, a 1987 Buick Grand National. The tuned exhausts rumbled as he listened for even a hint of a miss.

The car represented Buick's attempt to attack the limited "muscle car" market in the mid 80's. Buick had built the car for national stock car racing sparing no expense in building a really sweet street rod. To qualify as a stock car for the race circuit Buick had to sell the GN through dealerships, so they used the car as an incentive for their outlets. High sales performance won a Grand National for the dealership and they advertised it to attract customers. The car was a collector's item on the show room floor.

Jac often wondered about Buick's marketing strategy because they discontinued the car in 1987. They had a bird's nest on the ground, like the 1957 Thunderbird that Ford squandered. Only Corvette continued the limited edition hot car down through the years and they made a fortune on the line.

The GN developed 250 HP with a turbine/intercooler system using state of the art computers for fuel injection and spark advance on a small block, 3.8 Liter V-6. A $200 investment in a computer "prom" chip boosted the turbine to 22 psi and a 300 HP engine. Jac used titanium, aluminum, and Lexan windows where possible to lighten the car to 2900 pounds. Oversize 8-1/2" wide tires with flared fenders and a totally blacked out trim enhanced the brute strength appearance of a powerful street muscle car. Dark, tinted windows capped the black effect.

Jac liked to yell when he poured the coal to it, "Grab ah root and growl." Extended spoilers reduced ground effects. Delving into General Motors's tests showed instability above 125 MPH, so they installed a shutdown there. The modified prom unit by-passed the shut down. A simple rear mounted stabilizing wind vane enabled the car to top-end safely somewhere above 150 MPH.

Jac enjoyed "taking" the locals at stoplights when there was no danger. His conservatism wouldn't allow sure enough hotrodding.

However, it did occur one time in high school while driving his first car. Jac spent some time at the police station with his ever-present buddy, Vinson Dye. Vince still worked for GrandJac on the ranch. But they had grown apart when he went to Texas University.

GrandJac's influence kept them out of the pokey for that night. GrandJac's wealth spread throughout the community giving him an "inside track" with the local law. So it was just a stern lecture from the Police Chief and Grandpa.

***

Shift relief took only 5 minutes. There wasn't a lot going on, a few industrial injuries, a kid with asthma, another with a broken arm, and two elderly people with symptoms that needed to be explored. Jac grabbed Eddie Broussard, a male RN, and impatiently waded through the cases. What is the status on Meloney kept hammering at him.

As Jac walked by the area nurse's station, he heard Soe's voice. He spun around. "Where's that coming from?"

The nurse at the station answered. "It's coming from ICU 101 over the monitoring system. We can listen to the patients in ICU with this monitoring system if we want to by turning it on room by room. Sometimes it helps us when we get an alarm or a call from the room." She explained.

"Thank you, I didn't realize we had that feature."

That's the reason Jodie was so curious about Meloney last night, Jac mused with raised eyebrows. *We talked about a lot of things. I better check on her right now. If she has recovered, Jodie doesn't have much of anything except hearsay.*

Jac directed Eddie on two more patients and went to ICU to see Meloney and talk to Soe. As he entered, Meloney was sitting up in bed, looking him straight in the eye. For some reason, she had turned her gown around with the ties in front.

"I knew you were coming. Look, I'm feeling fine and I want to get out of here."

Jac smiled with raised eyebrows. The feeling came back. He seemed to be encompassed with her in an envelope. Time notched down a step. She really looked good. Good color in her face, alert eyes and clear speech told a lot. He stopped, admiring her attractiveness, even without makeup. High cheekbones, heavy eyebrows, full sensuous lips gave her a Latino flare. The nurse had helped brush her dark brown hair and it hung to her shoulders and curled out in an attractive background to her oval face. Her breasts pushed out against the gown. He knew she had a fine figure. Wow, what a change from last night as he envisioned her on the gurney in the rain and wind!

Meloney blushed and looked away to Soe sitting quietly in a chair, watching the scene, eyes darting back and forth from Meloney to Jac.

Ducking her head a little, smiling, Meloney spoke in a quiet confident voice. "Thank you, Dr. Jac, you're very kind."

She cocked her head and held out her hand. Jac took a deep breath; all he could do was stutter.

"How did you know I was coming? What do you mean?"

"Well, aren't you going to shake my hand, Dr. Jac?" Meloney's lips twisted in a sweet smile.

Jac stepped forward tentatively, smiling. "Yes, of course, Meloney." Grasping her hand, he was surprised at her strength.

Meloney pulled him down and kissed him full on the mouth, leaned back laughing at his reaction of surprise.

Jac stumbled backwards and felt his mouth, trying to mask his desire as time clicked back to normal. "Wow, you have really recovered quickly, Meloney. This is extraordinary. I'm amazed! You really may be ready to get out of here!"

Obviously jealous and amused, Soe stood up jabbing his finger at Jac. "Did you hear what she said, Jac?"

Jac scowled at Soe, hands akimbo, *here we go again! Soe is becoming a pain in the butt. Now, he's possessive of Meloney!* "What do you mean, Soe? I think I heard what she said."

"She read your mind, Jac. You were ogling her body and she knew exactly what you were thinking." Soe glowered. "Don't you see what the brain enhancer did to her mind? She now has telepathy! I came in here about 3 PM, Meloney knew I was coming, knew what I was thinking, and even anticipated what I would say when I walked in!"

Jac waved his hands ineffectually, trying to say something, trying to stop Soe for a moment.

Soe moved about the room with his fingers laced together, cracking his knuckles. "We must keep this absolutely quiet. I have to explore the boundaries of Meloney's capability. I have to determine if she has other ESP skills." Soe continued pounding his fist into his hand.

Jac held up his hand again, glaring at Soe. Meloney tried to follow his train of thought.

Soe ignored him and kept on yammering. "Meloney, I know you are having fun with this toy. But both you and I are in real danger if this capability gets to the wrong people. Just imagine what the press would do with something like this. The world would rise up and engulf us. Some for us and most against us. Some would want the power to control others but most would fear it because they don't want anybody knowing what they are thinking."

Jac shook his head in wonder as he glared at Soe. He started to say something but Soe was off again with his rambling on the outer edges of space.

Soe paused for a moment gathering his thoughts. "You can generally assume there is a skeleton in everyone's closet, so to speak, so privacy is paramount.

"I've got to establish a foundation for this remarkable talent. The most startling thing is that anybody might attain these talents! Think of a world like that!"

Soe unconsciously grabbed his knife from his pocket and snapped it open. He looked guiltily at them. Flipped it closed and dropped it into his hip pocket. He mumbled, looking down. "I've got to stop that."

Jac let out a gust of air as he stepped forward patting the air down. "Stop Soe, stop, just calm down." Speaking quietly as he leaned toward the two of them. "The nurses' station can eavesdrop on this room. We must get out of here. Here's what has to happen now. Let's get Meloney out. I'll check her over and release her from MCH. The two of you can go to my place temporarily and hang out until I get off shift tonight. We haven't told anybody about this. So nobody knows, except possibly Jody, the nurse." Jac pleaded spreading his hands.

"If reporters are snooping around about the wreck, they'll more than likely come to MCH and inquire. I'll handle that. Meloney was not hurt seriously. She has been released to pursue her life, no big deal."

"What do you think? I'll fill out a report that the hospital will have available to meet the public, okay?"

Soe and Meloney nodded agreement. "Yeah, that sounds good." Soe answered as quietly as he could.

"Okay, Soe you leave the room while I check out Meloney. I'll get her out of here. Wait in the lobby. Go on, Soe." Jac smiled as he shooed Soe out the door. *Maybe I can make him jealous; that turd!* Jac stood beside Meloney with his hand on her shoulder, looking like the cat that ate the canary.

Soe glared at Jac. "Okay, okay." He hesitated to say something more, then turned to go.

Before Jac could say anything, Meloney said coolly. "Doctor, I trust you. Go ahead and give me a check up."

Needless to say, Jac was taken aback. Because that was his thought when he approached Meloney. *This is definitely going to take some getting used to.*

Scanning the monitors for vital signs, Jac found all normal and in range. "Okay, that's good. Let's look at the contusion, Meloney." Carefully pulling the tape away from her forehead revealed a red line with black stitches. No swelling or dangerous signs of infection were obvious.

"Remarkable! A large Band-Aid will cover it satisfactorily. We can remove the stitches in a day, Meloney! It normally takes five days for a simple cut like this to close satisfactorily."

Jac removed the EEG leads, the cardio leads and the IV. In so doing he had to open her gown and pull the tabs on her chest, side and back. He was definitely cautious about looking at her breasts and having any thoughts. He tried to think professionally about her body and his inspection.

Meloney had a bruise across her shoulder and redness across one breast where the strap had restrained her when she hit the water. Jac pressed lightly and asked, "Does that hurt?"

Meloney smiled at him, "It's not real sore. I can move around easily."

"Do you have any other pains?"

"My right ankle hurts, Dr. Jac." Meloney indicated as she straightened her leg under the sheet.

"Yes, we noticed that last night and X-rayed it. There are no broken bones. I believe it's just a sprain. You could have twisted it when you hit the brake pedal and fell forward when the car hit the water. Let's see it, Meloney."

Meloney pulled the covers aside and in so doing pulled her gown off her body. She lay quietly, completely naked. Jac carefully pulled her gown back over her and glanced guiltily at her face.

Meloney was smirking, trying to keep from laughing. She finally giggled and said in a quiet, sweet voice. "Dr. Jac. You must maintain a professional manner, even in your mind!"

Jac took a deep breath as he stared into her eyes. "Meloney, you've got one hell of a body and I am finding it very hard, I, I mean difficult to maintain my professional cool." Jac slapped his forehead and rolled his eyes as guilty thoughts raced through his mind. *I don't even know this girl. That wasn't appropriate, I can't talk to her like this.*

A feeling of brotherly love came over him. He felt he had known Meloney for years, even back to childhood. *Son of a gun, she is transferring these thoughts into my head,* Jac realized. *She is trying to make me feel comfortable. Or intimate, like a brother and sister might feel.* "Meloney, this is going to be one hell of an experience. I don't know the rules, I hope you do."

Meloney sat up on the side of the bed and lifted her arms over her head, again baring her body from top to bottom, "Dr., please look at my ankle."

Jac smiled, shaking his head. *If you think it, you said it out loud.* He turned to her ankle. It was bruised and blue, slightly swollen. He lifted it and twisted it slightly from side to side. This time he said nothing, just thought the question. "Does that hurt?" To his surprise, he knew that it didn't hurt much and there was nothing serious.

Meloney, he thought. *Please stand up, put your weight on the ankle, and walk around.*

Meloney rolled out of bed with Jac's hand on her arm, and stood teetering slightly. *I'm 5'-7" tall and weigh 135 lbs.,* Jac heard in his head.

She took a step forward putting her weight on her right ankle with little apparent pain. Then she walked around the room, limping slightly. She smiled mischievously at him as she gathered her gown around her after reviewing Jac's thought.

Jac grinned slightly as he shook his head in wonder. "Meloney, there is nothing wrong with you that I can find. Your blood work was fine. You report a sore ankle. My greatest concern is the brain/coma condition, but your EEG is fine. Do you have any loss of time or memory concepts?"

"No."

"Okay. I had your clothes washed and dried. Your bag is in the closet. I don't know what the water might have ruined. Your purse and personal things were set out to dry. I hope you can recover them. Get dressed and wait here."

Jac stood with his hands on his hips as he looked at her with a faint degree of awe.

He broached the haunting question, the one uppermost on his mind. "Do you feel anything, Meloney? I mean, like we've met before or something like that? Or maybe something is supposed to happen? I can't explain it. I have this feeling. It's something weird, like déjà vu, about you and this whole happening. It's— just beyond me. It's— just gnawing at me." Jac stuttered trying to find the right words.

Meloney's sweet lips twisted in a slight smile. "I know what you are talking about, Dr. Jac, but I can't explain it. Actually, I seem to get the feeling from you or someone or somewhere else.

All I can say is; it's very strange. But, everything is strange right now. And I like it! Hopefully, time will tell." Meloney tilted her head in a questioning air and gave that disarmingly sweet smile again.

Jac nodded, looking to space. Then, boring into her eyes, searching for some connection. "I don't know. Meloney, last night——."

"Yes, Dr. Jac, that had to be a remarkable experience seeing life return to me in my eyes." She chuckled slightly. "You should have seen it from my side! Soe knows something about this but he will have to tell you. I can't pick it up."

Waving his hand in resignation. "Okay, Meloney, thank you for being honest with me." Jac left the room to fill out the various forms still wondering. *NDE. Mindreading! Wow, for craps sake, unbelievable. Acquired from a computer program. Can everyone get it? Déjà vu, Atlantis, rapid healing. I better catalog these happenings. My life went from medical/cars to outer space in 18 hours! I don't even know how to participate. I'll just have to hang on and watch.*

***

Meloney stared after him. Through the door, it seemed. "Well, yes, I'm sure we will find out, Jac. You see. I didn't bring anything but me. Whatever it is, is here." she whispered, cryptically.

Meloney gurgled. "Wow, look at that. They cut my clothes off. But they washed them and returned the rags to me, how thoughtful!"

She selected clothes from her bag while she reviewed the past as she had become accustomed to. She lived in her head, it seemed. Idly, she surveyed the few clothes she had brought. "They don't seem to be ruined. That's good."

Back in her head, *it's a metamorphosis! I can't believe how forward and extroverted I am! I feel so confident and self-assured,* as she looked in the mirror. *This mind thing is changing my views of life and myself!*

Throughout my life I have been introverted. A closet kid. Scared to venture forth. That's why I studied psychology in college. Now, overnight, I am changed. Almost reborn. Fantastic!

Plus, my injuries are healing very rapidly. I'm a new person and I like it! Imagine what it would do for people. I wonder if Soe is right? Can anyone gain this talent? Projecting an image to the world, *Hey World, what would you do with it?*

A wide smile crept across her face as she checked herself out in the mirror. We'll just have to see what Dr. Jac is talking about.

***

While completing the discharge papers, Jac found that Meloney had very good health and car insurance polices that were going to take care of all the hospital expenses.

"I'm sure Soe will be glad to hear of that." Jac murmured as he thought of last night and the Hospital release form that Soe threw a fit over. *If I sign this, I'm responsible for everything. Hell, Albert, I didn't take her to raise!*

It's this or nothing, Soe, the Hospital can't take chances.

Jac returned in about 20 minutes with Jody, the floor nurse, and a wheel chair. All patients of this nature must exit the hospital in a wheelchair. Meloney had dressed in blue jeans, a light sweater and jogging shoes. She had a coat on her arm. Jody wheeled her out to the lobby to confront Soe as he paced up and down the lobby with a scowl streaked across his face.

Soe glared at Jac. "What in hell took so long, Jac? What were you and Meloney doing in there?"

Meloney answered before Jac could say anything. "Dr. Jac gave me a complete inspection, Soe. That's hospital rules, and I passed with A's. Let's get a pizza. I'm starved."

Soe grinned like a smitten school kid as Meloney smiled and patted him on the arm.

Jac ushered them out the Emergency Doors and ramp to the parking lot. Night had fallen with a sharp coolness. Soe had grabbed her bag from Jac in a possessive move like a little kid.

With her arms to the sky as if thanking the Lord, Meloney inhaled a deep breathe. "I'm happy to be alive, Soe. I'll tell you later just how happy I really am." She cut her eyes to Soe, smiling.

Jody stared awestruck at Meloney. "I am amazed at your recovery, Meloney——, uhhh. I wish you the best. Take care." Jody mouthed the last as she cast a penetrating glance at Soe. Wheeling around, she pushed the chair up the ramp to the emergency doors past a young woman in a quilted coat.

"Meloney?" A plaintive voice called from the ER doors at the top of the ramp, "Where are you?"

They all turned back to the lighted door and saw a girl standing silhouetted in the swinging doors.

"That's Carol Ann." Meloney exclaimed with a lilt in her voice, "Hey, come down here. What in the world are you doing here, Carol?" She yelled.

Jac interrupted, hurriedly. "I can't explain right now, Meloney. It's a long story and I have to get to work. Soe, here's my house keys. Y'all go there, get settled down. I'll be there by 12:30 if everything goes well here. There're three bedrooms. Plenty of room for everyone to be comfortable."

Carol ran down the ramp and hugged Meloney. "Christ, I thought I had lost you! The crazy doctor was looking for next of kin!"

Meloney grabbed Carol, "It was very serious. C'mon, let's get out of the cold and I'll tell you about it."

Jac gave Carol the 'once over'. *Look at that, a real sweetie-pie.* She was an attractive and vivacious little thing, bright blonde.

"Don't y'all leave before I get home, you hear?"

Jac turned to the cute blonde. "Carol, I'm Dr. Cochran. I'm the crazy doctor that called you last night. You made good time and I appreciate you coming out here. I'm sorry I upset you last night on the phone, but it was a very serious situation. A coma is, ah-, well, very dangerous. But, as you can see, Miss Meloney is A-OK. This is Soe. He will take care of y'all. Go with him to my house."

An engaging smile greeted Jac as he extended his hand to Carol. Eye contact seemed to last longer than the moment required. "I'm so glad you brought her back, Dr. Cochran. You don't look crazy!"

Jac turned. "Well, that's a story in itself." He commented with a twist to his lips as he walked up the ramp to the ER doors. Hanging on the door looking at the three with elation bubbling through him. *This is it! This could be my new family! We just seem to click; maybe Meloney is influencing something. Anyway, I hope it works out!*

***

Soe grimaced in a sneer as he trotted to his Nissan compact and wheeled it up to the ramp. "Carol, get your rent car and follow me. It's not far to Jac's house." Soe directed as he opened the door for Meloney.

That 'shit' is getting all the credit for Meloney. I can't believe it. He's luckier than a two-dick dog! 'Daddy Warbucks' has more money than Fort Knox, he's 75 and Jac's gonna get it all. Well, he's in for a surprise!

Meloney smiled sweetly to Soe as she slid into the compact car. *What's he talking—, thinking about?* "Soe, this mind thing, this whole thing has just been dazzling. I feel like I have been reborn into another world, even another body! The anticipation of exploring it is just gnawing at me. I can't wait!"

Soe leaned over the wheel starting the car trying to hide his ecstasy. This event culminated all of his expectations from the last two weeks. Hell, the last two years! His sponsor pointed him into an overwhelming concept and he brought it to an explosive conclusion. As frosting, it was with a beautiful, vivacious, sweet young thing! *Wow, she was a charmer!*

Soe whispered, somewhat hoarsely, trying to control his voice. "Meloney, I'm so happy for you. I just know this is going to work out and be a major event in our time!"

Meloney stared at Soe. "Yes—, I believe you're right," with a penetrating, questioning look.

***

About ten miles of freeway in the evening went quickly as Soe exited and continued to a modest subdivision. Soe motioned for Carol to park in the street as he guided his car to a stop to one side of the main drive behind the house.

Carol grabbed her single bag of emergency supplies from the small rent car and walked to the house on a concrete sidewalk.

41

Soe stood on the small 'stoop' fumbling with Jac's keys in the dark. His head snapped up at Meloney's urging to watch a car pass slowly on the street. Two men stared at the house and the trio. In the semi-darkness from a streetlight at the corner of the block nothing could be determined. Straightening to full height, Soe put a belligerent stare on the car. It continued to the corner and made the turn.

"Meloney, did you see something, sense something? How did you get my attention?" Soe asked, swinging the door open and flipping the light switch.

"I receive images, feelings. I can't explain it. It just pops in my awareness. I thought—, I wanted to tell you. But I don't think I touched you, I don't know. This thing is unbelievable! It's so easy to sense, feel another person, almost meld with them." Meloney stammered.

"What ARE you talking about?" "Meloney, has something weird happened to you?" Carol demanded. She was so used to nurse-maiding her roomie through life, almost directing her actions and thinking. *The terrible accident that killed Meloney's parents, Heavens, that was right here!* It pushed Meloney into hiding. Even now, Carol found herself mothering her best friend, two plus years later.

Later! Appeared in Carol's mind, it seemed.

Carol snapped a glance at Meloney. "What? Okay, okay."

***

Jac's house looked just like all the others in the neighborhood. A small tree, shrubs and a minimal flowerbed dressed the front yard. Inside, it was clean and orderly. Jac spent most of his time reading, outdoors, exercising, or in his garage working on his cars. A shelf against one wall was filled to the top with books on a multiple of subjects. Several pictures of Jac with his parents and his grandfather covered another wall. Magazines on medical topics and cars covered the typical coffee table in front of the sofa.

Grabbing the telephone, Soe ordered two large pizzas. "Meloney, hey, ya'll want a beer? I sure do. Jac keeps a few in the frige. Meloney, you're not on any meds and I think you are completely recovered. You can have a beer."

Soe nonchalantly grabbed the beer as he looked the girls over, "Sit down, get comfortable. Boy, that beer hits the spot, huh? Carol, what did 'ol Jac do to you last night? Scare the hell out of you?"

Carol straightened up from a slump on the divan, took a drag on her beer eyeing Meloney and Soe. *What am I doing here? Let's play it out, it's like a step into another world! These two doctors are interesting specimens!*

"Yeah—, he really did. I get this call, are you Carol Marsh? Yes, can you give me next of kin for a Meloney E. Graham? You can imagine what goes through your mind about then. Meloney's dead. No, she's just in a coma. My God, we need next of kin to perform radical surgery or something. It scared the crap out of me. So, I rushed out here, flying any puddle jumper available. Then driving all the way from Dallas to find Miss Meloney is just perky. Nothing is wrong! Look at that, a Band-Aid. Is that where Dr. Jac entered your brain?"

Carol cut her eyes to Meloney for the rest of the story.

Meloney grimaced, casting a penetrating eye on both of them. "I know you were scared. You can bet I was scared. I was DOA at the hospital! I was trying to get to Marian in a terrible storm. The wind and rain were just beyond imagination! It almost blew me off the road. I'm approaching a bridge and some nut is clear over in my lane. The night turned to day as a lightning bolt hit nearby and this guy is gonna ram me head-on." Meloney stood up gesturing her arms.

"Involuntarily, I reacted to the right, driving through the bridge railing into the river and drowned! The windshield caved in like a piece of cardboard and the car flooded in seconds. I still think I could have got out but the seat belt latch was jammed." Meloney paused, eyes glazed over staring into nothing. "A piece of cardboard from a candy wrapper did it! A diver pulled me out after 10 minutes and I was frozen dead!"

Meloney gasped. "It is absolutely vivid in my mind. It's as if I'm watching this from afar like a movie!"

Meloney chugged the rest of the beer and wiped her chin. "Ahhh, that was good—! The ambulance took me to Marian Charity Hospital where I was stone cold dead. DOA!"

A quirky smile twisted her mouth. "Carol, did your mother ever tell you to wear clean underwear in case you had to go to the hospital?"

Carol shook her head in disbelief. "Meloney, what has happened to you?"

Meloney giggled, "My clothes were wet. You can imagine how difficult it would be to get them off me being limp as a rag. Well, they just cut them off, my new jeans, blouse, everything. They stripped me like skinning a pig—, with scissors. There were three men and three women staring at me lying naked on the table!"

She watched Carol for a reaction. She smirked, getting what she wanted. "Dr. Jac revived my body but I was brain dead or in a coma. He stuck a big needle right through my chest into my heart!"

Carol sat upright frozen rigidly, eyes fixed on Meloney's face. Her hand flittered across her mouth.

"If you think that is strange wait for the dream." Meloney stared at Carol. She seemed to be in a trance. Soe appeared much more casual.

Unconsciously, she felt the bump on her forehead as she stared into nothing. "Yes—, I cut my head on the steering wheel and I hurt my ankle."

Turning back from space, Meloney locked eyes with Carol. "I fell into this bright tunnel of light. I went before God and reviewed my life. It was indescribably beautiful and peaceful. I wanted to stay there forever."

Mouth gaping, Carol sat forward, hanging on every word. "Good Lord." she gasped. "That's really fantastic! I—— I can almost see it. How do you know all of this?"

Meloney put the empty beer can on the coffee table as she sat down next to Carol on the divan. Grabbing her hand. "I woke up in Intensive Care and could read people's minds! I can read your mind right now! Carol, you think this is all an hallucination and I'm sick in the head from the wreck, don't you!" She mesmerized Carol with burning dark eyes.

Carol put her hand in front of her mouth as her eyes locked with Meloney's. After a pause she blurted out. "OH, WOW! I believe you can read my mind. That's exactly what I was thinking! Are you in my mind, NOW?"

Soe interrupted as he sat forward on the edge of his chair, trying to contain himself. He clasped his hands tightly to control his outward emotions. "Carol, this is no happenstance. It actually has occurred, maybe because of the bump on her head and the coma state."

Soe quickly looked at Meloney. Catching her eye, he signaled that that would be their story.

"Meloney has demonstrated this mind reading capability on several occasions." Soe continued quietly. He fumbled for his knife, then gripped his hands tightly again in front of him. "I'm most interested in it because I'm studying neurotransmitters of the brain in my research here at the college."

Carol interrupted shaking her head, looking first at Soe and then at Meloney. "Meloney, this is just too much-. What about school? What about this boy you were coming here to meet?"

"Oh crap, I'm glad you reminded me, Carol. I'll call Kevin, now. Let's see, where is that number. Carol, all my stuff got wet in the car. Dr. Jac dried it out————. Here it is."

Meloney hurriedly stepped to the wall phone in the kitchen and dialed Kevin. An answering machine came on.

"Kevin, this is Meloney. I'm in New Orleans with car problems. I don't think I will be able to make it this holiday. I'm sorry I didn't call you last night. Things have just been hell. I'll call you at spring break. I'm sorry, okay?"

Meloney smiled a little shrugging her shoulders as she looked to Carol and Soe for understanding. She hesitantly hung up the phone.

The phonebook hanging on a hook reminded Meloney of Bobby Williams. Somehow she knew that he lived here in Marian.

"Hey, I haven't thanked Bobby Williams for saving my life. Remember, he was the diver that dove down to the car, cut the seatbelt and pulled me to the surface."

Carol stared wide-eyed as she waved at Meloney. "I don't know what you are talking about, Meloney. Clue us in." Carol twisted around, "Hey, Meloney, is the wreck story in the local papers? Isn't Kevin here in town? Do you think he might see the story and know you are here, but you are lying to him?"

The doorbell rang, a distracting ding-a-ling. The thought disappeared in the excitement.

"That's the pizza, girls. Just a minute." Soe yelled.

He grabbed the two boxes as he handed the kid two twenty dollar bills. "Thanks, Pal, I appreciate the late delivery. Lets eat while it's hot, girls. Anybody want another beer?"

Soe slid the boxes onto the kitchen table.

Meloney jumped up spinning around with her arms in the air. "Carol, it's over with Kevin. I'm so excited about this mind thing, I'm going to stay out here and explore it with Soe. I think I can go back and finish this semester of school. All we have are finals, anyway."

Carol grinned at her exuberant roomie. It was such a pleasure to see Meloney happy and excited about her life. *For two years, I have pulled and tugged Meloney out of the pits of self-pity after the terrible death of her parents—. What a coincidence, they were killed in a car wreck right here in Marian! Maybe we can visit the site or do something to help her sweep it away and get on with her life.*

Soe grabbed three more beers and smiled approvingly at Meloney.

Within ten minutes and no conversation, the pizzas were down to two strips. Soe looked at the last of the pizza longingly. "What the heck, let's save this for Jac. He may be hungry. He's just a growing boy, ha, ha."

He walked into the living room and plopped down in Jac's recliner. "Y'all come on in here. We need to rest after the battle with the pizza."

Meloney sighed. "I haven't eaten since yesterday noon. Boy, that was good!" She sat forward on the edge of her chair grinning at Carol. "I'm changing my name, Carol. Soe and Jac are acronyms and I like the idea. So from here on I'm going to be Meg instead of Meloney Eleanor Graham. What do you think?"

Carol asked with arched eyebrows. "Meg, what do I think?"

Meg laughed, "I can see that you're getting caught up in this thing and you're excited about it."

Carol stared at her with a funny twist of lips, maybe a little jealousy showing. "Roomie, you have changed-. But I like the new Meloney or Meg!"

Soe clapped his hands in delight. "I agree with you, Carol. I see a change even in a few hours. I don't know what she was like before, but she has become more outgoing! A happy little extravert."

Meg grinned from ear to ear. "I'm just what I want to be, now!"

"I'm so happy for you, Meg. It's been a long time coming. Soe, where did your name come from?" Carol asked leaning back on the divan, throwing her arms to both sides. Carol gave no notice of Soe staring at her large breasts jutting out.

Soe grinned mischievously enjoying the attention from the two good-looking women. "My name is Shawn Olin Etheridge and I have always gone by Shawn. When Jac came here in June from Galveston Med, I kinda took him under my wing. He was a brilliant nerd, a skinny bookworm. I put him on a weight training, exercising program and pulled him out of the closet to some extent. Hell, he's gained from 165 to 220 pounds in six months!

"I consider Jac my best friend. We do a lot of things of together.

"Would you believe that Jac has three degrees? ME, EE, a minor in chemistry and an MD and he's only 25 years old?"

Carol gurgled, "My Lord, how did he do it? He must be as brilliant as you say! Hey, what's the skinny on you, Soe?"

"Well, let me finish my name story, Carol. I liked the acronym idea so I became Soe. People razzed the hell outta me, so I changed the pronunciation to Sue instead of Soe. I still get a lot of ribbing from friends. Others, I slap the crap outta."

Meg chuckled, "I'll bet you can, too. You look like you have been weight training for a long time. I see you are 5 foot 11 and weigh 230 pounds."

Carol poked Meg. "Is that some of that mindreading stuff, Meg?"

Meg laughed. "Could be, could be. You better be careful what you think, roomie."

"Well, c'mon, Soe. Finish your life story." Carol demanded with a cute smile.

Soe waved his hand deprecatingly. "There's not much else. I graduated from Cal Tech in computers and electronics and went on 'til I got my MD. I'm pursuing research here at Marian College in neurotransmitters; brains, that is. One of the leading researchers in the country is here because of his family and the Collinga Foundation that is funding his research. He could work anywhere he wanted to." Soe leaned forward towards Meg. "I've spilled my tale. Let's hear yours, girls."

Meg crossed her arms over her chest. "I sure don't have that kind of credentials, Soe. I'm an only child going to Virginia Tech. I'm a senior in psychology. Two years ago, my parents were killed in a terrible wreck right here in Marian. All I have is Carol. She adopted me and pulled me through the hell of the last two years."

Carol had waited impatiently. She sat forward. "My turn, Soe. I'm from Pennsylvania. My daddy has a hardware store there. I have a little sister in high school. I'm a senior majoring in business. And Meloney, I mean Meg is my best friend. We are roomies.

"And, frankly, it has been hell pulling Meg out of the dumps. That's why I'm so happy for her in this new situation. I hope and pray that it continues."

Soe grinned, relishing the moment. "Hey, I think that's just great, girls. We know each other. Poor 'ol Jac doesn't know anything. Ha! Secondly, I have no worries about Meloney's, I mean Meg's recovery from this accident or her psychological trauma concerning her parent's deaths. We shall see a rebirth of the MEG!"

Meg held up her hand, scowling at Soe. "Well, maybe. I hope so. Go to the end of the hall or whatever is farthest and think of something as you walk away."

Soe shrugged as he looked at Meg and walked slowly down the hall to the back bedroom. "Sure."

Meg called out. "Come back, Soe. I've discovered something."

Soe returned with a quizzical look. "Yes?"

"I can only read your mind about 15 feet away, Soe. When I think back to the hospital I couldn't pick up anybody in the lobby, but I could in the hallway. It's possible I'm losing it or it's declining." Meg said, hanging her head.

Soe leaned back in his chair putting his hands behind his head as he looked at the ceiling. "Hmmmm, well, maybe so——, Meg. We'll do some testing in my lab tomorrow. I'm tired. Why don't we go to bed? Jac can take care of himself when he comes in. Leave the pizza in the oven."

The girls nodded. "Sure, I think we are both tired," Meg added.

***

The bedroom with two singles suited the girls. Soe went to the bedroom with a double bed.

Carol closed the door, flipped her bag on a bed, turning to Meg. "These are two real hunks. I can't imagine falling into such a situation." She giggled. "Which one do you want, Meg? I want the other one."

Meg smiled at her exuberant friend's ever interest in the opposite sex. "They're both fine specimens and both are very intelligent. I'm going to wait a little to see how this mind thing works out with Soe."

Meg settled on the bed eying Carol. "This is something you don't know, Carol. Jac brought me back to life on the gurney in the Emergency Room. I was stone cold, dead. Soe used his EEG/computer to bring my brain back to life with a special program. This has truly been one heck of an experience, these last 24 hours. I know it will affect me for the rest of my life."

Meg paused, staring off in the distance. "You know, Jac did not bring me back to life. He declared me dead. I was actually dead for maybe 15 or 20 minutes. The more I think about it, I was dead from sometime in the water! Somehow, I came back to life and Jac pulled me forward. Soe thinks it is an NDE. A near death experience, a rare occurrence that's unexplainable."

"Good Lord, Meloney, I mean Meg. There sure is more to the story, huh? This thing is sci-fi, but it's real!" Carol exclaimed with arched eyebrows.

"Yes, there is more. I don't know all of it, but tomorrow I will go to Soe's lab and maybe I'll learn more." Meg promised. "You see, I can't read Soe's mind about this, because he won't think about it. Apparently, all I can read in people's minds is what they are thinking at the moment."

Meg paced about the room casting sharp looks at Carol, voicing her thoughts. "I was very concerned about losing the ESP, but Soe isn't worried. I read his mind a little bit ago. He knows his program will boost it tomorrow. Here's another thing. I healed or got well very rapidly. Dr. Jac was very surprised at my condition this afternoon. He didn't say it, but he thought it. My ESP or whatever this phenomena is may be responsible for rapid healing."

Meg flopped on the bedside facing Carol. "This is startling, Carol. This mind reading thing has completely changed my perspective of my fellow human beings. I thought I was the only one feeling self conscious, inadequate, ineffective and so on. Everyone has the same feelings and is struggling to find their identity. I could help people with this gift. The world is far brighter than I ever thought.

"And, Soe says everyone has ESP capabilities. Maybe his program can turn everyone into a psychic. Wouldn't that be something?"

Carol sat through the tirade shaking her head, eyes locked on her friend, sighing. "Well—, maybe—, that has to be exciting for you because of your psychology interests. To me, this whole thing is just beyond the edge of the world. I can't even get an overview of the accident, the death, the revival, the ESP and now this rapid healing. What's next?"

Shaking her head, sighing again. "Whoaha, Meloney, I mean Meg, your world jumped three levels in 24 hours. I feel like I don't even know you. I only know the old Meloney. But, I'm very happy for you. I almost want to be a part of your new world. It really sounds exciting!"

Meg scooted over and hugged Carol. "I'm not going to leave you out, roomie. You put up with me for two years, nursing, begging, demanding that I return to reality. I'll pull you into this world, count on it. It's going to be unbelievably exciting, I just know!"

Carol hung her head as she stood up and moved to her bed. "Ahhhh, yeah, I know you will. Let's sack it. I've been flying or driving since last night at this time. I am pooped!"

Carol striped to her panties and bra. "What are you going to sleep in Meg? Your nothing as usual?" Carol asked with a grin, showing a little of her usual enthusiasm.

"Sounds good to me," Meg replied.

Carol unhooked her bra and let her breasts loose. She was well endowed, her breasts hung down pendulously as she bent over pushing her panties off and stepping out of them.

Stretching her arms over her head and spreading her legs, she arched her back. "You never told me which one you wanted, Meg." Carol giggled.

"Go to sleep, Carol, I thought you were tired. Let's get a few things settled before we attack." Meg scolded.

She turned over and pulled the coverlet up around her neck. *WOW, what a day! What has happened? I can't even begin to comprehend the whole thing. And it just keeps getting bigger and more complex. Jac, Soe and I are somehow immersed in this thing, like a mudhole. The excitement, the anticipation, it's awesome! Come on tomorrow! These covers sure do feel good. I don't think I will ever get warm again!*

Despite the lengthy time without sleep, Carol's mind raced to comprehend Meloney's newfound gift. *Mind reading! Apparently, telepathy, too! And much stronger than anything I have ever heard of. Everybody has it or can acquire it! What would I do with it? What a power base if only a few had it. It is just pure sci-fi! I'm going to get it, some way, some how!*

Carol's life centered on a stable family in Pennsylvania. She acquired her father's exuberant personality and her mother's voluptuous body. The combo created a smart, perceptive, talented, extravert ready to take on the world to laud her being. She freely admitted that she wanted the attention and strove to get it. Telepathy would only expand the thrill.

THE ENHANCERS

MONDAY DECEMBER 19TH

Carol awoke at 7:30 and rolled out of bed, stretching her strong body. The full-length mirror inside the closet door answered her young boisterous ego. Going over her youthful body in minute detail with a critical eye, she patted her cropped blond hair. It angled down from the back to her chin framing an oval face with a cute perky nose and full red lips. *I'm gonna get one of these men*, she decided as she looked at her clothes.

Smirking, she slipped into panties and a light robe. Leaving it open, she walked down the hall to the living room to peek through a crack in the door. Both Jac and Soe were following a TV jazzercise program with vigorous activity.

As could be expected if you knew Carol, she yelled, throwing the door open. "Wait for me."

Both men turned to look at her framed in the doorway with her robe open and her breasts hanging to each side just under the robe. The string panties did little to cover the dark vee at the bottom.

Soe lost his rhythm, stopped and stared. He recovered and looked away, mouthing. "WOW."

But Jac didn't miss a step. "Come on in, we've just started, Carol." Jac yelled over the music. *I knew it; she's a little flirt, just begging for attention!*

Carol turned slowly with her arms over her head and disappeared down the hallway, grinning impishly.

Meg looked fit dressed in shorts and halter coming down the hallway. "That startled them, Carol, particularly Soe." She giggled. "Get something on and let's join them."

A shower felt good after a 20-minute workout. Meg's foot limited her, but she found that it was getting well as she worked out.

***

The gathering in the kitchen area enveloped Jac with thoughts of his wish for a family. There is chemistry working here. *I hope*

53

I can pull them together and they will stay. Pessimism crept in, *that's a real long shot!*

"Here's what we have for breakfast, gang. Cereals, milk, OJ, toast or I can fix bacon and eggs. Name your poison."

Cereal was agreed upon as Jac glanced at Meloney. "Let me look at that cut on your forehead, Meloney," Jac said as he stepped towards her.

Meg held up her hand. "I've changed my name to Meg. It's an acronym like yours. So from now on I'm Meg, what do you think, Jac?"

"Sounds good to me, Meg. I like short names." He continued looking as he reached for her head. He turned her head to the kitchen light and examined the sutured cut carefully. "We can take the stitches out this afternoon, Meg. It's basically healed. You really don't even need a Band-Aid unless you want one."

Meg pulled Jac down giving him a big hug and kiss. "I never thanked you for saving my life, Dr. Jac. I owe you and Soe everything." Meg said with extended eye contact as she leaned back from him hanging on his arms.

Soe stepped forward with an envious smile. "Well, here I am, Meg. Thank me, too."

She whirled around and grabbed Soe by the ears pulling him to her. "Soe, thank you ever so much. We still have a lot to explore with this brain thing." She kissed him passionately.

Soe stepped back grinning. "Wow, I'll save you again this morning, Meg."

Carol jumped up, eyes sparkling, clapping her hands. "I want to be saved, too, you guys!"

Jac had stepped back and watched the action. Soe's envy was barely concealed.

Leering at Carol as he turned to her. "You do need saving. I'll say that much."

Carol smiled sweetly, eyeing Jac coyly. "Yes, my mamma thinks so, too, Dr. Jac."

Breakfast over, they all moved to the living room with coffee.

Meg announced, "I've got to get my car thing settled. I'm sure it was ruined. The engine was running when it hit the water. Almost surely it sucked water into the cylinders and blew the head off. I'll have to buy another one."

Carol snapped to attention. "Meg, you don't know a thing about cars, much less engines. Where did you get that idea?

Meg pointed to Jac, triumphly. "He told me, Carol. He knows all about engines!"

"More mind reading, huh?" Carol sniffed.

Jac grinned, "A new frontier to explore. ESP in action. Meg, the insurance agency was notified the next morning. They have an office here in town. You can find out from them about the car."

Meg called the office and identified herself. "Can you tell me anything about my car?" Meg's face flushed red and a scowl creased her brow. "What do you mean, $8500? That car was worth $12,000. It was only a year old!"

The agent's noncommittal response wasn't any better. "Well, we have to go by the book, Miss Graham. I'm sure you could get a settlement from the other car's insurance carrier if you could find the car or driver. I understand that they left the scene of the accident without reporting anything. That's a felony. They are going to be lying low, hoping they won't get caught."

"Thank you for your sincere consideration." Meg spit, "You have been so helpful. I hope I can return the favor in the near future so that we may have closure."

"Ah, Ma'am, ah, Miss Graham, I know you are upset. That isn't some kind of threat is it?"

"You are a service organization, selling insurance, helping the public. Why don't you reevaluate your presentation to the public and your clients?" Meg suggested caustically. "Do you think I'll buy insurance from you in the future? Maybe I'll meet you face to face so we can really settle this!" WHAM, the phone crashed in his ear.

"Wow, Meg," Carol mouthed. "That's not the Meloney or Meg I know. You put the hockey stick on his butt!"

Soe waved his hand trying to get her attention. "Don't kill him yet, Meg. I've got a car and I would really like to work with you for a couple of days if you can stay here. When you have to go back, we'll go buy a car. I know some dealers that will be fair with you."

"That's fine with me, Soe." Meg replied with a dejected sigh. "Finals start the 2nd of January. I need to be at school no later than December 28th to cram. This is the 19th of December. We have several days and I want to work with you." Meg lifted her head and smiled.

"What are you going to do, Carol?" Meg looked at her inquisitively.

Carol stood up and unconsciously crossed her arms over her breasts pushing them out. "I have to leave. My parents are expecting me for Christmas. I'll turn the rent car in and fly to Virginia and school. That's where my car is.

"However," Carol's eyebrows rose as she looked at Soe. "I would like to see Soe's lab set up and watch this stuff he's going to test on you. This mind reading thing is really exciting. I'll bet I could ace my finals with it." She giggled as she twirled around.

Jac looked at the three of them with his hands in his pockets and then stared at the floor. "I'll clean up the kitchen, wash the dishes, wash the clothes and vacuum the house."

They all looked at Jac realizing they had completely left him out.

Carol quickly stepped up to Jac putting her arms around his neck looking up into his face. She asked in a seductive voice. "You poor baby. Are you L-O-F?"

"What's that mean, Sweetiepie?" He encircled her with long arms and nuzzled her neck as he pulled her in close.

"That's 'left out feeling,' Jac!" She giggled. "Oh—, you are so strong. I just love strong men." Carol murmured as she batted her eyes and slowly disengaged herself dragging her hands down his arms.

Jac's stare demanded eye contact as he held her hands. *I wonder how far this might go?* There was certainly chemistry snapping between them.

Meg looked at Jac. *All the way, Bigboy!*

Jac shot a startled glance at Meg and dropped Carol's hands. "Okay, let's go to Soe's lab and play with Meg's brain, y'all."

Jac's eyes dragged back to Carol again as he put dishes in the washer. *She is just cute as a bug! Seems smart and I love that extraverted personality! Meg is the real charmer with that somewhat laid back personality. But she put the whammy on me yesterday with that brother feeling!*

They all filed outside in the cold. Jac announced, "I'm taking my car because I'll have to go to work after lunch."

Jac turned to Meg. "Go with Soe. Carol can ride with me."

Pushing a button in his pocket, the garage door opened and started the GN.

Carol gave Jac a startled glance. "How'd you do that, Jac?"

He held up a little black fob on his key ring, smirking at Carol. "Push the button and it goes. Some late model technology, Carol." He looked at Carol for a reaction as he pushed another button on the fob and both doors opened slightly.

Carol grinned impishly cutting her eyes at Jac. "Just what-all does that thing do Jac? Does it lay the seats down, too?"

"That's ah hell of an idea, Carol. I'll have to think about that. However, it does trigger a theft alarm, also." Jac grinned as he let his eyes slide down her body.

Carol caught the body survey and turned for a profile as she looked the car over, then she jumped in the seat.

"Hey, these are real nice seats. Is this leather, Jac?"

Jac shifted into reverse, backed out, and headed down the street after Soe. "Yes, it's leather——, of course." He grinned at her, rolling the car along slowly. "I took these seats out of a Ford Explorer. They're about the best I've found in American cars. General Motors has always had really crappy seats. They're both uncomfortable and unsupportable. I think they make them for gimlet butts." Jac sneered at her with a twisted grin. They moved slowly down the residential street approaching an access road to the freeway.

"The Ford seats are firm and mold to your back and legs with air operated pads."

Carol laughed as she leaned against the door watching Jac. "Go on Jac, tell me what you really think. Don't hold back."

Jac cocked his head smirking at her. "Well, the GM seats are made for small people. What kind of car do you have? You might not fit a GM seat."

"Ha, Ha, Bigboy. You been looking at something sweet?"

Jac watched her, grinning, as he entered the freeway and gassed it.

Her head snapped back and she grabbed for something to hang on to. Carol's startled gasp rushed out. "Boy, this car has some get up and go. What is it?"

Jac smiled and stepped on the gas again, revving to 5000 in third, slamming Carol back again.

"Get your seat belt on, Carol."

"My lord, Jac. This is some hotrod!" Carol yelled excitedly, "What will it really do?"

"That's enough for now, Carol, we really don't have enough road to demo this car. But it will scare the pants off you." Jac looked over his shoulder at her as he steered the car with his right hand.

"Ha, I want to see that." Carol grinned her impish smile at Jac and poked him in the ribs.

Jac's eyes crinkled into a grin. "Don't start anything now, Carol. We've got things to do."

"That sure sounds like some kinda promise to me, Jac." Carol looked coyly at Jac, whispering huskily.

Jac wheeled the car into a parking spot next to Soe's in the private parking area, making extended eye contact.

"Carol, have you had any peculiar feelings about this event with Meloney, me or Soe?"

Carol stared at Jac for a moment. "What do you mean, Jac? When Meloney left Friday, I had a feeling. A premonition, I guess, that it was a bad deal. I can't explain it. Something terrible did happen to Meloney, but it seems to be okay now. Is that what you had in mind?"

Jac shrugged looking out the window past Carol. "I have had a strange feeling, maybe déjà vu like, ever since the emergency call came to the hospital. Then Soe performs this mind enhancer deal on Meloney and basically brings her brain back to normal with ESP. He tells me it was preordained! I'm still drifting in a fog, wondering what it's all about. You talk about premonitions; I really have one about this whole thing. Anyway—, it has brought the four of us together in a capsule of time and I'm happy about it!"

Jac shrugged again smiling slightly, looking to Carol for understanding.

Carol put her hand on Jac's arm as she met his stare. "Maybe it is preordained, Jac. I have heard of meetings made in Heaven. Maybe we are supposed to do something significant in the future."

Grimacing, a stern stare, Jac opened the car door. "To the future, Carol. Arm yourself. You are forewarned!"

***

They ran up the stairs to Soe's lab and found the door open, Soe standing in the middle of the entrance staring.

He turned to Jac. "Someone has broken into my lab and scattered stuff everywhere." They looked over the lab. Equipment was pushed over and onto the floor. Paper, books, and a tray of floppy disks were scattered.

Soe fumed. "I wonder what they were looking for? I don't have anything here that is worth anything except sales at a pawnshop. Maybe some junkie was trying to find money or steal some electronics that he could sell for dope money." Soe clenched his fists. "I sure would like to meet the shithead for a few minutes."

"C'mon, let's clean it up. Please help me if you will. I want to get to Meg's situation as soon as I can." Soe sighed quietly as he bent over picking up his scattered floppies.

All of them pitched in and restored the lab to some semblance of order in a few minutes.

Soe sighed again as he clenched his fists. "I don't see anything missing. I don't know what's going on, but it sure

THE ENHANCERS

pisses me off. I'd like a few minutes with the bastard that did this."

Soe had grabbed his knife out of his hip pocket. He nervously snapped it open and closed, clack-clack, clack-clack.

Jac examined the doorjamb and lock. "I don't see any marks that indicate that it has been forced open. Could you have left it unlocked, Soe?"

"Hell no, Jac. I'm damn careful about locking up when I leave."

"Do you want to call the Police? Maybe check for fingerprints?"

"Let's just forget it for now. I don't think they can do anything anyway." Soe answered waving his hands in resignation.

Carol and Meg quietly took seats in available chairs listening to Soe cursing. Meg sent a message to Carol. *Just cool it. It will clean up.*

Carol shook her head, mumbling. "This is unbelievable."

"Well, it's working fine," Soe announced after the set up and check out procedure on his computer.

Snatching his keys, he retrieved the EEG equipment from a locked drawer and his disks relating to Meg's miraculous recovery.

"I think I'm ready. Let's get started. I'm over it girls. Thanks for the patience. Meg, sit here in this recliner chair and let me attach you to the EEG. You won't feel a thing." Soe hustled about the lab.

Jac and Carol took seats nearby watching Soe move in precise steps. He obviously knew what he was doing. The quietness hung in the air as each one of them anticipated something startling. The monitor flickered with data, then brain scans, and then it lapsed into an X-Y coordinate screen, white lines on a blue background.

"It all looks good, Meg. I'm going to run a normal scan on your brain and expand it very slightly."

Soe watched the screen. After entering instructions from the computer keyboard, a series of waveforms appeared on the

60

screen and marched across in a continuing sequence. More instructions produced the background waveform Jac had seen in ICU.

"Last night I was concerned about your recovery from the coma. But I think you are perfectly okay, Meg. I don't see anything of concern.

Jac mentioned, looking at Meg. "The only thing we might do beyond this is an MRI scan of the brain, Meg. But your EEG looks very normal."

"You're right Jac. Anyway Meg, here we go."

Meg finally got a word in. With a little bite, she said,

"Well, it's about time you put your stamp of approval on the new product. As an inventor, you must believe!"

Soe snapped up to look at Jac then Meg looking somewhat baffled. Then he realized Meg was joking. "Ah—, yes, Meg. In any experiment, closed loop control must be implemented. Here's the final test." He spun around in his chair as he entered more data. The screen changed again to reveal an enhanced carrier waveform.

"This will stimulate your brain EEG signals and you may get an increase in ESP senses."

A startled gasp exploded from Meg's lips. "Oh crap!" She gripped the arms of the chair tightly, squirming around, twisting and turning. Her eyes stared into space, her face contorted into a grimace.

"I can see what happened in the wreck. I see the other car coming at me, crossing the line, and the driver looking up!" Meg's lips pulled back in a snarl.

The energy emanated from Meg in an invisible aura encapsulating Jac, Carol and Soe. In their mind, they could see, hear, feel Meg's fright, fear, terror as the ghastly scene unfolded.

"It's a man and he's drunk or asleep and he's waking up, trying to jerk the car back into his lane. He brakes, slides to a stop and turns back watching my car go through the railing into the water." Meg panted, eyes staring into the black night as she strained against the chair arms.

"He gets out, looks around, gets back in the car and drives away.

"Hey, wait. I can see the license plate. It's JVC 299, Texas. It's an old car, maybe back in the 80's."

Meg leaned forward as if straining to glimpse something. "I can see what he sees through his eyes and feel what he feels. He's drunk and scared. He is driving fast and trying to get away before anybody sees him.

"He says something———, 'Ahhhh, better him than me.'"

Soe forced himself to swing around and slap 'escape' on the keyboard. Meg wilted into the chair gasping for breath, her face wet with beads of sweat, her eyes darting to and fro.

Jac snapped forward the first to recover from the vivid drama. He felt her neck for a pulse and peeled back an eyelid. Meg panted heavily with eyes dilated staring into nothing. Gaining control of his own emotions, Jac watched Meg calm. Her pulse dropped in a rush and her eyes focused on him. *Look at that recovery! Almost instantaneous! I'm telling you this is going to be a whizzer!*

"You okay, Meg?" Jac asked as an afterthought.

Meg started babbling again, eyes snapping, arms waving. "Unbelievable! That was so real! I was in his head and experiencing what he was feeling and seeing. I was jumping back and forth between him and me!"

Carol brought a glass of water for Meg. "Yeah, it was REAL! You carried us along with you, Meg. We saw it just like you did, I guess. It was scary, Meg. This is far more than the movies! How in the world does this thing work, Soe?" Carol demanded frowning at Soe.

She continued, as she looked from one to another. "Do you realize what this thing did? It gave us a look into the past through an actual witness's eyes, even feelings. This is almost incomprehensible! I wouldn't have believed it if I hadn't experienced it. And you're telling me it might work on everybody? This thing is more significant than the atomic bomb! Hang on. World. Half the population will kill the other half!"

Carol threw up her hands scowling at Soe. "You, I mean you and Meg, maybe us—, are sitting on a twist in the world's direction!

She turned and pointed to Jac and Soe. "From your looks you experienced the same thing I did, huh?"

"That's a very perceptive observation, Carol." Soe wheeled his swivel chair around to face the trio. "It's really a peek into a possible future world where there is no privacy."

Meg sat up, alarm in her voice. "I didn't realize you were tied directly into my mind! I think I can control it better next time so you won't be involved.

"Things keep popping into my mind. The night nurse at the hospital, her name is Jodie Barker. She knows something about this machine and she told some people about it. She listened to our room conversation and called someone named Sammy and told him about me and my recovery. Sammy promised to pay her and asked a lot of questions about the ESP capabilities."

"Good Lord, how do you know that, Meg?" Jac exclaimed staring at Meg.

"Apparently, the program stimulated my memory. I can see her listening in on the intercom to my room when you were first using the EEG on me. She called this Sammy. In fact, she called him twice. She told him everything." Meg answered, alarm still in her voice.

Meg turned towards the lab bench and extended her hand with the glass. It floated over to the bench and set down.

"Hey, did you see that?" Jac shouted. "How in the hell did you do that, Meg?"

Before Meg could answer, Soe held up his hand, casually waving it. "Stimulation of this carrier waveform somehow enables a person to perform ESP phenomena, telekinesis for example. I could do some slight telekinesis while under the computer stimulation, but the computer is not activating her brain now. She is much more powerful than me."

Clasping his hands to control his excitement, Soe sat forward in his chair. "Ahh—, let's try something else, Meg. See if you can transfer a thought to someone else's mind under control."

Meg closed her eyes and sat very still.

Soe snapped his fingers. "Ha, I got it Meg. You told me to turn the computer back on and try some more stimulation, didn't you?"

Meg grinned. "Yes, I used it earlier on Jac. I want to look at something else that is hanging on the edge of my mind. It's just beyond reach. Turn it up a little, also. I really don't feel anything unusual." Meg glanced around the room at the trio staring at her. She could feel and sense the excitement and a quiver of jealousy among her friends.

Soe clicked the keys again and the carrier waveform appeared on the screen. "Now I'm going to increase the power a few microvolts, Meg."

Meg lunged upright in the chair, clutching the arms with white knuckles and staring into space. She began talking quickly. "I can see two men opening your door with a key. One of them is wearing a uniform, like, maybe a janitor here in the building. The other man is wearing a suit and an overcoat. Overcoat is turning on your computer and trying to get past the password. The other is just watching."

Meg paused in her monologue staring into space.

"He's, ahh, he's put a disk in the slot and it's activated your computer. He's scanning your files. He's found a file on me and he's copying it to his disk. He's scattering your equipment and trashing the lab. Both of them turn and leave. They are both wearing rubber gloves so no fingerprints will be found. They never talk so I can't hear them. I can't get in their heads to read them."

Meg's head turned as if she were watching them walk out.

Soe clicked instructions and the scan on the screen diminished to a normal pattern. Meg relaxed and her eyes focused again. She was shaking and clammy with frightened sweat.

"Wow, that was some experience!" She declared loudly. "I was there, amongst them. I thought they could see me!"

Jac patted her and gave her a coat. "Just lay back and let reality come back. You're here in the lab with us, Meg." Jac said soothingly. "This time you did not include us in the picture. Whatever is happening, you are gaining control very rapidly. Were their faces clear? Could you identify them?"

Carol stared open mouthed at Meg and demanded. "Boyhowdy, I've got to try that machine, Soe."

Soe held up his hands. "Sure, Carol, we can do it. But first, let's review and try to figure out what's happening here before we dash off in another direction.

"First of all, they didn't get anything from my computer. I saved the program, data and Meg's experience to a disk and I locked it in the cabinet without naming it." Soe counted with one finger up. "From what Meg told us, they didn't get into the cabinet and I don't see any signs of entry. That's two. No one has a key except me. And three, apparently the janitor is in on the break-in. He has a key to my lab door. I don't know what to do about this situation. But, maybe Meg can ID these turds so I can put a little Mexican Taco on them!"

A wry sneer spread across his mouth as he looked at the three of them for help. He stood up leaning on a tabletop.

"We've got something going on here that's beyond me. It's almost as if someone has been monitoring my research and they're trying to steal it. I've got to think about this."

Meg had been anticipating an opening. "Yes, I can ID them if I see them again, Soe, Jac, but all I have is a face."

Soe shook his head as he looked at the floor.

Jac quipped. "It ain't on the floor, Soe. No use lookin there."

"Yeah, I know, Jac. Hey, what do y'all think happened here with this last scene?" Soe looked up and swept the crew with a questioning stare.

Jac and Carol shook their heads. "Damned if I know." Jac answered.

Meg spoke up. "I felt like I was pulling the scene from the surroundings or the things they touched. Their presence seemed to still be here, somehow."

Soe had sat down again and spun the swivel chair around to face them. "I've read about psychics who could visit a scene or touch objects and get feelings and visions of the past. But they usually weren't very clear, not nearly as clear as Meg has described."

Patting the computer keyboard, he fixed his gaze on the two witnesses. "I think the program I have here is stimulating the Quark wave effect in Meg and enabling her to use latent psychic talents. It's possible the accident and coma she experienced enabled the program to bring forth ESP in her to a higher level than in someone else. I tried it on me and it had a minor effect, as I told you."

Soe looked for confirmation, scanning Jac, Meg and Carol.

Carol asked. "What is the Quark effect you spoke of, Soe?" Carol's head tossed as she stared at Soe. "Hey, that's ah hell of a story, Soe."

"What do you mean, Carol?"

"It's kinda crazy." Carol pointed to Meg. "Almost as soon as I got the words out of my mouth, I had this story about Clark or Quark or whatever and the psychic reading in my head. The whole thing."

Meg laughed. "I picked up the story from Soe and sent it to you, Carol. Maybe that's the explanation. Maybe we have latent ESP talents and the EEG activates them. Let's try this thing on Carol and see what she can do."

Meg rose out of the recliner with almost no effort. She seemed to float to a vertical standing position.

Carol gawked at Meg. "For crap's sake, Meg. You almost floated. You might be able to fly! Soe, I sure do want some of that!"

Meg grinned impishly. "Yes, that might happen!"

Jac returned with sodas for everyone.

Meg grabbed the Diet Coke. "That's a good idea, Jac, I need some caffeine. I am washed out, thank you."

Soe connected Carol to the EEG wiring and keyed the computer. The screen lit up with a normal brain wave scan.

"Watch this, everyone has the same wave forms." Soe turned to Carol and signaled. "I'm going to start the sequence, Carol."

Carol showed no signs of awareness.

"I'll increase the signal strength." Soe looked expectantly at Carol.

Carol held up her hand. "I think something is happening, I can feel your presence. It's really weird. I know where each of you are without seeing you.

"I'll try to move the soda to me." The can remained stationary for a moment; then suddenly it moved to the edge of the bench top and fell to the floor. It rolled over to the recliner and rocked back and forth. "That's all I can do."

Soe tapped again on the keyboard, increasing the signal strength.

Carol yelled out. "Ahhhhhhhhh" as she gripped the arms of the chair, staring wide-eyed into space.

Soe quickly killed the signal as Carol lay back in the chair sweating, visibly shaking.

Jac was at her side immediately checking her pulse and looking in her eyes. He stole a glance at the screen. Her EEG scan had returned to normal. Jac patted her and asked. "How do you feel, Carol?"

Carol stuttered. "I could pick up hundreds of people's feelings. They were just pouring into my head, bombarding me with fear, hate, aggression, love, every kind of emotion. It was overwhelming. I couldn't stop them or separate them. They washed over me like a wave!"

She shuddered and gripped her shoulders, shaking her head with her eyes closed.

Soe patted Carol on the shoulder, "Carol, I'm terribly sorry about this. I just don't know what will happen with this concept. I tried it on me and had those intense feelings of awareness you mention. Apparently, it affects each person in a different way."

Soe looked at Jac. "Do you want to try it, Jac?"

"Yes, I would really like to see what it does to me or for me." Jac answered firmly.

"Carol, can you stand up?" Jac asked as he held out his hand. Carol struggled up, and with help, moved over to another chair.

"Give me my soda. I'm drained."

Jac settled in the chair as Soe attached the EEG connections. "I'm ready, Soe."

"Here we go, Jac."

Soe and the girls watched Jac closely.

Jac held up his hand. "Wait a minute. I can see inside machinery. I can see how it works. It's fascinating. I can see inside your body, Soe. I can look at your organs like your skin is transparent. This is incredible. This is better than x-rays or MRI or cat scans!"

As Soe increased the signal a few microvolts, Jac grabbed the arms of the chair, staring wildly. "Now I'm getting the feelings and emotions Carol was talking about!"

He gritted his teeth, grimacing with his eyes squeezed closed.

Soe killed the signal and Jac relaxed, breathing heavily.

"For crap's sake, that is one hell of an experience! Ahhhh, Carol, I can see why you did a flip." Jac wheezed, looking at her. "This might be a great torture tool. It wouldn't take much to convince somebody and it wouldn't leave any scars, ha, ha," Jac ended.

"What have you been reading, Dr. Jac? I would think you could pull up all kinds of drugs to eviscerate someone's mind?" Carol snickered.

"That may be possible, Carol. But today's analytical talents can detect those drugs to parts per billion. It's very difficult to hide."

Soe started to say something, but Meg interrupted him. "The way this thing is developing I will be able to read their mind, maybe without even their knowledge. Put me back on the EEG, Soe."

Soe looked at her curiously and again started to say something. Meg held up her hand motioned for him to go ahead.

Soe shrugged, hooked her up and keyed the computer. Everyone was watching to see what Meg was up to. Meg turned her head and motioned him to turn it up a little bit. Staring into space, Meg gripped the arms of the chair tightly. Suddenly she motioned Soe to disconnect.

Rising from the chair she went to Soe's desk and began writing on a pad. They all gathered around the desk, curiosity rampant.

"There is a bug in the room and the room has been entered more than once. Go outside in the hallway."

Gathering beyond earshot, Meg said breathlessly. "I had this scene in my head about another break-in and I wanted to check it out. The same two men have been here before and I believe they copied your disk on your EEG manipulation. The overcoat man put a transmitting microphone under your desk, Soe. They could be listening to everything that has happened today."

Jac stood with arms crossed glaring at Soe. "What in hell is going on here, Soe? Do you have industrial spies dogging you for this EEG thing? How could they already know? This thing developed in the last 24 hours."

Soe held up his hand and said quietly. "Let me get my bug sweep and clear the lab, first."

He reentered the lab, went to a drawer and rummaged through finding a small black box with a light on it. Walking around the room, he pointed it, panned it and leaned over his desk.

"Ah ha!" he mouthed, as he carefully pulled out a tiny box with a small antenna and put it in a beaker on the bench. Grabbing a bottle of concentrated hydrochloric acid, he grinned as he poured it in the beaker and watched the box dissolve. Further sweeping revealed another bug of a different kind under the bench counter top. Soe deposited it in the beaker of acid, also.

Soe motioned them back into lab. "I believe I've got all the bugs. The phone could be tapped. But it has to be done in the phone switchboard room somewhere in the building."

Amid the babble of everyone trying to talk at once, Soe held up his hand and addressed them. "Calm down. Just cool it for now. We have a great deal to talk about. There are strange things going on. It looks like someone is monitoring my progress here and maybe they have stolen some preliminary information on my original disk. They probably have been listening in on today's events and they now know that we have really advanced with the EEG concept."

"Also, my locks are no good. I certainly don't want to keep anything valuable here, data, or anything else.

"Finally," Soe said with a deep breath, "we could be in some danger. These people are very serious. It looks like they either bought the janitor or replaced him. We need to have Meg look at the janitor and see if she recognizes him. I can check with college personnel and see if he is recent, also."

Jac poked his finger at Soe. "That's just scratching the surface, Soe. We have several problems. We have a drunk and his car to turn over to the Police. Secondly, can you or can we continue to work here? They know us but we don't know them. Remember Meg's report about the hospital? They know where we are, but we don't know where they are." Jac waved his hands to make his point.

"I don't think the police would be any help in this situation. There's nothing concrete here but the break-in and we've cleaned that up. Hell, we're two-blocked!"

Carol stamped her foot as she sputtered. "Meg, you call the police and tell them about the license plate. Just say that you woke up and remember seeing the plate on the front of the car. Maybe they'll catch the bastard and put him in jail."

Carol grabbed Meg's arm. "Meg, how in the world do you keep the wave of feelings out of your head that Jac and I experienced?"

Meg looked at the floor and then at Carol. "I can feel them but somehow I can push them back and they disappear. I guess I concentrate on something else that's more prominent in my view. This whole thing is really weird. It needs a lot of exploring before we can be sure about specifics."

Meg turned towards the bench. "I think that each time my mind is stimulated, I get stronger ESP capabilities. Just look at this."

A drink can shot off the lab bench into her hand as if it had been thrown. It twirled to the ceiling and stayed there, spinning around. Meg grinned at them as it floated down like a feather and settled on the bench.

Soe's face lit up. "You see, that's just what the reader said about Atlantis. They had all the ESP skills and the energy supported them. Meg has that energy activated in her and I think it's getting stronger very rapidly."

"Meg, can you see into the future?"

Standing very still, Meg seemed to peer into the distance. "No, I can't get anything about the future. I don't know how to look or probe. If I get anything, it's more of a premonition."

Jac had held his breath waiting for Meg's answer. He sighed heavily. "We've blown most of the day. I'm hungry and I have to go to work soon. Soe, why don't you take your bug detector and sweep my house and your house. Check the phones, they are probably bugged, too.

"What we really need is some professional help." Jac paused for a moment. "I think I'll talk to my grandfather about this."

"That's okay, Jac, I'll talk to him." Soe offered casually with a slight wave of his hand.

Jac stepped back startled, glaring at Soe.

"What the hell does that mean, Soe?"

"Well, if you remember, Collinga Foundation is carrying most of my expenses. So, I have been reporting directly to Jac senior." Soe answered quietly with his chin jutted out.

"Well, kiss my naked ass. You are full of surprises. What else is there, Soe?" Jac demanded with obvious jealousy.

"That's about it as far as I know, Jac. Don't get your panties in a wad." Soe laughed in an attempt to defuse the confrontation.

The girls giggled. Carol grabbed Jac's arm. "I'm with you, Dr. Jac. Let's eat."

Soe made a quick cell-phone call to someone and spoke quietly with his head turned away. "Now is the time. We're leaving to get something to eat."

Grabbing his computer disks, Soe slipped them into a leather pouch that fit over his shoulder. Locking the door, he ushered them into the hallway. Announcing. "Hey, let's eat!"

On the front steps of the building, Soe stopped them. "Ahem, uh, y'all better be on the lookout. We don't know who are what we are dealing with. If you see anybody watching us or following us, alert all of us, okay?

"Let's get some sho nuff Texas food for the girls, Jac. You know the Chili Bar, don't you?"

"Sure. Carol and I will follow you. Take off." Jac answered brusquely.

Carol glanced sideways at Jac as they were driving to the diner. "Soe seems to be real tight with your Grandpa, Jac."

"Yeah, and I intend to find out what's going on. This whole thing is new to me." Jac agreed gritting his teeth. "I first got a glimpse of Soe and GrandJac's relationship yesterday. I don't know how far it has gone or what all is involved, but I will find out!"

Jac snarled, "Did the weather give you any trouble driving from Dallas? These Northers blow through here every three to five days making our weather cycle like a yo-yo. See, it's finally clearing off."

Jac knew that he was talking to avoid thinking of the confrontation with his grandfather, but he would have to face him. GrandJac used his Collinga Foundation to fund most of his pet projects. The whole town was a charitable write-off. From what Jac could see, GrandJac enjoyed giving money to most everyone in need. Jac's little awareness said that Grandpaw had a great deal of money. Well, anyway, the Foundation was a good tax write-off and still gave him some control of the contributions.

"Well, I did notice it was windy, Jac, but I was driving with the wind and across to some extent. It wasn't bad. The rain had stopped anyway." Carol answered looking at Jac to see his reaction to trivia.

Jac had never had any interest in GrandJac's financial affairs. He just knew they were large, very large. His parent's estate had provided him with quite a bit of money to pursue any of his interests. But schooling, auto mechanics, and now being a Doctor consumed all his time. He had little interest in blowing money just for the thrill of it. *Humph, Soe, GrandJac, Collinga, brain stimulation, Meg, ESP and déjà vu, new challenges. Oh, yes, don't forget about this blonde bombshell next to me!*

Jac's stare returned to Carol with a grin. "What tha hell. It'll wash out. My single greatest concern is this déjà vu thing. It is much more that it seems, I think. Why don't you solve it, Carol?"

"I can understand your concern Jac. I'm just too far out of the loop at the moment. This looks like a Meg/Soe play. You think the DJ is big, I think the ESP is big. It's just absolutely beyond imagination!

"Yeah, logically, it is the biggest and most important thing in our time. I can't imagine where it will go." Jac acknowledged flicking a glance at her as they pulled into the restaurant. "If the public became aware of it, they'd storm the gates!"

***

Steam rose from the heaping bowls of chili as Carol and Meg gingerly poked at them. The jalapeno cornbread wasn't much cooler, but the sharp tastes teased their taste buds.

Meg smiled at the two men. "Yes, it is very good. Carol likes it, too."

Jac smiled. "Giving us a read, Meg? I guess this is the first time you've been to Texas, Carol?"

"Yes, and it's exciting and spooky. I'm a little scared of all this spy stuff with Soe. And, of course, Meg, the new Meloney, just in from Mars, ha, ha."

"We'll talk to Grandpaw. He can get this crap cleared up in a New York second, Carol."

Jac rubbed his chin, eying Meg. "Meg, this mind reading capability can easily be an invasion of privacy, and there's nothing anybody can do about it."

"That's very true, Jac. It can easily be abused. However, I can only read your thoughts right now." Meg paused for a moment. "It seems that you can block your thoughts and my reading. But I don't know how you do it."

Carol interrupted the direction of the conversation,

"Well, can you use it to see if anybody is watching us here in the restaurant?"

Meg slowly panned the room with piercing eyes and smiled.

"There is no one spying on us for the EEG capability. However, that group of boys is very interested in Carol's body, particularly her sweater effect."

Carol spun around and stared at the boys who quickly looked away.

Jac smiled as he nudged Carol's arm. "Like Joe Namath says, Carol. 'When you got it, flaunt it'. Now take a deep breath for your fans."

Carol slapped Jac on the arm with a coy smile. "Are you one of my fans, Bigboy?"

Jac rolled his eyes as he ogled her sweater. "My Mama told me about these things. But she never said they'd be so big."

Carol blushed.

Meg laughed as she pointed a finger at Carol. "That's a first, Carol. Someone got your goat and you blushed."

Soe watched the parlay of words and caught Meg's eye. He wasn't particularly amused. "Meg, can you read these people? The ones here in the restaurant and determine what they are thinking, specifically?"

"Yes, I can." Meg averred. "Take that one at the cash register. He doesn't have a job and is broke. He's desperate and may take up stealing.

"This tool could have very wide ranging effects on our society. It might curb the hell out of crime in many forms, even before the event."

"Which reminds me." Meg declared, eyes snapping, "I want to get that bastard that ran me off the road. Soe, let's go to the Police Station."

Jac stood up abruptly and grabbed the check. Something just didn't seem right with Soe. "Get the table, Soe, I'll get this. I've got to go to work. I hope you can nail the turd, Meg, good luck."

***

The girls and Soe jumped in Soe's little Nissan and drove down town to the police station.

Jac went to work with suspicions developing.

***

The police dispatcher at the front desk listened carefully. He called an Officer forward to meet with them in an adjacent room.

Meg stepped forward. "My name is Meloney Graham. This is Carol and Shawn. They are friends of mine, Officer."

"Hello, Miss Graham. I'm Sgt. Harold Whitner. How can I help you? Please sit down." The Sgt. waved to the table after he shook hands.

Meg sat across the table facing Whitner. Sticking her chin out, she stated. "Last Saturday night, I was run off the road at a bridge into a river by a hit and run driver."

Soe held up his hand. "That was on Hiway 42 at the Marian Creek Bridge, Officer."

"Yes, thank you. I'm familiar with the accident."

Meg continued as she turned back from Soe. "There was a bright flash of lightning and I saw the license plate on the car. It's Texas JVC 299 and the car was tan or brown."

"That's very helpful, Miss Graham. Please wait a minute." Sgt. Whitner rose and left the room.

Carol touched Meg's arm. "That lightning flash is a good point, Meg. You didn't tell us about that."

Meg turned to Soe and Carol. "I think I mentioned it. But the more I go back in my mind to review the scene, the more I see, the more details come out. I hope we can get this guy."

Sgt. Whitner came back in the room with a sheet of paper. "That's a good number, Miss Graham. Can you describe any more of the car?"

Meloney read his mind and knew this was her man. "Yes, the car looked old. Maybe a Buick or an Olds in the 80's."

"That's very good, Miss Graham." Whitner answered with a tight smile. "The description fits, the car owner is William Cleaver. Was there actual contact with Cleaver's car? Did he hit you?"

"Well, no, I don't think so. I dodged off the road to avoid a head on wreck. He was completely over in my lane. I could go to his side or go to the right. I guess I acted instinctively, steering the car to the right."

I really don't care if this turd is caught or charged with hit and run. I'll hunt him down and give him a trip he'll never forget!

"He has a record of alcoholism and is currently on probation. If it were Mr. Cleaver, it would explain why he left the scene. We will follow up on this and contact you."

Soe gave his and Jac's phone numbers.

Sgt. Whitner stood up and reached for Meg's hand.

"I'm amazed at your rapid recovery, Miss Graham. My report indicates that you were in critical condition Saturday night. Now you have a Band-Aid on your forehead."

Meg smiled slightly as she met Whitner's eyes. "Yes, I have two brilliant doctors who snatched me from the jaws of death!"

Carol giggled and poked Meg in the ribs.

A curious twist of Whitner's face brought no response from Meg as they filed out of the room. A vivid image appeared in his mind's eye of a beautiful woman clad in a white filmy robe fleeing from a monster's jaws spread wide dripping slimy drool. The woman had her hand extended towards two men in white coats standing in the distance on a dark hill.

In the hallway, Whitner suggested. "If this man does admit to this, you probably can get some help from his insurance on your car and hospital costs."

"Thank you, Officer Whitner, I'm sure he will admit to it. I hope I can meet him. In fact, I'm looking forward to it." Meg held Whitner's eyes in a cold stare for seconds beyond normal.

Officer Whitner stepped back as he reached for his mouth, expelling a gasp. The same monster appeared again, crunching this William Cleaver through the body, blood spraying from dripping jaws. "Ahem, yes, of course, Miss Graham. That may be possible. Thank you for coming in."

***

"C'mon, girls, it's 6 O'clock dark. Let's go to Jac's shed and plot against our enemies."

Soe patted Meg. "That was real good, Meg."

Carol skipped along beside them, giggling. "Meg, we—, you are going to get this turd and I hope you can fix his little wagon. He needs to be off the streets!"

Soe nodded, "Amen."

***

The Nissan glided onto the freeway as he accelerated to road speed. The freeway lights illuminated a large black Lincoln pulling up beside them in the inside lane. Soe glanced at the car; darkened windows showed nothing.

Alarmed, Meg moved her hand to her mouth, yelling. "They are going to try to run us over the rail on the overpass ahead. Soe, you've got to do something!"

"Fasten your seat belts, girls. Let's see what happens." Soe quickly bent over and retrieved a model 59 Smith and Wesson 9-MM automatic from under the seat.

"Oh shit," Carol screamed. "We're going to be killed!"

Meg squirmed in her seat. "They have guns, too, Soe."

Soe rolled the window down on his side as they rolled up the slope of the overpass. The Lincoln stayed beside them in the inside lane. Soe did not look at them to indicate that he knew anything. *This is great! Our enemies have come into the open. We can ID the bastards!*

Suddenly the Lincoln swerved ahead and across in front of them. An evil sneer crossed Soe's face as he slammed on the brakes and dropped behind the Lincoln as it veered into his lane.

"Get the license plate, Meg." Soe demanded brusquely.

Meg clutched the dash in the right front seat.

Carol braced herself in the back seat moaning. "Do something, Soe. They're gonna hit us!"

The Lincoln swerved back into the inside lane and braked hard pulling up beside the Nissan again. In moments, they were at the bottom of the slope. Soe quickly exited on the available ramp. The Lincoln rolled on down the freeway a short distance. Suddenly it ran off the shoulder of the road, through the grass, and onto the access road ahead of Soe's car. Soe turned right on a side road behind the Lincoln just past the exit lane. He gunned it to the next turn and turned right again.

The Lincoln slammed on the brakes, spinning around in one motion and accelerated back on the access road going the wrong way.

Two on-coming cars swerved wildly, one on each side of the Lincoln, veering over the shoulders. The one on the right slid into the curb turning over onto a concrete apron in front of a convenience store. Sparks showered out from the iron grinding on the concrete. It came to rest smashed into a parked car. The other car braked and slid up the side of the grassy slope of the freeway to a stop.

The Lincoln slid around the corner where Soe had turned and raced to the first intersection, hesitating.

Meanwhile Soe had turned right again and approached the access road where he turned right and drove down one block to the convenience store, pulled in and stopped.

"Get out, go inside to the back of the store. Get on my cellular phone. Call 875-2220. Tell them where you are and we need help. You're at Pecan and the Freeway, Westside." Soe yelled with an evil cackle.

Meg grabbed the phone and the two them charged into the store.

Soe got out with the 9 mm and walked over to the wreck where people had gathered. He kept the gun under his coat in his belt as he turned to watch the road. The lights surrounding the parking area in front of the store dimmed towards the street. The crowd at the wreck milled around in the semi-darkness.

The Lincoln rolled down the access road slowly. Seeing the Nissan in the parking area, it pulled into the curb beside the car one space over.

Soe moved back into the crowd and watched. Initially, no one got out of the car. Slowly the door opened behind the driver and a man got out dressed in blue jeans, a leather jacket and a ball cap. He had a light unshaven beard. Long, brown hair hung out from under his cap. With his right hand in his leather jacket he looked around, went to Soe's car, peering through the window. Another quick glance around the parking area showed nothing. He started towards the store snickering at the wreck.

An ambulance whining down the freeway with siren blaring and lights flashing shattered the night. Leather coat man looked back at the ambulance, hesitating as it exited at the Pecan exit and rolled towards the store.

Soe walked rapidly out of the crowd towards the leather coat man with both hands at his sides.

"Hey," he yelled, as he neared the man.

Leather-coat turned towards him, scowling. "What you want, Fatboy?" Soe walked right into him with a left hook to the jaw and a leg behind his leg. He fell heavily with his head smacking the concrete and lay still.

Turning quickly to the Lincoln even before the man hit the ground, he smashed the driver side window with the 9-MM pointing into the car. The tempered glass shattered in a thousand pieces as he stuck his gun in the face of the driver.

"Have you died lately, fuckhead?" Soe hissed as he looked over the inside of the car. There was a Mac 10 9 MM automatic on the back seat and the driver had a .45 automatic in his lap. No one else was in the car.

The small driver's neat moustache quivered over his van dike beard. Thin, tight fitting gloves grasped the wheel in a panic grip. A tailored suit and tie did little to hide the tension in his thin face and body. Small fragments of the shattered window covered him like a snow shower.

"Ahhhh." he belched. Jerking back from the 9 mm stuck into his cheek, his dark eyes stared wide at Soe.

With eyes locked on Soe's, his right hand slid down the steering wheel towards the .45 auto in his lap.

Soe said quietly, "I sure hope you go for it. Please, I'm going to shoot across your nose and eyes. It'll blind you and make you look like a mole!"

The man quickly moved his hand up the wheel again.

Soe stuck a massive arm in the car and clamped his big hand around the man's thin neck. "You gotta name, shit for brains, before I pull you through this window?" Soe's scowling countenance would have scared a small child to death.

"Carlos Garza." The man gagged. "Ahhhh—! Don't hit me! Don't hit me! You're choking me!"

"Who do you work for, suckdick?" Soe pushed his face into the car, breathing heavily on the thin Latino.

Carlos gasped and struggled in vain as Soe tightened down even more.

"I don't even know his name, man. He paid me $5000 to hit the girl." Carlos gagged out with eyes protruding and saliva drooling down his chin.

Police had arrived in the parking lot and were trying to control the crowd, the traffic, and assist the EMT's with the people in the overturned car. They hadn't noticed Soe and the Lincoln, but they were kneeling down by the man in the leather coat.

A pickup truck pulled up on the far side of the lot. Two men got out and walked rapidly towards Soe and the Lincoln. They quickly sized up the situation. One got in the Lincoln from the right side and picked up the .45 in the driver's lap. Soe released Carlos and stepped away from the car.

The other man stepped quickly to the police, shaking his head. "Gawd a'mighty. John Duey's done it again, Officer. He's a friend of mine. I'll take care of him."

The man was tall, over 6 feet and wore boots and jeans with a western cut jean jacket.

The big man spit a stream of tobacco juice to one side. "Ya see, officer, John has seizures if he don't take his medicine. Hell, we've found him in the front yard after a night uh drinkin. I'll take him home."

The policeman asked. "Do you want the EMTs to look at him, Mister? He's got a nasty cut on his chin and mouth."

"Naw." He replied shaking his head. "This happens once a week. I'm really gettin tired of picking him up. He fell again, the dumb shit. Don't worry about him; you have your hands full with the wreck. I know how to help my buddy, John Duey. He just needs to take his medicine on schedule. Thet mashed mouth'll remind him for ah while."

The big man reached down and pulled John Duey to his feet. Soe stepped in, supported him, and they poured him into the back seat of the Lincoln. The man got in the driver's seat of the Lincoln and started the car.

Soe stepped up to the car as he looked over the two hit men. "Give me a call when you got it settled."

Soe went into the store and retrieved the girls from the back where they were talking excitedly about the events.

Meg turned to Soe grabbing his arm. "The man in the leather coat was going to come into the store and shoot us in front of everybody. He didn't care who saw. We didn't know what to do!" Meg continued talking rapidly. "All of a sudden his mind went out like a light bulb. All I could get from the driver was fear. He was scared. His mind was chaos!"

"What in hell did you do to them, Soe?" Carol whispered as they rapidly walked to the front of the store.

Outside on the store apron, Soe glanced at them with an evil smirk. "Well, the first one I adjusted his head. I could tell it was crooked, when I straightened it he passed out from the pain. I squeezed the second one's neck 'til his eyes bugged out. Boy, I enjoyed that!"

The girls giggled delightfully and hugged Soe on each arm.

"Let's get the hell out of Dodge." Soe suggested.

They quickly got in the Nissan and backed away from the crowd surrounding the wreck. The EMT's were loading the last victim into the ambulance.

"There's some work for Jac." Carol quipped.

"What happened to the Lincoln and the thugs?" Meg asked scanning the parking lot.

"Some of my support troops came by and hauled them off. We'll get a report later on." Soe explained grimly.

"We need to inform Jac of these events very soon because he may be in danger, too." Soe suggested. "Let's go by the hospital and tell him."

"You don't have to, I've already told him." Meg informed him, smiling smugly.

"WOW, that's just fantastic, Meg. You contacted Jac from here with telepathy? Son of a gun, if my troops can't get a straight story from the thugs, I'll have you sweep their minds. That's the easy way. I really want to work them over. I'm a little frustrated right now."

Meg looked at Soe for a long moment. "Yeah, I can tell. For the preservation of witnesses, let's just talk to them, okay?"

Soe looked at Meg, smiling. "Sure." He turned the car around and headed for Jac's house.

Carol sat forward in the back seat with her hands on the front seat. "Meg, if you can send a message to Jac, I'll bet you can read them like a book!"

***

Another surprise greeted them at Jac's house. Two men sat in a pickup truck in the driveway.

Carol stuttered, eyes wide. "Oh shit, is this more trouble?"

Soe motioned them out of the car, stating with emphasis. "They're on our side, let's get inside and talk about it."

The girls went inside while Soe talked to the men.

"We've been here for over an hour and swept the neighborhood for any 'visitors'. Can't find any. Soe, we'll stand guard through the night." The leader said as he stuffed his hands in his jacket.

Soe warned them with a wave. "Look for Jac. He'll be home from work about 12:30."

"Yeah, we know that. We'll keep an eye out for him, Soe." The leader acknowledged with a squirt of tobacco juice.

Soe went inside to find the girls milling around waiting for him with questions on their faces.

"Let's fix a pot of coffee, girls. We got some talkin to do." Soe suggested as he pulled his coat off.

Carol spun around, happy to ease the tension. "I'll do it, I know where everything is, Soe."

Soe pulled his sweep detector and proceeded to check the house, room by room; then he checked the phones.

"Everything looks okay, girls." Soe said as he waved them into the living room, "We can talk now."

Soe sat leaning forward, looking at the girls with a big grin. "Whatta ya tink, girls, ain't we having fun?" He had pulled the lock-back out and was snapping it back and forth.

Carol hesitated, squeezing her hands. "Well—, yeah, maybe. But it's more scary than fun, Soe. We don't know anything, really. It's like being in a sci-fi movie but it's for real!"

Meg just smiled. She already knew what direction Soe was going.

Soe held out his hands, palms up. "Girls, you can't go back to school because each of us has been marked by the opposition for removal. We have stumbled onto some new technology that the 'others' want very badly and will do literally anything to get. You saw tonight that they were intent on killing us though a hired hit man."

Soe gestured with his hands again as he got up and walked across the room.

"Meg saved our ass one more time with her mind reading. On the other hand, we have some very powerful allies that will protect us. If y'all go back to school, you would be out in the open with no one to help you.

"I think the one they really want is Meg. She has all the marbles. I was very surprised that they wanted to take her out tonight. We will need and we will have maximum protection from now on. That will take most of the heat off of us."

Carol looked at Meg, then Soe. "Soe, if they have the computer program and know how to use it, they may think that they can implement it with anybody. Meg would be a threat to them because she might be able to find them with her powers."

Soe spun around pointing the knife at Carol. "That's it, girls! They do have the program and plan on using it on somebody. That's very creative, Carol, good, good, good."

Whammm, Soe slammed his fist into his palm. "We must progress rapidly!"

Soe paced about the room with the gears cranking as he stared into nothing.

These girls are sharp. They will be an asset to the program. I'm just amazed at how rapidly it's moving forward. It's gonna stretch me just to keep up with the technology.

"I want to continue to explore this ESP phenomena and the carrier wave energy. I have more ideas about implementation. I want to condense the apparatus to something portable so we can be mobile and not tied to the lab."

Awareness, cognizance, recognition, experience. Meg observed the play of emotions in Soe and Carol. *Our life exists in our mind. Grasping. Pulling in these sensations. Analyzing them in light of our past awareness. Physical experiences feed the mind with emotions, sensations that create our experience, awareness, and thus, our perspective of our existence! I know I haven't formulated the concept to completion. But this unbelievable tool almost makes it like watching through a window with audio! We have always evaluated people by their actions and words. If they say nothing, we have only actions. A very poor second to judge them by. This phenomenon is almost like being a God! Maybe even influencing the people and circumstances to create a desired direction. I can't even comprehend the power it gives me or the others if they can exist.*

Turning her head, looking at Carol and Soe, she listened to the words, reading the emotions behind them. Meg coughed involuntarily trying to give the outward appearance of controlled casualness that the scene demanded.

Carol seemed to sense the tension, the undercurrents circulating, but she could not dissect them like Meg. She could only sense the emotions and cast out verbal rebuttals trying to pull forward enlightenment.

"You may enjoy all this cloak and dagger stuff, but it's scaring the crap out of me! Where are all the men and help coming from, Soe?"

Maybe a little bit of a sneer crept across Soe's mouth as he turned to face the girls from the center of the room. He folded his arms across his chest. "My primary sponsor is the Collinga Foundation funded by GrandJac. Jac's grandfather is the 'power behind the throne.' That's where the manpower and protection are coming from."

Clack, clack, clack went the knife. "Jac's grandfather is one of the wealthiest men in America. Wealth begets power. Make no mistake about that. I fully trust him to protect us from the 'others.'" Soe looked at both of them with assurance. "Think about wealth, power. They have always dovetailed. But here we have a new kind of power. Meg has brought forth power as yet undefined, but awesome in its potential!"

"Yeah, yeah, well, who in the hell are the 'others'?" Carol demanded in a sharp voice.

"GrandJac's team will flush them out in the open soon, Carol. You can count on that." Soe stated emphatically staring her down as he pointed the knife at her. "We already have two to work with. And I'm looking forward to that! HA, ha. Boy, they sure better come clean!"

***

Charles Wimberly, the janitor at the research center, grabbed the phone. *Ah yes, a call from Sam Friedman, 6:30 pm.* He dropped the sandwich and leaned back in the swivel chair flexing his arms over his head as he held the phone under his chin. The blond hair, blue eyes, high cheekbones accented by the square jaw pegged him as a Slav. Migrating from the northern edge of Russia with special skills enabled him to land a job in America's government forces.

"Charlie, this is Sam. I've got to get back into Etheridge's lab tonight. It looks like he found the bug."

"What do you intend to do, Sam? He'll probably sweep the lab every time he enters it. Particularly, if he has already found your bug." Charlie stated in a flat monotone.

"Well, I've got a new type of bug that only switches on and transmits when someone speaks. It's much more difficult to find with an ordinary bug sweeper. Secondly, I can turn it off remotely." Sam answered with a triumphant challenge in his voice.

"Hey, that's a clever idea you got there, Sam. Come on by about 8 and we'll get in the lab and set it up." Charlie answered slyly, thinking, technology to the rescue!

THE ENHANCERS

Charlie called his motel room. "Hey, Tommy, Etheridge found the bugs. The Jew wants back in the lab. Claims he has a new type of bug that energizes and transmits only on voice activation."

His partner, Tommy Silva, replied casually with a hand wave. "Yeah, I already knew that Etheridge found our bug. We're planning something different, but we aren't ready to put it in yet."

Charlie came back sarcastically. "Well God damn. I guess these Jew boys are better than we are, Tommy. It looks like you better get your ass in gear and do something before tomorrow morning. Etheridge will be back in here, and he might have another breakthrough."

"Charlie, you just sweep the floors like a good janitor and I'll have something by midnight." Tommy spat back at him. *That fuckin Swede could spoil a rotten egg,* Tommy thought as he turned back to his electronics project.

His slight build and his small thin hands were helpful for working on tiny electronics and crawling in tight spaces. The large expressive eyes seemed kind and caring. Tommy had used that trait more than once to woo a victim into complacency while he casually sent them to the Promised Land.

***

Sam Friedman pulled into the general parking lot at the college and got out with a knapsack like the students carry their books in. He didn't want to seem conspicuous to any students or campus guards. Walking briskly across the parking lot in the cold night air, he entered the research building where he approached the guard in the lobby.

I'm surprised I haven't heard from Carlos. I put him on Etheridge and his girls two hours ago. This bug will get the final snitch on Etheridge. I, we, can move on from there. I really don't like working with this janitor. He's got the damndest eyes. I believe he could kill without any remorse. But, he would be a good hand to have in the field! All I have left is to snooker this stupid guard with my pass, place the bug and get out of here.

"Hi, I'm Jeff Blundell, research assistant to Dolphlin Scott on the third floor. I've just been assigned here. Here's my ID and

86

pass." Sam offered confidently as he looked around the complex. The lobby lights had been dimmed, shadows stretched across the white floor from the guard post light. *If you didn't know better, it might seem kinda spooky here, awful quiet.* The guard scanned the plastic laminated pass and scrutinized the picture as he held it up in the light comparing it to Sammy. He sniffed at the "Dapper Dan" standing with an air of condescension in front of him.

"Okay, Mr. Blundell, you're cleared to enter. Be sure to check with me when you exit. All personnel in the building must be accounted for after hours, okay?"

"Yes sir. I will certainly do that, thank you."

Sam went up the stairs, turned onto the second floor and proceeded to Soe's lab. The door was unlocked so he stepped in expecting to see Charlie. Charlie was at the far side of the lab standing beside some man Sam didn't recognize. Neither said anything or showed any recognition of him. Sam quickly spun around to get out the door. He found another man standing in his way with a .22 caliber revolver with a silencer. Apparently, he had been behind the door. Sam could smell the Copenhagen snuff on his breath.

The revolver pointed at his chest. He spoke quietly in a Texas drawl. "Sam, do you want to die here and now or do you want to take a ride with Charlie and my friend?"

Sam's arrogant sneer told it all. "Okay, cowboy. I'll take a ride right now, "Bubba." You better be careful with that gun. I just might take it away from you and stick it up your ass!"

"Bubba" didn't say anything. He just moved the gun slightly and fired. The gun sounded like a book being slammed shut.

Sam yelled. "Hey, ahhhh—, you crazy fuck! You shot me!" He clutched his side.

"Now Sam, do you want to continue to be a smart mouth? I got seven more rounds with one in the hole. Enough to blow your liver out your ass." 'Bubba' challenged.

Sam didn't say anything else. He glowered at the man momentarily then opened his coat and looked down. His shirt was wet with blood on his right side. Popping the buttons open on the shirt revealed a blood soaked ribcage. He could see a crease like a cut across his side and blood continuing to ooze out.

"Bubba" casually grabbed a handful of paper towels from the bench top. "Here, stick this against the crease. You ain't hurt." Sam pressed them against the wound as the pain seared across his rib cage like a hot poker.

Before he could complain or reply, the tall scraggly looking gunman poked him with the silencer. "We're going out the service door in the rear, Sam. Charlie, come along." 'Bubba' ordered as he stepped aside and motioned Charlie forward.

The other 'cowboy' never said anything. He had a gun in Charlie's back as they walked by. Sam gasped as he turned, glancing at Charlie, then 'Bubba' while holding his side with the wad of paper towels.

"Don't even think it, Sam, Charlie. I will perforate you like a flyswatter." 'Bubba' emphasized stepping back, holding the pistol dead on.

The service door opened on to a dock platform overlooking the parking lot. Stepping down a short stairwell, they approached a fourdoor pickup truck. 'Bubba' pulled two sets of handcuffs from his coat as he moved to Sam and Charlie. "This is the next step. Ya'll want to cooperate?

Charlie's jaw took a set and the blue eyes glittered as he stared at 'Bubba.' The other 'cowboy' with 'Bubba' stepped back holding his .38 S & W silenced revolver. "I don't care, Charlie, whether you live or die. Make your move!"

Charlie still didn't say a word. Glaring at 'Bubba', he finally extended his hands in front. Sam followed suit.

"How'd y'all get past the guard, bullies?" Sam muttered.

"Sam, don't you fret over some little thing like thet. You need to conserve your energy. You may bleed to death!"

The big cowboy named 'Bubba' sneered. "Naw, that ain't gonna get it, Charlie, turn around. You just don't look too cooperative."

Cloth bags over their heads completed the nabbing as they were hustled into the truck. The truck snaked through back streets in Marian for about 15 minutes before turning into a large warehouse building.

***

Sam and Charlie were helped out and herded into a room with a one-way window looking into another room. The light dimmed as Sammy and Charlie were debagged. Hard hands pushed them down into chairs facing the window. In the other room Carlos and his friend were seated at a heavy wooden table facing the window. Cuffs attached them to rings on the table.

"What's your name? You, next to Carlos?" A voice echoed with frightful assurance.

"You can kiss my ass clear up in the red, fuckface." The man spit out, his face twisted into a defiant sneer.

Without a word, two men stepped forward. They looped a rope around his neck and snatched it up tight until he was gagging. A third grabbed his left hand and held it palm down on the table while the second drove a 40-penny nail through his hand into the table with a single blow from a large wooden mallet. He screamed and fell back as the rope was loosened from his neck.

He gagged and coughed. "Jesus Christ, you son-of-a-bitch! What the hell is this?" he screamed again. "Ahhhhh." Fear twisted his face now.

"What is your name?" the voice repeated again, deadpan.

"Vernon Wiley." He gasped, rolling his head around and grasping his left wrist with his right hand. A pool of blood had formed under Vernon's hand, flowed to the edge of the table and dripped in his lap.

Carlos feebly pulled on his handcuffs. His face distorted into a grimace of fear with his lips pulled back. *These some-bitches are playing for keeps!*

"When I ask a question, I want the truth. Do you understand?" the voice spoke quietly and firmly. "If I think you are lying, further persuasion will be implemented."

A man stepped forward and put three more nails on the table with the mallet and bolt cutters. Nothing was said. Vernon and

Carlos stared at the tools, their faces revealing their worst thoughts.

"What was your plan tonight with the three in the Nissan?" the voice asked.

Carlos stuttered out. "We were supposed to kill the dark headed girl and scare the hell out of the other two. Maybe shoot them but not kill them."

"Who hired you? Who directed you?" The emotionless voice asked.

Carlos looked around the room wildly, fear staring from his eyes. "I don't know. I met this guy in a bar a few days ago. He said he needed a hit job and asked me if I was interested. I sure as hell wasn't going to admit anything to him until I checked him out. I told him I'd get back with him at the bar. So I left and did some snooping around. This cat checked out with several contacts of mine. No one knew him personally, but he was okay. So I got back with him and we agreed on $10,000. $5,000 up front and he would furnish the guns and car."

"Where did Vernon come in?" the voice asked.

Carlos sighed, relaxed a little. *Maybe they won't nail my hand to the table.* "Well, I needed a second gun, so I picked up Vernon in a bar. I knew he was just out of the can and needed some money. That's the whole story, I swear to God, man." Carlos finished with his eyes wide open and staring.

"Vernon, you have anything to add?" The voice asked.

Vernon sputtered, grimacing with pain. "That's just the way it was, so help me God."

"Describe the hire man, Carlos." The voice ordered.

Carlos swallowed hard and whimpered. "He told me if I got caught and fingered him, he'd cut me into slivers and pour alcohol on me. Then he'd set me on fire."

"Heh, heh, hey! He sounds like my kind of man." The voice stated with a bit of humor. "That's really better than what I had in mind. I just plan to cut your fingers off one by one. Then maybe some other things." The voice continued firmly.

Carlos jerked on the handcuffs and gasped, raggedly. "Hey, man. Wait a minute. Just give me a minute. Ah—, yeah. I think I can describe him." He sucked in a big breath and spit out rapidly, "Yeah, I got it. He's maybe 5 foot 10, weighs 150, has curly dark hair, wears glasses. He dresses neatly, wears a suit and overcoat. I think he's a Jew. Looks like one, anyway." Carlos looked around the room, hoping he had satisfied the voice coming from a speaker on the wall beside a TV camera.

Another man stepped forward and handed papers to someone out of view. "Here's their rap sheets."

"Well, let's see here, boys. Just what do we have? Hmmmm, it seems Vernon has robbery, dope, manslaughter, DWI, and assault convictions. He's real bad. Carlos is a pimp, dope pusher, rapist, etc.

"Neither of these guys has ever worked for a living. They are sores on society." The voice condemned harshly. "I don't want to waste the gunpowder to blow them to hell and be faced with the coyotes eatin the bodies.

"I got it! We could test our hogs! Starve 'em a week and they will eat a man in 30 minutes! Bones, clothes, everything! Live or dead! Whatta y'all think? It's that or Singapore, boys?"

Carlos gasped. "Ahooo, man! You wouldn't do that! I'll-, I'll take Singapore." "Me, too." echoed Vernon.

"Okay, put them on the next boat to Singapore with no papers of any kind. Let's see if they can survive in the strictest society currently out there."

The voice seemed to be pointing a finger at them. "Are you aware of Singapore's public caning policy, boys?" The voice asked, blandly. "Last year, a kid spray painted some cars as a prank and got 20 lashes. He spent the next week in the hospital healing his back where the flesh was bitten off."

The voice paused a moment to spit snuff. "You see, they use Rattan cane that splits when lashed across the back. It spreads and bites when retrieved. It removes a slice of flesh each time. Many times, the criminal must be healed in the hospital so that he can take the rest of his caning. I wonder what they would do with some of your crimes? Castration, amputation, whipping 'til death might be the sentence."

Carlos and Vernon sunk down in the chairs hanging their heads abjectly.

"Bring in our new guests." The voice ordered.

Sam and Charlie were ushered in the room through a connecting door.

Carlos reeled back trying to get his hands up to protect himself, yelling. "Oh Shit, that's him, that's him!" He snatched at his handcuffs trying to get away.

Sam glared at Carlos, spitting. "You weak piece of shit. You'll never make Singapore. You're gonna get sliced to the bone and fed to the buzzards."

"Now, now, Sam. Is there no loyalty among trash like you and Carlos?" The voice asked caustically, burning in his ear.

Sam lunged forward towards Carlos. Someone behind him gave him a push. He fell heavily on the table in front of Carlos and Vernon. Both Vernon and Carlos fell back as far as they could. Vernon screamed with pain from jerking on his hand. Sam was picked up by two men and stood to one side with Charlie who witnessed the whole scene quietly.

Another man came forward with a crow bar, a block of wood and pried the nail out of the table using the block as a pinch point. Vernon screamed again as the nail was pulled from his hand. He bent over double holding his hand with his right hand as blood poured from the wound.

Two of the men stood him upright and handcuffed him.

The handcuffs on Carlos were detached from the ring in the table and snapped over his wrists. Both were herded out the door behind the table.

"Let's get Sam and Charlie settled in here, men." The voice ordered. Each was uncuffed on one hand from in back.

Charlie spun around, kicking at one of the men. Sam tried to break away but two of the men picked him up by the arms and slammed him down on the table face first. Gasping for air, he lay quietly as he was cuffed to the ring in the table.

Charlie had backed away into a corner crouching low, slowly moving his hands in circles.

He hissed, glaring evilly. "You bastards may get me but I'm gonna teach you a lesson." The cuffs dangled from his right wrist.

The voice stated flatly. "Shoot him in the face, we don't need him anyway. We got little Sammy Friedman!"

One of the men turned to a cabinet, removed a 12-gage pump shotgun and jacked a shell in the chamber. The click-clack of the slide rattled off the bare walls.

Without a pause, he fired directly at Charlie, over his head. Flame and smoke sprayed out of the barrel into Charlie's face, the lead shot ripping a hole in the wall behind Charlie. Sammy gasped, air rushing out his mouth as the concussion and thundering noise swept over him.

"Ahhhh." Ripped from Charlie's chest as he plummeted to the floor seeking protection for his ears with his hands.

"Don't shoot, don't shoot." He screamed as he twisted on the floor.

Gasping for a breath, Charlie watched two sets of boots stop beside him. Large hands encompassed his head, picked it up and slammed it back into the floor, cutting his left eyebrow, letting the blood flow. The rough hands grabbed his clothes, arms, neck, pulling him erect. The left eye had swollen almost closed.

"Now are you ready to behave, Charlie?" one of them asked as he held his head in a vise-like grip.

"Yeah—, yeah, okay." Charlie stammered out.

The man circled his head with a thick arm, bending him over. He dragged him to the table where he was forced down and handcuffed to a heavy steel ring bolted through the table.

"I'm glad you did that, Charlie. I know you had some piss and vinegar in you and you had to get it out." The voice laughed sardonically.

"Well, Sam, I guess you're from the Saul Friedman clan, huh? Hell, you might be one of the three surviving sons from 'ol Saul himself. Is that right, Sam?" The taunting voice prodded grating on Sammy's nerves. "This must be one hell of a caper to get a

Friedman out to do the dirty work directly. Y'all have always hired your dirty work done so you don't soil your hands."

Sam spoke with quiet intensity as he glared up at the window. "Jac, when Saul hears of this stunt you pulled here, he'll get on you like ugly on ah ape. You can't even imagine what's going to happen to the rest of your life in the next 24 hours."

"Sam, I really do appreciate the warning and I'll take it to heart. Hell, I might send you back and throw myself on Saul's mercy."

The voice continued relentlessly. "I guess you can appreciate Saul's mercy when he blew up my son's house 15 years ago and killed Jason and Patricia. He would have killed Jac, my grandson, too. By chance I picked him up for the day. Do you remember that, Sam baby? Do you think I have forgotten that, maybe forgiven 'ol Saul for that, Sam?" The voice demanded intensely.

Sam blurted out. "Hell, I was not involved in that. I don't know what happened there. Besides, you burned down three of his homes and killed 6 of his men after that, you shithead. What do you call getting even, Jac?" Defiantly Sam shot back at the voice.

The voice pounded into him. "Sam, the point you must remember, if you are capable, is that the family was not part of the feud until Saul killed my only remaining family. It's total war, now, Sam, and you're caught up in it. Now, here you are trying to kill my people again. This must be one hell of a toy Etheridge has discovered."

Sam didn't say anything, just glared defiantly at the TV camera mounted on the wall.

"Your remorse is so evident, Sam. You are certainly a loving individual."

The voice intensified as it addressed Charlie, "Who the hell are you and what are you up to, Swede?"

Charlie raised an eyebrow, but remained quiet glaring at the camera. One of the men approached Charlie, pulled his wallet from his pocket and spilled it on the table. As he pawed through the papers, he snatched up a plastic laminated card.

"Aw shucks, Charlie. Here it is, Theodore Wesley with the CIA." He scanned the rest of the papers. "That's about it. Looks like he's from Washington D.C."

"Well Theo, tell me what's going on." The voice stated without rancor.

Theo spoke calmly, "The CIA is funding Etheridge's research and we have a right to know what we're paying for. We don't think he is keeping us informed, so we decided to check him out."

Sam glared at Theo, wide eyed. He blurted accusingly, "Well kiss my ass. The fucking government is in this, too! You asshole, I thought you were the janitor. The CIA is an offshore agency. What the hell are you doing working inside the U.S.?"

The voice informed Sam. "Theo replaced the janitor about a month ago. Apparently the janitor became ill and is still in the hospital with an unknown disease. That's the CIA for you. Poison some poor 'ol boy to get him out of the way. The end justifies the means. What did you do to the janitor, Theo?" the voice demanded.

"I think he was given some mercury. Nobody would think to check on that." Theo offered blandly.

The voice came back sarcastically. "That's real nice of you, Theo. Mercury poisoning is a neurotoxin, permanent nerve and brain damage."

"Well," Theo answered calmly, "Etheridge is into some breakthrough technology that he doesn't even realize the magnitude of. We are about to take it over as soon as I file my report."

"So you haven't filed your report yet, Theo?" the voice acknowledged with a lilt.

Theo didn't acknowledge anything.

"Are you working with somebody local, Theo?" the voice demanded, changing the direction of questioning.

Theo stuck out his chin and quipped. "That's for me to know and you to wonder about, Jac. Is that what you call him, Sam?"

"Yeah, that's 'ol Jac. John Cochran." Sam informed him, attempting a little bravado. "And if you don't know of John Cochran, you better get your ass in gear. Cause he's gonna jerk a slipknot in your ass and you are gonna shit out your ears."

Blue fire arced across the steel ring to Theo's cuffs. Theo screamed and jerked upright. He tried to get away from the table thrashing around on the floor, knocking the chair over. He continued to scream and jerk spastically under the table releasing his bladder and puking in large gagging coughs. When the rigors ceased, Theo hung face down with his hands behind his shoulders still attached to the ring.

Kicking back, jerking at the cuffs and ring, Sam stared horrified at Theo puking and gagging on the floor.

"What in hell did you do to him? Jesus Christ, that was terrible!" Sam's voice quavered with fear.

The voice spoke calmly, "Heavy metals in the body short-circuit the nervous system and your whole body can go into convulsions. It's a terrible death, Sam."

"Theo," the voice asked calmly. "Do you remember who you are working with here in town?"

Theo gave no response, his head hung down between his arms. He lay there as if dead. A man came over and felt his pulse in his neck. Turning Theo over on his back, his head flopped backward. Puke and drool dripped out of his mouth. His eyes stared blankly into nothing.

"He's dead." the man said, "He may have slipped a cyanide capsule in his mouth when he was uncuffed. I can smell it. That's fairly standard for CIA's first line henchmen."

Sam spit out indignation. "Good God, a government agent and you killed him, Jac. You Goddamn killer! You'll pay for this. I'll see to it!"

"Sam, all I can think of is fire. The fire that burned my children to death. Did you know that the fire trucks couldn't get to their house because a big truck blocked the road? Do you think all that was a coincidence?" The voice pounded home the point. "Fire, Sam. Think about it, fire. Think of being burned alive. Think about hiring a thug to kill a young girl. Just to stifle a life that might bring something new into the world that you want to control. Saul and your family are power mad. You obviously will stop at nothing to fulfill your desires for control. Power. For your own selfish ego."

Sam stared into the video camera with widening, knowing eyes jerking ineffectually against the steel chain between his cuffs.

***

"Still pretty cool out there, girls." Soe exclaimed as he rubbed his hands together. "Hey, is the coffee ready?"

Jumping up, Meg checked in the kitchen. "Sure is, Soe. Want some?"

"Well, I thought the men outside might want some since they are going to be staying here all night, watching for the bad guys." Soe replied.

"What do you want to do? Give them a thermos and some cups?" Meg asked.

"I see you have been reading my mind again, you little Sweetie."

"Ha, ha, that might happen. You better be clean!" Meg bustled around in the kitchen. Found a stainless steel thermos, cups and some packages of sugar and cream. She filled the thermos and took a tray out to the men in the driveway.

Carol stood up. "Soe, let's get some before it's all gone."

Outside, Meg found one on the phone talking and the other around in front of the house, sitting in a lawn chair behind some shrubs.

He stepped forward and took the tray. "That's very sweet of you, honey." He said in a Texas drawl. "It's gonna be a long cold night."

Meg looked at him in the light from a street lamp on the corner. He was big, maybe 6 foot 4 or 5, his face like wrinkled leather. A heavy sheep wool jacket, blue jeans, boots, gloves and a Texas style cowboy hat dressed him out. *Dipping snuff and stains around the mouth seemed to mark the Texas cowboy. That's really a filthy habit, ugh.* Meg observed.

"I'm sure glad you're on our side, mister."

The deep-set steely eyes crinkled a little, maybe a smile. "Well, you betcha, honey. We're the good guys. You run along, now, honey, before you catch cold. I'll get my pardner over here and give him some cawfee."

Meg turned and went into the house.

"Heavens sake—! Soe, Carol, I've got to tell you something." Meg stuttered as she rushed into the living room. They both looked up at Meg, startled.

"What in the world is it, Meg?" Carol asked as she went to her, grabbing an arm.

"I want some coffee. It's cold out there." Meg said as she hurriedly looked about the room.

"I've anticipated that Meg." Soe offered. "Here you are."

Meg grabbed the coffee and sipped it to see how hot it was and then swilled it down.

Meg started out excitedly. "Aah, I needed that. One of the men was on the phone talking to someone and I could read his mind. Some of his friends caught two men in your lab, Soe. They took them to the same place here in town where they took the two men in the Lincoln. Apparently they are all working together against us." She spit out as she crossed her arms hugging herself. "They are questioning them about their plans concerning us.

"I took coffee to the man out front and I could read his mind, too. He was hoping someone would come by tonight and start something. He wanted some 'action.' I sure am glad he's on our side. He is one mean looking man!" Meg scowled at Carol and Soe as she sat down.

Soe grinned sucking in a deep breath. He clinched his fist clutching for his knife. "Ha, it looks like our team has flushed the enemy out into the open, Meg. That's exactly what we need. We'll get a report by the time Jac gets home. Let's fix some supper and wait up for Jac. It's 10:30 now. He'll be here by 12:30. Let's hit the fridge or the freezer and have something for him when he gets here."

"You betcha." Carol said, standing up and moving toward the kitchen. "I can cook. My mama demanded that I learn while I was growing up. Let's see what 'ol Jac has stock-piled." The girls moved into the kitchen as Soe paced the living room flipping the worn lock-back. Clack, clack, clack.

Carol spied a package of dried spaghetti in the cupboard. "Y'all look for ground meat. We'll have spaghetti and meatballs."

"Here's ground beef. No, wait, this is ground turkey. Hell, it'll work, girls. I'll thaw it in the microwave. Carol, season it heavily. It's just a carrier for the sauce anyway." Soe laughed.

"Digging in someone's kitchen is like going through their underwear drawer. You know that Carol, remember? Here's the salt and pepper. Yeah, there's the sauce in a jar. Ragu, yep, 'It's in there.' Jac knows how to shop." Meg nodded to Carol, knowingly.

"What's the underwear comment, Meg? I haven't heard that one?" Soe inquired.

"Oh, it's a kinky psychological study we did in school to study personality traits and their impact on behavior. For example, your knife flipping is a dead giveaway to your lack of confidence and tension in this situation. It's also a relief mechanism for the tension. You subconsciously want to hurt, kill the enemy and protect yourself."

"Sounds like the psychologists got the world figured out. I wish they'd fix it."

"You may not like the fix I put on it, Soe. Us psychologists really don't have it. We just like to give that impression and boost our little egos in your eyes."

"Okay, okay, you two war-birds. Kiss and make up. Gimme the defrosted meat, Soe. We're in the home stretch." Carol admonished.

Thinking of Jac, Soe called the hospital, "Come straight home for supper, Jac. We have some news."

It sounded like Jac was going to reach over the phone and grab him by the throat. "What tha hell is going on, Soe? I get this mind message from Meg saying that you were going to be killed. But then everything is okay. What is it, anyway?"

Soe laughed easily. "It's okay. Just come on home and we'll fill you in, Bigboy. There have been some serious developments tonight. By the way, there will be two dudes in the driveway. Don't throw a wrench when you pull up."

Shortly after 12 midnight, Meg waved her hand. "There's Jac, now." Soe and Carol could hear the rumble of the turbocharged V-6 GN sprinting up the driveway and darting into the garage.

Carol clapped her hands. "Shitty witty, I love that car, Meg! You've got to ride in that machine. Jac said it'd scare the pants off you."

"No, he said it'd scare the pants off YOU." Meg shot back, emphasizing the "you" as she pointed to Carol with a knowing grin.

Carol crinkled her eyes in a grin as she stared at Meg. They seemed to communicate without Soe.

Jac stopped briefly to talk to the two men outside and then came on in through the side door. Carol met him at the door with his western hat on tilted back and a big smile.

"I jest cooked yore supper, Big'un. You jest sit over here and get some vittles." She pushed him towards the kitchen table and a chair as she turned to the stove and filled a plate of spaghetti and meatballs from a big bubbling pot. Jac admired her figure from the rear as she spun around, the hip-hugger jeans fit like they were painted on. *Yes, she certainly is a healthy young woman.*

Meg and Soe came in and pulled up a chair at the table along with Carol.

Meg laughed. "Isn't she a sweet girl, Jac? Stayin home and fixin yore supper?"

A slight blush suffused Jac's face as he grinned because he knew Meg had been reading his mind again.

Soe nervously rapped on the table with his fingers as he fondled his knife. "I just got off the phone with some of the troops. We need to go to GrandJac's ranch in the morning and get briefed."

Jac looked at him kinda walleyed. "Whatta ya mean the troops, Soe? And another thing. I'd like to know just what kind of relationship you have with my grandpa?"

Soe laughed easily at Jac's obvious jealousy. "We'll get it straightened in the morning. How's the spaghetti?"

Jac smiled to himself and relaxed. "Hell, it's damn good. Carol's a good cook. I will hate to see her and her sweater go back to school."

Carol spun around with her arms over her head. "I can't help it if I got it all. I'm a product of my mama."

Meg smirked. "She's modest, too."

Carol put her arms on the back of the chair and faced Jac, sticking her chin out. "Soe doesn't think we ought to go back to school. He thinks there is too much danger for us away from here."

Jac leaned back in his chair glaring at Soe. "Just what tha crap is going on, Soe? I'm tired of being in the dark. Put some words on me, man."

Soe shuffled his feet, looked away and turned back to Jac. "Well, it's a long story and I can't cover all of it. Your grandpa will have to fill in a lot of it.

"For my part, it revolves around this brain scan thing I'm working on. You know all about that, Jac. You're in on the ground floor." Soe nodded.

"What you don't know is that there are two factions that want the technology bad enough to kill for it. You know, they bugged my lab, broke into it and stole some of my technology. But I don't think they are as deep into it as I am. Really, they can't be. Secondly, they don't have Meg. She is unique to the program and is capable of taking it to unknown levels."

Soe waved at Meg, grinning. "They tried to kill her tonight just to stop my progress. I called GrandJac earlier today for help and he responded in spades. He put two men in my lab and they caught the two who were bugging the lab."

Soe stood up and leaned on the back of the chair. "The men have been identified as CIA and a member of the Friedman clan. Friedman hired the two hit men that tried to kill us on the freeway. As you know, the CIA is funding my research in a small way and does deserve to know what is going on. But they sure as hell don't have to break into my lab, steal my data and bug it as they have done."

Soe hung his head. "The really terrible thing is the fact that they poisoned our old janitor just so they could take his job and have the run of my lab. Poor 'ol Roy Jones has been poisoned with mercury and probably won't ever recover.

"I'm sure GrandJac has told you about the Friedman clan. That's about it, Jac." Soe spread his hands.

"There're lots of holes in your story, Soe." Jac looked skeptically at him. "I only know that Grandpa has been in competition with the Friedmans through the years, in business. But I sure as hell don't know what's going on with them now. How do you know about the janitor and all this stuff, anyway?"

Soe studied Jac for a moment, then looked away, shaking his head slightly.

Jac paused as he reviewed the information. "What's happened to the four men? Are they going to be turned over to the Police?"

Soe scowled at Jac, looked away again, then replied with a chilling air of finality. "Ahh——, no, I don't think so. I understand the two hit men are going to Singapore for rehabilitation. The other two, well—, ahh. The CIA man felt threatened and committed suicide with a cyanide capsule in his mouth."

"Jesus H. Christ, Soe!" Jac shouted as he stood up taking a deep breath. "What in hell are you and the girls getting into? That's unbelievable!"

"Jac—, Jac, just calm down. It isn't just me and the girls. It's you too. You are right in the middle of it. GrandJac will explain in the morning." Soe's eyes demanded eye contact as he backed away from the table holding up his hands palms outward.

Jac took a deep breath, sat down and leaned back in his chair. He ran his hands through his hair and let the air out with an explosive gust. "Okay, okay, Soe. I can see I'm way behind in some serious goins on around here. I'm looking forward to a long talk with grandpa in the morning. Let's get some shuteye and go see the 'ol man' first thing. Shit, I can't believe it!" Jac stood up waving his arms in resignation, terminating the meeting.

***

Carol stayed in the kitchen. "I'll be along in a minute, let me clean up a little here."

Meg turned to help but Carol waved her on, stating. I'll be there soon. This will just take a minute." She put up the rest of the spaghetti, loaded the dishwasher, and wiped the table and counter. Scanning the kitchen, "I believe I've got it all." She peeked down the hall towards the two bedrooms Soe and Meg were in. Soe's light was out and it looked like Meg had left the nightlight on.

She turned and walked across the kitchen, down the hall to Jac's room. He had just gotten out of the shower and was standing in the middle of the room drying his hair with a towel. He looked up, startled, to see Carol come in scanning him up and down.

"Wowowee!" she exclaimed with big eyes as she caught Jac's eye. Jac smirked and draped the towel across his front. "Well, I'm just a country boy from Texas, Carol. Can't you tell?"

"As I said, Jac, wowowee—! May I use your shower? Meg is using the other one." Carol asked with her head cocked to one side and a tiny smile creeping across her lips.

"Well—, sure." Jac said a little hesitantly. "Let me get some clothes on. The towels are in the cabinet. Help yourself."

Jac pulled on shorts, turned on his reading lamp, turned off the overhead light and got in bed. After thinking about it he jumped out of bed, shucked off his underwear and slipped under the covers again. The bathroom door creaked open as Carol peeked out. With a nervous little giggle, she came out of the bathroom wrapped in a beach towel, sidling over to the bed. Holding the towel to her neck, her eyes crinkled as an impish smile crept across her face demanding attention.

"Yep, just as I thought. I was hoping. I didn't dare ask—," Jac stuttered, sliding over in the bed pulling the covers back.

The large towel cascaded to the floor revealing Carol in all her youthful glory. "Well—, I guess—!" she answered authoritatively sliding into bed and under the covers.

Jac and Carol both started to say something simultaneously; then laughed. They lay facing each other. Jac reached over and pushed a wisp of hair out of her face then put his hand behind her head, pulled the two them together and kissed her passionately. He felt her full warm lips. "Ummmmmm, what a sweet mouth you have, Carol."

He held her head in both hands and pushed her away to look at her. Her radiance shown through enlarged and glistening eyes.

Carol's hot breath puffed on his face as she licked her lips. "Meg said you wanted me. Well, I want you. So-, whatcha gonna do, Bigboy?" Thirty minutes of frantic physical love left them exhausted, panting and sweaty.

Jac rolled over and gazed into Carol's eyes, panting. "Yeah, I wanted you—, from Saturday night. You are one hot mamma, little girl. I've got to shower again. You got me inna lather!"

Carol joined him, showering together. Carol grabbed him, smiling as the shower pounded in her face. "Be careful with that thing, it could go off in your hand." Jac croaked hoarsely. "Carol, hey Sweetiepie, we have to get some sleep tonight. It's already 3:30."

"Okay, okay." Carol answered begrudgingly. Jac encircled her with his arms and pulled her in close. She pressed her body against his and laid her head on his hairy chest as she looked up at him. She could feel movement as she continued to hold herself against him.

"You hot little pussy. You don't give up, do you?" Jac smirked as he bent down and kissed her. He cupped his hands on her rump and hoisted her up. Carol coiled her legs around his body and sighed with delight. Five minutes of shaking and quivering and it was over. They leaned against the shower wall and let the water cascade over them.

Jac kissed her on the nose. "We've got to get to bed, Carol. Let's go now." They stepped out of the shower, dried off and jumped in bed. Both were asleep in a minute.

TUESDAY DECEMBER 20TH

Jac woke to the raucous sound of the jazzercise video at 7:30. He rolled over, snuggled Carol's breasts and sucked on her nipples. They quickly grew hard. Carol grabbed him around the neck and pressed her body against him.

"Okay Bigboy, you started it." Carol whispered in his ear as she hunched him with her hips.

Jac disengaged from her and chided. "We have a lot to do this morning, Carol. Is this all you ever think about?"

Carol threw back the covers and lay naked with her legs spread apart. "Well, I like to eat-, sometimes-, in-between!" She smirked, watching Jac ogle her.

Jac got out of bed and extended his hand to her. "C'mon, you o.s.u.l. Hussy, we got the world to save."

Carol jumped out of bed with her breasts flopping up and down. "What in the hell is osul?"

"'Over sexed, under loved,' everyone knows that, hussy. C'mon get your ass in gear." Jac teased her as he pulled his shorts on.

Carol turned her back to him and purposely bent over from the hips to pick up her panties on the floor.

Jac declared. "I was right. You're just an osul hussy," and swatted her behind.

Dressing quickly, they went to the living room where Soe and Meg were exercising to the video.

Jac yelled over the video with a wave of his hand. "I'm too tired to jazz, let's eat." Soe and Meg grinned but kept dancing a fast pace.

Carol quickly cooked a dozen eggs and two pounds of sausage with a stack of toast. "World warriors need hearty breakfasts." Carol declared as she poured orange juice for all. The crowd devoured breakfast and chased it with coffee.

"Haaaa, good stuff, Carol. You're handy to have around. Let us shower and we'll be back to tackle the world."

Jac stepped outside with coffee, eggs, sausage and toast for the men. "We're going to the ranch in a minute."

"Thanks Jac. We'll tag you." The men jumped in their truck and backed into the street.

***

With a flick of his hand, Jac opened the garage door and cranked his GN with the remote. Carol, Soe and Meg filed into the garage. Sun slanted through the door windows glittering on metal.

Carol yelled, pointing across the GN. "What in HELL is that?" Machine tools, toolboxes, workbenches and welding equipment lined the back wall and third bay.

Jac walked over and stood beside his experimental car with his arm resting on the top rail. "I'm building a car with my ideas I've had since school. Have ah look."

The hard top was off the car so most of the interior could be seen. Jac flicked on the overhead lights as he surveyed the responses from the girls.

"It doesn't have a steering wheel." Carol squeaked as she prowled over it.

"Yes it does." Jac stated and pointed to a small hand sized wheel sunk in the dash. "I started the car with the idea of using today's technology avoiding the stereotypical car design.

"The dashboard is soft and padded. It pulls up and out in front of you, so that you can sit back comfortably. It positions all-ways for comfort. You rest your arms on it in a comfortable position and steer the car with either hand through a small retractable wheel set in the dash. It's an electro-hydraulic controlled steering system that can be manipulated with one finger. It's called drive-by-wire, like modern airplanes. The dash acts as a crash pad with air shocks in the event of a wreck. It is completely retractable for exiting and entering the car."

Jac turned to see if Carol understood. Getting no response, he continued.

"The seats are fully adjustable with air pads and electronics to conform to your body as you like it. They are typically firm and give a feeling of being contained comfortably. The headrest can move forward and contain the head for relaxation. Armrests are adjustable if you don't rest them on the dash, which is preferred." Jac smiled at Carol's bewilderment.

Carol smirked at Jac. "You mean like a Ford seat system?"

"Yeah, that's right, Carol. All controls are touch pad under the right hand. That's the radio, air conditioning, door locks, windows, wipers, washers, turn signals, cruise control, instruments, you know.

"The gearshift is a multi-position toggle switch under the left hand just like a conventional shift lever. It's also electronic controlled." Jac wiggled his left fingers to illustrate.

"With a little practice, you never have to take your eyes off the road to look down at instruments and controls. The only instrument is the speedometer, which is reflected onto a dark spot on the windshield directly in front of the driver, but low down. The other instruments are keypunched for a vocal reply. Any deviation in instrument reading is a vocal warning or caution. All monitors on the car are vocally alarmed, such as open door, savvy?" Jac looked at Carol. "Hey, give me some feedback. Do you follow?" Shrugging, Jac added. "The tach readout can be vocal if you want. That way you just have to watch the speedometer. Or, it can read out on top of the speedometer, the two superimposed."

Jac leaned inside and punched a button on the keypad. A very sexy female voice asked, "Jac, do you want an instrument readout? Insert your initiator—, you know how."

Carol leaned against the door staring at Jac with budding jealousy. "Who was that? She sure does sound friendly. How did you dream all this up, Bubba?"

Jac smiled a sly grin, continuing. "She's a professional. The foot controls are fuel and brake, one under each foot and set on either side of the foot well in a comfortable position. You can rest the foot on each pedal and bend the foot down to actuate."

Jac grinned at Carol, "You may like this one, Short Stuff. The mirrors are located at the top of the windshield directly in your line of sight. Through fiber optics, miniature TV cameras and mirrors, you can see to each side and a full view of back without turning your head. There are no blind spots with this mirror system. Also, the side mirrors have been removed as unnecessary. They act as windbreaks anyway and make the car look like some kind of eared animal."

Carol glared and slapped Jac on the arm. "What's with the Short Stuff, Bubba? I'm 5'-5", I'm not a runt! I guess that mirror fetish is more of that seat fetish?"

Jac laughed out loud. "Well, at least I got your attention. Yes, I don't like the 'bat wings' hanging on the side of the car.

"The frame is titanium alloy. The body is aluminum and polyurethane plastic. The windows are Lexan and will not break except under extreme conditions.

"The suspension system is four wheel independent with adjustable height and stiffness control. The brakes are four wheel disc with electronic antilock control."

Jac looked at Carol pausing. "Do you wanna know about the engine?"

Carol nodded, mouth agape.

"Okay, it's powered by a mid-engine aluminum 4.0 liter V-6, hemi-heads, dual overhead cams and electronic fuel injection with turbo. All functions on the engine are computer controlled. The engine develops 425 HP at 6500 RPM. The transmission is aft of the differential and is automatic with four speeds and overdrive. Oh yes, the differential is fixed with in-board brakes and swing axles.

"Fuel economy is 35 miles per gallon at road speed. The car weighs 2200 pounds, fueled. Possibly you've noticed? The car is very aerodynamic to reduce wind friction at speed.

"Since the car is going to be an eye catcher, I spent a lot of time on this feature, Carol." Jac continued with a little smirk. "The car is very anti-theft. At rest, all wheels are locked. The windows are unbreakable. There are no keys and all openings are controlled from inside such as hood, trunk, gas tank and doors. The doors are electronically actuated by remote. The remote is the ignition key. If the car is molested, it screams, in a pleasant voice, 'Get the fuck away from me, shithead, or I'll give you a shot in the shorts,' at 125 decibels in five languages."

Jac keyed another button for a demonstration.

Meg laughed and clapped her hands. "That's so cute."

"Jumping chickens!" Carol exclaimed. "That's the wildest thing I ever heard of. Does it really scream like that on alarm? Is that the same voice I heard earlier, the— ah, 'the professional'?"

Jac threw back his head, laughing. "Well—, yes it is. The alarm is programmable. It will say anything you want it to say. I thought that was appropriate. What do y'all think?" Jac waited for a response about his pride and joy.

Carol shook her head, awed. "I am very impressed, Jac. First at you and second on how you got it built. It looks finished. What is that color?"

Jac laughed as he ran his hand over the hood. "Thank you, Carol. The color is powder metallic blue with wisps of light pearly-silver drifting through it in a mirage effect. A lotta of time in that paint job!"

"It's really a beautiful car, Jac. And it is very well engineered." Meg added quietly.

"The car is drivable now." Soe emphasized. "I have driven it and it is one hell of a performer. It hugs the road like a snake and it will scat. It'll make you hang on with both cheeks."

"I want to drive this car and the other one, too, Jac." Carol demanded. "I just love cars."

Jac replied. "That's possible, but you'll have to get checked out first. Neither of these cars is ordinary and they will require some careful driving at first."

Soe seconded that statement. "Carol, they will scare you."

Jac stood up signaling the inspection was over. "Let's go see Grandpa at the ranch. I'll take Carol in the GN. Soe, you take your car 'cause I have to go to work later."

Driving through town traffic gave Carol time to ask quietly as she studied Jac's profile. "Do you really think Soe was telling the truth about the captured men last night? It sounds like some kind of Mafia gang war deal like you might see on TV."

Jac nodded, a scowl across his face. "Hell, I don't know, Carol. I know almost nothing about Grandpa's dealings, business or otherwise. I lived with him for six years before I went to college. But I sure didn't see anything like what Soe is talking about. We'll know soon enough."

***

Carol sat forward. "Wow! This is some ranch, Jac."

"Yeah." Jac answered turning in on the paved driveway, through the gate to GrandJac's sprawling ranch house.

The whole complex was situated on a long rolling hill. Land dropped away about 600 yards out on three sides. The house was set back from the road about 200 yards with a grassy field in front. A ten-foot chain link fence surrounded most of the complex. Most of the area in front of the house was paved for parking cars. Two large metal buildings were off to the left side and looked like car or machine stalls. A heliport was on the opposite side with a runway stretching away in the distance. It appeared that the runway and large concrete apron nearby could accommodate a good-sized airplane. Metal buildings spread around the runway apron.

Transmission towers stood far behind the house with more metal buildings surrounding the towers.

On the left behind the machine stalls were 20 residences on two streets. Power lines entered the property to the left about four hundred yards out and went to the buildings by the towers. There was no visible sign of a water supply. In the distance behind the complex there appeared to be a high tech sewage plant.

Wide paved roads connected all facilities. There were no trees of significance, just bushes and shrubs around the houses. Lights on poles and buildings were capable of illuminating most of the areas at night.

Jac parked beside Soe and all exited.

Meg spun around taking in the complex. "Jac, this is one hell of an establishment! Did you live here?"

Jac leaned on the GN, looking over the area once again. "Yeah, I lived here since I was ten when my parents were killed in a fire. I went to college at UT and medical at Galveston. I've only been here at MCH for 6 months."

"Did you go to high school in Marian?"

111

"Well, some. I graduated when I was 16 due to home schooling credits and went on to UT. I tested out of a lot of basic credits at Texas. So I concentrated on technical credits such as mechanics, chemistry, electronics, and premed. I went to school year around so I could finish early."

Ugh." Carol grunted. "That must have been hell. I need the breaks like spring and summer."

Jac smiled as he ruffled Carol's hair. "I'll bet you do. You need to maintain your image among the fans."

Carol blushed. "Hey Bigboy. My fans need relief, too!"

"Well, I wanted to finish so I plowed through it. Now I can laugh and play and be gay, ta, tah, ta, tah, like my little sweetie, here."

Carol glared at Jac poking him in the ribs. "Don't get caught up in the 'Consuming Danger of Assuming', Bubba. I just might flush you."

"Oh hell, Carol. You'd crawl through broken glass to get back to me. Wouldn't you?"

Meg stopped the power struggle and one upmanship. "C'mon, you two. Put up the sabers and let's see Jac's little shed, here."

As they watched, the two men in the pickup drove by to one of the houses back of the metal buildings. Jac led the way up on the porch and opened the door.

Two men talking in the entranceway turned to Jac. "Hi Jac. I know 'ol Soe, but who are these two sweeties?"

Jac grinned as he said hi to Duncan and Morris. "Would you believe I found them? Yes, I found these gals walking down the road so I picked them up. I don't know who they are. I think they're pickups. Hell, they look like trucks."

Meg stepped forward and grabbed Morris's hand, shook it. "That's bullshit and you know it, Morris. I'm Meg and this is Carol. Jac hired us to nurse him back to health. He's starving living by himself. He's very inept in the kitchen and just recently became potty trained."

Meg turned to Duncan and shook his hand and placed it on Jac's arm. "He needs guidance. Show him where the toilet is."

Meg continued. "As the world knows, man has a narrow window during his life span when he has bowel control. He's born crapping his pants and he dies crapping his pants. Jac is very fortunate. He has just entered that narrow window and he spends a lot of time playing in the toilet."

Duncan and Morris guffawed. Duncan stepped back. "Jac, you got your hands full here! Wow!" Cutting his eyes as he looked the girls up and down.

Carol grinned at Meg. "Hey Meg! You would never had said that before your rebirth!"

"I agree Carol. I have changed. I think for the better!"

Before Jac could come up with a rebuttal, Morris asked cocking his head to one side, continuing to eye the girls. "Y'all here to see the big bore coon?"

"Yeah, is Grandpa up and moving about?" Jac asked staring at Meg awestruck.

Grandpa Jac came around the corner of the hall in that moment with a big smile and grabbed Jac's hand. "Howdy, son. Good to see you. Introduce me to your girlfriends."

Jac spun around and pointed to the two girls. "Sho nuff. This is Meg and this is Carol. They are schoolmates back East out here on some peculiar business."

GrandJac shook their hands and turned to Soe shaking his hand, "Hi, Soe. Wal, y'all come on back and let's get up to snuff on what's going on."

Jac mused to himself. *That's a tattletale! Maybe 'ol Soe has already briefed Grandpaw. There's an awful lot left un-said.*

They followed GrandJac to the hallway end and turned left down a staircase into a huge office like room. A big desk, chair and credenza backed to a wall with chairs and sofas set around the room.

A beautiful Latino woman, possibly in her 50's, came in with coffee service and set it on a round table on one side of the room. She wore a traditional long Mexican dress in bright reds, yellows and blacks.

"This is Annie, girls. She is my light. She led me out of the dark. I love her for it and many other reasons." GrandJac explained as he placed a hand on Annie's shoulder.

Annie smiled at the girls and winked at Jac. "I know Soe. He's boring. Hi Meg, hi Carol. We'll have time to visit. Sit down, please."

She stood in the background waiting to serve the group.

GrandJac was tall, maybe 6-3 or 4. He had a shock of white hair parted down the middle and shaped on both sides down to his ears. Craggy dark eyebrows, high cheekbones, and deepset, dark eyes peered out at the world. A prominent nose and thin lips with a bushy moustache hovering over them completed GrandJac. He had about two days of gray beard stubble covering his cheeks. The casual western cut jeans and shirt fit him perfectly.

GrandJac poured himself coffee with big hands and took a seat in a comfortable leather chair beside the round table.

Annie offered coffee to the guests. "Would you like anything else?" She glanced at Jac.

Jac whispered to Annie. "Do you have any of those, ahhh——, cinnamon rolls, Annie?"

"Sure do, Jac." She giggled. "I knew you were coming so I made some just for you."

She hustled out and returned in a moment with a tray of steaming hot rolls, plates and forks.

"Thank you, Annie. I want these girls to try something really special. Poor 'ol Soe's on a diet and can't eat things like this."

Soe stood up and moved to the table. "I'm going to miss lunch so I can have one of these, Annie. C'mon girls."

They quickly obliged.

Carol licked her fingers. "Boy-o-boy, Jac, how did you stay slim with something like this around?"

Jac pushed the plate to her. "Get the last one before Soe snaps it up, Carol. You and Meg can share it."

GrandJac looked at Soe, deadpan. "Bring me up to date on the EEG machine."

Soe shuffled in his chair nervously looking at Jac. "Well, ahh, there's really nothing new except Meg, here. I haven't had time to follow any ideas because of other activities, as you know. Meg has some very strong ESP skills." Soe continued, waving his hand towards Meg. "And I want her to demo them."

Without a word, a coffee cup left her hand and floated to the table. The empty roll plate and fork followed.

GrandJac snapped upright, eyes staring vacantly. "My lord! She's in my head. She told me in an instant all the activities she knows about for the past four days. This is unbelievable! It's incredible!" GrandJac stood up and paced around with his hands to his temples.

He turned swiftly with a penetrating look. "Are you reading my mind, too?"

Meg's expressionless face stared at him as he stuttered. "She says she can only read my current thoughts. Who in the hell knows about this? Wait. I already know that the lab bugs may have let the cat out of the bag to the CIA and Friedman."

GrandJac moved to the chair and plopped down expelling a gust of air. "This is really going to take some thinking through!"

Jac interrupted in a strong voice, "Grandpa, bring me up to date on what's happening. Soe, here, knows more than I do about Friedman and me and a hell of ah lot more."

"Okay, Jac, I agree. It's time you got the picture. I agree with Soe. You girls are in some danger and can't go back to school. Not now and maybe never." GrandJac stated spreading his hands.

Meg eyed Carol with a thought. *Hold on; let's get the story!*

"Here's the story." GrandJac paused with an air of conspiracy as he sat forward in his chair resting his elbows on his knees. "I get this story as a hand-me-down through the family from my great grandfather dating back to 1868, a very important year. I can't trace our family past great grandpa Jac when he was a full-grown man at that time. He just appeared and our tree started." GrandJac looked at each of them as he spread his big hands expressing the unknown.

"It seems that he was traveling west in a wagon train going to California. A band of Commencheros from the Civil War attacked them in the prairie west of Kansas City. I'm sure you've heard of them. They were looters, outlaws, preying on wagon trains, small towns, and whoever or whatever they came upon.

"As the story goes, Jac and the family shot the hell out of the looters. Killed every one of them but one who got away over a hill. There were four brothers and a father who made up most of the gang. Grandpa Jac killed all but one. This group of thugs was a family called the Friedman gang who had been terrorizing Kansas, Missouri, and the territories in that vicinity."

Carol, Jac, and Meg sat in rapt attention listening to GrandJac tell a great story. Soe seemed to already know it as he listened casually, leaning back in his chair.

Jac looked first at Soe and then GrandJac to see any interplay between them. Soe feigned boredom or casualness.

GrandJac watched his audience carefully. "Even though several of the family were wounded, Grandpa led them on to California where they started an empire that exists to now.

"The lone Friedman, the one that got away, declared war on the Cochran's. The families have been at war, a feud, ever since.

"The wars always were in business in one form or another. There were raids, fires, sabotage, thefts, murders of employees, court cases, you name it. It's been one hell of a fight for the last 130 years."

GrandJac stood up with a long face thrusting his hands deep in his pockets as he stepped back.

"Fifteen years ago the Friedmans killed your mother and father in a setup house fire, Jac. That was the first time family members were attacked since 1868 that I know of. If they killed others, it was a very subtle plan through Doctors, hospitals, and drugs. When that happened, I set the hounds loose on Friedman. I tried to kill his whole family. I burned three houses and killed 6 of his bodyguards. I was insanely furious. But even more so, I was terrified with the loss. Jac, you were the last of the clan. I absolutely had to protect you.

"I don't think I got a single one of the Friedmans.

"Things have been rockin along fairly smoothly until Soe here discovers this power wave and stimulated ESP phenomena. Apparently, Friedman and the CIA have been spying on Soe for the last month, at least. They certainly have some of the technology and are aware of its power through Meg, here."

GrandJac had walked to the corner of the room in semidarkness and turned, looking at the group. "Since I have funded Soe through the Collinga Foundation, he has kept me informed of happenings and I have helped where I could. That's most of the story Jac. That's why girls, you are in serious danger. Friedman will stop at nothing to get the upper hand on me through this EEG machine and develop a power beyond imagination with both ESP and the power wave. The CIA is another matter, entirely.

"Last night we captured one of the Friedmans in Soe's lab. I want Meg to visit him and sweep his mind."

Jac thought as he hesitantly held up his hand. *The power wave, what does he mean by that?* He started to ask but GrandJac kept on talking.

GrandJac turned to Meg holding out his hand. "Honey, I'm real sorry you are caught up in this thing. There's nothing nice or pleasant about it. It's just plain 'ol evil at work. I hope you can understand it for what it is."

Meg stared hard at GrandJac. *What does he mean, the cycle has started?*

Meg's strong voice silenced GrandJac for a moment. "I know exactly what it is. From the viewpoint of your thoughts and feelings, I'm sure I can get the same from this Friedman. What is going to stop the feud forever, GrandJac?" Are we the new generation to carry the feud forward in your name?" Meg's eyes and voice penetrated into GrandJac. "Look how many lives are entwined in this thing, just festering evil and hate on both sides."

GrandJac rocked back and sat down hard in his chair as a wave of guilt and remorse swept over him. "Believe me, little lady, I am sincere when I say that I can stop it now and let the past rest in peace, if Friedman can do the same. It has directed most of my life. I'm not proud of what I have done in the past. But, if Friedman can cleanup, I can too."

GrandJac leaned back in his chair and ran his big, gnarled hands through his hair. "I feel like I've been to church, to confessional!" He stated fervently. "Meg, you have some unbelievable powers. I can't even comprehend where you are going to go. The powers in place will fear you, hate you. They will mercilessly hunt you down and kill you. If Soe can develop his machine so that other people can do what you do, there is indeed a brave new world out there.

"What if the world could read minds? What if it happened over a very short time period? I can't even start to imagine the ramifications!"

Jac stood up, his face distorted almost to tears. "Grandpa, why didn't you ever tell me about all this? I might have been able to help or I might have got in the way and got killed. This is the damnedest thing I have ever heard. I can't believe you kept the truth from me on mother and dad. Just two days ago I gave one of your cards to a poor woman. She praised you as the kindest, most generous man she knew of. I agreed. Now I find out that you are in a death feud, killing people, plotting to destroy your enemies."

Jac threw up his hands in despair and sat down.

GrandJac sighed as he hung his head with his elbows on his knees. "I did what I thought was best at the time, son. I have protected you from all this crap down through the years. I didn't want you to develop the hate and bitterness that I have. With you not knowing, you were happy, carefree. You brought me the joys that I missed. I think you are the better for it. Maybe, with Meg's help, we can get Friedman to quit. That way, you won't have to carry the burden of hate all your life. I pray it can happen." *Of course, if little Sammy can't do this, he's gonna die!*

GrandJac stood slowly, stiffly. Sighing, his hands slapped his sides as he moved around the table. He stared off into some unknowable distance contemplating what he was to say next. *This thing is almost getting out of control! I've got to calm Jac down and keep the forward progress moving. Jac must stay here. Carol cannot drag him away. This truce and forgiveness of Sammy and the Friedmans might convince Jac I'm mellowing. He's so naïve and idealistic he'll go for it. He just can't leave now; I don't know what would happen.*

"The Cochrans have made a fortune down through the years." GrandJac waved his hand ineffectually as a mournful scowl crossed his face. "A strange quirk of events happened that enabled us to profit from investments in most of the markets. I—, ahhh, we are invested in most industries. You must learn this trade to continue the Cochran family."

GrandJac looked at the girls and Jac apologetically. "The money has brought me little solace. My wife is dead. My children are dead and my grandson faces a greater challenge than imaginable. Some pleasure is derived with the charities here in Marian. I am very pleased to help the people here any way I can. In the last few years, Annie has pulled me through—. I thank God."

GrandJac faced Jac as sorrow streaked across his face. "I'm really not too proud of my life, son. Or the way I handled it. You have already had more fun and pleasures than I had in growing up. Dad pulled me into the business early. I grew up quickly and learned to fight and hate, kill without remorse."

Jac sighed at GrandJac "I'm trying to understand, grandpa. Give me time to adjust to this new world."

Jac smiled inwardly. *Then this is the déjà vu that has been bugging me. Meg, Soe, GrandJac, and who knows who else or what else are balled up in this thing. It's rocketing forward, possibly out of control. Soe definitely knows more that I do and GrandJac is in it to the hilt. Somehow, I'm mixed in it, not just Meg. I don't believe I can trust grandpa or Soe 100 percent anymore. The fundamental concept of déjà vu is that it has happened before. I haven't got that page of the story yet.*

Carol sat tensed without saying anything, eyes darting back and forth to each party as they spoke. Soe remained nonchalant with his arm over the back of the chair and his legs crossed, seemingly unmoved by the epic of the Cochrans.

Carol leaned forward in her chair speaking intensely. "Why am I in danger? Why can't I live my own life?"

A little bit of smile, maybe a sneer graced GrandJac's thin lips. "Carol honey, the other side doesn't know what you know or don't know. Their best strategy is to take you out of the picture. Just to be safe. That's how they think. Honestly, if you could develop ESP skills, you would be much better off in protecting yourself from these bastards." *That's a hell of a good idea. I'll talk to Soe and get them interested in making a conversion. We can try it on Carol and see if it works. It's something we have to know anyway, can any man be converted to Quark ESP skills?*

Carol's eyes glittered as she squeezed them to slits looking at Soe and Meg.

Jac's face contorted in a frown. "What is this challenge you speak of Grandpaw?"

GrandJac sucked in a deep breath. He looked at Soe and then Jac. "We shall see as time unfolds. Come along. Let's go visit our enemy, Sam Friedman. I hope with Meg we can see what he has to say."

Just as I thought, an evasive answer. GrandJac is punching the buttons. Soe may know the whole scheme, but he sure as hell won't tell. It's beginning to look like this thing is revolving around Meg and me! Meg is the déjà vu. She came here and initiated it. Yet she might not know it or what part she plays. I sure as hell don't know anything.

Outside, the foursome trailed GrandJac to the metal buildings on the left and entered a side door.

GrandJac turned to the group holding up his hand. "Here's what we are going to do. Sam is in a room with a one-way mirror so you can watch him and hopefully, read him, Meg. I will question him to direct his thinking."

Soe grabbed GrandJac's sleeve. "Let me 'talk to him' first. He's the one that wrecked my lab. I'd like to return the favor, ya know?"

Meg interrupted. "Hold off, Soe. There are bigger issues here than trivial revenge over the lab."

A grunt of disgust echoed from Soe.

Sitting down in the darkened room, they looked through a window at Sam Friedman lying on a cot. A sorry sight greeted them. A weak little man in a rumpled suit and blood stained shirt turned to a sound at the door. A table and chairs were in the middle of the room.

GrandJac went through a second door and into a hallway where the cell door was. He and Morris entered the room.

Sam quickly got up watching them closely. GrandJac sat down at the table and motioned Sam to do likewise on the other side of the table. Sam took the seat cautiously, holding his side with his left hand as he sat back from the table. Sam had a bruise and bloody scab above his right eye where he had been slammed into the table. He fingered it with his right hand.

GrandJac looked him over with a sneer as he shook his head. *Boy, does this piece ah shit need to die.* However, he dove right into his quest. "Sam, I'm getting old and tired of this fucking feud our families have been in for over a hundred years. Do you have any interest in reaching a truce and maybe peace between our families?"

Sam kinda smiled and squirmed in his chair. "Why, ahhh—, hell yes, GrandJac. That might be an interesting mission."

"I can't forgive you for killing my children, but I can let it slide in the interest of peace."

"You may not know it, but you killed two of our family when you went on that terror sweep fifteen years ago. So maybe we are even in a sense. Paw never did explain why he did that, anyway. I was only 20 years old then."

"Okay, here's the plan, Sam. I'm going to send you home to present my offer to Saul. See if you can sell it. I would like to have peace. We can meet and negotiate a settlement."

Sam got up with a smile on his face. "You bet, GrandJac. I'll do that now."

They shook hands. The man led Sam out the door. Outside, he gave Sam the keys to his car, letting him drive away.

GrandJac returned to the viewing room. Sitting down heavily with a sigh, he cocked his head. "What was Sam really thinking, Meg?"

Meg shook her head with disgust. "I see what you mean about evil, GrandJac. He thinks you are old and soft. This is finally a chance to beat you once and for all. If they can get you in the right spot, they will kill you.

"Sammy's driving ambition is to get control of the EEG capabilities. With them, they will be invincible.

"They think Jac Jr. is a pussy. They will kill him to stop the family line.

"Also, you did not kill any Friedman in your attacks 15 years ago.

"He is so evil, I want to spit to get the thoughts out of my head." Meg twisted around with her arms clasping her shoulders and a sour sneer on her pretty mouth.

"Ha, that supports my assessment of Sam and his tribe." GrandJac affirmed nodding. "You see son, the kind of animals we're dealing with? That attempted murder last night is in line with their thinking and plan. They will stop at nothing, Soe, Meg, to get this power you have.

"Soe, I think you ought to move your lab out here and you girls ought to stay here. I have confidence my men can protect you here. They can't bug this place. Whatever technology they have, they won't get any more!" GrandJac said with ringing finality.

Soe glared at the window, then GrandJac. "I wish I coulda slapped him around a little. You know, just an opener. He really needs an ass adjustment."

Meg turned to Soe with the air of a commander, "Wait your chance, Soe. We won't be safe at school and we won't be safe at Jac's house. We have a breather right now while the negotiations are being set up. We should move today."

Soe nodded as he looked at Meg and then GrandJac. "We'll get some help here and do it."

GrandJac dialed a phone from his pocket and talked for a moment. "There's a pickup truck outside with three men. Go get your lab, Soe."

Carol stood with her hands on her hips. "Well, we got that straightened out. Now, are we going to get our things at Jac's house? I've got nothing but what's on my back. What about Jac continuing to work at the hospital and live at home?"

Carol sniffed as cynicism swept over her. *This is an absolute can of worms. It's just like some movie script, but it's for real! I guess I'll play along, for a while anyway. Maybe Jac and I can get something going and escape this nightmare! Jac is the best part of the pie and I want him!*

GrandJac answered Carol with a nod. "We need to keep up a normal front as much as possible, Carol. But I think you ought to be here tonight. I have men out there looking out for Jac, routinely. Why don't you go home with Jac after lunch, pick up your and Meg's things and drive back here? Jac can continue on to work."

Jac looked at Carol to see her response. On the surface, it appeared that she agreed with the whole plan. No questions asked.

***

Sam drove the three hours to Dallas and his father's estate, elated, thinking about how they could swing this deal and kill GrandJac too. Waving at the guard, he drove through the high gate and stonewalls up to the parking area beside the three-story house. Beautifully landscaped trees, shrubs and flowerbeds surrounded the colonial. Tall white columns guarded an expansive front porch. Long thin windows looked out draped in white frilly curtains.

Sam paid no attention to the beautiful colonial house that he had lived in all his life. He accepted his life-style without ever thinking about it. Daddy had always had money and he doled it out to the three boys. They lived in an affluent state, the envy of their school chums when they were growing-up.

He walked rapidly to the front door and entered. A black maid met him in the hallway. "Good afternoon, Mr. Sam. May I help you? Oh—, Mr. Sam, you are hurt. Your shirt is bloody!" Sheila exclaimed in a shrill voice as she reached for Sam. "How can I help you?"

Sam waved her off. "I'm okay, Sheila. I need some coffee and I need to see Daddy."

"Of course. Mr. Saul is in his office. I'll bring coffee." Sheila hurriedly turned away.

THE ENHANCERS

Sam strode rapidly down the hallway and turned right into a huge room with high ceilings. It was finished in dark mahogany paneling. Pictures of the family covered one wall. A bookcase filled another wall. An inset cabinet with glass doors stood behind a beautiful dark walnut desk. The cabinet was filled with a fine collection of pistols and rifles dating back to the early 1800's. Swords from that era adorned the walls on each side of the cabinet.

Daddy Saul sat behind the desk talking on a phone. He looked up as Sam rushed in. Miss Sheila brought coffee in, set it on a service table and left after Sam waved her away.

Daddy Saul's small frame and potbelly were concealed behind a black vest, long sleeved white shirt and black string tie. Thin hands with carefully manicured nails protruded from the sleeves. A large diamond ring glittered on his left hand and a heavy gold watch draped his wrist. His receding hair was curly brown cropped close. It descended down long sideburns to a manicured beard accented with a neatly trimmed moustache above full lips. Beady black eyes peered from behind rimless glasses. He had a broad, hooked nose that he was rubbing as he watched Sam pour coffee. He carefully cradled the phone and turned to a cabinet behind him where he poured himself a generous glass of sherry. The phone clattered in its seat.

"Sam, my boy, you look excited. What has you stirred up?" Saul inquired in precise English. "By the way, is that a black eye? Hey, son, is that blood on your shirt and your jacket? Who did that to you?" Saul demanded sitting forward over his desk.

Sam held up his hand. "Wait a minute, Daddy. Let me tell you what is going on. I got more information on the EEG system, first. Second, I met with GrandJac and he wants to have negotiations to settle our feud, forever." Sam blurted out looking for admiration from Daddy.

Saul looked critically at Sam. Leaning back in his chair. "I believe you have left some details out. Please start from the beginning."

He tipped the sherry glass and carefully sipped twice, licking his lips while watching Sam expectantly.

124

Sam knew that he couldn't fool Daddy Saul. "Uh couple uh weeks ago, I made contact with the janitor in Etheridge's building. I put a bug in his lab and found that he had made some real progress on his EEG machine. I told you about the janitor, you know."

Sam jumped around nervously in his chair. "Saturday night, a girl died in a car wreck. She drowned, and little Jac and Etheridge brought her back to life with strong ESP skills—, using Etheridge's program. I got a copy of his computer program so I put a hit on the girl. That fell through." Sam paused for effect, but Saul gave no indication.

"GrandJac's men captured the janitor, the hit men and me. He tortured one hit man to get the truth. Nailed his hand to the table. I got shot in the side fighting to escape." Sammy paused for effect, watching Saul.

Saul nodded and muttered, "Hmmmmmmmm."

"It turned out that the janitor was a CIA operator trying to get the same data I got. Well, he got tough and GrandJac tortured him 'til he bit down on a cyanide pill and died right there."

"Right there in front of everybody, Sammy?" Saul parroted.

"Yeah." Sammy blurted out, looking to Daddy Saul for feedback.

Saul gave no indication of reaction. He nodded, "Yes?" expectantly, urging him on. He listened passively, shot his cuffs and steepled his fingers throughout the long dissertation while looking for inconsistencies that Sam had a habit of generating to cover his faults.

Saul prodded. "What happened to the hit men, Sammy? You left that out."

"'Ol GrandJac sent them to Singapore on one of his ships to be rehabilitated."

Saul harrumphed. "Tell me about the girl's ESP talents, Sammy. This is a pretty wild tale."

Sammy grinned. "All I got is verbal discussions on tape from the bug, Daddy. The girl's name is Meg and she could levitate a coke can, maybe more. She could read the past from the objects in the room and she could send thoughts to people. Yeah, she could read your mind, too."

Saul looked at Sammy directly for the first time. Piercing beady eyes, sarcasm laced his next question. "Do you think all these ESP talents are the result of Etheridge's EEG machine on the girl's ahhh, Meg's mind?"

Sam stood up waving his left arm as he replied excitedly. "It seems crazy like, but it's the God's truth, Daddy. I have it on tape from bugging Etheridge's lab. I didn't actually see it but I have the conversations on tape and I have copied his programs from his computer that controls the power."

Saul took another long sip of the sherry. He leaned back in the big, high backed leather swivel chair as he continued to hold the tips of his fingers together while looking through Sam.

Sam ducked his head and sipped his coffee.

"So, old GrandJac wanted a peace offering, maybe a settlement. Wanted to stop the feud as he said." Saul repeated. "Hmmmm, tell me more of the actual setting of your conversation with GrandJac, Sammy."

"Well, I was in a small room with a bunk, table and chairs. GrandJac came in, sat down and immediately began talking about stopping the feud."

"Were there any windows or places where this Meg could see you, watch you, Sammy?"

"Yeah, there was a window. No, it was a mirror on one wall looking at me. I guess she could have been looking in from a dark room. Hey, I betcha that was a one-way mirror, Daddy!"

"Hmmmm, by the way, how is old GrandJac looking these days, Sammy?"

"Well, he is getting quite gray. He's stooped a little, but he still has the fire in his eye, Daddy." Sam said hoping for recognition from Saul.

Saul continued the questioning. "When GrandJac was talking to you about the peace conference, what were your thoughts?"

Sam spoke up quickly. "The first thing I thought was, this may be the time we can get GrandJac outside away from his guards and kill him. Then we could kill Jr. and wipe out the family. You see, Daddy, old GrandJac was really ready to settle up. I could tell by his whole attitude. I think we can put a plan together to clean 'em out once and for all." Sammy rose from his chair waving his arms, looking at Daddy for approval. "Uhh, that hurts." Sammy exclaimed grabbing his side.

Saul looked at Sam pensively. "What if the girl, Meg, was mind-reading you, Sammy? What if she's really that good?"

Sam's jaw dropped as he put his hand up to his mouth. "Oh shit Daddy, that could have been happening. If that's true, then they know what I was thinking and planning."

"Yes, Sammy, you could have fucked up. Think about that. Maybe she knows everything you know. Yeah, Sammy, the more I think about that the less I like it." Saul pointed a finger at Sammy.

"What are you going to do now, Sammy?" Saul posed the question as if Sam were running the show.

Sam paused a moment, wrinkling his brow. "We've got to get the EEG thing working. I'll get our technician on it. I got copies of Etheridge's programs. If we can make it work, I'll test it on myself."

Saul frowned at Sammy, shaking his head. "No, don't do that. It might be advisable to test it on someone else and if it works, kill him. Then we can use it. It just might destroy your brain, Sammy."

"Yeah, yeah, Daddy. That's a good idea." Sammy answered snapping his fingers. "I'll get on it now."

Sammy left, Saul watched him go, shaking his head.

"You better have someone look at that bullet wound, Sammy. It could get infected." Saul called after him.

Well, well, well, it has finally started. All these years of planning, anticipating. I really wondered if I would live to see it. Ha, ha, this is going to be fun! I'm going to let my program continue to run. They must be exterminated!

         ***

Tommy Silva finished the assembly of the miniature TV camera and sound system that he intended to install in the ceiling of Etheridge's lab. It had a battery pack and long play tape recorder for the video and sound. Since it transmitted no radio waves, it was undetectable. Even so, he had wrapped it in heavy aluminum foil to shield it from any stray electrical transmission.

He called the number for the janitor's phone in the service area. It was 11:30; Charlie should be there. There was no answer. Tommy drove over to school and parked in a remote area of the research-building parking lot. He walked to the building, approaching it from the rear where the service entrance was located.

Charlie's car was parked near by. Tommy looked it over. It was cold and no one was in it. The doors were locked. He called Charlie again on his cell-phone and got no answer.

Well, where in the hell is that buttwipe? Tommy grumbled angrily. *I've got to get this thing in tonight.*

Tommy went to the front of the building and tapped on the door to get the guard's attention.

The guard came to the door and inquired, exasperated. "What the hell is going on, it's midnight?"

Tommy pulled phony ID for the local Police Department. "I had a call from the janitor. He wanted to talk to me."

The guard let him in. "Let's go get Charlie and find out what the hell is going on. If he is having a problem, he should call me and the Campus Police, first." He informed Tommy in a loud voice.

They proceeded to the service area and scanned it. Then they got on the building speaker system and called for Charlie. No answer.

Tommy suggested. "Let's look in Charlie's locker and the service area."

His locker was in order and his coat was hanging up. The service area was neat and clean and the outside door was locked.

"Thank you, Officer, I'll have to look elsewhere."

Outside, Tommy walked to Charlie's car. *What tha hell is that dumb Swede up to?*

From about 30 feet, Tommy could see Charlie sitting in his car. "There the stupid shit is, sitting in his damn car!" He trotted over to the car and jerked open the door. Charlie slumped forward over the wheel, head lolling to the side. Tommy pushed Charlie's head back and looked into vacant eyes.

"Hell, he's dead and the damn door's unlocked!"

Tommy quickly checked his pulse as he stared at a bruise over one eye.

Well, shit, he's been dead and even getting cold and stiff, Tommy observed as he pushed him back. *Someone put him here while I went inside.*

Tommy carefully panned the parking lot and surrounding area. *They are probably watching me right now.* Nothing was obvious.

Turning back to Charlie again, *I believe the dumb S.O.B. used his cyanide capsule. Now why would he do that?*

Tommy flipped open his cell phone calling the home office.

"Call 'the boss,' Tommy." The terse reply came back.

"The boss'" sharp, clipped instructions rattled in Tommy's ear. "Get Charlie and the car away from the campus and out to the wrecking yard rendezvous where he can be picked up. Wait there until another operative comes and helps you clean things up. Get your car away from the campus. I want a full report in the morning. You better find out what happened to Theo. It could happen to you."

Tommy sighed. "Yes sir." He closed the phone. "Boy, it's going to be a long night. The new guy will have to come from Dallas at least."

As it turned out, two new guys had to come from Washington DC and it was midmorning before things began to shape up. One of the operatives drove Charlie and his car to Dallas where Theo was flown to DC for final clean up. They picked up Tommy's car at the campus and went to the motel room where Tommy and Charlie had been staying.

"We're to call the Administration building at the college and inform them that Charlie has been called home for a death in his family last night around midnight. He will be gone at least a week." The new agent informed Tommy, scowling.

Tommy grabbed the shirtsleeve of his new partner, Dan Reynolds. "We have to get back into the Research building and get the bug receiver that Charlie was using. It's probably in the janitor service room. Really, the best thing to do would be to get the temporary janitor job that will be needed to fill Charlie's absence."

More calls were made and strings pulled to get Tommy in as the temp janitor for tonight. He had to report early for training.

Dan told Tommy, demanding eye contact, "The boss wants the girl. She's the key to the puzzle along with the computer programs you taped. We have to pick her up somehow. Got any ideas?"

Tommy shrugged, "All we can do now is locate her and make some plans from there. She's been staying at Dr. Cochran's house."

Dan answered with a wave. "Sure, let me see if I can pick her up there."

***

Jac and Carol left after lunch in Jac's GN. Sitting in the parking area in front of GrandJac's house, both stared at the other. Finally Jac brought up the subject haunting them.

"Carol, the best of this crazy unbelievable mess is that I have captured a family! You and Meg have pulled us into a tight knot, something I've always wanted. The worst thing is the power lust! The end justifies the means. I don't have a clue to where this thing is going. But, I believe some of these strange feelings; you know this déjà vu crap I've mentioned is surfacing. Meg seems to be the catalyst. GrandJac and Soe are right in the middle of it, somehow controlling, directing the play. Do you have any observations or comments?"

Carol scowled and put her hand on Jac's arm. "They are killing people. Shooting people, supposedly the bad guys! This is really scary! I think we ought to fall in with the theme and watch it carefully. Try not to think about it. You know Meg can read your thoughts. I'll try to get a feel from her later."

Jac suggested, "Okay, that's a plan. Let's coast for a day or two. It's developing like a cancer! I just can't believe this attitude of casualness about the violence. GrandJac must be one mean dude and apparently has been mean all his life. I grew up

130

in it and never knew anything! It sure seems like GrandJac is determined to control this ESP power for himself. The Friedmans are the same, just absolute power! I think there is more to come. Best I can tell, Soe is the actuator. It's beginning to look like Soe has caught the power bug, too.

"Ahhhh, tell you what, you drive the GN back to town and get used to how it handles. We can turn your rent car in. I have two cars, so we'll be fixed for the road, okay?"

Carol pushed the crazy thoughts away and clapped her hands. "Hot dog, I just love cars, Jac. I want to see what this moochine will do!"

Jac grinned; her extraverted personality enveloped him. He knew he was tumbling for her, hard.

***

Carol looked the shifter over, the pedals, the instruments and moved the power seat up to fit her. As she strapped her seat belt and lowered the tilt on the wheel, she patted the accelerator pedal. The engine whined up to 3000 rpm, the exhaust pipes giving off a throaty rumble.

She turned to Jac, eyes dancing. "Buckle up, bigboy."

Jac leaned against the door and watched. She was wound up with excitement. Her eyes were big and that cute perky mouth was twisted into a tight smile.

Carol held the brake as she pulled the console shifter back into overdrive. The car lurched against the brakes as the 2000 pound torque converter/transmission caught. She released the brake and gassed it a bit. The car leaped forward as if catapulted and snapped Carol back against the seat.

Jac reached for her hand on the wheel. "Go easy on the gas, gal. The car has a Positrac differential and lots of rubber on the ground. It won't spin the wheels easily. The wheel is 2.3 turns lock to lock with progressive response and the suspension is hard."

Carol nodded as the car rolled along at 40 on the Farm to Market road.

"You've got some room up ahead, kick it and hang on." Jac laughed.

Carol gritted her teeth and stepped on the gas pedal, hard. The GN kicked down to second gear; lurched sideways as the tires grabbed the pavement. There was little time to notice the tack rev to 5000 and see the boost gage jump to 22 psi. The turbine whined at a high-pitched scream even over the noise insulation.

Carol hung on the steering wheel and watched the road and the speedometer. In seconds the GN had shifted through 2nd, 3rd, and slammed into 4th at 115 mph, continuing to accelerate. She got off it at 125 mph. The narrow farm road flashed by like a ribbon in the wind.

"Hold it steady, Carol, you can take the curve ahead." Jac shouted above the wind noise and exhaust rumble.

The hard suspension system held the car virtually flat as Carol powered into the curve. Seemingly feeling the road, she gassed it again halve way through. The GN squatted slightly gripping the pavement easily negotiating the curve at 135 mph.

Carol let the car drift to 80 mph shouting. "Wowowee, what a machine!"

Jac smiled proudly. "Where did you learn to drive?"

"My daddy has always had Corvettes and I've driven them for 7 years, even did some drag racing."

Jac nodded. "When we get into the edge of town, spin it around some corners and see how it handles. I think you will be surprised. Corvettes have always under steered."

As they approached town, they could see a new housing development on the left. The concrete streets were in and two houses were going up at the far end of the proposed subdivision.

Jac pointed. "Here we go, Carol. Pull in here and drive around some of these blocks."

Carol giggled. "Boy, this is my day!"

She gunned the GN into the entrance, accelerated to the first corner, braked, and slide around the corner, giving it the gas in the turn. The GN responded perfectly and straightened out shooting down to the next corner. Again, Carol gassed it through the turn and braked hard. The GN screamed to a stop with the anti-locks working perfectly.

Jac reached over and ruffled her hair, hollering. "Gal, you're good, I'm impressed." Carol's eyes twinkled as she leaned over and kissed him.

She drove conservatively to Jac's house and pulled into the drive. "Let's get our bags and I'll be on my way. I assume you are going to drive the HM, Jac?" Carol asked tilting her head to one side and smirking.

"What's the HM, sweetie pie?"

"Why, the 'home made,' of course."

"You little stinker. Yes, I'm going to drive my Tiger."

They gathered Meg and Soe's things in one bag and Carol's in another.

Jac and Carol's eyes locked in the bedroom as she began unbuttoning her blouse. Twenty minutes later, they were exhausted, lying across the bed.

Jac rolled over and nuzzled her neck. "Carol, watch the interplay between Soe and Grandpaw. Watch Soe. There is something going on that we're not privy to. I don't think even Meg can pick it up. This whole damn thing is being orchestrated by Grandpaw with Soe doing the running. You know, I asked you if you could pickup any feelings about the happenings? Can you?"

Carol twisted to look at Jac. "I'm not getting any déjà vu, haven't since Meg left school. I guess I'm just not psychic at all, Jac. I'm sorry I can't help you, but I will watch Soe and I will talk to Meg. She will tell me if anything is going on."

Jac sighed, kissed her passionately as he fondled her breasts. "You really have some nice thumpers—, Ahhhhh. I've got to go to work, you hot mama. I'm showering and checking it to you."

"What's a thumper, Bigun?"

"When you jump up and down, your breasts slap your rib cage causing a deep thumping, echoing from your chest cavity. Can't you hear it when you exercise in the morning?"

Carol smirked as she lifted her breasts and let them fall. "I think it's a man-thing, Bubba!"

Carol followed Jac to the garage and watched him get in the Tiger. The dash was completely forward, so it was easy to slide into the car by hanging on the roof frame over the door.

Jac motioned to Carol, "Put the top on, it's not heavy."

Carol picked it up, "It sure is light. I'm surprised! It fits perfectly, Jac. You did a wonderful job."

Jac snapped several clips inside. "It's titanium. These side rails are crash/frame supports.

I didn't do it all, needless to say. I had these ideas in school and spent a little time on them, but to get it finished in six months, I had to farm out some of it."

Carol nodded, grinning, "Sure, I knew you weren't that good."

Jac glared at her. "I'll get you for that, puddle jumper!"

By squeezing a lever on the left side, the dash moved easily out and up. Jac could rest his elbows on it and reach the small steering wheels with either hand.

"Here's the way you start it, Carol." Jac pushed the remote into a slot on the dash while pushing a button on the keypad. The engine revved into life with a pleasant burble. A woman's voice listed instrument readings and reminded Jac the door was open.

"Well, let's go, girl. Get in your machine and we'll blow this joint." Jac snickered as he shifted the car into overdrive with his left hand on the small toggle lever and rolled outside.

Carol backed the GN into the street. Jac pulled beside her giving her a hard stare as he gunned the motor. Carol grinned and gunned the GN's motor.

"To the corner." Jac pointed and watched her.

She slammed the gas pedal down and the GN jumped forward. Jac goosed the Tiger and in an instant it was ahead of the GN and screaming down the street. Jac braked hard as the GN pulled along side.

Carol rolled the window down and yelled. "I want that one. That's mine, Bubba." Jac grinned as he pulled ahead of her and around the corner.

***

Carol rolled the GN through the neighborhood, onto the access road, and accelerated up to speed on the cross-town freeway. She pushed the radio button, caught a country-western station. *I guess I'll check out the local music.*

A red Pontiac Firebird pulled up beside her on the right and matched her speed. She glanced over and saw the window down on a cold day. She could see the driver looking at her. He couldn't see her, she knew, because of the dark tinted windows.

An arm poked out of the backseat behind the driver with a pistol aimed at the GN. Carol slammed on the brakes and fell behind the FB. The FB changed lanes trying to get in position beside her.

Strangling the wheel, Carol scanned the freeway for police. Fear flushed her face. Adrenalin flooded her heart and breathing.

Carol's scan showed no cops, light traffic. She gunned the GN, shot past the FB and ran it on up to 110 mph. She could see the FB accelerating and coming up behind her. Carol was weaving through traffic that was doing 55 to 70 MPH. A few saw her coming and tried to switch lanes making it even harder. She braked heavily twice when she and the other car switched lanes together. She gassed the GN around them and looked back. The FB was almost on top of her.

"Catch me if you can, toadstool!" Gasping, she pushed it to the floor and held on past 125 mph. The FB fell back with Carol frantically trying to dodge traffic.

She picked up her exit sign beyond the next overpass and braked hard switching to the outside lane. The FB anticipated and moved over into the right-hand lane.

Carol exited and made the right turn onto the Farm to Market road. She had to swing wide to miss a car and cut back sharply into her lane to miss an oncoming car. The GN slid sideways and Carol fought the wheel to get it straightened out in her lane. She looked in the mirror and saw the FB run off the shoulder of the road to miss a car. Mud, rocks and grass spewed into the air as it slid down the ditch. But they got it together and back on the road.

Carol muttered grimly, "Okay, asshole. Lets see what you can do now." A small bit of confidence had returned. She knew she could out drive them with the GN. Traffic was thinning out rapidly. Pressing the pedal to the floor, she hung on the wheel as the engine screamed through 3rd and 4th gears. She whistled past five cars at one time, the twin exhausts thundering.

Ahead, an oncoming truck and a car in her lane blocked the two-lane country road. Braking hard, she swung onto the shoulder on the right, half on and half off the pavement. The GN bucked through the soft ground from the rains.

Carol almost lost it in the ditch on the right. The powerful engine spun the wheels in the soft shoulder spraying mud on the car behind her. The heavy tires caught on the pavement shooting the GN to the other side of the road. Fighting the wheel, she gunned it again. The GN responded, jumping back onto the pavement. With the turbo screaming, it straightened out shooting ahead, mud spraying from the rear tires. The car she had passed on the shoulder braked hard to a stop. The driver screamed out the window honking his horn.

The FB blew past the stopped car almost catching up with her. An arm was hanging out the right window trying to get off a shot. The white puff of smoke whipped away but the bullet struck the rear window and bounced into the sky.

Carol gripped the wheel fiercely as she pushed the GN past 130 mph. The FB was rapidly lagging back.

"Oh shit, here's that long curve!" Carol yelled as she tried to gage the road and an old pickup truck puttering along in her lane. It looked like it was standing still as she bore down on it, braking hard. Switching to the on-coming lane, she blasted past the truck at 110 mph.

Carol stole a glance in the mirror and saw the air draft shake the truck almost sideways. The old farmer stared wide-eyed through the windshield at the black car disappearing ahead. The FB blew past him. He ran off in the ditch waving his fist out the window.

Carol could see GrandJac's ranch ahead and the entrance road racing to meet her. She braked hard and held onto the wheel as she approached the entrance. The GN seemed like it was going to plow up the road with the front bumper.

She jerked the GN through the entrance road and gate doing 70 mph with a big slide out into the field. Rocks and mud sprayed from the under-frame as she gunned it again and accelerated to the house. The high-pitched scream of the turbo and raucous roar of the twin exhausts alerted two of GrandJac's hands inside the house.

They ran out the front door and saw the red Pontiac Firebird speeding down the road.

Carol screeched to a stop on the paved apron, snatching open the door. Trembling, gasping, almost falling out of the car, "Those assholes tried to kill me. They shot at me!"

Morris ran to his pickup truck and snatched the door open, grabbed a mike and called the County Sheriff on the Police radio band. "This is Morris at the Cochran Ranch, a red Firebird on Farm to Market road 1495 is going west at high speed. Armed and dangerous, shooting at us."

He turned to Carol grabbing her arm to steady her. "Miss Carol, you're shaking like a leaf, honey."

Carol hung on Morris's arm, panting. "Those bastards were shooting at me. Jac's car saved me!"

Morris grabbed her shoulders. "Easy, easy, Miss Carol." She calmed down as her breathing returned to normal.

"Thank you, Morris. I'm sure glad you were here." Grabbing a big gulp of air, "Ahhh, I've got some bags here, can you help me?"

"Why, shor-nuff, Miss Carol. Let me get 'em." Morris stepped forward and grabbed all three in one hand and led the way to the house.

Duncan stepped outside onto the porch. "Miss Carol, give me the keys and I'll move Jac's car so it can't be seen from the road."

Duncan came back in the living room in a minute. "I found where a bullet hit the car on the back glass. The glass is Lexan. It's used for bulletproof protection in Banks. All it did was 'star' the plastic. Looks like Jac's ideas are paying off, Miss Carol. It just might have saved you from getting shot."

"Well, the car saved me—, really." Carol stated firmly, "That buggar is unbelievably fast and one hell of a road hugger.

"Do you think the Sheriff can catch them? They were trying to kill me, you know!"

"The Sheriff will put out an APB for them. They better hide. That car is easy to spot." Morris nodded as he spit a stream of tobacco juice across the flowerbed."

***

Annie appeared in the doorway. "Hi, Miss Carol. Come inside and I'll show you your room."

Carol answered. "I have Meg's bag and some stuff for Soe, also, Annie."

"That's just fine. We have a room for each of you." Annie led the way down a hall off the living room.

The house had four bedrooms in the west wing, each with a bath. A large rec room with exercise equipment was included. Carol, Soe, Meg, and Jac were all situated in that area.

***

Soe left the ranch with the three men in a double cab pickup truck and headed into town to the college where they backed up to the service entrance. Soe went around through the front door to open it up. With the extra help, Soe was able to load the important parts of his electronics gear quickly. He had to leave quite a bit of equipment. Thinking about it, *that was good. It may fool someone into thinking that I'm still working in the lab.*

As Soe passed through the service area, he thought of Charlie bugging the lab. *Maybe he left his receiver here somewhere.*

Soe suggested. "Let's find the bug receiver if it's still here, men."

Ten minutes of detailed searching found the unit in a box of paper towels in the storage room. A neat hole had been cut in the back. A small LP tape recorder/receiver still had the tape in it.

Kendall, the man who found it yelled to the others. "Hey, here it is. Y'all come here."

138

Soe grabbed it, elated. "Good work, Kendall, we'll just take this and let them go fishing."

They left through the service door and drove away in the truck.

***

Tommy Silva drove into the parking lot as Soe and the truck pulled out. He recognized Soe from pictures Charlie had taken. *Looks like he's leaving with a gang! I wonder what he's doing?* Through habit and training, Tommy noted the license plate and make of the truck as it pulled away.

He reported for work, met the janitor supervisor, Russo Vidalli, in the lobby where his training started. Standard procedure, cover the tools and walk down the hallways discussing each lab and what to do. As they passed Soe's lab, Tommy asked about it in particular. The supervisor opened the door with a master key and they entered.

Tommy asked, scanning the room. "Does someone work here? It sure is a mess."

Russo replied. "Yes, this lab is in use and we have to clean it just like the others. As for the mess of equipment, don't touch it. That's the way the scientists are sometimes."

***

With training ended, Tommy started his rounds of cleaning and proceeded to Soe's lab. After looking it over, he decided that Soe had pulled out. He called his new partner, Dan, and gave him the license plate to checkout. He started searching the service room and Charlie's locker for the bug receiver. Twenty minutes later he discovered the unit in the paper towel box and the fact that the tape was gone.

Hmmmmmm. Looks like Etheridge or someone found the unit and took the tape only.

Tommy called Dan again and asked about the truck plates.

"Yeah, I got the ID on the truck, Tommy. It belongs to John Allen Cochran located on FM 1495."

"You know I told you about the truck leaving as I pulled in. Well, that was Etheridge moving his lab out. He almost surely found the recorder and took the tape. All we got is a verbal between Theo and me now."

Tommy answered shaking his head. "Naw, that's not right. We have the computer discs Theo copied from Etheridge's lab. We need to get them to Dallas for review."

"It is even more important to capture the girl, Meloney Graham, now." Tommy demanded. "The boss wants the girl. Make some plans. I'm stuck here with this janitor job. Do something."

Dan reported, "I went by the Cochran house and watched it. No one came or went. Maybe they are at the old man's ranch on FM 1495?"

Tommy sighed. "Hell, watch that place, that's all I can think of."

***

Soe stopped off at a safety supply house and picked up four hard hats on the way through town.

He'd been thinking. *How can I implement the EEG concept? The hard hats could hold the electrodes and the user would put the hat on for contact. I could use a laptop computer for controls and the individual would have the ability to run the program himself.*

Morris pointed to one of the stalls on the left as they entered the ranch. "Those buildings have a garage door on front and will make a good work place, Soe."

"Sounds good to me, Morris, let's do it."

The men moved in more benches from a stall next door and helped Soe set up his lab. He immediately went to work on the headgear idea he had and found that it would work fine. He programmed a laptop computer from his discs and wrote a program so that the arrow keys would control the brain stimulation.

***

Night had fallen and a cold wind whipped out of the north. Soe thought, *It will surely freeze tonight, Brrrrr,* as he zipped up his coat.

He hurried to the ranch house and through the front door, feeling the warmth inside. The living room was large with stuffed chairs and sofas around a large center table made out of the root burl of a huge cypress tree. A glass top enabled you to see the wood support. A large fireplace and hearth made from Austin chalk sat in one corner and a crackling fire of oak burned brightly. A 48" TV console and entertainment center stood against the wall on the left of the fireplace. Seating allowed everyone in the room to enjoy the fire and the TV center.

Carol and Meg were settled in big leather easy chairs watching a TV show. GrandJac relaxed in his favorite chair by the fire sipping a drink.

"Hi y'all. I've got my lab moved out here and set up. Boy, it's getting cold outside."

Carol whirled around in her chair and immediately started telling Soe about the car chase and the shooters.

Soe grinned and held up his hand. "Whoa there, girl. I already know about it. Meg told me as soon as I walked in here."

Carol pouted. "For crap's sake, Meg, I wanted to tell Soe."

Meg laughed and interjected. "It would take you 30 minutes and we'd miss the end of the show."

Carol flounced around in her chair. "Okay, okay, let's see the show."

Annie came in looking expectantly to Soe. "Can I fix you supper, Mr. Soe?"

"Annie, you rang my bell, thank you." Soe grinned broadly as he followed her out of the room.

***

Eating an apple, Soe casually drifted into the room where he could feel the heat from the fire. His eyes were drawn to the girls. He admired their bodies as they lounged casually in the big chairs.

Meg turned to him and smiled. Soe turned red, because he knew she had read him. A thought popped into his head, it seemed to come from nowhere. *You're a hunk, too, Bigboy.*

Soe wondered how far this mind thing would go. *Do you want to try the portable unit tonight?*

141

Meg stood up and turned to Soe. "Let me get a jacket and we'll test it."

Carol turned, scowling. "Aha. Secrets and conspiracies going on here, I want to go, too."

She and Meg returned from their rooms with jackets. Soe waved at GrandJac. "We're going to my new lab to test some equipment."

He waved them on, saying. "I'm enjoying the fire. Y'all go solve the world's problems."

GrandJac watched Soe as he walked across the room. Soe looked back catching his eye and holding it for a long moment.

***

"Here, Meg. The hat fits this way and you can adjust the strap to pull it down for a firm contact. We may have to use the chinstrap. We'll see. Here's the control system." Soe indicated, as he strapped the portable laptop over her shoulder and let it hang on her right hip where her hand could easily reach the keys.

Meg keyed the on button and felt for the four arrow keys as she stared into space. Keying the up button, she turned slowly as if on ball bearings. Soe could see she was resting lightly on the ball of one foot. Soe and Carol watched, awestruck. Meg turned towards them and Carol slowly rose in the air about a foot, then Soe floated up beside her. Soe moved about, waved his arms and continued to float. They slowly settled back to the floor.

A thought entered their heads. *This is so smooth compared to the other tests. I seem to have so much better control.* Meg continued in their heads. *I can feel the presence of other people who have been in this room. I can see them and feel what they feel.*

Meg stared into space floating gently about the room in a vertical position about a foot off the floor.

The sensation of power that I have is incomprehensible. I feel like I could lift a car or something very heavy. I feel like I could communicate with someone across the world. She paused for a moment, *I feel like I could look at earth from space and see tiny details on the ground.*

The sensation of power seems to emanate from my fingers. It's as if I can point my hand and make things happen.

Meg turned and faced Soe lifting her arm towards him. Soe stumbled back falling heavily to the floor with his arms pinned above his head gasping for breath.

Carol screamed, jumping forward. "Meg, Meg, what are you doing?"

With no indication, Meg fell to the floor, then to her knees, her head hanging down. She crumpled over in a disheveled pile of clothes and lay inert.

Soe struggled to a sitting position. He rolled over onto his hands and knees with his head hanging down. "Jesus Christ, I have never been hit that hard before." He gasped.

Carol ran to Meg and tried to turn her over. "Help me, Soe!" she yelled.

Soe slowly crawled over to Meg, took off the helmet and checked the computer. The battery was dead.

"Damn, I forgot to charge it."

"What—, what are you talking about, Soe?" Carol demanded. "Help me with Meg. Help me turn her over, damn you!"

"I'm trying, Carol. She kicked the shit outta me!"

Soe rolled Meg over on her back with Carol holding her head. She was breathing but maybe unconscious. Her slack mouth hung open. Her eyelids fluttered over vacuously staring pupils.

Soe gripped the table struggling up where he grabbed a first aid kit from the tabletop. Kneeling down to Meg, he spilled the contents on the floor.

"There it is—, the little shit." He panted.

Grabbing an ammonia ampoule, he broke it and passed it under her nose. Meg rolled her head and pawed at her face with her hand. Both Carol and Soe heard Meg say, *Get that away, I'm okay—, I think.* She blinked her eyes into focus and struggled to sit up. Soe and Carol helped her.

"I can't believe it—! I felt like I fell from space to earth when the computer quit!" Meg gasped out loud as she leaned on Soe's arm. "I think I've had enough tonight, Soe."

Soe exclaimed wildly, waving an arm. "Wal—, I hope to kiss a pig, girl. You slapped the living shit outta me. I have never been hit that hard. It was as if my whole body was hit at once, all over!"

Carol laughed uncontrollably, sitting back on her haunches. "You crazy butts. You scared the crap outta me-. But maybe ya'll are okay, huh?"

She got up, dusting off her pants. "Ha ha, I feel just fine, come on, 'kiss a pig.' Lets get Miss Piggy over to the house and get her some caffeine. She looks like she just had a high enema and is all washed out."

That brought out a giggle. Soe shut down the lab and plugged in the computer to charge the battery. Helping each other, they made it to the house.

"Coffee sure hits the spot." Meg exclaimed, holding up the cup to Soe and Carol. "Let's wait up for Jac and tell him about tonight's experiment."

Soe agreed. "You betcha, Meg. I want you to put the double whammy on him like you did on me. I want to see how tough he is."

Meg laughed. "I'm very sorry about that, Soe." She patted his arm looking for forgiveness. "It seemed as if I just waved my hand at you and fiery power leaped from my fingers. I don't know what it is or how to control the intensity."

Carol scrunched down in the big sofa like chair. *I am in some kind of crazy world! I get in a road race, get shot at, coulda been killed. Everybody just takes it like eating a pickle! Meg finds a new kind of power. One that will knock you down with a wave of her hand and it's all okay! I'm gonna haft to get Jac to give me some emotional stability pills. I'm right on the edge of the world!*

*** *

GrandJac had retired, so the girls turned on the TV and caught the 11:00 news. Local news dealt with another mysterious disappearance of a young girl in the area. She had left home the night before in her pickup truck to visit her girl friends at a local teen hangout. About 1:30 or 2:00 AM, she left them in her truck. The truck was found today parked on the side of the road with the keys in it and her purse on the seat.

THE ENHANCERS

The report went on to state that this was the latest in a series of teen girl abductions and/or disappearances.

Meg watched the news intensely. She could feel something about the case but she couldn't put her mind on anything specific.

Carol turned the channel over to a late night talk show. Soe went in the kitchen and popped some popcorn in the microwave for the troops.

"Carol, I can pick up glimmerings of something else out there between Soe and GrandJac, but they mask it very carefully. They are very good at protecting their mind's privacy. I don't think it's anything to worry about, though. I'm trying to stay aloof from the interplay. I, we still don't have an overview of this thing. Let's just let it coast and watch, okay?"

Carol nodded as she stared at Meg. "Looks like you can read me like a book. As you already know, I can't see anything. This is Jac's idea. The whole damn thing is really scary."

***

Jac's evening shift seemed normal. It had the many kid illnesses, colds, sore throats and runny noses. As usual, another bug, a stomach virus, was going around knocking a lot of people out of work. Doctor work was very gratifying. People were helpless with disease. It always gave him pleasure to ease their pain. *I believe that is one of the reasons I have always wanted to be a doctor.*

Jac gave four more "Let Me Help" cards to needy patients. It was pleasing even if it wasn't his money. In two days, his family world awareness had grown 500%! *Here, a benefactor to the needy, donations to the hospital, the schools, the city, the police, firemen and many other charitable contributions. GrandJac had created a separate job and office in town with the Foundation's backing just to address charitable contributions. Yet in business, particularly with the Friedman's, he was mean, vicious, cruel, a street fighter. I certainly don't know my grandfather as well as I thought, maybe not at all.*

GrandJac has fallen from grace. He has feet of clay. What was the real personality of the Cochran clan? Are we the bad guys? Time will tell.

Work slowed towards midnight allowing Jac to make shift change on time. With mind rambling, he changed to street clothes. *I'm glad I have the Tiger. It will be fun to run the freeways home to my sweetie. WOW, she is one package of dynamite! This ESP thing is absolutely beyond the edge. Somehow, I still feel bound up in the drama. I can't step away and look at it objectively. I can't see. I can't anticipate what will happen. It's react as it happens.*

Trotting across the parking lot stretched his legs, it felt great. Tiger stood ready, *man, I love that car!* The tight fitting seat felt good as he pulled the dashboard up to him in a comfortable position. With the engine revving to 1500 to get warm Jac snapped the seat belt and shoulder harness across his chest. The five point aircraft harness held him firmly in the seat so he could use his hands to operate the car without the concept of "hanging on the wheel." Jac pushed the climate button just to listen to the woman's voice state, "The cabin temperature is 70 degrees F." Pushing the "Report" button gave an overview, "All systems normal."

He flicked the shift toggle in OD, let off the brake and stuck his index finger in a hole in the miniature steering wheel on the right. The car steered easily with his fingers wrapped lightly around the wheel or the forefinger like a knob.

Driving out of the parking area, he accelerated onto the feeder street and up the freeway ramp to the inside lane. The rev up of the engine rattled through the exhaust pipes like a motorcycle accelerating. Jac cocked his head to catch the reverberations. *Am I a motorhead? Ha, ha. Hell, admit it. Live it!*

A red Pontiac Firebird from the parking lot matched his maneuver pulling up beside him on the right. Glancing over, Jac could see a black man driving, looking at him. Jac gassed it a little to 80 mph and lowered the suspension system. The Pontiac lagged back, but quickly accelerated up beside him.

Jac snickered, "Ha. I guess these boys want to run. That just suits me fine." Surveying the freeway forward and back, it was pretty clear. More big trucks in the right lane than anything. At least no visible cops. Jac gassed it again kicking it to 120 mph. The road rushed at him like a wild freight train because of the cab forward feature of a mid-engine. Whipping past a few cars that might have been doing 75 mph, he looked back and saw the Firebird hauling ass accelerating up to him. They topped the next overpass at 120 mph. Car dodging had become very serious.

Tightness across his nape begged to be rubbed. *Just what are these assholes trying to do?* A snap glimpse caught the window down and someone sticking a pistol out. The white smoke and crack of the bullet against his window occurred simultaneously. The radiating star in the Lexan gave him the impetus to gas it again.

"Shit fuzzy, these bastards are trying to kill me!" Jac screamed. His face twisted into a snarl. "Well, these cats have to be near top end. I'll blow them off the road!"

Already the Tiger accelerated through 145 mph and weaved around two more cars. The Firebird lagged back and Jac grinned. "I knew they were peaked out." He snapped a glance in the mirror system overhead.

Racing up the slope of the next overpass, he rocketed over the top at 130 mph, almost airborne. "JESUS CHRIST!" he screamed. An 18-wheeler with a big box trailer stretched completely across the three lanes of freeway at the bottom of the overpass.

Jac had no chance of stopping and no place to go. It looked like he only had time to die. Reactively braking and in an instant, he lowered the suspension to ground level. The Tiger flattened like a squirrel jumping on a tree trunk. It slid under the box sideways, tires smoking, still doing 115 mph! The car bottomed once. White titanium fire blew out the back as the frame cross members scraped on the concrete.

Standing on the brakes, he grabbed a look in mirror. The Firebird didn't have a chance.

It plowed into the box in a ghastly shower of shrapnel, dirt and glass particles glittering in the lights. The lower body, from the hood down, went under the box frame. The top half was cut off flush with the windshield/hood joint. The lower wreckage careened down the freeway sideways another two hundred yards and crashed into the railing coming to rest, smoking. Steam poured out from the hood.

Cutting the wheel sharply, Jac gassed it, spinning around with tires squealing. In seconds he was beside the wreckage calling 911 giving pertinent information. Snapping the belts loose, he slapped the emergency latch on the dash. Pushing it forward, he jumped out of the car.

The strong smell of gasoline permeated the air as he approached the Firebird hulk. Dripping from the gas tank in a steady stream, it spread across the pavement searching for cracks to invade.

Funny how you notice things in situations like this, the gasoline wet the concrete, soaking into the pores. Water would never do that!

Yellow sodium vapor lights suspended 40 feet on thin stanchions turned the scene into a macabre horror flick. No windshield. Blood smeared across the seats and back over the rear deck. Apparently two people had been in the front seat and had been cut in two at chest level. The bodies were in the car and their heads back at the truck!

"Fuck ah duck! Look at that!" The trunk of one still had a beating heart. Blood welled up out of the chest/neck area in pulses.

A grunt or moan came from somewhere. *Holy shit, don't tell me the head is talking in the back seat!* Jac peered behind the seat back that had been smashed back into the back seat. In the glary yellow light, he could make out a Latino crouched down on the floor, mumbling to himself. Blood saturated his clothing and the back seat.

Jac squeaked in a high-tension shrill voice. "Hey, can you move? Are you hurt? You've got to get out of the car. It may catch fire."

The Latino raised up staring at Jac with eyes dripping blood. "How—, how, did you get past the truck? We had it planned. You had to crash!"

Jac stepped back, glaring. "What do you mean, planned, asshole? Were you trying to kill me? Run me into the truck?"

The Latino pawed ineffectually trying to crawl out of the car across the jagged metal and glass. Jac grabbed his arm, but he still slipped in the blood and fell across the rear quarter panel's ragged edge. He screamed as the metal tore into his chest and stomach. Jac virtually lifted him out of the car and in the process saturated his front with blood.

"C'mon, shithead! Help me. The damn car could blow!" Jac yelled as he dragged the Latino away from the car and laid him down on the concrete.

He quickly stripped his coat and shirt away to inspect the man's chest and stomach. He had three deep flesh wounds that were bleeding profusely. Jac pushed the shirt and coat down on them as a compress bandage to stop the bleeding.

Sirens screaming and red lights flashing announced ambulances and police cars converging on the scene from both sides of the truck. Jac stepped back as an EMT rushed up to the man on the ground.

"He has lacerations on his torso and he might have internal injuries from the crash."

A second EMT ran up recognizing Jac. "What tha hell, Doc? Are you hurt, you're covered in blood!"

Jac replied as he waved his hand at the Latino. "No, I pulled this man out of the car and he leaked on me."

Two policemen arrived, panting, as they looked the scene over. "Ahh. Are you—, are you the one who called in the 911, sir?"

Looking down his front clothing, Jac wiped his hands on a clean spot, answering quietly. "Yes."

"We'll need a statement from you. Can you come over to the car? Are you hurt?" The first officer asked as he grabbed Jac's arm. Jac went with them to the cruiser and told them who he was and what had happened. He failed to inform them that he was racing 50 to 75 MPH over the speed limit.

Jac asked curiously, eyeballing the officer. "Where is the driver of the truck?"

The policeman admitted. "We don't know. We haven't located him yet."

He turned, looking at Jac's car incredulously. "What you're telling me is that you went under the box? I've got to see your car!"

Jac led them to the car where they stared openmouthed at the interior. "How in the hell do you steer it, Doc?" one asked.

Jac waved his hand. "Just a minute. I've got to go so I'll show you." He slid into the car grabbing a towel from the floor to keep the blood off the seats. He lifted the dash panel up to himself as he cranked it up. The demo continued as he raised and lowered the suspension system and turned the wheels with the hand wheel.

"That's the damnedest thing I have ever seen, Doc. Be careful on the way home. We may need some more information. We'll call you in the morning."

Jac eased the Tiger over the next overpass and gunned it on down to his exit on FM 1495. Releasing a little pent-up tension felt good as he revved it up to 100 mph and cruised out to the ranch. *Shit, two more dead men! I just don't know what to do or who to go to. This thing, whatever it is, is out of control! So far, 'they' have died, but the odds are that we will fall, too!*

***

As he entered the hallway and turned into the living room, "Hey, I see you guys stayed up for me." Jac shouted with his arms outspread.

Soe and Carol looked up screaming. "Ahhhhh, ughh. Jac, did you commit hara-kiri?"

Jac looked down at his front. He was bloody from his chest to his knees. Meg just grinned because she already knew what had happened.

"I'm okay." Jac laughed as he realized what he might look like. "I got a hangnail on the way home and when I bit it off, it bled. The popcorn smells good, any left?"

Meg interrupted as she stood up. "This could last all night, let me fill y'all in." She proceeded to tell Carol and Soe about the race and the wreck and tell Jac about the experiment with her. That took about 30 seconds. They sat there looking at each other.

Carol exclaimed. "I'll bet that red car is the one that chased me."

"What's that mean, Carol?" Jac asked suspiciously, scowling at her. In a moment, Meg had filled him in on Carol's race.

Jac stared in awe at Meg. "Girl, you are really getting into this thing, aren't you?"

Meg nodded, staring quietly at him.

Jac looked at his family, then Carol. He sighed, shrugged, "This has been one busy day. I'm beat; I'm going to bed. I'll eat in the morning."

He pointed at Carol with an accusing finger. "I'll look my GN over in the morning. If you scratched it, I'll spank your rear end."

Carol's chin stuck out. "Ha, ha, I scratched it, so let's get it on, Bubba! Looks like you care for that car a lot more than you care for me. I'm gonna go out there and key it right now!"

"If that happens, you're gonna be called the red-butt baboon!"

"That's enough for me," Soe laughed, "let's sack it."

Jac nuzzled Carol's neck as he squeezed her shoulders. "You little pixy. You just stay in trouble don't you?"

"What's that mean, Junior? You're no better!"

***

Soe had finished showering and donned his underwear, which he slept in. When he entered the bedroom, Meg was standing there in her robe. Soe asked, startled. "Meg, is everything all right?"

Meg approached Soe putting her arms around his neck. Her robe fell off. She was bare. Soe could see her proud breasts jutting out.

"Soe," she said with a little smile twisting her mouth, "I'm very sorry I hit you tonight. You have done so much for me and I repay you by knocking you to the floor, crushing you!"

Soe encircled her body and pulled her in close. Meg pressed herself against him. He bent down, cradled her in his arms and laid her on the bed as he looked into her glistening eyes. Meg reached up and grabbed him, pulling him down onto her craving body.

Soe whispered. "I'll take a whipping any day for this. I wanted you from the moment I saw you in the hospital, you sweet thing. Hold on a moment, let me get my shorts off." He quickly stood up and shucked them off.

Meg grabbed him again, laughing. "I know that, Soe, I can read your mind. It's like an open book—, on some things."

Soe eased down on top of her and kissed her gently for a moment, then passionately.

Meg's mind reading and levitation capabilities introduced a new form of lovemaking. Soe was goggle-eyed after 30 minutes of strenuous exercise. "Meg, this is definitely patentable. No one, and I mean no one has any concept of what I've just gone through."

Meg giggled as she grabbed him around the neck and pulled him down for another kiss. "That's what it's all about, Hunk. Different strokes for different folks."

WEDNESDAY DECEMBER 21ST

Meg woke to a cowbell ringing in the hallway. Soe looked at his watch, 8 o'clock. Crawling out of bed, dressing in sweats, they staggered down the hall to the rec room. Jac and Carol were dancing to a hot beat with an exercise tape on TV. Twenty minutes of stretching, exercising finally got Soe back to normal. "Ugh—, I needed that," Soe admitted.

Annie clapped her hands. "Y'all come to breakfast. I have it all ready for you." She smiled proudly at her new family as she winked at Jac.

***

"Let's catch the morning news. I usually watch local and then national." Jac suggested as he walked into the living room with his coffee.

Local news had big coverage of the bloody wreck with the 18-wheeler on the freeway. Authorities could not find the truck driver. The two men killed were from Dallas and the third was a local, still in the hospital.

Meg scanned the group. "I'll bet I can read the man in the hospital. We might get a better picture of our enemies. What do y'all think?"

Before any one could answer, the phone rang. Officer Whitner asked politely. "Miss Graham, this is Officer Whitner, I got your forwarded message for this number. If you can come down to the station, we can finalize your accident investigation and report."

Jac answered, looking over at Meg with a grin. "I'll tell her, thank you."

Jac shouted, standing up. "Hey, let's go gang. We may have an opportunity to see Meg's killer. C'mon, we can go in the GN."

Outside, Jac walked around his car with meticulous scrutiny. Mud covered it from the hood, across the top, sides and back resembling a mudder that had rolled.

"Carol, I'm going to have you wash it, you little twerp." Jac laughed as he poked Carol. "And remember, if it's scratched, your ass is grass."

As they got in the car, Carol leaned forward from the backseat and slapped Jac on the back of his head. "You better watch it, Bubba. We'll armwrestle for who's on top and I have never been beaten."

Jac leaned forward looking over his shoulder. "I'm gonna— —, I'm gonna spank you, twerp." Meg and Soe grinned knowingly at each.

At the police station, Carol demanded. "Give me the keys and I'll go wash your car. There's a place right down the street. You better get off of that twerp crap, John Allen."

Jac blew a kiss at Carol as she drove off.

***

Meg led the way as Jac and Soe followed up the steps to the dispatcher's desk. "We are here to see Officer Whitner."

Whitner came forward to the lobby. "Come with me, Miss Graham. We can handle this at my desk. Y'all are her friends. You can come along, too." Officer Whitner sat down behind his desk and shuffled a few sheets of paper. "Miss Graham, I have some good news for you. The hit and run driver confessed. He did have insurance, so you can recover your costs and maybe some type of settlement. I need you to sign this form. It's the accident report. See here. You have given the license number and car description. That's very important."

Meg scanned the other papers and found that the driver was the William Cleaver, local to Marian mentioned earlier.

"Is this Cleaver in jail, Officer Whitner? Could I see him? Speak to him?" Meg asked casually as she signed her name. She stood up and looked Whitner straight in the eye demanding an answer.

Officer Whitner met her stare for a moment and glanced away. "Ah—, yes, Willie is in jail here. He can't meet his bond. However, I don't think your meeting would be productive. Willie is remorseful and frankly, he is not well. He is an

154

alcoholic and is having a very difficult time 'drying out', you understand?"

"Yes, of course, I understand. I was hoping I could pour gasoline on him and offer him a cigarette. He needs direction in his life. I believe I could give it to him." Meg said quietly as she seemed to mesmerize Whitner with a penetrating stare.

Officer Whitner jumped up holding his hands in front of his face as he staggered back against the wall. "Ahhhhh—, Wow—, ahh. I can see him burning. He is screaming and running!" Whitner snapped upright and shook his head. "That was the most vivid picture, imagination, or whatever I have ever seen short of the real thing. Just you saying the words, Miss Graham, and I was there. Forgive me, I can't get over it."

Whitner rubbed his face and eyes and ran his hands through his hair. Jac and Soe watched the event passively, without expression, as much as possible.

Whitner picked up the papers and placed them in a folder as he tried to regain his composure. "Miss Graham, that's it. Here are papers that will assist you in your insurance claims. I'm sure you are joking about Cleaver."

"Yes, of course—certainly. Thank you, Officer Whitner for your help. I can't imagine what set off the thing you saw. I was just idly dreaming of revenge. It's not often you get to make a round trip to death." Meg exclaimed casting a side-glance at him.

Officer Whitner recoiled once again. "I didn't realize it was that bad. You seem so healthy—, well—, now, Miss Graham."

***

The scene was interrupted by a policewoman walking by with a box in her arms going towards the evidence room.

Meg spun around as she pointed to the policewoman. "Stop, stop, I want to see that box!"

Soe turned around quizzically, looking at Meg, *What the hell, girl?*

The woman, alarmed, had stopped as if nailed to the floor. Meg stepped forward grabbing the edge of the box, staring in. There were two things, a woman's purse and car keys.

THE ENHANCERS

"Those are the things you found in the abandoned truck yesterday." Meg stated flatly as she stared at them intensely.

Soe stepped forward quickly grabbing Meg's arm. A nervous smile twitching across his face. "Ahhh, uhhh—, she has some psychic powers that appear at random times, uncontrollably."

Officer Whitner answered quickly. "Ah ha, I can believe that. Maybe she can help us. Let me call the officer in charge of the investigation. Please wait here, both of you." as he pointed to the policewoman and Meg.

Soe leaned into Meg's ear as he tightened his grip on her arm. "What are you doing, girl? We don't need this kind of publicity!"

"I can't help it, Soe. It just came to me and I must follow through." Meg answered as she pulled away from Soe's grasp.

Nervously Jac looked at the two of them as he ran his hands through his hair, shuffling his feet. *Here we go again—, that strange feeling is creeping up on me. I'm beginning to get a picture of this déjà vu feeling. When something new or different comes along, it starts. Like as not, it's associated with Meg.*

Detective Brandon came around the corner, "Hi ya'll. I'm Brandon, Detective Brandon. "Ya'll come on in. We can talk in my office."

Brandon led them three doors down as he swung his short, chunky body behind the desk and plopped in a worn swivel chair. Running his right hand through heavy brown hair growing down onto his forehead, he shuffled a few papers. Brown eyes looked expectantly at Meg and her followers as they paraded in, sitting down in available chairs.

Meg sat rigidly straight upright with a determined line to her jaw. *I better give Brandon a little show for cover.*

"What's the relationship between y'all?" He asked as he read the looks on their faces.

Meg waved her hand acknowledging Soe and Jac. "These two men saved my life from a car wreck and drowning last week. This is Dr. Cochran and Dr. Shawn Etheridge. Maybe you read about the car that went in the Marian River last Saturday night?

156

That was me." Meg said as she started wringing her hands and wiping them on her jeans.

"They have helped me regain my memory and get back to reality. You see, I was pronounced dead at the scene. Now, I have flashes of events I can't explain. Dreams and blips of things I don't understand, you know? When this lady, this policewoman walked by, I had this uncontrollable urge to look, to touch the items in the box, you see?" Meg nervously played with her hands and twisted her mouth, her eyes darting about the room.

Brandon spoke soothingly as he watched her twitching. "Yes, I have heard of situations like this. But I have never met anybody or worked with a psychic, Miss Graham. Absolutely anything you can give us would be helpful. Can you tell me anything about the events surrounding the truck?"

Soe and Jac looked at each other as they got a thought simultaneously. *If we go public and get enough attention, they won't dare attack us.*

Meg nodded, wagging her head side to side. "Yes I understand. Let me see the box of items, okay?"

The police officer offered the box to Meg. Meg tentatively picked up the purse and car keys as she stared off to one side.

She spoke quietly, hesitantly. "The girl, Sue Ellen, pulled off the road because a boy flagged her, okay? He was beside his car with the hood up, see? She thought she recognized him from school, maybe? It was a brown Datsun in the 80's. The boy was white. He was wearing jeans and a dark coat and ball cap. He was slight build, got it?" Meg opened her eyes spreading her hands. "That's all I can see now, maybe I can help later, okay?"

Brandon sat forward in his chair, eyes alight. "That's a hell of a lot more than we have from anything else. Thanks, Miss Graham. When can we get together again?"

Soe stood up placing his hand on Meg's shoulder. "This kind of thing tires Meloney greatly. She is just a few days from death's door. Let us call you when she is rested."

Brandon's nervous energy propelled him around the desk where he grabbed Meg's hand. "Please try again and call me.

You have certainly filled in some blanks. We found car tracks in front of the pickup in the dirt shoulder. We suspected another car, but that's all we have." Brandon volunteered. "Thank you for your help. We will follow up on this lead."

***

Soe, Meg and Jac left the station to find Carol in the freshly washed GN, smiling, waiting for Jac's approval.

Nothing was said until they got in the car. Soe's exasperation bled through in his voice. "Do you have any idea what kind of mess this is going to turn into? The police can't keep a secret. There is always somebody who will take a payoff and leak the story to the press. When they get it, it's 'Katy, bar the door'."

Scowling, Meg shot back. "We have been the target of murder, bugging and car wrecks and each time we have escaped by the skin of our teeth, Soe. I think if we go public, the press, the police, and the community will protect us. They won't dare try anything. Because we will be public figures!"

Carol yelled. "Hold it, hold it. What the hell is going on?"

In an instant Meg had told her about the purse and seeing something about the abduction. "Oh shit." Carol said as she jumped around and faced Meg in the back seat. "If we are pointed out in public, we will be targets for drive-bys, snipers, knifers, or anything else, Meg."

"Well, it's too late." Meg said with finality, sticking out a determined chin. "I think I can help the police here. This may be a serial killer according to the news. Besides, some strange force I can't explain is pulling me into it. It's like I'm in a whirlpool. I just have to follow it.

"Finally," Meg continued intensely, "think of what can be done with this mind reading concept. If it's put to good use in a proper manner, it can solve a world of problems."

Carol snapped back. "Yes, I agree with you, but 99% of the people involved don't want the information out. Just think of revealing everyone's closet skeletons."

Meg had calmed down a bit. "Well, that's right, but it would have to be used very carefully and honorably."

Jac shrugged resignedly looking in the rear-vision mirror at Meg. "You must be above judging people. When you dig up the information and review it, you almost have to be a saint!"

Soe countered, "If this thing can be transferred to another person, we really have a can of worms. Whoever has it has vast powers. He better be a saint, as you say.

"Personally, I think any person can be transformed. We already know that everyone has latent ESP powers. Just think of it: 'YES, YOU TOO, CAN HAVE THE POWERS OF ATLANTIS. COME SEE SOEJAC ENTERPRISES AND ENTER THE 21ST CENTURY WITH THE POWER OF THE GODS!'" Soe laughed, waving his hands for effect.

Jac asked, incredulously. "Do you really think it can be transferred, Soe? It turned me and Carol on our ear."

Soe shrugged. "It's a possibility, a strong possibility. We know so little. We have just touched the surface of this power."

Jac turned around starting the GN. "Well, okay, let's use some of it and go by the hospital. We'll sweep the cat I pulled out of the car last night, y'all."

***

The hospital was a short distance down the freeway. Jac exited and parked in the Doctor's lot. Approaching the information desk, a smile crept across his face. "Hi Liz, where is the Latino who survived the car wreck last night?"

The desk nurse looked up. "Oh, hi, Jac—, uhh—, Dr. Cochran, you mean the one you pulled from the wreck—? Yes, he's in 232."

Jac smiled as he turned to the two girls, "Thank you, Liz. This is Carol and Meg. They are visiting from the East Coast. You may remember Meg, Meloney Graham. She was in the car accident last weekend."

Liz nodded her head, smiling, then a quick look at Jac. "Yes, yes, of course, uhh—, Dr. Cochran. Hi y'all. Meloney, you just look great. You seem to have no ill effects from that terrible wreck. That's wonderful."

"Thank you, Liz. Yes, I bounced back very quickly with the help of Dr. Jac and Dr. Etheridge. Elizabeth, your voice is very familiar. Have I heard it before, maybe on a recording?"

Liz glanced at Jac again with a quick smile. "Well, maybe, I have worked with Jac on a special recording. I do certain kinds of audio commercials on occasion."

"Thanks again, Liz. We want to visit the survivor of the wreck, okay?" Jac waved as he ushered them to the elevator.

"Sure." Elizabeth sighed as she watched the foursome enter the elevator. *I'll bet Jac will take one of those wholesome girls and disappear off the available market.*

Carol punched Jac in the ribs. Letting a little sarcasm drip. "Elizabeth certainly is a pleasant girl and she has a beautiful voice, Jac, uhh—, Dr. Cochran."

"Carol—, ugh, you poke hard. I haven't been living in a monastery, you know." Jac answered, grabbing her around the head and pulling her to him.

"C'mon, it's to the left." Jac said as they hesitated on the second floor.

"Here's what we're going to do," Jac whispered secretively. "Carol, you go in the room and pretend to be a reporter asking about the wreck. We will be outside and Meg can sweep him. Meg, you direct Carol's questions if he isn't thinking about what we want to know."

Carol laughed. "Ha, ha, this is going to be exciting. I'm a reporter!"

Entering the room quietly, Carol saw a dark skinned Latino propped up in bed watching TV. He had three bandages across his chest and stomach. Carol stepped up to him introducing herself. "Hello, I'm Tina Waverly from the local paper. May I ask you a few questions about the terrible wreck on the freeway last night?"

"Sure."

"Thank you." Carol answered crisply. "First of all, what is your name and where are you from?"

"I'm Juan Rodriguez and I live here in Marian."

"What is your occupation?"

"I'm a cement finisher and work construction on houses."

"Tell me about the accident last night. Who were the other two men in the car?"

"I don't know. One was called Jimmy and the other was Duane. I met them in a bar last night. I think they were from Dallas. We pulled onto the freeway and this dude in a fancy sports car wanted to race. So we got it on."

Juan stared at Carol's chest without any awareness of his ogling.

Carol smiled, urging him on. "Yes?"

"Well, yeah. You know, they scared the hell outta me. They were driving over 120 mph and we came over the overpass and the truck was across the street. We couldn't do nothin. I ducked down in the back seat. Next thing I know this guy is pulling me outta the car and he drops me on the wreck and I get cut to pieces."

"Oh, that was terrible, Mr. Rodriguez. Do you think the man saved your life? I understand the car caught fire."

"Naw, I coulda got out. He wasn't helpin."

"Did the men in your car say anything about the guy in the sports car?"

"Naw, we was just going to another bar and that's when the race started."

Meg prompted Carol. *How long were they in the hospital parking lot waiting for Jac to pull out?"*

"Mr. Rodriguez, were y'all waiting in the parking lot when the sports car pulled out?"

"Well, yeah, we were sitting there drinking a beer." Juan replied evasively.

"Were you waiting for the sports car to pull out, Mr. Rodriguez?"

Juan stared at Carol a little more closely with his chin jutting out. "What are you trying to do? Hang something on me? Go on, get outta here. I got nothing to say." He waved his arm. "Go on," he demanded. Carol turned and left.

Outside, Meg filled them in, eyes snapping. "The two men from Dallas came here to kill you with the truck setup. They were prepared to scare you by shooting at you and drive you over the overpass into the truck."

Meg sneered. "This trash, Juan, and his buddy stole the truck and his buddy parked the truck on the freeway. He left. They had cell-phones to control timing. Juan and Julio, the buddy, were paid $1000. Juan went along because he wanted to see the wreck. Julio parked the truck one overpass early. That's why the Pontiac didn't stop in time."

"There is nothing we can do about this." Jac exclaimed, hanging his head, dropping his hands resignedly. "Shit, the police won't act on it because there is no physical evidence. These bastards tried to kill me! Imagine the killings if this hadn't occurred at midnight. I wonder how many cars would have topped that overpass and not been able to stop? I think justice was served with the beheading of the two in the front seat!"

Meg turned to the door, glaring. "Well, we have one to dance. Juan should pay."

A terrible scream echoed from the room.

"What the hell was that?" they all said looking at Meg.

"I think all his stitches pulled out. He'll be in pain for sometime and it will make an ugly scar." Meg replied nonchalantly.

A nurse ran down the hall glancing curiously at Dr. Cochran as she entered to room.

Carol smirked. "Well, there are some benefits from this power. Justice can be rendered instantly. For instance, that can come in handy on the freeway. You better not cut me off, shithead!"

Jac grabbed Carol. "You little vixen, you'll be a terror with this power, won't you?"

Carol poked Jac. "We'll be the 'Better Be Good Boys' like the DPS boys."

***

As they exited the hospital, Jac made a point of surveying his car. He walked around it, feeling the fenders. After cranking the car, he grinned at Carol. "You did good, Twerp. I'm proud of you."

Carol snorted. "That twerp shit is gonna stop, you hear me, Hillbilly?" Jac grinned as Soe and Meg hee hawed.

***

Lunch looked like another Mexican restaurant. It was one that Soe recommended because it had authentic style and not Tex-Mex.

Soe explained. "In the old days before refrigeration, food was preserved by smoking, hot peppers and salt. The salt and hot peppers were used to kill the bacteria. It was typically stored in cellars for coolness. Hot tamales were prepared so that they could be carried into the fields and eaten without cooking or heating."

The girls enjoyed the hot, spicy food and drank a gallon of ice tea to quench the heat.

***

At the ranch in the lab Meg put on her hard hat and turned on the computer. She demonstrated to Jac how she could levitate him.

"I'm suitably impressed, Meg, Soe. Where do the powers end?"

Soe looked up from the computer. "Jac, we honestly don't know. We don't even know what other powers there are. I have a very good inkling that there are more surprises in store."

Jac nodded knowingly. "Yes, I suspect there are."

Meg nodded as she smiled at Jac and adjusted the hat. "Soe, we need to miniaturize the computer and headgear so I can wear it in public and not be so conspicuous."

"Yeah, I know, I'm thinking on that. Just hold on."

Surveying the head strap, Soe positioned the electrodes so that they would contact the scalp when pressed down. A sophisticated hand computer game machine made a good base for the memory program. The joystick had to go. A variable potentiometer replaced it. Using a small case, he attached a belt for hand control at the waist. The head strap fit under a ball cap and wires ran down the back under a coat. Meg could be relatively inconspicuous in public.

Jac and Carol watched Meg manipulate the Quark Enhancer, as Soe named it, floating around the room.

Jac got up. "I wish I could stay and play, but I've got to go to work."

Soe started for the door. "We better brief GrandJac about our recent events."

Jac scowled as he pulled on a coat walking through the door. *Soe and GrandJac sure do fit hand in glove. I'll bet there is a whole lot under the iceberg.*

***

GrandJac looked up from papers with the phone stuck in his ear. He covered the phone with a big hand. "I'll be free in a minute, y'all sit down. What's happening? I haven't seen y'all lately?"

Soe started the story, but Meg held up her hand. GrandJac leaned back in his chair, wide eyed, shaking his head. "That's the damnedest thing I've ever seen or heard. Y'all sure have been busy. Let me see this levitation thing, Meg."

GrandJac floated up in his chair, came over the desk and set down in front. Gripping the arms tightly and leaning back, "Heaven's sake, I believe you, Meg!"

GrandJac looked his chair over and leaned forward. "Ahhh-, let's talk about you going public. That could be a dangerous situation. First, here's a thought. I think Saul Friedman is behind all of this. Why don't you go to the wrecked car or the morgue and see if you can pick up anything on these Dallas dudes. If Saul is involved, I think I'll give him something for Christmas." GrandJac reared back in his chair and stared into a corner of the room.

Turning back to the trio, he waved a hand. "Second, if you stay here, I can protect you. But in the outside world, you will be vulnerable regardless of what measures I take." GrandJac spread his hands, looking at each one pointedly.

"It looks like the die is already cast. So here're some considerations: Wear a disguise. Wear bulletproof armor. Wear a Kevlar helmet. Do not get separated. Let me send some men to be with you at all times. Get in the public eye quickly. I will talk to various people at the government level and get you help. See Morris for protective gear."

GrandJac looked at Meg. "How do I get my chair back over there, Meg?"

"Simple, simple, simple, GrandJac. Here you go."

The chair and GrandJac sailed over the desk and landed softly as GrandJac clutched the arms grimly.

Meg looked at each of them. *This could become a big deal!* They left for the lab to design their disguise and talk to Morris.

***

With a wry smile, Soe turned to the group. "We better inform the necessary parties of our situation in case something happens. Carol, you need to call your folks. I need to talk to my professor at school. Meg, is there anyone you need to talk to?"

Carol grabbed the phone on the wall, dialed home. She shrugged as she grinned knowingly. "It's the AM as usual. Mom, this is Carol. I'm in East Texas visiting friends and have a man friend. I'll tell you all about it later 'cause I'm not coming home for Christmas. Oh, by the way, Meloney is just fine. She crawled up out of the grave hollering, 'I saw the light, I saw the light! I'm proud of her. Y'all have a great holiday. I love you, bye."

Meg and Soe grinned as Carol spun around with her hands in the air.

Soe called Professor Chaphin at Marian College. "Dr. Chaphin, I've moved my lab to Cochran's ranch. You know, The Collinga Foundation. I'll stop by in the morning and give you the details."

"See that you do, Shawn. You have been very lax of late." Dr. Chaphin snapped back.

Meg put her arms around Soe, smiling, as she rubbed noses with him. "I'm staying for Christmas."

***

Morris came in with bulletproof vests and military Kevlar helmets. Placing them on a bench, he turned to face the trio. "These vests will take a .44 magnum or a 30.06 at close range. But the force of the impact might knock you down, bruise you or even knock the breath out of you. The bullet will not penetrate the vest.

"The helmet is made of Kevlar. It's lightweight, but it will deflect a bullet. Always wear a chinstrap to keep the helmet in place. Again, the impact of a bullet might jar the hell out of you, but it will not penetrate. The face shield is Lexan and will deflect a bullet to some degree except for a straight on strike." Morris rattled off the specs like a drill Sergeant.

Carol stood up waving her hands, interrupting Morris. "Let's get long leather coats, sunglasses, gloves and boots so we look like Darth Vader. Wear the collar up in back and we can tuck our hair in our helmets. No makeup and never smile." She clapped her hands, giggling.

Soe ignored Carol as he turned to Meg. "I've been thinking. I can put the entire unit in the helmet with no knob Meg. You can adjust it with telekinesis. The battery will have to be inside your vest or somewhere nearby with wire up to the helmet. Otherwise, the helmet will be too heavy."

Morris chuckled, standing with his hands on his hips. "You kids don't realize how serious this is. You're going to make a game of it---. I hope that's all it is."

"C'mon Morris," Carol chided. "Are you going to be our BOG? Let's have some fun. What are you going to wear? I'll tell you what, Morris. You and the other BOG's wear blue jeans, boots, cowboy hats, cowboy shirts and those heavy sheepskin coats with the fur inside and the collar turned out. I think they look sexy." Carol said as she poked Morris.

A big grin spread across Morris's face as he ogled Carol.

Soe turned, scowling at Carol for interrupting his pontification on the controller. "What the hell is a BOG, Carol?"

"Body On Guard. Everybody knows that, Soe." Carol laughed loudly. She loved to poke Soe's little ego. "The military and the goviment make acronyms outta everything. So can we." Carol averred in a Texas drawl.

Carol stood up to catch everyone's attention. "The way I see this thing, the power can be used by the criminal jurisprudence system to solve all crimes of any nature. The crime scene can be dissected by an Enhancer and pertinent parties brought before the Judge or a panel who are Enhancers. The charged suspect tells his story and the Judge or panel reads him and corrects lies and omissions. There will be no circumstantial evidence. The real story will be told, as true as it can be. You will be guilty or innocent, black or white. The only thing left will be sentencing. There will be no jury or long drawn out trials with red herrings and bullshit to confuse the issues.

"The law can be drastically simplified. The main legal issue is protecting the accused rights. What questions can be asked?"

Morris interrupted, grinning sardonically. "It sure is gonna put a lot of lawyers outta business."

Carol nodded, "Yeah, that's right. The weak link will be the fallibility of the Enhancers. They must be pure of heart, always. A very difficult thing to do when large sums of money and power are at their fingertips."

Meg looked at Carol with owl eyes. "That's pretty impressive, RM. What if the accused is a person with Enhancer powers? He might be able to mask himself and fake the answers."

Carol threw the question back to Meg. "You can tell us more about that than we can ever surmise, Meg. You have the power. What is RM?"

Meg smiled sweetly. "Carol, that's room-mate, get with it. I think it will be a problem."

Soe smirked at Meg giving it back to Carol. "What if the person is mentally ill in some way and truly believes what he is thinking and saying? Meg, do you think you can read a person and be absolutely assured that he is telling the truth?"

Meg shrugged. "I have so little experience in this area, I can't be sure of either question."

Soe added. "I see a major problem. Who and how will the Enhancers be selected? So far, in my opinion, only people who have had a 'near death experience' are capable of becoming Enhancers. That might create a very select list of candidates with most any kind of morals."

Surprised, Carol asked, a trace of sarcasm creeping into her voice. "When did you arrive at the NDE connection, Soe? Has new evidence come forth that you haven't told us about?"

Soe stared at Carol critically. "It's the only tie I can make that seems positive. Her brain was in a very relaxed state and I was able to enhance the Quark Wave without harm to her. Her other physical conditions, drowning, chilled body, bump on head still may be significant. But I don't think so."

Meg leaned forward with her arms on her knees. "I think the biggest worry will be powerful people and organizations obtaining their own readers for corrupt purposes. I really worry if we should let this power out."

Carol snapped back. "Well, to-de-do, girl. You're the one that introduced it to the police, Meg. Yeah, and to the world, too, according to Soe."

Meg shook her head. "Yeah, yeah, I know. I'm hoping it will give us some protection. Public exposure, I mean. Secondly, we will get a peek into some of our concerns about using the concept in the law."

Meg sighed wishfully. "Can you imagine what this tool could do for humanity? No lies, no corruption, just honesty and love. It could be a utopia. Think of what could be done for the mentally ill. The psychological basket cases, anyone with mental dysfunction?"

Carol paused as she stared at Meg. "That's awfully theoretical, Meg. Well—, what the hell. We're committed. Let's get it on."

Morris had sat through the whole discussion glancing at each as they made their pitch. "Kids, ya'll are unbelievably idealistic and naïve. When the real hosses find out what you got, they'll just come get it and send ya'll to the next stage. A hole in the ground!"

No one said anything as they looked introspective.

Soe busied himself with modifying his Enhancer equipment to fit inside Meg's helmet. He looked up occasionally at Morris and the girls with an air of tolerance. As he neared the final twist of wire, he stared at Morris. "Hey, ya'll. We ain't got to the end of the tunnel yet. There might be a few surprises for the 'hosses!'"

Carol's exuberance returned as she jumped up and down. "Yes, Soe. That doesn't surprise me at all. You still have six aces don't you? Well, c'mon, c'mon. Let's get downtown and pick our outfits."

Morris shook his head as he stood up to go. "Soe, I hope you and the girls got it, cause hard ball is startin." He walked out. "I'll get ya'll outfitted, anyway."

Meg stepped forward and placed her hand on Morris's arm. "Thank you, Morris. I know you will be there when we need a backup."

"Okay, okay, Carol. Let's go." Soe finally agreed. "Let's take the GN to the Mall. That will be the best place to shop."

***

Meg interrupted. "This is possibly the only time I will be able to meet Bobby Williams and thank him for saving my life. I would like to call him and try to meet with him. Do we have time?"

Soe and Carol echoed. "Well—, sure, let's try, anyway."

A quick call to the Williams's home phone got a baby sitter. "He's not here. He took his wife and older kids to the Mall for Christmas shopping. Can I take a message?"

Meg answered. "We're going to the Mall. We'll catch him there, thank you."

Carol stared at Meg. "I guess you know what he looks like and can contact him mentally, huh?"

Meg smiled, "Yes."

"Meg—," Soe and Carol stared. "How will we find him? You'll have to show me, us what he looks like."

"Don't worry about it, ya'll. We'll find him." Meg answered with a grin.

***

Parking illustrated the extent of the crowds to be expected in the Mall-- full to the curbs. Carol exclaimed. "I am always amazed at the last minute shopper frenzy. Now, here I am right in the middle of it."

***

Dan Reynolds watched the ranch all night from a hill about a half-mile away.

He called in to the apartment in the morning. "Tommy, I'm whipped. It's 10 AM. Get your butt out here and relieve me. Best I can tell the whole crowd is living here at the ranch."

Tommy arrived, relieving Dan about 10:30, then to the police station, the hospital, the Mexican restaurant and back to the ranch.

On top of the hill again, Tommy called in about 3 o'clock. "Dan, I've got to go to work. You will have to take over the surveillance."

Dan laughed sarcastically. "No you don't, Tommy. If Etheridge is not at the lab anymore, there is no need for you there. You just stay put and call me if something develops. I'm getting some sack time!"

The next happening occurred about 8 pm. "Hey, the two girls and Etheridge are driving out in the black car. If they go to town, we may have a chance. I'll follow them and let you know."

Dan met Tommy after a brief call from the Mall. They considered their options.

"The Mall's going to be very crowded. We might get a chance to drug her if she gets away from her buddies." Dan suggested. "I have a shot of knockout drug in a syringe that we might use. All we can do is play it by ear. Let's go. I sure as hell don't want to face her when she's alert!"

***

Shoppers milled, wandered, charged through the wide Mall hallways assaulting the stores. The mass of bodies radiated heat making the enclosed area hot.

A first opportunity to look at humanity in the raw. Can this tool really be used for the benefit of mankind? Is it really practical? It's like having a universal cure for a human malady. Who, what, how will it be administered fairly?

Meg stood quietly, feeling and reading the jumbled thoughts and emotions emanating from the throng. Her capabilities had continued to grow and strengthen. She could single out people and sweep their minds. It was startling and, at times degrading, to see people in the naked state. *The privacy of the mind and one's thoughts create a world we are comfortable with. Staring into a person's mind and his deepest feelings and thoughts is very distracting.* Meg tried to think how such a world might operate. *Maybe people could develop skills of hiding their feelings and thoughts from the prying of mindreading. Then again maybe they could clean up their act and make the world a better place by not having those thoughts. So, so naïve. It ain't possible!*

Meg mentioned the concepts to Soe and Carol. "For example, look at that young couple over there. Would you say they are in love?"

Carol glanced at them. "Yes, they are obviously in love. Look at the way they touch each other, look at each other."

Meg grimaced. "The real truth is, she's in love and he is infatuated with her body. He doesn't even know what love is. It's a relationship destined for the rocks with a lot of heartache."

Carol snipped. "That's just like a man. Completely sexually oriented."

"In my senior psychology class on sexuality, we had to write a paper on the male concept, 'A hard penis has no conscience.' I see it in action, now!"

"Ha, ha, there's a lot of truth in that, Meg. An interesting way of expressing the primordial drive of procreation." Soe commented, smirking at Meg.

"Hey, that's pretty good! That cleans up my statement. It justifies man's attitude. He can't help it. Bullshit!"

Meg continued. "Well, whatever. Among other things, this tool would be great in psychological counseling."

Carol dropped another axiom. "There will have to be one hell of a lot of Enhancers to solve the world's problems. The more I think about it, they better be bulletproof!"

Meg mused. "When I look into the minds of these people, I lose my respect for the human race." "Less than 10% of them have any charitable thoughts or dignity about them. The depravity of the world is overpowering. It would be so easy to wipe out everyone with evil thoughts."

Carol asked pointedly. "Holy crap, Meg. How many would be left?"

Meg turned to Carol and Soe. "I'm rapidly becoming very cynical about the human race."

Soe sneered at Meg. "Welcome to the real world where it's a dog fight for your space. With security in the mind and material wealth, it's easy to be magnanimous. Not many have it."

Soe sighed as he put his hand on Meg's shoulder. "Envy, greed, selfishness, lust and hate. Five of the seven deadly sins track man with tenacity. I'm sure you are seeing a lot of that here." Soe sneered at the two girls. "Now that we have identified the problem, we can move on—. We're with you, Meg! You have to find Bobby Williams. We don't know what he looks like."

"I think I can find him. If he has brought his children, or some of them, they might be in the toy section."

Carol blurted. "That's a rare dissertation from you. Soe, very insightful."

"C'mon gang. Let's get our Vader outfits." Carol demanded, changing the subject.

With Carol's urging, they picked out long, black leather coats, high boots, thin, black leather gloves, black jeans and shirts. Carol led them over to the sunglasses and picked large framed dark glasses.

"Jac will have to come here tomorrow and get his outfit." Carol stated, grinning like the Cheshire cat.

***

Meg stopped the two with her hand. "I feel or sense we are being watched. Look around and see if you see anybody suspicious looking." Meg turned slowly scanning the crowds, trying to pick up the feeling again.

Soe spoke tersely, "Point him out and I'll fix his clock."

Meg admitted with a sigh. "I can't pick it up again. Maybe I was wrong."

Carol interjected. "I'll betcha you're not wrong. With all this crap going on, we have to be targets any time we're in public."

Meg pointed. "I'm going over towards the toys. Ya'll look there." She indicated the children's clothes with her finger.

Glaring at the two of them, Carol demanded. "Let's get the hell out of here. If anybody seems to be following us, Soe will smash his face."

Meg ignored the suggestion and struck out towards the toys.

The crowds of parents, children and last minute shoppers created a mob, particularly in the toy section. Meg walked slowly among the melee down one aisle and the next. *Bobby Williams is here. I can sense it.*

A queasy fear nagged at her, *I'm being watched!*

She felt someone punch her in the side with a stinging sensation. Spinning around, a man was reaching for her as she seemed to be falling. A black world enveloped her. She screamed to Soe but no sound came from her mouth. The man caught her and another man supported her from the other side.

A last thought. *The crowds of people hardly noticed. Maybe I fainted. It's uncomfortably hot in here.*

***

Meg's scream pierced Soe's mind like a blinding light. Spinning around towards the toy department, he ran through the crowd knocking shoppers down and out of the way.

Like a charging fullback, he yelled. "I'm coming, Meg!"

It's so clear. Meg is guiding me. At the second aisle he turned sharply, staring, searching. *I know she is here. I can feel it! Meg, Meg, where are you?*

He charged down the aisle scrambling past the parents and kids. She was nowhere to be seen. The escalator loomed before him. Instinctively he ran towards it. At the bottom of the stairs, a short stocky man seemed to be fighting with two men. A woman was between the two men, hanging limp.

Soe bolted down the escalator stairs three at a time, screaming. "You bastards, I'll kill you with my bare hands!"

The two men turned, looking at Soe charging down the stairs like a bull elephant. One reached in his coat as if to get a weapon, maybe a pistol. Soe catapulted off the last stairs, airborne, to land on top of him. Meg dropped to the floor in a heap. Dan jerked a small automatic pistol from his coat and waved it at the heavyset man, "Get back! Get back!" He pulled Tommy from the pile of Soe and they swiftly scurried through the crowds to the exit doors. Soe gasped for air as if he had the breath knocked out of him. The heavyset man grabbed and pulled him upright.

"Hey, this is the girl I pulled from the water Friday night! Those men were trying to carry her off! What's happening? Who are you?"

Soe gasped. "They were trying to kidnap her! Are you Bobby Williams?"

"Yeah, yeah, I'm Williams. How did you know?"

He bent down beside Meg, felt for a pulse in her neck and peeled back an eyelid. "She's alive. She has a pulse, but she's unconscious. Thank God!" he gasped.

"Williams, we came down here to see you. But we don't have time right now. We'll catch you later." Soe panted.

Carol appeared in her Vader outfit, coat flapping as she fought her way down the escalator. "What is it, what is it? Oh shit!" she screamed.

Soe picked up Meg like a baby, charging ahead. "Carol, Carol. Lead the way to the car. I think those two men drugged her. Let's get her to the hospital."

Bobby grabbed his wife. "That's the girl I pulled out of the river, Martha. Something has happened to her again. They said they were looking for me!"

Needless to say, it was a problem getting the limp body in the two-door GN. Carol finally got in the back seat and Soe put Meg in the passenger seat. Carol held her shoulders by hanging over the seat.

Carol had grabbed their bags of clothing as she ran through the store. Tossing it in the trunk cleared room in the car.

Soe blasted the car onto the freeway and accelerated to the hospital with emergency flashers blinking. Sliding to a stop in the Emergency Area, Soe grabbed Meg and ran into the hallway, yelling. "Get Dr. Cochran here right now!"

***

The nurse paged Jac. "Dr. Cochran! Emergency space one, stat."

Jac stepped out in the hall and saw the anguished plea on Soe's face.

Carol yelled. "Jac, Jac, help us!"

"Get her on a gurney. What's happening?" *I hope this is not some relapse from the Soe treatment or near death experience, but it wouldn't surprise me. Meg's recovery has been just unbelievable!*

Panting as he laid Meg on a gurney, Soe blurted out. "There were two men in the Mall. I saw them. I think they drugged her. They were trying to carry her off when I yelled at them. They dropped her. She may be injured."

Jac checked her pulse, blood pressure, and heart rate as he peered into an eye. "She seems to be just unconscious. Her vitals are good. Let me try something."

He broke an ampoule of ammonia and waved it under her nose. Meg twitched a little and feebly tried to paw it away.

A piercing thought struck all three of them. *The dammed CIA shot me with a tranquilizer in the back and tried to kidnap me. Get me a shot of coffee or caffeine. I've got a terrible headache!*

Jac turned to a cabinet and grabbed two Tylenol and a bottle of No-Doz. "Break the No-Doz in half. She doesn't need that much." He shook out a pill and sat Meg up. Soe had grabbed a cup of water and between them they got the pills down Meg.

Jac ordered, glancing back down the hall at one of his emergencies. "Sit her in the lobby and let the pills take effect. I think she will be okay. Watch her closely and call me if you see anything."

Carol and Soe sat beside Meg watching her crawl out of the haze of the tranquilizer drug. In a few minutes she could talk and after 30 minutes, she seemed normal.

A heavily built man walked hesitantly into the lobby scanning the people waiting. Upon spying Soe, Carol and Meg, he stepped forward rapidly.

"Pardon me, Sir, I'm Bobby Williams. I saw you briefly in the mall toy store. You said you were looking for me?"

Soe stood up extending his hand. "Yes, I'm Dr. Etheridge. This is Meloney. You saved her life last Friday night. This is Carol, her roommate from school. We wanted to find you and thank you for your extraordinary efforts."

Meg stood up as she hung on Soe. "Bobby, I had a dream of you saving me in the sunken car. You had to cut the seat belt to get me out. Your headlight was shining in my eyes and I fell down it in a tunnel of light. I think it pulled me back from the other side."

Meg babbled on, reaching for Bobby's hand or arm. "On the roadway above the river, you were very skeptical of me surviving. You told the helper that I was dead. You had seen several men like me and they never came back."

Bobby stared at Meg in awe. "That's exactly what did happen, Meloney. I'm stunned at your recovery. It has to be a miracle!"

Meg stepped forward and hugged Bobby, "Thank you. Thank you for your daring dive pulling me out of the car and the river, Bobby. I feel like I know you as a brother."

Meg glanced over to the door. "That must be your wife and children. Please let me meet them and tell them what a brave man they have caring for them. I must have your address, Bobby. I want to thank you in other ways."

Martha and two small boys came forward as Bobby introduced them. "We have a baby girl at home.

"I'm home on leave for Christmas. I'm a marine diver out of Houston. So the dive to save you wasn't anything."

Meg laughed quietly. "It was a lot more than you can ever imagine, Bobby, to me and a lot of other people. Thanks again. Thank you for your address. I'll be in touch. Martha, you are so lucky to have a man like Bobby here. He is truly above and beyond the general cut of male fluff out there."

Meg said goodbye and waved at the two boys as they left the Emergency exit.

***

176

Martha looked back at Meg as they exited the door. "What an unusual thing to say, Bobby. It's as if she has an insight into the male being. But, I have to agree with her, you are something special. That was very courageous to dive into that black water to save her. She is a pretty thing, isn't she?"

Reviewing Meloney alive and well, he had to agree she was a beautiful young lady. What a dramatic change from the bedraggled thing he pulled from the water! "Yes." Bobby agreed carefully. He didn't need any jealousy cropping up.

***

"I'm glad we made contact," Meg sighed, "That was so important to me. I want to do something for them, Soe."

Meg sat down looking off in the distance. "I don't know anything about the abduction attempt. I can't even remember their faces. That drug knocked me down in seconds and wiped my mind. I can't remember calling to Soe." She shook her head, "I feel okay, now. Soe, thank you again for saving me. You are my hero!"

Soe touched Meg's arm. "You called me. You don't remember? The scream nearly blew my head off! Just think how close you came to disappearing, Meg. It can happen in an instant. We must always be on guard."

Jac returned as frequently as he could within the bustle of the ER room problems. "I don't think she got a full dose, otherwise she would still be out. Her coat may have restricted the needle and injection."

It took a full hour to get up to snuff before Meg felt strong enough to say. "I think I'm okay, gang. Let's go."

***

Soe asked, cocking his head at Meg. "As long as we are here, do you think you could read the car wreck bodies without the Enhancer equipment? The Morgue is downstairs."

"I can try."

Carol snipped, looking down the hall. "Yeah, and we can tell Jac what we're doing, too, if we can ever get his butt out of ER." Carol snatched Jac as he moved quickly from one room to another. "I want to see my man in his outfit like this!"

Jac grinned and kissed Carol on the cheek. "I'll bet this whole thing is your idea, huh, Carol?" Carol smirked. "We want to see your bodies, Jac."

Meg filled him in on the evening's events as Jac led the way downstairs to the Morgue.

Jac shook his head, sighing. "Meg, this thing is getting dangerously close to total war and death for all. Can you handle it?"

Soe put his arm around Meg for moral support as Meg spoke forcefully. "I'm learning, Jac, that there's lots of evil out there. I was so naïve last week in my little cocoon thinking I was going to save the world with my psychology degree. For right now, I think I can handle the bad guys. Maybe not kill them, but certainly kick their butts!"

In the basement through two wide swinging doors, Jac nodded as they approached the attendant and found that no one had claimed the bodies. Fortunately they were not yet autopsied.

The attendant pulled open a drawer and slid the sheet off a body.

"Here's a first look, Meg—, the real thing!" Jac grinned maliciously.

Horrified, the girls gasped and stepped back with their hands to their faces. A badly crushed head lay on the tray next to the torso that was mangled from the shoulders up. Dried blood covered the head and upper torso.

"Gruesome is as gruesome does." Jac quipped.

Soe coughed and looked away. "God, did they ever eat a plate of shit, wow!" Meg turned away and closed her eyes.

Carol left the room with her hand over her mouth. "I think I'm going to puke." She gasped.

Meg said quickly. "We can go now. Let's get the hell out of here, ugh! What is that awful smell?"

Jac smiled wryly, "I don't believe we can use the body in med-school either."

Carol leaned against the wall pressing her face against the cold plaster. "Lord, that was terrible." She whispered through clenched teeth. "Jac, that could have been you. That car saved your life!" She went to Jac and hugged him. "Let's get outta here, now."

Jac laughed, "I sure do like the hugging, Sweetiepie."

"Ah poke in the ribs is all you gonna git, Bubba." Carol snapped back.

Upstairs in the lobby, Meg turned to them. "Saul Friedman paid them to kill you, Jac. Carol wasn't the target at noon today. They couldn't tell who was in the GN. He wanted another accident like your parents. He planned the whole thing and hired these thugs to carry it out. He is evil, evil, evil."

Soe spoke up. "Meg, you were able to read the body without the Enhancer. You are getting stronger by the hour. I am suitably impressed!"

Meg gritted her teeth. "Maybe I will be able to ID those shitbirds who shot me."

Carol challenged, "Jac, go to the mall in the morning and get your outfit just like ours. We're going public tomorrow at the police station. We're going to have BOG's, too." Carol looked expectantly at Jac to see if he would respond to the acronym.

Jac replied casually. "Is Morris going to be a BOG?"

Carol turned to Meg accusingly. "You told him, didn't you, Meg?"

Meg grinned, "Let's go to the ranch, gang. I guess Jac is psychic, Carol."

Soe and Jac laughed. Pouting, Carol glared at them.

"Hold it for a minute," Meg continued. "I guess our enemies are defined. The CIA and the Friedman gang from 1868. We really need a plan, don't y'all think?"

Carol demanded. "Yeah, yeah, we're gonna do it. Meg, tell him my idea about how to use the Enhancers in the criminal justice system."

Jac looked intently at Carol. "That's very perceptive, Sweetiepie. I'll have to think on that for a while."

***

At the ranch, GrandJac stood in the glaring light of the front porch anticipating a report. Very little happened in Marian that GrandJac didn't get word on from his many allies.

Pacing back and forth with arms outspread shaking his head, "You will be conspicuous in those rigs, kids. You'll either attract a crowd or scare the hell out of the crowd."

Meg floated before GrandJac, hanging in the air. She gave him the details of the tranquilizer shot and Saul's plan to kill Jac on the freeway.

"That doesn't surprise me at all," GrandJac affirmed. "The CIA is just as desperate as Friedman, and their true colors are coming out. Saul sure does need an ass kickin and I guess I'll have to do it."

Carol popped out. "What'cha going to do, GrandJac? Jerk a slipknot in his ass so's he'll hafta shit out his ears?"

GrandJac looked at Carol reprovingly. "You have really picked up this Texas slang, haven't you, young lady?"

"'When in Rome, do as the Romans do,' GrandJac."

"Thanks for the idea, Carol."

GrandJac had a mysterious look as he turned into the house. "Let's go to bed, kids."

Carol shot back. "We haven't had supper yet. We're going to the fridge."

Soe waved a hand. "I'm going to the lab and finish Meg's helmet. If you would be so kind as to bring me a sandwich, I would appreciate it, Meg." He swatted Meg on the behind as he walked back to the lab.

Meg watched as Soe quickly finished the installation of the enhancer circuit in the helmet. "Hey, Honeypot, go onto bed. I'll be there soon. There is no need of you hanging over my shoulder."

***

Returning to the house, Soe checked the bedrooms. All were apparently asleep. Walking quietly, he moved to the opposite side of the house and knocked on GrandJac's door. "GrandJac, this is Soe. You still up?"

"Yeah, hold on a minute. I'll get my robe."

The two moved down the hall to a small file room filled with metal cabinets and computers.

Soe grabbed a swivel chair. "GrandJac, this thing is getting sticky. Tonight, Meg hit me with the white wave and nearly killed me. She doesn't have any idea what is happening to her. Is this still a go? Are we already too late to stop it? I need some direction."

GrandJac sighed grabbing his knees. "Soe, it is on track. We must get all information and programs from Friedman and the CIA. Kill any people with the programs that cannot be stopped. I think I, we, can control it. I think we can stop the cycle if we can stop the release of the programs to those two. If the program gets beyond our control, then it will cycle just as I have told you." He stood taking a deep breath. "This can be the greatest thing ever for man, but we must have absolute control, okay?"

Soe nodded. "Okay, but give me some guidance as it progresses."

GrandJac touched Soe's arm, "Do you think you can convert a human to this ESP? From what I can tell, Carol wants it and would be a good guinea pig. She would be an asset to our group and it would give her an inclination to stay her. I'm concerned about her dragging Jac off and out of the track. Until this thing clears, Jac must stay here so that I can influence him."

"I really think it's possible, GrandJac. I'll get it going tomorrow or the next day." Soe commented without any conscience.

This thing, this concept, or whatever you want to call it, is progressing just like GrandJac told me four years ago. I can't believe he can call the future like this. I feel bad about hiding behind him and not telling Jac. Jac is going down hard. I just know it. But, if GrandJac is right, it's preordained. There is nothing I, we can do but ride the wagon and watch. However, it would be a fantastic tool for humanity. Just like grabbing an atomic bomb and holding it in your hands with impunity!

THE ENHANCERS

THURSDAY DECEMBER 22ND

For one of the few times, the whole family gathered in the large atrium off the kitchen for breakfast. Annie proudly served the clan her usual big farm breakfast and sat down to enjoy coffee.

Soe outlined the day. "I have to brief Professor Chaphin on our program first. Then we need to go to the police station."

Meg interrupted, "I have money from my parent's estate. I want to give some to Bobby Williams, Soe."

GrandJac smiled, placing a large hand on hers. "Meg, you are very sweet and thoughtful. I have taken the liberty to intercede on your behalf. Mr. Williams and family will receive a beautiful bouquet of flowers and $500,000 this morning. That's tax free, of course. I hope that meets with your approval?"

Meg and Carol gasped. "Good Lord, GrandJac, that's fantastic! I was thinking I could spare $1000." Meg stammered as she reached for GrandJac.

GrandJac's eyes twinkled mysteriously as he waved his hand casually. "It's a small down payment on a very large debt from the past. My family has benefited tremendously from it."

GrandJac looked at Jac. "Stay behind so I can get some information."

***

Soe, Meg and Carol left in the GN dressed to the gills in their new Enhancer garb.

"This is our first public performance, gang. Let's make the most of it." Carol demanded. "That looks good, Meg. Helmet, glasses, black coat, pants, boots and don't forget the black gloves. They are intimidating. See, the public can't see any skin if we put the face shields down. Soe, you look like something from medieval times. Let's get 'em!"

***

GrandJac turned to Jac. "Do you know anything about animal tranquilizers and the chemicals used, Son?"

"Sure, there are several liquid anesthetics that are used. What did you have in mind, Grandpaw?"

GrandJac waved his hand casually. "Oh, nothing special. I've an idea. I want the fastest acting one available, Son. I also want a volatile one or one that can be used as a gas."

Jac cocked his head with curiosity. "Sure, that would be Triexylene methyl chloride."

"Can you get me something like a pint or half pint or tell me where I can get it?" GrandJac asked as he sat forward.

Jac volunteered. "It's available from the medical supply house the hospital uses. I can get it. You can buy it through the business, no problem. What do you have in mind?"

GrandJac rubbed his chin. "Well, I think it's time we returned the favor to Saul. I let Sam go a few days ago and now I want him back. As you can see, Saul didn't respond to the truce offer. He was smart enough to realize Meg could read that brilliant Sammy.

Sammy leaves home every morning for his office in his bulletproof car with bodyguards. I think I'll just surprise him."

GrandJac looked at Jac for help. "His car has Lexan bulletproof glass. It will deflect a bullet easily but it's also easily machined, isn't it?"

Jac really didn't want to get involved. He answered in a very neutral manner. "I believe that automotive Lexan has glass either on the outside or sandwiched in between in some way, Grandpaw. Thinking about it, I'd say it's on the outside to protect the glass from scratching. Lexan is easily marred."

"That's good information, Son. We'll have the tools," GrandJac answered with a determined jaw.

***

The town of Marian, 30,000 population, benefited greatly from the Collinga Foundation. A very well accredited four-year college served the surrounding communities funded by the Foundation and a mild tax base. Professor Chaphin came to Marian to perform research on brain wave electrical phenomena with substantial grants from Collinga. Dr. Shawn Etheridge was attracted to the environment with help from GrandJac several years ago.

Dr. Chaphin's arrogant superiority provided a difficult atmosphere for Soe, but he stuck to it. Urging and help from GrandJac made life bearable.

Entering the research building with Meg and Carol in full regalia created a stir at the security guard's station. The few remaining students watched to see if something special was to happen. A quick trip up the elevator to Chaphin's office turned out to be uneventful.

"Dr. Chaphin, this is Meg and Carol. They are friends from Virginia here for the holidays." Soe spoke graciously. "Last Saturday Meg was involved in a very serious auto accident and suffered a blow to the head. I used my brainwave stimulation program while she was in a comatose condition and upon recovery she has developed remarkable ESP talents. I'll have more details in my monthly report. But I thought you might like to meet Meg." Soe spoke quietly with calm assurance.

Dr. Chaphin said nothing for a very long moment as he looked at the three dressed in their black attire. Finally, he sat forward in his chair and hunched his small frame up on the desk with his elbows and arms crossed. With difficulty, he was able to control a contemptuous sneer curling across his generous lips.

"What's with the black garb, Shawn? Is it Halloween?"

Soe could barely keep a civil tongue as he waved his hand as if warding off a fly. "No, no, it's nothing like that, Dr. Chaphin. There is a little skullduggery going on and we have taken a few precautions. It will be in my report. I thought you might like a demo of Meg's ESP talents, Dr. Chaphin?"

"Well, I suppose so." Dr. Chaphin sighed with a sneer as he leaned back in his chair crossing his arms on his chest. "Let's see what you have—ahh, Meg——, is that it—, Meg?"

I hope Shawn has something. It will be the first thing I've seen from him. He's a bust!

***

A thought crashed through Soe and Carol's mind. *He's an arrogant little shit, isn't he? I wonder who made him God?*

Meg smiled sweetly as she looked at Soe and Carol, then turned to Dr. Chaphin. Chaphin's chair shot up into a corner of the room and tilted forward so that he had to hang on with all his strength to keep from falling out. He screamed with his eyes protruding and mouth agape as he clung to the arms of the chair. A wet spot appeared in his crotch and trickled down his trousers.

The chair plummeted back to the floor and nestled behind the desk. Dr. Chaphin gasped and slid the chair up under the leg well as he pawed at his glasses and tried to regain some composure.

"Ahhhhhhh!" Chaphin panted. "That didn't happen. It couldn't happen. I don't believe it happened!" Chaphin stared wild-eyed at the trio, his mouth working.

Meg looked surprised as she turned to Soe and Carol. Then she leaned across the table into Chaphin's face. "What is he talking about? What are you talking about, Dr. Chaphin? I haven't given my demonstration yet. Are you ready, sir?"

Chaphin jerked his hands up in front of his face. "No, no, no more. I'm impressed, please go!"

"I'll be in touch, Dr. Chaphin." Soe waved as he ushered Meg and Carol out of the office. "Let's go to the police station, girls."

Carol pulled on Meg's sleeve. "What in the world did you do to him, Meg? He pissed his pants!"

Meg flashed a picture in their minds of Chaphin sitting in the lead seat of a roller coaster coming out of a looped spin, leaving the rails, sailing across the carnival and crashing into the Ferris wheel a hundred feet in the air.

Meg laughed heartily. "You got to see it from an aside. You ought to make the ride up front with him. He really has good control. I expected him to soil his pants. The little shit!"

Carol snickered, jerking on Meg's sleeve. "You're getting mean and hateful, Meg. But, that's what it takes to fit in this nightmare we're living, isn't it?"

"What's that mean, Carol?" Soe asked, sneering. "I thought we were just having fun exploring a new realm of science!"

Carol snapped back, giving Soe a little push. "You're right, Soe. We have stage two of the new atomic bomb and they want it. They got the program but don't know what to do with it. Best thing to do is to come and get it from us. See, it's perfectly clear!"

Meg finally got a word in before the barbs got too bloody. "A concept we studied or discussed in school pointed out that any society that did not pay the dues in the development of new technology, would not, could not appreciate their find. They would abuse it because they did not have history to present the ramifications. Thus, they would die by the sword! The new sword, that is!

"This professor went on to say that our generation is progressing so rapidly with new technology, we would kill ourselves shortly. Well, we got the new tiger, but where is the tail?"

Carol and Soe stopped to stare at Meg as they reached the car. "Wow." Carol blurted. "Meg, that's profound, deep! What did you do, snatch that pontification from Dr. Soe?

Soe bowed to Meg. "Very erudite. Since we can't do much about any of it, let's go to the police station."

***

Saul Friedman's family arose every morning at 5:30 and met for breakfast at 6 am. Mother used to prepare breakfast herself, but now they had a live-in maid/housekeeper staff that handled all household chores.

The oldest of three sons, Sam, was 35. The children descended to age 25. Saul and Sam ran the many businesses and made the decisions.

Sam mentioned casually at the breakfast table, "I read in the paper that there was a horrendous wreck in Marian a few nights ago, Dad."

Saul looked at Sam, fish eyed. "I haven't seen it. Were there any details?"

"Well, some." Sam replied. "An 18-wheeler apparently got crosswise in the road and a car ran into it. It killed two people in the car. A third was hospitalized with multiple cuts."

"That's terrible. Did the article give any names?" Saul asked as he buttered his toast.

186

"Just said that the two men were from Dallas and the third was from Marian." Sam answered resting his hands on the table as he looked at Dad.

"Those big trucks sure can be dangerous." Saul remarked. "I hope it wasn't one of our trucks."

Sam sat up straight at attention. "Matter of fact, it was one of our trucks. It was stolen that afternoon from our terminal in Marian. The thief got away. Our truck wasn't particularly damaged. The box was hit low on one side. Our people in Marian are handling the details, Dad." Sam finished with a shrug.

Mother and the two younger brothers looked at each other and then Saul. The tale had the usual trappings of a cloak over a much greater event.

After breakfast, Sam prepared as usual to go downtown to his office. He had a brief meeting with Saul on business matters and went to the garage where the family's bulletproof stretch limo ticked over on the apron.

Sam rode in the back with two bodyguards. One more rode in the shotgun seat beside the driver. Their standard procedure was to exit left from the estate gate, wind through the residential streets to a thoroughfare and onto the freeway to town.

There, the car drove inside the building parking area. The bodyguards got out, looked the area over. If clear, Sam exited immediately into the building and a private elevator to the penthouse office suite.

Today was SOP, left turn to the stop sign two blocks down where a large moving van hesitated. If someone had noticed, it might have seemed odd that no traffic on any of the streets could be seen.

Almost immediately a second truck pulled directly behind the limo, against the bumper and pushed the limo into the truck ahead before the driver could react. With precision timing the back doors flew open in the front truck. Five men dressed in black and ski masks jumped out with automatic weapons. Five more appeared from the back truck.

The bodyguards, trained commandos, pulled pistols while the driver snatched up a phone to call base.

"These thugs can't hurt us. They can't get in the car and can't shoot through the windows or sides, Mr. Friedman. We'll have support troops here in two minutes from the house. Ha, ha, we're going to kill some stupid asses today!"

Sam swung his head wildly from side to side. "You better watch these turds. There're probably from Cochran's clan!"

One of the attackers jumped on the hood of the car with a portable power drill and immediately began drilling a hole in the windshield with a carbide drill. It ate through the glass and plastic in 5 seconds. A second attacker was ready with a canister and nozzle which he stuck through the hole and released a cloud of gas in the car.

Panic ensued inside the closed, sealed tomb as Sammy screamed. "Do something! Stop him! Stop the gas! Shoot the bastard!"

The bodyguard tried to put his finger over the nozzle but was only partly successful because the attacker quickly moved it around. In seconds the powerful anesthetic had the passengers unconscious.

The forward van pulled ahead, dropped a ramp and the rear truck pushed the limo up the ramp and into the van. The doors were closed and the van drove away. The whole operation took no more than two minutes. The men divided equally into the two trucks and drove off in different directions with hi-fives.

***

The call to the estate roused four guards who raced down the long estate driveway in one of the family cars. The shotgun rider phoned the gate to open ahead so they could drive straight through. Next, he phoned the car. "We are one minute out, Mr. Friedman. Remain calm. They can't hurt you, but we will hurt them!" The rider cackled as he jacked a 3" magnum into the assault shotgun.

As they rounded the last turn and approached the exit, a large box 18-wheeler pulled across the driveway exit against the gate. Slamming on the brakes proved ineffective as the full size

Mercedes slid into the side of the box doing 40 mph. The hood went under the box wedging the car to the windshield, crushing it in. Failure to use seatbelts resulted in a jumbled mass of humanity crammed into the front seat. The shotgun fired through the dash and instrument panel shredding the wiring and ignition system.

"Get off my back!" The driver screamed as he forced the door open clawing his way out of the air bag. "C'mon, c'mon, we only have seconds." He yelled as he sidled past the cab of the tractor/trailer jammed into the gate and wall. "God damn it! Lookit that, it's one of our trucks from Marian!"

Friedman Industries painted on the door stared him in the face. Clearing the tractor brought forth a chilling sight. An empty road, no cars, nothing. Just a squirrel running across the boulevard unaware of the first of several tragedies to happen to the Friedman clan.

***

Soe parked in the police station parking lot, a short walk to the entrance. Upon entering, the dispatcher took one look at them and pushed a buzzer. Five policemen burst through the doors with guns drawn pointed at the trio.

Before anything was said, Meg whispered mentally. *We are the Enhancers. We are here to help you.*

The police looked at each other as one said. "Did you hear anything? I think I heard something in my head."

Soe spoke up. "We are here to see Lt. Brandon. He knows us."

"I heard that, I think." Said one of the officers.

"What the hell is this wild getup y'all have on?"

They heard a soothing voice in their head. *Be calm, we are not here to hurt you.*

"Okay, okay, I think I hear you. Sit down. I'll get the Lt."

Brandon appeared in a few seconds and laughed at the attire. A voice whispered in his ear, it seemed, as to who they were.

"Okay, I got it. Boy, y'all sure stirred up the troops. Come on in." They trailed through the offices to Brandon's stall and sat down. "What's with the getup, kids? You look like something from Star Wars."

Soe answered perfunctorily. "We think we can solve several of your crimes. We could very well become hit targets. So we want both recognition and protection."

Brandon leaned back in his chair with an air of doubt. "That's strange, just what are you going to do to solve my cases or how are you going solve them?"

Meg answered from behind the shield. "Let me look at evidence and sites of any case you want to work on. Give me a try."

Brandon shrugged and hunched in his chair. "What the hell. I'm willing to try anything on some of my cases.

"By the way, we appreciate the tip on the abduction case. It may break soon. We found the brown Datsun. It was stolen and abandoned in a parking lot."

Meg stated. "That's a good start. Let me look at the pickup truck and the Datsun."

"We can do that, Meloney. They are in the Police impoundment area." Brandon rose from his chair. "Come with me."

"Do you have any evidence in other cases here that I can look at?" Meg prompted him.

"Okay, Yeah, come with me to the evidence room." Brandon answered as he led the way down the hall.

Other police officers and employees stared as they paraded by. He stopped by a row of file cabinets, pulled out five folders and continued to the evidence room.

"Don't touch anything in here unless I hand it to you." Brandon cautioned.

"Here is a knife from a burglary and murder six months old and here are pictures of the scene. We haven't been able to generate any substantial leads."

Meg held the knife and looked at the gruesome murder scene of a woman sprawled across a bed soaked in blood. She closed her eyes and slowly floated up spinning in the air. Her eyes were unfocused and the pupils enlarged. It seemed that a small wind swirled around the long black coat as the hem lifted and fluttered.

Brandon stepped back with his hand before his face as he gasped. "Whoa man—, hey man. What the hell is happening? How do you do that?"

Meg spoke in a monotone. "The woman had a secret lover who no one knew about. He is from Dallas. His name is Mark Castorville. He killed her to break-off the relationship. He may still have things stolen from the house in his possession. He took a gold broach studded with diamonds that was quite valuable. Look for it." Meg settled to the floor and turned to Brandon with her eyes open.

"What else do you have?" She asked as if nothing extraordinary had happened. Brandon staggered back grabbing for a chair. "Let me get a tape recorder. This is fantastic!" He hurried out and returned in a minute with a small recorder.

"Now then, tell me again about the murder I showed you."

Before he could blink, the information slugged into his head. He reeled back, goggle-eyed.

"Ahhhhh—. Here is another one we need help on." Brandon opened another folder and gave Meg video pictures of a robber in a convenience store, a grocery store and a bank.

"This guy wears elaborate disguises. He lost his wig in a robbery when a customer tried to wrestle him down. We didn't get it on video however, and he got away. Here's the wig."

Meg held the wig and spun around on one toe. "His name is Joe Luzano and he lives here in Marian. He works as an itinerate carpenter. He has also robbed several homes and raped a woman in one of the homes. She didn't report the rape for fear he would come back. You can pick him up at the 'Dew Drop In' bar where he hangs out when not working. His disguises are in a case in his car trunk."

Lt. Brandon frantically thumbed through his folders and pulled pictures of a random drive by shooting scene.

"This is fantastic, this is great, Meloney! Here, all I have are shell casings from a 9-mm auto and general descriptions of the van."

Meg scrutinized the pictures, read the description and held the shell casings in her hand. She slowly drifted down the aisle with her hand outstretched and stopped in front of a bin with a pistol in it.

"There is a gang war between the La Machos and the River Rats. They are bent on killing each other for several reasons. First: initiation rites for new members. Second: revenge. Third: territorial disputes. Fourth: women. You have a serious gang war situation here and all they understand is violence and power. Your swat team ought to instigate a confrontation with them and kill 8 or 10 of them. Then give them ultimatums about behavior."

Lt. Brandon shook his head exclaiming loudly. "Good Lord, Meloney! We can't do something like that. That's outrageous. We are supposed to protect the people!"

Meloney replied. "If the police are tough, they will fear them and curtail their activities. I will set the scene if you want me to, Lt."

Meg floated back to the Lt. and hung in the air in front of him, staring into space. Drifting down, she looked directly into Lt. Brandon's eyes.

Brandon threw up his hands in front of his face. "Awwww, ugh!" He gargled as he stepped back as if to protect himself. He stammered. "I saw a gun battle between us and the gangs and we killed them like shooting ducks."

Meg stated vehemently. "They play rough. Give them some of their own medicine."

Meg terminated the case solving with a terse demand. "Take me to the car impoundment area."

Trailing Brandon out of the evidence room, they went out the back of the building. A chain-link fenced area of about four acres faced them. There were cars everywhere.

Soe remarked. "Looks like the police are in the car business, Lt. Brandon."

Carol laughed, turning to Meg. "Maybe you can get a car here, Meg."

Lt. Brandon went to a small building and read a log of cars and their locations. "Okay, I've got it. Let's go over to the eastside."

On the way he explained. "We impound cars for a number of reasons; evidence, parking tickets, theft and so forth."

They stopped by an S-10 pickup and Brandon opened the door with keys he had picked up at the building.

Meg sat in the car with her hands on the wheel and slowly rotated her head back and forth. She stepped out. "Take me to the Datsun."

Lt. Brandon turned to the left but Meg turned to the right and walked down about 30 cars to the brown Datsun. The car wasn't locked. Meg opened the door and sat inside. After a moment, she hung her head and sobbed uncontrollably.

Soe handed her his handkerchief as he slowly pulled her out of the car and held her. Meg hung on him sobbing.

"Let's go, let's get out of here. Come on, Carol." They turned and retreated to the gate with Brandon trailing behind.

***

Tommy Silva drove to Dallas with his new partner, Dan Reynolds, for a briefing with the D. E. A. (Drug Enforcement Agency) Regional Director. Mark Weatherby, Deputy Director of the CIA in Washington, DC, had made a deal with the Director of DEA to handle some chores for him and the CIA onshore.

On the way, they discussed the case again.

Tommy initiated the review, taking a deep breath. "I can't believe Theo voluntarily used his cyanide cap. That's pretty far out. Then there is the missing tape. The tape recorder was still there. The lab looked like they had moved out. I guess they did because I haven't seen any activity in the last two days."

Tommy stared out the window seeing nothing. "Etheridge must know that he was being bugged and moved out. The truck that moved him out apparently belongs to John Cochran there in Marian. I don't think he knows who is doing the bugging, though."

Tommy paused again. "You know, there is the possibility that Etheridge identified Theo as the "bugger" and somehow caused Theo to pop his cyanide cap. That possibility is very dangerous. And, I haven't seen or heard from the 'Jew boy' as Theo referred to him. Theo stated in his notes that this guy came to him with lots of money and wanted to bug the lab and search it. Both Theo and Abbe, that's what Theo named him, copied the floppy discs locked in the cabinet. I have the discs now. We'll see what they have to say in Dallas."

Dan answered, changing the subject. "Yeah—, we missed our chance to get the girl in the Mall. She must have somehow called Etheridge. But I sure didn't hear her. Did you?"

Tommy shrugged. "Naw—, we couldn't afford to have a scene in the store with that many people around. We had to drop her. We damn sure didn't want a fight with Etheridge right there at the foot of the escalator. As you can see, the only way to neutralize her is with a tranquilizer. You cannot face her when she is awake.

"Hey, do you think she could have made Theo pop his cyanide cap? He told me she had developed very unusual telekinesis powers that morning in the lab. That was on the tape that disappeared."

***

The DEA director, Wilson Williams, listened closely as Tommy and Dan brought him up to date.

Dan asked, "Do you have anything on Theo?"

Wilson stared at both of them as he paused for a moment. "Theo used his cyanide cap. He had a lot of gunpowder debris in his face and minor burns on his wrists. That gave the indication that high voltage passed through steel handcuffs or wire wrapped around his wrists."

"Hell, maybe he was tortured." Tommy's mouth twisted in a sour turn, "And he chose to die."

Wilson nodded, noncommittally. "That is a possibility. But there was little evidence of physical abuse to his body. The gunpowder in his face makes you think he was shot at close range. But there are no gunshot wounds of any kind. He had a

194

bruise over one eye where he was hit with something. We don't know anything definitive." Wilson ended, shrugging his shoulders.

Wilson adjusted his big frame in the creaking swivel chair. "Let me tell you why Etheridge is under surveillance. He was sponsored by a small grant from the CIA. They are interested in brain wave research. The National Science Foundation was used as a sponsor also just in case he filed different reports.

"Etheridge had filed a report a month ago that looked promising. Weatherby, CIA, wanted him watched. We are directing local operations for Weatherby."

Wilson called an agent. "Here's a name, Wally. Run a check on a John Cochran in Marian."

Continuing his twenty questions, Wilson glared at them. "Tommy, Do you think you can dig up anything on this Abbe that Theo was working with?"

"Well, we might. He was in a rent car according to Theo. He was very closemouthed about his business."

Tommy shuffled through the hand written notes Theo had left.

"Here's something that I missed on the back of a page." Tommy volunteered. "He traced the rent car to Magellan Rentals out of Dallas and a Sam Friedman rented the car."

Wilson called again. "Wally, check out Sam Friedman in Dallas."

Wally returned shortly with a computer printout two and a half pages long on John Cochran. Wilson snorted as he laid it on the table. "Look at this! John Allen Cochran is one of the richest men in the U.S. He has vast holdings in almost every business field there is. Oil, mining, shipping, railroads, electronics, stock markets, banks, automotive, aircraft, news media, you name it."

"Here's the word on Friedman." Wally said as he stepped in with more papers.

Two pages of details defined the Friedman family as one of the richest families in the U.S. with holdings just as broad as Cochran's.

Wilson closed his fist, grabbing the sheets and glaring at the two. "Looks like we hit paydirt. We have two very powerful entities trying to get something Etheridge is working on. We need to see what is on the discs you copied, Tommy. Let's let our boys have a look."

Stepping next door, he yelled. "Wally, take this to Salvador in computers. Tommy, go with him. Tell him to be careful with it and find out what it is."

***

Salvador cleared his computer and inserted the first disc. It came up in machine language that was unintelligible. The other one did the same.

Salvador leaned back in the swivel chair. "Tell me about the discs. Where did they come from?"

Tommy put his hands on his hips. "Best I can tell, it's a computer program that does something to the human brain through an EEG machine."

Salvador nodded. "Okay, let me work on it with our lab and I'll see what I can do. Let me have a copy of the notes. Maybe they will point me in the right direction."

***

Wilson stepped out into the hallway. "Tommy, come on back here. The 'Boss' wants the girl, Meloney Graham, captured. She's got to be taken alive for support with the computer discs."

Dan Reynolds acknowledged, nodding. "Yeah, that was our primary mission when I left Washington. We had a slim chance in the Mall last night. But it didn't work out. I actually shot her with a tranquilizer. But Etheridge was on us from nowhere before we could get her out."

Wilson asked perfunctorily. "So what, the two of you couldn't handle him?"

"Yeah, we might've handled him. He's an exercise nut. You know, weight lifting, heavily built. But we had the girl and the Christmas crowd in the mall. It would've been a big brawl and attracted the police. We decided to drop her and get a better situation."

"Okay, Y'all got any ideas?"

Tommy quickly blurted out. "I think the whole bunch of them moved to Cochran's ranch, lab and all."

"Okay, Tommy, follow up on Etheridge. See if he moved to Cochran's place in Marian and put a watch on him. Once we know where they are and where the girl is, we'll make some plans to take her. Dan, do some checking on this Sam Friedman here in Dallas. Get to it, men."

***

Soe, Carol and Meg walked rapidly with Soe partially supporting Meg. Lt. Brandon followed them through the aisles, eyes a glitter, seemingly unaffected by Meloney's condition.

"Thanks for the tips, Meloney. Come back when you are feeling better. I will give you the results then."

In the parking lot, Carol stepped up to Meg as Soe escorted her rapidly to the car. "Meg, what is the problem? I haven't seen you act like this. Tell me, maybe I can help."

Meg continued to sob and shudder uncontrollably. Carol and Soe drove back to the ranch holding Meg, trying to console her. When the car stopped in GrandJac's yard, Meg finally spoke in a halting voice as she sobbed.

"Ughhh, it was terrible! The emotions just overwhelmed me. I felt like I was in a cold, black pit naked with slimy hands pawing me. I was screaming, clawing, trying to get out. But the hands pulled me back again and again."

"Good Lord, Meg, that's horrible. Unbelievable!" Carol cried as she tried to hug Meg. "Did you see anything like you did with the other past reviews? That sounds like the scenes I saw when I was tested."

"Yes, I saw the whole thing. I saw Sue Ellen get out of the truck and go to the boy." Meg began crying, shaking, again.

Soe interrupted. "C'mon inside. We're home, Meg, hang on." Carol hugged her close.

Soe opened the door helping Meg into the house. Jac came forward expecting some excitement from the morning's events.

One startled, quick look at Meg and Jac ordered. "Take her to bed, Carol. I'll be there in a minute." Jac returned with a bottle. "Here, take one of these sleeping pills. It will relax you.

Carol handed her a glass of water and Meg gulped it down. She lay back and sighed. "It's going to take some time to get over that." She dozed off while they watched.

Jac led them into the living room and sat down with Cokes, demanding, scowling at them. "What brought this about?"

Soe gave a brief review of the morning and psychic readings of the crime scenes.

Carol answered glancing at both of them. "We'll just have to wait until she awakens and is feeling better."

Shaking his head in wonder, Jac muttered. "I can't see where this thing is going. It's just a ball of boogers rolling down hill out of control."

Carol smirked, patting his arm. "Jac, that's pretty darn descriptive!"

"What have you been doing, Jac?" Soe asked, moving to another subject with no apparent recognition of the problem.

"GrandJac thinks it's time I started getting involved in the business so we spent time going over various things."

Soe looked into the distance, ignoring Jac's explanation. "I think I can record some of Meg's energy. I'm going to the lab and experiment."

Carol watched Soe leave. She turned to Jac with a sly grin. "Lunch won't be ready for 30 minutes. Do you want to arm wrestle, Bigboy?"

Jac grabbed her arm, dragging her down the hall. "I'm going to get you caught up, you little pixie!"

***

Soe worked through lunch and into the afternoon with the computer and discs he had recorded earlier with Meg.

Stumbling through the door late in the day, Soe groaned. "Ahhhh, I'm bushed. C'mon supper. How's Meg?"

Carol rose up from the recliner, yawning. "She woke up about 4 o'clock and is feeling much better. I'll get her." She disappeared down the hallway.

Meg came in, sat down at the table and stared at Soe. "Okay, we can try it after supper. I'm feeling much better."

THE ENHANCERS

Carol swiveled back and forth between them. "I wish you would let me in on the secret."

Soe answered with a slight smile. "Hang on girl, we'll have something for you soon."

"Let's go to the lab." Soe proposed directly after supper. "Meg, I believe I can record your images on video. I have written a program that will take your brain waves and manipulate them into usable electrical signals for a VHS tape."

***

In the lab Soe connected two leads to Meg's helmet system and turned on a TV monitor.

"Here, Meg. Put this on and read something here in the room."

Meg turned the unit on with telekinesis and slowly floated in the air. The monitor responded with squiggly lines in color. Soe tapped on his computer and the lines tried to take shape. Further adjustments continued to clear the picture. Thirty minutes elapsed before a clear picture came in of Morris talking about the bulletproof vests. Remarkably, the monitor even had sound. The picture twisted and swirled, the sound faded in and out with distortions. But it would clear up and bring back the past in remarkable clarity.

Soe switched on the tape recorder. "Meg, you can see the results on the screen. Can you modify the signal to clear it up? Try it with the Datsun or the truck from this morning."

Almost at once the truck appeared with Sue Ellen in it pulling onto the shoulder. The picture appeared to be what Sue Ellen saw looking through the windshield at the Datsun and the boy in the glare of headlights. The boy smiled and waved as he walked forward to the door. The door glass rolled down.

Sue Ellen stared cautiously out the window. "Hi, what happened to your car?"

The boy continued to smile, seemingly very pleasant. His slight build was not threatening. "My name is K. C. McDonald. My car just quit. I don't know what is wrong unless it's the throttle linkage. I need someone to push the pedal down while I watch it under the hood. Can you help me?"

199

Sue Ellen felt much more confident as she quipped. "Sure, I can do that. Where do you live, K. C.?"

"I live in Marian over on Maple Street not far from here."

"Do you go to the High school?"

"I graduated three years ago. What's your name?"

"Sue Ellen."

"This will just take a minute, Sue Ellen, if it works. I sure would appreciate your help?"

K. C. walked back to his car and waited for Sue Ellen looking into the headlights.

Sue Ellen made up her mind. *This won't take long. He looks okay. I've got to get on home. This is all I will do.* She got out of the car and walked to the Datsun. The picture looked down at the rocks on the shoulder and the dirt ahead by the boy's car.

K. C. stood by the raised hood. "Let me get under the hood and you push the gas pedal down."

Sue Ellen sat in the car with her hands on the wheel and pushed the gas pedal, yelling, "Can you tell anything?"

He yelled back from under the hood. "Shift the car into gear."

Sue Ellen felt for the floor shifter as she glanced down at the console. She put her hand on it. A Taser released 200,000 volts into her hand. She blacked out, slumping in the car seat.

Instantly, you saw the scene from K. C.'s eyes. The truck pulled to the side of the road with the headlights glaring in his face. He could see it was a young girl in the cab. The scene repeated itself from K. C.'s view. When the girl touched the shifter and K. C. heard the spark, he closed the hood and went to the door. Sue Ellen was slumped over the wheel to the right. He pushed her over to the right side seat and looked at her as he ran his hand in her blouse and fondled her breasts.

K. C. took a towel, a can of Diesel starter fluid and sprayed it into the towel. He placed the towel over Sue Ellen's face and gave her a good snoot full of ether.

Starting the car, he drove away, down the road in the direction the car was parked. You could see him looking in the rear vision mirror and glancing around as he passed intersections of other roads.

In about two minutes of driving he came to a dirt road leading into the pine trees on the right. Flicking the lights to parking, he drove down the road for about 100 yards and stopped. Pushing the door open, he stood, stretched, grabbed his crotch and went around to the right side where he jerked the door open. Sue Ellen's limp body slide easily out as he dragged her around to the front of the car in the parking lights. There he taped her mouth with gray duct tape, taped her hands over her head and stripped her clothes off. He didn't bother to pull her blouse overhead. Taking a large hunting knife, he slit it up the front. Another slash cut her bra in front.

She lay naked on the ground in the light. K. C. dropped his pants, fell on her and plunged his penis into her as he spread her legs. You could hear him panting. He shuddered and dropped forward for a short time, jerking.

He straightened up on his knees and pulled an ammonia ampoule out of his shirt pocket, broke it and passed it under Sue Ellen's nose. She snapped her head away and opened her eyes. You could see her eyes widen and see her try to scream. She brought her arms down and tried to hit K. C. He grabbed the knife and slashed her throat with one powerful swing. Blood sprayed out of the huge wound as Sue Ellen thrashed around on the ground.

K. C. got up, pulled his pants up and watched until Sue Ellen lay still in a large pool of blood. With little effort, it seemed, he caught her hands over her head and dragged the body a short distance into the trees to a shallow grave where he had a shovel. There, he quickly shoveled dirt into the grave.

He returned to the car with the shovel and picked up Sue Ellen's clothes. Gasping a big breath, he bundled them in a ball as he plunged his face into them snuffling in ecstasy.

Grabbing the shovel, he covered the blood in the road with dirt.

He looked briefly at his handiwork and returned to his desire. He grabbed the clothes again and buried his face in them as he bent over and ejaculated in his pants.

After tossing the clothes and shovel in the Datsun, K. C. got in the car and drove into town to a Wal-Mart parking area where he parked near the door. He put the clothes and shovel in another car beside the Datsun. Grabbing a towel, he wiped the car down inside and out. The scene faded out as he got in the other car and drove away.

Soe and Carol watched the whole thing transfixed without saying a word. Meg settled to the ground and fell in a chair, sobbing. Carol ran to the door and vomited, gagging, hanging on the doorjamb.

Soe turned the machine off and took a deep breath. "CRAP, does that son of a bitch ever need to be gutted and dragged behind a truck until there is nothing but a wet rope."

He went to Meg and slowly raised her up so he could hug her. She cried on his shoulder for a minute longer and slowly regained her composure.

Meg shuddered. "I could feel all of the emotions, his thoughts. He is mentally deranged, sick. It's my first look at a psychopath's mind. I don't want anymore. It was unbelievably horrible."

Carol came back in, grabbed a towel off the bench and wiped her mouth. "Meg, that had to be the awfullest experience in your life. Lordy, how did you stay with it? Didn't you want to run screaming to get away?"

Meg finally gasped. "The only reason I could stay was to get enough information so that trash can burn."

Meg reached out for Carol and clung to her. "That's the Kevin I came here to visit."

Carol choked. "Ahhhh, my Lord, that could have been you!"

Soe slammed his fist into his palm. "We'll get that festering sore. This tape will fry him! I absolutely guarantee that if the law can't get him, I will!"

Carol sputtered. "I thought he was in Tyler, Meg. What's he doing here in Marian?"

Meg hung her head answering limply. "I thought so too, all I had was a telephone number. I thought he was in Tyler."

Soe spit. "Oh hell, he could have a phone in Tyler with call forwarding to here. We don't know what he was up to, either here or there."

Soe escorted the girls to the house and sat them down by the fire. Annie appeared. "How about some hot chocolate. It's real special!"

"Hey, that sounds fine, Annie!" they chorused.

Soe got up. "I'm going back to the lab and make a copy. I'll be back in a minute."

***

As he stepped out of the house, Morris grabbed his arm and whispered. "Hold it, Soe. We've got company out there."

Billy Joe, another of the men who lived at the ranch and took care of GrandJac's "errands" handed a nightscope to Soe. "Look to the right of the gate."

Soe looked through the scope. He was amazed at the picture. The view was a greenish yellow with about 4-power magnification. He could see clearly across the field 200 yards away.

A car was parked down the road to the right and a man sat in the roadside borrow-ditch looking at them with binoculars. Apparently they were not nightvision. If they were, he gave no indication of being watched.

Soe asked. "What are you going to do?"

Morris grinned. "We have a surprise for him."

As Soe watched, a pickup approached very slowly from the right without lights. It stopped behind the car and four men got out. The dome light did not come on when the door opened.

One stayed by the car and three walked down the road quietly towards the man in the ditch. When they were about 20 yards from the man, he turned and saw them and attempted to run. He couldn't get out of the ditch fast enough. The men were upon him in seconds. Soe watched the whole thing through the nightvision glasses.

The men had a gun on the spy as the pickup truck drove forward, picked them all up and drove into the yard. The spy was taken to the prisoner room and handcuffed to the table.

Soe went inside and told the girls about the incident.

They jumped up, eyes alight. "Let's go see who it is!" Carol demanded.

In the dark observation room GrandJac and two men sat discussing the situation. Tommy Silva hung his head dejectedly and leaned on the table. His slight build heightened the dejected posture. He wore casual slacks, sweatshirt and a heavy jacket.

GrandJac picked up a mike and spoke quietly. "What is your name, Mister? What are you doing out here spying on my house?"

"I was taking a piss when these guys jumped me. That's all I know." Tommy replied.

Meg hissed quietly. "His name is Tommy Silva and he works for the CIA. He is here to try to learn more about you and Soe."

GrandJac continued, sneering. "Tommy, the CIA is not going to be too pleased to hear that you were caught while pissing in the ditch observing us. Why are you interested in Etheridge to the point of bugging, stealing, and now spying when you will get science reports routinely with your funding program?"

Tommy snapped to attention and began looking around. *I wonder how much they really know about the CIA's operation?*

Meg filled them in on Tommy's meeting in Dallas.

GrandJac rattled him again. "Wilson is going to be unhappy with your screwup here, Tommy. You don't have anything and already you've blown your cover."

Tommy twisted around and stammered out. "I guess the girl is reading my mind, huh? That's how you know so much? You can kiss my ass. You won't get anything else. I won't think of it."

Suddenly his hands jerked up hard against the cuffs and his head slammed down on the table three times. He looked up dazed, with blood running from his nose and a cut over his right eye. Blood dripped onto the table making a puddle between his hands.

A thought slammed into his head from Meg. *We already know everything, Tommy. I was just thinking of the janitor you poisoned with mercury. His life is agony and will be agony until he dies.*

Tommy reared back pulling, twisting on the cuffs. "Shit, what kind of people are you? How do you do that? You know I didn't poison the janitor. That was my partner, Theo."

Yes, I know that Tommy. But you were an accessory and condoned it to get what you wanted. It would seem that the CIA is not content to share any technology. They want to steal it before it is available to anybody else. Meg put a little pressure on Tommy's mind. His eyes stared as he quivered with convulsions.

Suddenly Meg sat bolt upright. *What's this idea about capturing me, Tommy? You were one of the men in the mall last night that drugged me, weren't you?*

Tommy squirmed and looked away. "That's not my idea, that's Wilson's. I was just following orders. What the hell are you doing to my mind?"

Tommy, you shall pay, Meg spit ominously. *I see you have two small children at home, Tommy. You are a loving Daddy.*

Tommy found himself on the freeway at rush hour. He was standing on a dividing line with cars darting by him driving 70 MPH. They were honking and dodging. Tommy ran to the side and a car swerved across a lane and piled into another car. The door blew open and a child flew out into his arms. He could see two cars bearing down on him. They were going to hit him! He tried to run across another lane and a huge truck hit him squarely in the chest mashing the child, his child, into a bloody pulp. He was covered with blood from the child and there was another one in the middle of the lane. He grabbed his other child and looked into the grill of a pickup truck. It smashed the child against him and again he was saturated in the child's blood. He screamed and screamed as the cars smashed him again and again with his children in his arms.

He found himself in the room crying hysterically hovering over the table. A phrase kept ringing in his ears. *You are a*

205

disgrace to the human race, Tommy. You killed 20 children. But the most important thing you must remember is that your children will never be safe again from kidnapers. Spend some time thinking about that, Tommy!

Meg had been sending the same thoughts to the others in the room, so they were up to date. They looked at Tommy with disgust.

Soe stared in awe. "That is so vivid! Meg. You, we can destroy a person's mind!"

"Yes. It's something to think about. What do you want to do GrandJac? I think the CIA ought to come forward and pay for the janitor's life as a minimum. Secondly, they ought to come out in the open and approach us on level ground." Meg suggested as she turned to GrandJac.

GrandJac placed a gnarled hand on Meg's shoulder, "You are mature far beyond your years, little lady. With this power you are far beyond the rest of the world. Again I say, this power is possibly too much for our times. But it could do so much to straighten out the world. It could be a deterrent stronger than anything yet in existence, particularly if it were administered impartially. In the wrong hands it would create anarchy beyond imagination." GrandJac sighed as he patted Meg.

GrandJac finally spoke after a long pause. "Meg, I think you are right. Let's give the CIA an opportunity to be honest and forthright. Let's send Tommy back with a message to the CIA to get their shit together and come see us."

Meg turned to Tommy and relayed the message to his brain with a little further stimulus. He staggered upright rolling his head around wild-eyed. Tears still streamed down his face mixing with the blood giving him a ghoulish appearance.

A man entered the room and uncuffed him. Tommy put his hands to his temples and looked at the glass.

"I'll pass the word. You can count on it." He said with emphasis. A door opened and he walked out and across the front field through the gate to his car.

GrandJac stated firmly. "See, I told you that these people are dangerous. I think the CIA is more dangerous than Friedman. They are after you, Meg, and the technology."

THE ENHANCERS

Meg stared off to the distance, "They better come prepared for a trip to hell. If I get a chance, they're gonna get a free ticket!"

Soe watched Meg with a degree of awe. *This will get out of control, I feel it!*

Soe turned to GrandJac and suggested that he come to the lab and see the video that Meg had made tonight.

***

The girls turned to the house, "We're going to the house and ask Annie for some late supper."

Carol grabbed Meg's coat sleeve. "What do you really think, Meg? You are getting stronger and we are sliding deeper into some kind of pit. Can you see anything down the road?"

"Nothing, Carol. I'd tell you if I could."

***

GrandJac watched the tape and hung his head in shame and disgust.

"First, think of this as a tool to correct wrong. And secondly, think of clearing filth like this off the streets. Administration of this power is almost incomprehensible. I just really don't know where to start. Your current program of going public will absolutely scare the hell out of everyone, innocent or guilty. But it is a tickler to test the waters. Let's continue for a few days and watch closely."

THE ENHANCERS

FRIDAY DECEMBER 23RD

For the morning, Jac remained at the ranch with GrandJac to continue his training. Soe, Carol and Meg drove to the Police Station and asked for Lt. Brandon. The dispatcher grinned. She was accustomed to their attire.

Lt. Brandon rushed into the lobby grabbing Meg's hand. "I was hoping you would come back. The information you gave me yesterday was correct and we have made arrests and solved two crimes! Come in, come in. I want you to consider helping us on other cases."

In a conference room, Lt. Brandon turned to Meg, a questioning stare. "I've forgotten your names. Please introduce yourselves to our Police Chief."

The room held five policemen seated and the Chief. Meg had erased their names from everyone's memory.

"Our names are unimportant." Meg stated as she stood to one side of the room. "What we have to show you is an introduction to a new world, hopefully an honest and loving world. It certainly won't be a world you are familiar with and it won't tolerate many of the sins of our society. And—, maybe a world obsessed with fear. We need feed back from you, the people, the media, the government, everyone."

The men sat without saying anything. Several smirked or sneered at each other. A policeman rolled in a VCR and TV receiver on a stand and set it up at the end of the room.

"Here you are, Chief." He commented, turned and left the room.

The Chief remarked. "Did I ask for this?"

Lt. Brandon recognized the cynicism of the officers. He waved his hand, suggesting quietly. "Just be patient, men."

Without a nod, Soe stepped forward and turned on the equipment, inserted the tape and pushed play. The tape began with Sue Ellen slowing down and pulling off the road. The officers stirred and sat upright. They could see the brown Datsun in the headlights. Soe, Carol and Meg watched their reactions as the tape unfolded its gruesome tale. All were intensely alert. Some grabbed the table. Others pawed on their clothing, fumbled with their face.

When the tape went blank, they all yelled at once. "Where in hell did that tape come from? That's the Sue Ellen case. Who is the kid? How did you get something like this? Who in hell are you?" Pandemonium reigned.

The Chief rose holding up his hands for quiet, demanding. "For God's sake, that is unbelievable! Tell us about this tape. What is your name?"

"We are the Enhancers!" Meg's voice seemed to echo in the room. "Through electronics and ESP, we can recapture scenes from the past or present."

Soe stepped forward and connected Meg to the VCR's input ports, inserted a new tape and pushed record. Instantly, a replay of the room and the men watching the tape's end appeared on the screen from Meg's perspective at the front of the room.

The officers hardly moved, as if stunned. "Lord help me—, us, what is this thing?" One finally choked out. "There will be no secrets here!"

A policewoman came in and handed Meg a file and pictures of a case dealing with a car theft ring. Meg studied the pictures and slowly floated into the air with the VCR leads trailing her. In a moment, the TV screen lit up with a scene at night where a Latino stuck a door shoe down a window and opened a door on a new car. He quickly sat in the car and used a locksmith's tool to pull the cylinder in the column and replace it with another. He drove away in 45 seconds.

Another scene appeared in a warehouse where the car was parked and five young men, Latinos, blacks and whites worked on stripping the car. Several more cars were parked and two more were in various stages of being stripped.

A quiet pall hung in the room as the officers stared at the video and then at Meg. No one seemed to be able to formulate a question or make a statement.

The chief stuttered. "This could solve hundreds of crimes. Maybe all crimes, maybe stop crime before it started! Who—, what——, how——, I don't understand. Wait, wait don't go. Please, this is incomprehensible. You have to——."

Meg settled to the floor. "You have seen the beginning. We will be in touch."

Meg turned on her heel, stepping quickly across the room to the door. Her entourage followed without any word, nod, or acknowledgment of the policemen gaping, pawing after them.

Lt. Brandon sprang to life running after them, begging. "I must be able to contact you. We have several more cases, whole bunches of cases you can help us on."

***

Meg spun around to Lt. Brandon, eyes glaring, penetrating into Brandon. "The city jail is here in this building isn't it?"

"Yes——, yes, it is." he stuttered as he tried to decide what or how to address the Enhancers.

Take me to the cells so I can see the prisoners. Meg's voice echoed through Lt. Brandon's head.

Carol whispered. "What are you doing, Meg——? Ha, I know. You want to see the driver that killed you, don't you?"

Lt. Brandon led them through the offices to the jail section amid wild stares from policemen and workers. With a little help from Meg, they soon settled down and accepted the black-garbed Enhancers.

In the cellblock, Meg walked down the aisle looking at the inmates.

A thought burned through Lt. Brandon's mind as Meg paused in front of a cell. *I can determine right now whether each of these men is guilty and to what extent. Do you have any questions?*

Brandon eagerly stepped forward. "Yes, yes, give me any information you have on any of them." In seconds, Lt. Brandon had complete pictures of the crimes each inmate was accused of. Brandon grabbed his head as if it would explode. "Hey, hey, hey I can't handle it. Slow it down, Mr. Enhancer."

Meg spit sarcastically. "You will retain it, Lt., don't worry. This is the one I wanted to visit with." She announced as she stepped forward to the bars of a cell.

THE ENHANCERS

Willie sat on his bunk leaning against the wall with one boot on the bed, twisting his moustache. A toothpick hung out the side of his mouth. He waved a thin arm hanging over his knee as he spit on the floor, yelling. "Hey, Lt. what the fuck is the clown doing here? Get it away from my cage. I don't want to see it or talk to it."

In an instant, Willie was plastered against the back wall of the cell, spread-eagled as if he were nailed to a cross. His mouth hung open and his eyes bugged as he screamed an unearthly noise. In his mind he was flashing down a freeway trying to steer a car against traffic. The wheel was loose with slack as he twisted it left and right avoiding cars that were going to ram him.

A huge truck grill loomed in front as he jerked it to the right and plunged through a crowd of his construction worker friends on the job. Bodies sprayed over the area with heavy thumpings. His best friend, Vern, smashed against the windshield with his face protruding through a broken glass hole, screaming in his painful death throes.

"Willie, Willie, what are you doing? You are killing us!"

The car hurtled towards a heavy concrete wall. Willie couldn't see past Vern's crushed and bleeding body.

Suddenly, time stood still. Meg got a flash of a past scene where drunken Willie goaded Vern to pass a truck on a bridge and cause the truck to jackknife.

Meg screamed, pointing. "You sorry, worthless bastard, you shall pay the rest of your life."

Willie screamed, gasped, panted and cried as he shit his blue jeans. He flew forward and crashed into the bars, spun around and flew back to the wall and smashed against it where he slid to the floor in a spreading pool of blood, urine and excrement. His body twitched uncontrollably as terrible thoughts raced through his mind.

Lt. Brandon stood transfixed with his mouth agape and hand outstretched as if he could stop the assault. The Enhancers turned and filed out of the jail cell compound. Lt. Brandon trailed them rubbing his head, looking around as if trying to remember what was happening.

211

"What was that, Mr. Enhancer? I think one of the prisoners was hurt?" Meg finished wiping his mind of the event.

"You have information to close all the cases on the inmates. Get to work on them." Came the harsh reply.

The Enhancers continued through the offices and into the parking lot disappearing in the mind's eye of most watchers.

In the car, Carol grabbed Meg's coat. "Meg, what tha hell was the deal with Willie? You beat the shit outta him!"

Meg flooded their minds with the haunting story she had extracted from Willie.

***

Some two years ago, Willie and Vern were drinking beer and driving on a country road approaching a bridge. Vern was driving. An 18-wheeler was ahead of them seemingly blocking the flow of traffic.

Vern initially slowed but Willie goaded him. "Vern, you pussy, pass that fucking truck. All they do is block traffic. You ain't got a hair on your ass if you don't pass that truck, pussy." Vern paused momentarily, then gassed it around the truck to find another car in front of the truck. He had to pass it, too! And he just barely got back in his lane with an on-coming car bearing down on him.

Willie laughed hysterically and slapped Vern on the back as Vern cursed.

"You sorry shit, I coulda been killed." Vern glanced back in the rear-vision mirror and gasped, horrified. "Jesus Christ, Willie, that truck jack-knifed and smashed that car!"

Willie snapped back to look at the wreck. "Somebitch, man, we can't stop. The law will hang us by our balls. Get the hell outta here." Vern sped on down the road, trying to look back at the wreck.

"Man, we gotta go back." Willie put his foot on top of the gas pedal and mashed it.

"Get the hell outta here, Vern."

***

"Wow Meg, that's the wreck that killed your parents. This Willie shit killed your parents and you, basically, didn't he?" Carol screeched.

Meg couldn't speak. She just nodded as she held her face in her hands, sobbing.

Soe put his arm around Meg and pulled her over to him, speaking intensely. "I hope you fixed Willie, Meg. That cancer needs exterminating."

Meg's vengeful thought flashed through their minds. *He will never be the same again. Remorse will haunt him to his grave. Along with some serious scars on and about the face and body. I can't kill him, but he might commit suicide.*

Soe shook his head with disbelief. "This has really been one hell of an experience, Meg. Let's go to the ranch and let the police chew on the information they have. I have some other ideas I want to work on in the meantime."

He continued, "Meg, do you remember when you knocked me down the other night with a wave of your hand? Do you know how you did that?"

Meg thought about it for some time. "I seemed to extend my hand and throw or fling something off my fingertips."

Soe interjected. "Do you know how you levitate or move objects? You see, we have opened a controversy here through the police and we may need better control of these powers. The public is going bonkers when the media dumps this on them."

***

Soe wheeled into the ranch and parked behind the metal buildings. Morris and Duncan parked their pickup truck beside them. They had tailgated them to the station and home. Meg had brought them up-to-date on the events.

Soe turned to Morris. "Better be extra careful, Morris. We probably have turned over the ol' turd and the stink is developing."

Morris grinned. "Yup, Iah shore do believe that's gonna happen. Iah shore do like Miss Meg's method of justice. Swift and to the point."

A wry grin spread across Soe's face. "Yep, the bad boys may be in for a surprise." "Let's get Jac and ask him about something. Girls, y'all want a snack or a drink? I'm hungry."

***

They found Jac with GrandJac in his office discussing the automotive industry. Soe poked his head in. "Hey man, can we interrupt for a while?"

"Sure," GrandJac agreed, "Come on in." Soe and Meg updated them on the police visit.

GrandJac shrugged his shoulders. "There is no doubt. We are committed. We shall reap the winds of change."

Jac snapped around staring hard at GrandJac as that funny déjà vu feeling immersed him.

Soe turned to Jac, seeing the stare. "What is it, Jac? Can you come to the lab for a discussion?"

Jac raised an eyebrow to GrandJac. "Sure, go ahead, son. I'll catch you later."

"It's nothing, Soe. Maybe later. Meg, I'm glad you have the final on your parents. I can hardly imagine the coincidence of one person being responsible for all the deaths of your family. This Willie is walking death. I wonder if he has killed others?"

Meg nodded, a determined scowl streaked across her face, "Yes, it is a terrible coincidence, but I can live with it. You can bet Willie will live with it the rest of his life!"

***

The girls trailed into the workshop with drinks and chips. Soe grabbed a Coke and a hand full of chips as he turned to Jac.

"When we tried to enhance our brains, it was a disaster, but Meg has no problem. I think it has something to do with the 'near death event.' Somehow it conditions the brain. What do you think about one of us going into oxygen deprivation maybe to a blackout and flat line stage? Then using my program to enhance the brain?"

Jac stood up gawking at Soe, awed. "For Crap's sake, Soe, where do you get these ideas? Surely you realize the risks. Meg was chilled very quickly in an unconscious state. Her body declined to a very low metabolic state. Maybe the bump did something. I'm sure other factors came into play, but what I don't know.

"You must be thinking of the movie, "Flatline." It was a movie! Remember that. If you can find one of your school chums willing, we can experiment like in the movie. Think about what to do with the body afterward, though."

Startling everyone, Carol stood up after a penetrating glance from Meg. "I want to try it, Soe. You can use me as a guinea pig."

Jac looked at Carol realizing she was serious. "Carol, let me talk to you. Come in the other room."

Jac turned to Carol, put his hands on her shoulders. He looked down at her, felt her warmth. "Ahhh, you are so impetuous. This is a very dangerous experiment. Carol, I think a great deal of you and I don't want anything to happen to you."

Carol's eyes enlarged staring up at Jac. "I love you, Jac. But I feel like a third leg here. This is really Soe and Meg's play. GrandJac has pulled you out of the picture. So here I am, a tag along."

Jac circled her with his arms and hugged her close. "Carol, you are so sweet and perceptive, I love you for all of that and more."

He bent down and kissed her warm mouth. Tears rolled down Carol's face as she responded to Jac's caress.

Carol stammered. "I still want to go through with the test, Jac. You will be with me, I feel safe."

Jac grabbed her face and turned it up to him. "Carol, we are not in the world of 'Ignorance is bliss or what you don't know won't hurt you.' We are in a real, dangerous world. The more we learn, the more we realize how much more we have to learn. This deal with Soe and Meg is a classic example."

Carol glared at Jac as she stamped her foot. "I want to go through with it, Jac. Now."

They returned to the lab with Carol wiping her eyes.

Meg came to her and hugged her. "I'm so happy for y'all. I had to peek. I couldn't help it, Carol."

215

Carol laughed, grabbing Meg's hand. "Nothing is private, is it? I want some of that peeking ability, too, Meg."

Soe looked on curiously. "What the hell is going on? I'm L.O.F."

Jac spread his hands in disgust, "Carol is determined to let you experiment on her in a comatose state."

Jac faced the trio with hands on hips, a scowl across his face. "We are caught up in a bubble of technology and emotional events that we can't see beyond. It's whirling around us, encompassing us. We think in very short futures. We must step back and grasp for a broader view. We are like a fuse burning brightly, but very short-lived."

Carol hugged Jac. "That's a beautiful insight, my lover. But it doesn't get me a Meg kit, and I will have it if it's possible."

"Go for it, Carol. I think we can do it!" Meg encouraged staring at Jac with piercing eyes.

Jac didn't seem to acknowledge Meg's stare. He bent down kissing Carol. "Alright, but if there is anything I consider beyond my control, I'll stop it."

"I want to get some equipment and things from the hospital before we do anything. I must leave now to make shift change at 4 this afternoon."

"Wait a minute, Jac. Things may be getting sticky out there. Wear this bulletproof vest, at least. Already, the other side has tried to kill the driver of the GN and your car. That's you, for clarification." Soe demanded.

Soe caught the girl's attention. "Even though Jac hasn't read or heard of this technique, I have read of comatose technology being used for severe brain aberrations, mentally ill people, for example. The tests didn't lose anybody. But they didn't help greatly, either."

Jac shook his head at the inane statement. "Soe, come up with something more definitive."

***

Jac slipped the vest on with a light billowy jacket and climbed in a pickup with Morris. "To the hospital, James."

It was 12 o'clock. Jac would have to hurry to get his supplies back to the ranch and still get to work on time.

"Park in the emergency area. It's close, Morris. I'll get the stuff and bring it out." Morris remained in the truck and watched the area. He was surprised to see Eddie Broussard exit a car and enter the building. He normally worked the evening shift with Jac. What was he doing here 4 hours early? Morris got out of the truck and went inside.

Jac's medical bag sat on a table in front of the supply room. He stood by checking an oxygen bottle with a regulator.

Eddie approached Jac. "Hey, Jac Baby, I got something for you."

Jac turned around looking surprised. "Hey, what's up, Eddie?"

Eddie pulled a wicked looking knife from his coat sleeve and stabbed Jac in the rib cage. The knife ripped his coat and shirt in a big slash. Jac fell back against a table knocking glassware and supplies to the floor in a loud crash.

"What tha' hell are you doing, Eddie?" Jac yelled holding up his arm to fend off another slash.

Eddie stepped in and stabbed Jac again in the stomach. The knife slid off through his clothes, ripping them again. Jac lashed out with the heel of his left hand, catching Eddie on his cheekbone, tearing skin, snapping his head back.

Jac stepped back and crouched low, balanced on the balls of his feet. "Come on, shit for brains. Let's see how good you are."

Morris stepped forward and yelled. "Eddie, drop the knife or I'll gut shoot you." Morris was pointing a .357 snub revolver at Eddie. You could tell he meant it.

Eddie dropped the knife, growling. "Hell, I don't need a knife to take this pussy." He pivoted around swinging his leg and foot towards Jac's head in a vicious arc. Jac stepped into Eddie letting the leg strike his left arm and slide up towards his head. Ducking, he slammed his fist into Eddie's crotch. He could feel the soft testicles crush under the blow.

Eddie crumpled to the floor, gagging. Slowly he clawed to get away. "Hey, Eddie, I thought you were tough. Snap to it!"

Nurses and orderlies yelled to stop.

Morris waved the gun and yelled above the din. "We're gonna see this fight to the end. Just shut your faces."

Eddie got on his feet and crouched low, waving his hands in circular motions. Jac feinted with his left hand and drove his right hand with his fingers extended straight into Eddie's face striking his mouth and sliding across his cheek, leaving blood and raw flesh. Eddie rebounded with a right and hit Jac hard on the side of his head. Jac stepped back, looking dazed. Eddie stepped forward to deliver a hard right to the mouth. To his surprise, Jac drove his extended fingers deep into his solar plexus, driving the air from his lungs. He bent over gasping and gagging. Grabbing his belt and shirt collar, Jac picked him up bodily, slamming him down on the floor with a sickening crunch.

Eddie lay gasping and panting on the floor. Jac rolled him over with his foot. His eyes stared vacantly. Eddie was out cold.

Police rushed into the room about 10 seconds later with guns drawn. Morris had faded into the crowd and left the building. Everyone was talking at once, pointing and shouting.

Jac picked up his bag, supplies and set the table upright. Hardly panting, he looked at his hand and felt the knot where Eddie had hit him. Glancing down, he pulled at his coat. It hung in shreds.

The police picked up the knife with rubber gloves and put it in a plastic bag.

An intern asked the police. "Do you want to get Eddie off the floor?"

"Sure, let's get him up," one of them agreed.

The intern bent down and passed an ammonia ampoule under his nose. Eddie twisted away, opening his eyes, staring into the policeman's face.

They rolled Eddie over on his belly, handcuffed him and picked him up on his feet. The policeman read Eddie his rights from a plastic laminated card he carried in his pocket.

"You want to tell me what is going on?"

Eddie said nothing, hanging his head, scowling.

The policeman turned to Jac and asked him the same thing.

"Hell, I don't have any idea. Eddie and I work together. We have always been friends, I thought. He tried to stab and cut me twice with that knife. Fortunately, I was wearing this vest I got for a friend of mine. I was just trying it out. It's almost like he's on some kind of drugs. Better test him."

The policeman looked at Jac's shirt and coat, "You are one lucky man. You need to come to the station and fill out a report today, if possible."

"Who was the man with the gun? Several witnesses said he was the referee?" The policeman asked.

Jac just shrugged and turned to his supplies. "I've got to get these things across town as soon as possible."

Signing a requisition form, he carried an armload outside to the truck and returned for the rest. Jac sighed as he hung on the door handle looking around. *This shit just goes on and on. One of us is gonna git it, I just know it!*

"The keys are on the floor." Morris was lying down on the back seat with his hat over his face. "Home, James." He spoke quietly, sitting up. That brought forth a small chuckle.

***

Tommy Silva staggered to his car, drove to his motel room where he cleaned himself up looking in the mirror. "Ugh." Swollen nose, probably broken. Both eyes blackened. The cut in his eyebrow really needed something to pull it together. The ringing in his head from the Godawful stimulus Meg had given him pulsated with his heartbeat. The freeway scene continued to haunt him.

A voice pounded in his head continuously with an ominous warning. *You better see Wilson and spill your guts. You are on a timer!*

Tommy changed clothes and drove to Dallas where he waited in the parking lot for the office to open. At 8 o'clock he entered the building and went to Wilson's office. Several workers looked at Tommy with wide-open eyes, but nobody said anything.

***

Wilson ushered Tommy in and sat him down with a cup of coffee. "Looks like you ran into a wall, Tommy. Tell me about it." Wilson demanded. Wilson was a big, burly, dark headed, intimidating black man who had used those skills to move up the ranks.

Tommy told his story in detail.

"Why did you drive here to tell me? You could have called, you know." Wilson admonished with a rapid drumming of his fingers on the desk.

Tommy stammered, pleading, whimpering. "You don't understand. They want you and the CIA to come forward and meet them face-to-face. They want the CIA to admit they poisoned the janitor and pay him off. They are willing to give the CIA technology. I'm telling you, this stuff is powerful. That girl can slap you around and talk in your head. You can't hide anything from her in your mind."

"You sound like a salesman, Tommy. They really did a number on you. I don't know if we'll be able to use you again." Wilson interrupted as steely eyes pierced Tommy.

Tommy sat back in his chair, almost crying. "What-, what do you mean by that, Wilson?"

Wilson replied deprecatingly as he waved his hand towards Tommy. "You appear used up, Tommy. Go get some rest. Maybe we can talk about it."

Tommy sat forward, an anxious scowl on his face. "What the hell are you going to do about meeting with them and paying off the janitor?"

Wilson answered brusquely with a sweep of his hand. "Tommy, we can't play their game. You know that, for crap's sake. You are really screwed up."

An agent rapped on the door looking through the glass. He poked his head in. "Got some hot news, Wilson."

"Come on in, Steve. What's hot?" Wilson answered perfunctorily.

Steve ignored the attitude. It was Wilson's trademark. "Wally just called in from Friedman's place. Seems like a gang of masked men kidnapped Sam Friedman on the way to work.

Stole the entire car and his bodyguards, all of them. Kendrick tried to follow them, but was forced off the road into a ditch. He got the license plate on the truck. It was stolen from Friedman's own trucking yard."

Wilson reared back in his chair, taking a deep breath as he slammed his fist down on the table. "God damn it. These boys are making fools out of us. Look at Tommy here. They slapped the shit out of him last night over in Marian."

Tommy and Steve exchanged glances. "Boy, that looks bad, Tommy. I hope you got in your licks," Steve offered.

"'Fraid not, Steve. Tommy took a hosing there. On top of that, they brainwashed him. Fucked his mind up."

Wilson's disgust rang through his words.

Tommy's voice quivered as he tried to defend himself. "These people are really powerful, Steve. They can hurt you from a distance with their mind."

Wilson brushed the implication away with his hand. "That's enough of that, Tommy. Brief Steve on the situation. Steve, I want you to go to Marian and put Cochran and his gang under surveillance. See if they are the ones who kidnapped Sam Friedman. If that's true, we may have a war going on between these two powerful families. Find the girl, Meloney Graham and report back to me." Wilson slapped his hands palm down on his desk, looking expectantly at the two men.

Tommy and Steve recognized the termination and left the office together.

***

Wilson called Weatherby in Washington DC and reported in on the situation. He and Weatherby had a good laugh about the demands for restitution for the janitor or for collaboration. "That is so naïve!"

Weatherby continued, "Wilson, old Cochran has called me to tell of the CIA agent, Theo, involved in the break-in and data stealing. He failed to tell of Theo dying or what else might have happened. He definitely has some influence here on the hill, but he won't get any support. I'll see to it."

Wilson paused without acknowledging Weatherby's comments. "This ESP thing could be pretty damn powerful. I can't believe it's everything my man claims, though. I'll keep you informed." Wilson slapped the phone down in his usual abrupt style. Musing, *you know, I am going to stay real close to this crazy power thing. It might be the new wave of the future.*

***

Police Chief Thurmond put his best men on the Sue Ellen case. By afternoon, they had a confirmed ID on the boy in the video. The name and address he had given were false. Chief Thurmond briefed the Mayor informing him that he wanted the press involved in both the arrest and the finding of the body. "We can work this into next year's election, Wharton. Let's make the most of it, okay?"

"Alright, do it." Wharton answered.

The neighborhood turned out to witness local TV and press following the police to the boy's house where he lived with his mother.

K. C. snickered at the camera as the arrest and search warrant took place. "Have fun, you vultures." He screamed, spitting at the camera. Searching revealed the clothes of Sue Ellen and significant evidence in related cases. Thurmond's entourage continued to the dirt road in the pine forest and found the body, the blood pool, everything that was depicted in the video. Thurmond gathered the press as the crime scene team moved into the forest. "There's more, folks. We are gonna clean house on criminals today!"

Late in the afternoon, TV and press covered the exposure and arrest of a gang of car thieves and car strippers at a warehouse in town.

Mayor Wharton and Chief Thurmond held a news conference as a summation of extraordinary arrests and received accolades for solving four major crimes in two days.

One of the news interviewers asked about a rumor. "What are, or who are the Enhancers, Mayor Wharton?" The Mayor turned to Chief Thurmond and motioned for him to respond.

"Yes, we are receiving assistance from a group called the Enhancers." Chief Thurmond answered, curtly.

"How are they helping you?" the questioning continued.

"We are not ready to release that information at present."

"Who are they?" another question came forth.

"We cannot comment at present."

"Have they been instrumental in solving all of these cases, Chief?" The questions continued.

"No comment." The Chief replied as he turned to go. "When we are ready, we will release a statement to the press. That is all."

"Chief, hey chief, is it true one of your prisoners was badly beaten in his cell today?"

Chief Thurmond turned back to the assemblage, glaring at the reporter. "Yes, one of our prisoners was injured today. He was not beaten. An investigation has revealed that he apparently tried to jump off the top bunk in the cell. He fell. That's all."

The reporter held up his hand, trying to get a further word from the Chief. "Uh, Chief, uh, I understand the prisoner suffered five broken ribs, a dislocated shoulder, both knees torn, four broken fingers and severe lacerations about the face and head and he is in intensive care with brain damage."

Chief Thurmond turned steely eyes on the reporter for a moment, snapped a glance at the Mayor then spoke authoritatively. "Well, his injuries are serious. He fell on the toilet from the top bunk as I said. He is recovering successfully. It was a careless act on his part. He was in a cell by himself. There was no beating. He fell, understand?"

***

Two of the reporters in the pressroom turned to one another, smirking. "You've got to remember that line, 'He fell.' It's standard police coverage for any type of police harassment. Okay? Whoever that was, he really pissed someone off!

From the little information given, that asshole is covering up something pretty big. I bet you a steak dinner." Jerry declared to Hartzog. "Let's see if we can dig it out. 'The Enhancers,' this could be one hell of a story!"

Hartzog answered. "I know the gal who runs the evidence room at the station. I'll ask her. I've had several dates with her. She's ah good ol' gal."

That evening, Hartzog called Jessica Warren, the caretaker of the evidence room and visited with her. After some small talk about a possible date, Hartzog asked. "Say, Jessica, what in the world is this Enhancer thing that came out this afternoon?"

Jessica giggled, whispering conspiratorially. "We have all been sworn to secrecy, Hart. The Enhancers are solving these crimes. I can't tell you more."

"Well, I can certainly understand the necessity of confidentiality in dealing with informers, Jessica. You must protect them." Hartzog answered soothingly.

Jessica countered. "These are not informers, Hart. They are three people who just appeared here three days ago."

"I think it's every citizen's responsibility to report crimes that they see happen, Jessica. I'm proud we have people like that here in Marian." Hartzog continued as if he were waving the flag.

"These people didn't see the crimes happen. They somehow focused their mind or something on evidence and told just exactly what happened." Jessica whispered, surreptitiously.

"Isn't it wonderful that we have people, not one, but three people who came forward to help us, Jessica?" Hartzog goaded cautiously. Thinking to himself, *well, what the hell do we have here?*

"Actually, it was one girl or young woman who did it." Jessica whispered as she covered the phone with her hand.

"Golly, I'll bet it was exciting to be in on the ground floor hearing this young woman relate the crime in detail." Hartzog cooed with an edge of challenge to continue.

Jessica's voice raised an octave, demanding recognition. "Hart, you should have seen it. She made a video of the actual crime as it was happening. I saw it. The video showed this boy rape and slash the throat of poor little Sue Ellen. It was in color and sound. Ahhh, it was horrible. The boy is some kind of psycho. He smelled Sue Ellen's clothes and got off. It was beyond gross. When the jury sees this video, they will lynch him."

"Sweet Jesus, Jessica, aren't you proud to have the Enhancers on our side of the law?" Hartzog challenged. Thinking, *This is going to make one hell of a story!*

"My gracious, yes." Jessica answered, alarmed. "I can't imagine what would happen if they were with the criminals!"

Hartzog read the fear in her voice. "Well, I'm sure happy they're on our side, Jessica. I'll bet they'll be back to help us again real soon, won't they?"

Jessica covered the phone again, whispering. "They promised to come back, Hart." She rushed on. "You ought to see how they're dressed. They look like Darth Vader, all black leather boots, gloves, coats, and helmets. Their helmets have shields and they wear dark glasses. You can't tell who they are. It's real spooky." Jessica paused for effect. "The real scary thing is when the girl flies as she is talking."

Hartzog was almost at a loss for words as he tried to grasp what he heard. "Flies—, ahhhhhhh, ha, ah, yes, flies! Ahhh, I'll bet that is something to see! Jessica, I sure would like to see that. Why don't you call me the next time they come in? Would you do that?"

"You betcha, Hart. You'll just turn a flap, ha, ha. That's a play on words, Hart." Jessica laughed.

Hart's voice caressed her. "Jessica, you are so smart. I'm going to give you a big hug and kiss when I take you out for a steak dinner next week."

"You just call me, Hart, when you're ready," Jessica giggled, "bye."

Hartzog turned to Jerry and told him the details he had gleaned from Jessica. "I got it on the phone recorder. Boy, do we have a story here, Jerry. Let's go write it up. This could be an AP exclusive."

***

Jac drove the truck back to the ranch and parked it in back. He and Morris carried the supplies into the lab.

"Jac, you got any idea what come over Eddie? I'll bet 'ol Friedman is wrapped up in it somewhere."

"If we could get Meg on him, we'd find out, Morris. She can read a chicken egg and talk to it. We're going to have to hump it, it's 2!" Soe and the girls came out of the house with sandwiches for them.

Meg paused looking at Jac's shredded coat. "Tell them about it. Are you hurt?"

Jac felt the knot on his temple, "Just bruised. You tell them, we don't have much time."

Carol wrapped around Jac, pulled him down and kissed his bruise. "That jacket saved your life, Jac. Think about how close you came to not wearing it. I saw the look on your face when Soe suggested it."

"Well, you're right, it sure did. And I'm thankful to Soe and the jacket. C'mon, let's get this program in gear, if we are going to do so. I have to be to work at 4 PM."

***

GrandJac appeared and watched them set up the EKG, EEG, shock pads and gas bottles.

"Let me have your attention for a minute, kids. The Friedman's have made four attempts on your lives. This Eddie was surely in Friedman's pay today. They want the Enhancers and they want war. So this morning I collected Sam. He's visiting with us even now. You know, he's the oldest son. I thought having him as a hostage might slow Saul down. But he tried to kill Jac at the hospital."

GrandJac sighed, spreading his hands in resignation. "There are no boundaries. Jac, I don't think you ought to go to work today. Just call in absent due to the fight. Let's see what Saul will do."

GrandJac turned to Morris. "I want 'Ready Alert' 24 hours a day from now on. Check all supplies, etc. You know what to do, Morris."

Morris turned, immediately pulling a radio from his coat and began barking orders as he walked away.

Jac put his hands on his hips as he stared pensively at his Grandfather. "It sounds like we are going to war, Grandpaw." "I'll bet you're right, son." GrandJac threw back as he disappeared through the door.

A call to Ketchum, the hospital administrator, was an unpleasant chore. Jac had never been absent on the job. Now, here he was lying about it.

***

Jac's quiet, strained look quickly gathered the group. "Okay, here's the routine. Carol will be monitored with EKG, EEG and heart functions. She will be put under with nitrogen which will starve the brain for oxygen like Meg was. We can go to loss of involuntary functions like breathing and heart function. The brain will continue to live for a few minutes and then flat line brain activity. Effectively, she will be dead." Jac's tone and manner cast a pall over the group.

Jac paused again as he looked at Carol for go. "We can then administer oxygen, forced breathing and heart manipulation, then the cardio pads and/or adrenalin to get the heart beating again. Soe can stimulate the brain with his program. Maybe Carol will live and maybe she will have an active brain, maybe like Meg's or maybe she will be in a PVS, persistent vegetative state. A grinning vegetable."

"Heavens sakes, that's a graphic description." Meg exclaimed as she looked at Carol. "What are her chances, Jac?"

"It is absolutely beyond prediction. We are considering something that has not been chronicled. Maybe tried, but not printed. I personally don't agree with it at all, particularly on Carol. She is very special to me and I don't want her any other way." Jac hugged Carol and looked at her for a "no."

Meg suggested. "Maybe I can monitor her brain and we can reach an inactive level before clinical death?"

Carol listened very attentively with no smile as she hung on Jac, glancing surreptitiously at Meg. "You are so sweet, Jac. I know you care for me and want me as I am because I'm so sexy." She smiled that impish grin.

Jac bent down and kissed her. "I don't want you to do this, Sweetiepie. I know what I have now. I might have a carrot afterwards."

"Well, that settles it." Carol stamped her foot, "He thinks of me as a carrot, so let's get it on."

Jac threw up his hands, "Get your butt up here on the table, lie down and expose your big tits."

They lay a heavy blanket on the bench and propped her head with a pillow to get air passage breathing in an unconscious state. Jac unbuttoned her shirt and unsnapped her bra in front. Her breasts sagged to each side.

Carol cut her eyes to Soe with a sly grin. "Do you like mine better than Meg's, Bigboy?" Soe blushed beet red.

"Girl, you are a pistol. When you pull out of this I will find a way to embarrass you. In front of a crowd!"

There was a little nervous laughter as the EKG and EEG pads were stuck in place. The monitors were put through their paces and all checked out. Soe connected his computer inline with the EEG and inserted his data program. Jac prepared a syringe with adrenaline solution and greased the cardio pads. He checked the machine for function. All seemed in order.

Carol and Jac's eyes met again for confirmation. Raised eyebrows questioned her as he turned on the nitrogen and oxygen cylinders and checked gas flow rates through the rotometers and hoses. A faint hiss emanated from the masks.

Jac bent down and kissed her, "Well? I love you, Precious. Come back to me."

Carol stuck her tongue out at Jac. "You better be faithful to me while I'm away, Bubba."

Jac looked away and whispered a prayer, "God, please help us in this trial."

Again, a last look of questioning as he placed the nitrogen mask over Carol's face. No response—. She breathed normally and closed her eyes. In about a minute Carol began involuntary convulsions caused by suffocation. All three had to hold her to keep the mask on her face. Then it was over. She stopped as suddenly as she had begun, lying limp. The monitors indicated that her breathing and heart had stopped, but her brain still showed activity.

Throughout the termination, Meg had held Carol's hands, staring glassy eyed at her. Her sharp yelp, "Now!" made Soe and Jac snap up involuntarily.

"Okay, here we go." Jac jerked the nitrogen mask off, slapped the oxygen mask on her face and began pumping her chest with standard CPR technique. Standing upright, he struck her chest with the flat of his hand fortunately starting her heartbeat. He watched her chest to see if her breathing had started. It had not so he gave her resuscitation through her mouth and slapped the oxygen back on her face. She started breathing.

"Thank you, Lord," he gasped.

The EKG screen looked good so he turned to the EEG screen. It had never declined to flat line but Meg had indicated that it had reached the right point. Soe tapped on his computer and introduced his stimulation program. The screen quickly showed the Quark wave effect with the normal brain pattern superimposed. He left the stimulation on until Meg signaled stop.

The three watched Carol anxiously. All indications seemed normal, but she didn't wake up. Jac pulled back an eyelid. The pupil was dilated and staring into nothing.

"Well, she is alive. That's all I can say." Jac choked out and turned away with his hand to his mouth. *How in the name of God did I, did we get to this point? Is this the PVS stage? This is just idiocy. I'm not in control! Is Meg pulling some strings here?*

***

Steve and Tommy went to the coffee bar to get another cup. "Let's go to my cubbyhole, Tommy."

Tommy immediately began stressing how powerful this girl was.

"I was chained to this table and no one was around me. All of a sudden, my hands jerk up in the air and my head slams down between my arms three times. I could not stop it. I couldn't do anything." Tommy winced as he demonstrated with his hands. "She broke my nose and cut my head as you can see.

"Then she talked in my head and told me to report to Wilson. My head started screaming this Godawful high-pitched noise that varied in pulses with my heartbeat. When my heart beat faster the pulse increased. I knew my head would burst. Suddenly it stopped and I thanked God."

Tommy raised his hands to the air.

Steve watched Tommy as he sipped his coffee. "Tommy, Tommy, this is pretty far out, man."

Tommy held up his hand. "The worst was yet to come. I was on the freeway holding children and cars and trucks were smashing them against my body. I was covered in their blood. They all looked like my children!"

Tommy took a deep breath. "Last night we tried to capture the girl in the Mall. We shot her with a tranquilizer, but she got away. Steve, I don't want to go back and see her under any conditions."

Steve's face twisted into a conciliatory, supportive grin as he spread his hands. "That's one hell of a tale, Tommy. I know you believe it, but just think how improbable it is. They could have simulated all of that with electronics. The physical end could have been done with a wire to lift your hands. After the head banging, you don't know what happened. Hell, someone could have grabbed your head from behind."

Tommy sneered as bitter words spit out. "You dumb shit, you don't believe me, do you? You better get your head right when you go there. If this girl gets ahold of you, you will shit in your pants. I guarantee it."

Steve's weak laugh indicated he had some doubts. "Okay, okay, let's go over the rest of the case."

Tommy filled Steve in on the case from the beginning. "I suggest you get a copy of the file from records. But it doesn't even touch the part on what this girl can do, Steve."

Tommy sat back in his chair eyeing Steve as an unbeliever. *I hope this smartass gets caught and gets a taste of that woman!*

***

THE ENHANCERS

Inhaling large breaths through his generous nose, clinching his fists, Saul Friedman eyed his troops lined up in the garage. A rigor seemed to shake him as he paced back and forth. "What the hell you're telling me is in two minutes they neutralized the four guards in the car. Then they stole the car with Sammy and disappeared into nothing."

Butch Henry, the lead guard, tried to placate Saul as he held his hands palm up. "Mr. Friedman, we run into a truck at the gate. I was able to get out of the car and run to the corner. It was probably 4, maybe 6 minutes from the call when I could see down to the intersection. There was no limo, no nothing. The drive was blocked; we couldn't move the truck. The keys were gone, we were too blocked."

Saul threw up his hands and spun around on his heel. "If Sammy is hurt someone is going to pay." He whirled around and pointed to Butch. "You better get your ass out there and find Sammy and your friends, alive and well!" he screamed.

***

Saul stormed into the house and his office flipping open a codex file, snatching up the phone. "Eddie, this is Saul Friedman. I know you have been dealing with Sammy, but Sammy got his ass captured this morning by GrandJac. So I'm calling the shots. I want you to gut that Dr. Jac you work with, today, understand?"

The phone had awakened Eddie. He sat up in bed looking at the clock trying to get up to speed with Saul. "Ahhh, wait a minute, Mr. Friedman. Ahhh, what do you mean, Sammy was captured?"

Ol' Cochran came over here and kidnapped Sammy this morning." Saul shouted, waving his arms in frenzy. "But don't you worry about that. I want you to gut young Cochran today, you got that?"

Eddie stuttered, running his hand through his hair. "Gut—, gut him, you mean cut him with a knife?"

"Yeah," Saul shouted, "I want you to spill his guts. I want a bloody mess, so ol' man Cochran can see I'm playing hardball."

231

Eddie backpedaled quickly. "The only time I see him is in the hospital. You want me to cut him right there in the hospital? That's going to put me in a lot of view. I could get caught." Eddie pleaded, his voice quavering at a higher octave.

Saul picked up on the hesitation. "I don't know what Sammy's deal is with you, but I'll pay you $100,000 to cut that smart-ass Doctor. I want his guts on the floor, today. Understand?"

Eddie realized he might parlay this into a retirement package as he answered with assurance. "I can do that, Mr. Friedman. You'll read about it in the paper!"

Saul hung up and leaned back in his chair with his hands clasped behind his head and chin jutting out. *I'm going to get that shithead if it's the last thing I do.*

***

Snatching the phone again, he called Jacob Steinberg, his computer expert.

"Jacob, this is Saul. Did Sammy drop off some computer disks the other day with special instructions?"

Jacob was always very careful when he talked to Saul. He had a habit of laying traps for the unwary and springing them at very inappropriate times. He chose his words carefully.

"Yes sir, Mr. Friedman. He asked me to examine them and see what they contained. I did that and they have only machine language that is apparently directing another program or machine to do something. I can't do anything with them without knowing what the complete hook up was."

"That's it, Jacob? Nothing else has been done?" Saul asked with just a tiny lilt at the end.

Jacob could see a trap developing. "Mr. Friedman, Sammy was in a hurry and that's all he said. See what they were. I haven't been able to get in touch with Sammy to follow up. I've called twice for him, but he was out."

Saul shook his head in disgust. Sammy and his half-assed operation ran through his mind. "Well, here's the deal, Jacob. The computer apparently controlled signals from an EEG machine."

THE ENHANCERS

"What's an EEG machine, Mr. Friedman?" Jacob asked very carefully.

"That's an electro-encephalograph used to monitor the brain waves of a human." Saul stated with authority. "I'll call my doctor and we'll get something set up. Just wait a while." He finished, shaking his head and staring off into space.

***

Saul's call to Mory Abner, his doctor, hung on for 5 minutes.

Finally Mory answered the phone, carefully. "This is Dr. Abner, how may I help you?"

Saul recognized the soft pedal. "Cut the crap, Mory, this is Saul. I've got a really big deal here that might put you and me on top of the world."

"Oh?" replied Mory in his best doctor-patient voice. He knew Saul was up to some dirty work as usual.

"Come on Mory, listen to what I've got here." Saul demanded.

Saul outlined the history of the EEG machine signal development and the results with the girl in Marian.

"This girl can levitate objects, telecommunicate two ways at a distance, and has clairvoyance. She can read objects and look into the past. All of this is from computer stimulation of EEG signals of a human brain." Saul paused reviewing his sales pitch in his mind.

Mory answered carefully, very neutral. "None of what you are talking about is in the literature, Saul."

"I know that, God damn it. Listen to what I said." Saul spit back at Mory. "This research dick, Etheridge, over at Marian is doing it in his lab. He is on the cutting edge of new technology!"

"Okay, okay, I have the picture. Where do I come in, Saul?" Mory questioned carefully, trying to placate Saul.

"Well, I just happen to have the computer programs that control the EEG machine." Saul answered quietly, with a hint of smugness. "What I, I mean, what we need is an EEG machine hooked up to a human so we can test the programs and see if our human can develop ESP capabilities."

233

Mory caught the slip as he tossed the ball back, "That sure sounds dangerous. You, I, I mean we could harm a person's brain."

"Look Mory," Saul answered stridently, "I want this technology. I can put half a mil in your hands if we can take this program to fruition."

Mory coughed just loud enough to be effective. "Uhhh, that's a lot of money, Saul. There must be a lot at stake."

Saul spoke confidently. He could read the close. "Well, hell yes, Mory. There is a lot at stake. With this tool, I can, I mean we can control an empire with an iron hand. No one can fool us, trick us, lie to us, because we can read their minds, don't you see, Mory?"

Mory paused and offered a little bait. "I can get an intern at the hospital to scan a patient's brain with an EEG machine. Will that do it?"

"Hell no, I want an EEG machine in my lab with my computer and my technician and my doctor running tests on people!" Saul demanded, "That's half a million bucks, Mory."

Mory countered with a hint of demand in his voice. "If we can make it work, it'll be worth a lot more than that."

Saul knew he had hooked his fish. He asked carefully, "It might be, Mory. How much?" Saul smiled to himself, *that sly fish just got hooked.*

Mory hummed, "Ahhh, for one million, I'll get the EEG machine and we'll work in your lab. You supply the people and we'll do this at night. I can't let my practice suffer."

"Done," Saul declared enthusiastically, "let's start tonight here at my facilities, 7 PM."

Saul called Jacob, "Jacob, we're going to run some tests tonight at the lab with these computer disks at 7 PM. Be there."

***

The next call went to Butch, "This is Saul, give me an up-date on what you have found, Butch."

Butch put as much assurance as he could muster in his reply. "We found the trucks and the limo on the eastside of town, but no people, Mr. Friedman. They stole our trucks and used them to make the hit. That's ol' Cochran sure as Hell is hot."

Saul didn't even acknowledge the report. "Butch, I want you to pick up a couple of homeless on the streets. Clean them up and have them at the lab tonight at 7 PM. No drunks, got it?"

Butch almost sighed with relief in Saul's ear. He knew 'ol Saul was onto something else. "Sure do, Mr. Friedman. Do you want us to continue on this kidnapping?"

"No, let's wait for Cochran to make the next move." Saul answered sharply.

Saul thought to himself, *Ol' Jac will be jumping when he gets Junior's gutted body for supper!*

***

Jac choked back a sob as he looked over the two machines again, his mind racing. Her heart and pulse were okay. She was breathing. Her brain was normal. What else could he do? She was unconscious—, that's what it was! It was as if she had been KO'ed!

He turned to Meg, "What do you see?"

Meg stared into Carol's face. "She's doing fine, Jac. I think she needs some kind of stimulus to pull her out. Here, let me try to awaken her." Meg suggested, moving in.

She placed her hands on Carol's temples and stared into her face. She closed her eyes and bowed her head. For 30 seconds Meg concentrated and then she raised her head, smiling. "She's awake now." She stepped back to let Jac move in.

Carol's eyes fluttered open and the pupils focused. She looked into Jac's eyes and recognition showed. Jac bent down, kissed her and hugged her close. "You little squirrel. I'm so glad you pulled out. I sure wasn't looking forward to digging a hole to throw you in." Jac quipped.

"Will you stop fondling me in front of my friends, Doctor?" Carol demanded. "Get these things off me Soe. I know all you want to do is look at my breasts."

They all gave a sigh of relief and laughed. "She's okay, thank God."

Soe quickly pulled the various electrode contacts and leads off as Carol sat up, fastening her bra and buttoning her blouse.

Carol turned to Meg, "I know what you felt and saw in the light. It was an unbelievable experience. You don't want to leave. It's so warm, so comforting, so loving, so peaceful. It's really indescribable!"

She hugged herself, threw back her head, took a deep, deep breath and slowly sighed.

Jac couldn't stand it any longer. He stepped in and gathered her in his arms picking her up. "My little hussy made the big jump." Carol put her arms around Jac's neck and they kissed passionately.

Soe interrupted, "Don't drop your pants here, you guys. Let's see if Carol learned anything while she was away. I may want to get on the table now!"

Carol squirmed and Jac lowered her to the floor, steadying her, still holding her close. Meg's broad smile told what she was thinking.

Carol shouted. "Ah ha, you do think my tits are bigger than Meg's don't you, Soe?"

Soe turned beet red again. "Okay, okay, so what else can you do?" Soe's hair began to stand on end and flutter as if in a wind. He slowly floated up and over to Meg who grabbed him and the two floated around the room, slowly twirling.

Soe exclaimed. "Great, let's put the headset on you and give you the ability to amplify your strength."

They settled to the floor. Soe grabbed Meg's helmet and put it on Carol. He checked it for fit and fastened the chinstrap.

"You don't have to turn anything, Carol. You control the amplification with your telekinesis ability."

Soe was lifted back up and set down hard on the bench. "Whoa, girl, it's very sensitive."

Carol rose in the air and drifted around the room with her eyes closed. "I think I can do the same things Meg can do. I can feel the people who were here before us and I can read them. I can cull out all the extraneous emotions that try to pile up on you as they did the first time I tried it."

Soe leaned against the table with his arms folded across his chest sucking in a deep breath.

Carol interrupted him. "Don't even get started, Soe. Let's get a Coke. Man, I'm dry and I need the caffeine."

***

In the house, they picked a drink from the fridge.

Carol paused as she looked at the TV. "We need to turn on the TV."

As they walked in the living room, the TV lit up on the local channel.

A newscaster was giving full coverage to the Mayor and Police Chief's press conference on the solving of Sue Ellen's murder and other crime solutions.

When they got to the Enhancer question, Carol clapped her hands. "See, we made the news!"

The newscaster moved on to another local event, the attempted murder at the hospital. She gave the details that were released by the police. "A local hospital employee attempted to knife a local doctor at about noon. The attacker was arrested and the doctor was unhurt." No other details were available.

"C'mon," Soe demanded impatiently, "we've got some exploring to do." He spun around leading them to the lab.

Facing them, Soe took a deep breath. "I think your ESP capabilities are the result of the Quark energy you access in your brain. I don't have any idea how it works, but you have seen it on the amplified EEG screen. Somehow your brain can tap the energy form and you acquire ESP capability." Soe paced across the room while spinning on his heel, pointing. "You have trained your brain to do it routinely and the Enhancer helmet amplifies your powers.

"I think there is a difference between Atlantis and us though. I realize that Clark the psychic didn't describe everything in Atlantis, but he did cover the ESP capabilities in some detail."

Soe looked at them for a response. When he got none, he pointed to Meg. "Open the big door. Meg, I want you to put your helmet on and lift that pickup truck."

Meg obliged and with no visible effort lifted the truck.

"You see," Soe exclaimed jabbing his finger with eyes dancing, "I knew you could do it. You are controlling a source of energy that may be boundless!

"Remember when I asked you about knocking me down? I want you to try to shoot a bolt of power or whatever across the yard."

Filing outside in the dark back yard, Soe pointed to the 'back 40.' "Try in that direction."

Meg pointed her hand and a blinding white line of energy sprayed across the field, possibly 500 yards long. It lit up the sky like the sun.

"Cripes!" Soe exclaimed as they all stepped back shielding their eyes.

Soe fumbled. "Let me get a flashlight, I want to see what happened to the earth."

Meg held her hand high and a white light emanated from her fingers. It lit the whole area like day. Soe looked at the ground, there was a blackened streak about 4 feet wide tracing a straight line into the distance.

Carol was jumping up and down. "I want to try. Give me the helmet, Meg."

Meg loosened the chinstrap and handed the helmet to Carol. She quickly put it on and adjusted the strap to pull the electrodes in place.

"Is this the way you do it, Meg?" Carol held her hand up and white light seemed to fall from her fingers to the ground, dazzling the on-lookers. She moved her fingers slowly. The light flew across the field in waves. Where it struck the ground, dirt exploded like grenades popping.

Soe spoke very quietly. "Carol, let's shut down and go inside to discuss this."

Carol turned, floated towards the shop, a trail of light streaming from her hands. Landing there at the door, she unstrapped her helmet. A sigh of relief escaped from Soe.

Jac mused, standing outside as the others filed into the shop. *So this is the white power Grandpaw mentioned. Somehow, he knows what will happen, like it's already happened before. That's the déjà vu I've been experiencing. I must be wrapped up in it to the eyeballs, because no one else feels anything. At least, they claim they don't. But Soe knows. I'll bet Grandpaw pulled him in to be the actuator!*

Inside, Soe turned to the group taking a deep breath and sighing. "This power cannot be defined without major experimentation. It's beyond imagination. We can't let it loose on the world. We can't take a chance of it falling in the wrong hands. I don't think the people in Atlantis had this capability. I think the computer enhancement of your brain and the wave somehow enables, activates, releases, does something to this fantastic power." Soe spread his hands in resignation.

Carol held up her hand as if in a classroom. "If the story of Atlantis has any basis, maybe this is the power that blew them to hell! Do you think it has that much power?"

Soe paused, looking at each one. "Who's to say? We don't know. Don't dare test it. I think we need to—, ahh—. We must get my disks back from Friedman and the CIA. They may be able to implement something that will get them on the right track from my discs."

"Let's discuss this with Grandpaw." Jac suggested, eyeing Soe critically. "He might have some insights we don't have. If you remember, we talked about this phenomena being transferred to anyone. Remember that? It now appears to be possible. Also, NDE victims might be a logical choice. But apparently, anybody can get it. I agree with you. It must be shut down."

***

GrandJac sat by the fire sipping sour mash. "You missed supper again," he chided them. "Annie may have something she can heat up for you."

In a moment Meg had informed GrandJac of their latest accomplishment with Carol and the power they had experimented with.

GrandJac leaned back in his chair, setting his glass on the small table. "This does not surprise me for some reason. I have had a foreboding omen all day. I agree with you. This power must be suppressed. The world is not ready now and may never be ready. I only hope you can remain pure in heart and not unleash it on the world.

"The experiment with Carol supports my worst suspicions. This might be transported to most anyone. Initially, I thought these strange phenomena might be controlled, but I have lost faith. It is dangerous beyond our imagination.

"We need information about who has the disks." GrandJac added. "Let's go talk to our buddy, Sammy, first."

Jac stared hard at GrandJac. *Here it comes again. I've been here before. What the hell is it? GrandJac has the whole picture. Now he has admitted it. He thought he and Soe could control it just like Friedman and the CIA. Somehow, I'm an actuator. I'm being manipulated to reach a goal. I just don't, can't see what the déjà vu has or is in this ball of boogers.*

***

All five gathered in the interrogation room, waiting for Sammy. Morris brought Sammy, cuffing him to the table. Dapper little Sammy smiled confidently from the façade of his dark business suit and red power tie. The cut over his eye had closed successfully. He appeared in no pain from the gunshot wound to his side.

"Hi, Sammy." GrandJac announced cheerfully.

Sammy looked at the video camera smiling broadly. "I have trained my mind since the last time I was here. You won't read me this time!"

GrandJac sighed. "I am under the impression that you did not convince Saul to negotiate a truce. Now, I'm hearing that you are impenetrable. Shit, Sammy, you've outsmarted me again. I was hoping to get some information about the disks that you stole from the lab. What did you do with them, Sammy?"

Sammy laughed. "You can't make me think of those things GrandJac. I've trained my mind."

Meg and Carol laughed. "This poor sap is a push over. We've swept him to his childhood."

GrandJac answered stridently, " Damn it, Sammy, you're too much for me. Morris, shoot him in the gut with a .357 dumdum. Don't hit his spine, now. I want Sammy to enjoy all of it. He's of no use to us. He's just so smart."

Morris stepped forward as two men jerked Sammy to his feet and stood beside him.

One of the men pleaded. "Morris, don't blow his guts on me. This is a new shirt."

Sammy jerked on the chains whimpering. "Wait a minute, for God's sake! GrandJac, let's talk about this."

Morris pulled his gun out of his coat and pointed it directly at Sammy's gut. Wham, it went off. Fire shot three feet from the barrel accompanied with an ear-shattering bang.

Sammy crumpled to the chair, twitching and blubbering. He feebly pawed at his stomach. Then lifted his hand. Surprised, there was no blood. He straightened up, gasping. Looking down, he could see a blackened area where the powder burns had hit him.

Sammy blubbered, trying to reach his nose and wipe it. "Please, GrandJac. Get this maniac out of here. I'll tell you whatever you want to know."

"Sammy, we know the first word you ever said. You are pathetic." GrandJac intoned like a death knell.

GrandJac continued as a judge might read a rap sheet. "Sammy, let's review your most recent history. Breaking and entering, bugging, theft, poison of a human being, bribery to commit murder, bribery to commit murder, bribery to commit murder, and then there's Eddie Broussard. A likable person, but weak. You bought his soul so you could use him against Jac or whoever when the time came. Look at the lives you have ruined. What have you done to redeem yourself?"

Sammy glared at the video camera. "You asshole. I would love to kill you, you ol' fart. You should have died years ago. I'll kill you in a heartbeat if I get a chance."

GrandJac replied. "You'll get your chance, Sammy, real soon. Use your brilliant skills. Carol put it succinctly, 'When in Rome, do as the Romans do.' Goodbye, Sammy."

***

Morris and the two men uncuffed Sammy from the table, stood him up, recuffed him and led him out the door.

THE ENHANCERS

One of the four door pickup trucks out front stood by as they loaded and drove off.

"What is this, the last ride? You takin me out to kill me? Sammy sat up in the seat, hunching forward, deflated. "What's your name, mister?

"Morris, my name is Morris, Sammy."

Sammy smiled in the dim light. "Well, Morris, I know that old GrandJac has taken care of you. But you haven't been taken care of like I can take care of you. Morris, I'm prepared to put one million dollars in your hands and one million dollars in your buddies hands if you will take me to Dallas and let me go."

Morris looked sharply at Sammy. " Wow, that's three million dollars, Sammy. You got that kind of money?"

"I can get it in the morning, Morris. Cash in any form you want or I can put it in a bank of your choice. Where are we going, anyway?" Sammy asked expectantly.

"Hell, Sammy, we're going to Dallas."

"Okay, Morris, you're my kind of man!" Sammy exclaimed delightedly.

Sammy and Morris made small talk for a while. Finally Sammy fell asleep on the long trip to Dallas.

***

The door Sammy leaned against opened awakening him. The night was pitch dark. Multiple layers of stars could be seen through the canopy of trees. The truck seemed to be parked at some kind of gate on a high chain link fence. A sign read, "Deliveries, 8 to 4." Buildings inside the gate lined a paved road.

Sammy pleaded, getting a sick feeling in his stomach. "Where are we? What are we doing here? I want you to let me off at my home, Morris."

Morris said with an air of finality. "Well pardner, this IS home to a lot of things, but it's just not your home. However, I'm sure you will feel at home!"

One of the men took a large bolt cutter from the back and cut the chain holding the gate closed. They swung it in driving in with lights out. The truck moved slowly along a paved road that seemed to be behind chain link enclosures and small buildings.

Cameron slowed to a stop. "This is it. This is the backside where the caretakers work from."

Sammy was pulled out of the truck and his handcuffs were removed. Morris put on a helmet with nightvision glasses that folded down over the eyes. Hanging on the chain link fence fingers laced through the wire, he looked the area inside over very carefully.

It contained a concrete block building to the right and kind of rolling terrain with trees and what looked like a moat on the far side. The moat shouldered up to a high stonewall that had a fence and railings on top.

One of the men was busy picking the lock on the gate in the fence that opened into the field behind and beside the building. A second gate led down a fenced hallway to the block building. Sammy couldn't see much of anything. The only light was the reflection of city lights from the sky and faint starlight.

"What's that smell?" Sammy asked as he sniffed the air. "Are we at some kind of animal pen or at the slaughter house? It stinks."

Morris continued to hold on to Sammy's arm as he retrieved a flashlight from the truck. He walked Sammy over to the gate. Cameron stationed himself at the gate with a rifle.

Sammy could see enough to realize something crazy was going on. He turned to Morris, demanding. "What the hell is going on here, Morris? I thought we had a deal?"

Morris replied, assuredly. "Hell, Sammy, we do have a deal. I want you to remember the words, 'When in Rome, do as the Romans do.' That's 2000 years ago to be accurate. Now, here's the plan. You see that tree over there where I'm shining my light?"

"Yeah, yeah, I see it, so what?" Sammy spit out. "Well, this here is the lion cage at the Dallas Zoo. Now isn't that where you wanted to go, Sammy? Home in Dallas?

"Remember the Christians and the Romans and the lions and the coliseum back in Rome 2000 years ago?" Morris prompted as he leaned over into Sammy's face. "Well, Sammy, this time you're not up in the stadium. You're not of the ruling class. You're not up there with Cassius. You are a performer. That's why that tree is so important."

Sammy gagged out. "Awww——, Gawddamn, man, that's not fair. I don't have a chance."

"Yes, you do, Sammy. I'm going to give you a running start for the tree. If any lions spot you before you get there, Cameron will shoot them with the tranquilizer gun so you can make the tree. Ready, set, go!" Morris shouted as he pushed Sammy through the gate into the compound.

Sammy stumbled, fell to the ground, but he got up scrambling and clawing as he sprinted for the tree. He was halfway there when a lion came out of the blockhouse and spotted him. The lion charged across the ground with a loud roar. Sammy screamed, redoubling his efforts. The lion, a female hunter, was amazingly swift and would have caught Sammy if Cameron hadn't shot the tranquilizer gun. The lion stumbled and almost got Sammy as he was clawing his way up the tree. The lion fell to the ground at the base of the tree, twitching, trying to get up.

Morris motioned for the men to get in the truck. They closed the gates and turned the truck around. As they were driving back to the entrance gate, more lions came out of the blockhouse and ran over to the tree.

They could hear Sammy screaming. "Don't leave me here. We had a deal. Come back, come back!"

**

Steve Brownlee read the file on the Etheridge case and reviewed his conversation with Tommy Silva and Wilson. Then he drove to Marian. A city map acquired at a convenience store provided the town layout. The Wal-Mart parking lot provided light to read by. The radio spit out the 6 o'clock news in a Texas drawl. It appeared like the local police had solved four major crimes with the help of the Enhancers. The station played up the mystery of who or what the Enhancers were.

Steve snorted. *I wonder who the fuck the Enhancers are? Probably some gang getting even. Hell, I'll just drive out FM 1495 and look at Cochran's place. I won't stop because of what happened to Tommy.*

On the way, he stopped in at a diner and had supper. He overheard a conversation about the capture of the Sue Ellen killer.

"I'll bet that bastard is the one who has been killing the teenage girls around here." One voice stated emphatically.

"I sure hope so. If it is, he needs to be tortured to death." Another voice stated.

Steve smiled at the comments, *mob rule. I wonder if he's got the balls to do the torturing?*

Steve turned to the talker. "Hey, I hear they're drawing lots to see who gets to torture the criminal to death. You gonna get in it? Sounds like a good deal to me, Buddy."

Steve turned back to finishing his supper. Every once in a while he'd eye the talker to see if he'd make eye contact. "Hey man, good luck on the draw." Steve waved as he left the diner. It was very quiet at that table.

He drove by the college, the motel where the CIA had a perpetual room and on to FM 1495. As he was driving through a long sweeping turn, a blinding white light streaked across the prairie into the distance. In the glare, he could see buildings and the ranch house.

"Good lord, what the hell was that?" Steve muttered, eyes trying to adjust.

Slowing the car, he watched the buildings. In a minute, the area was lit up with another white light behind the same building. Steve watched fascinated.

They must have some kind of rocket they're launching.

He put the car in gear and was easing ahead when another weird light phenomena occurred. The light seemed to dance up and down across the prairie in graceful trails and finally disappeared. Every time it touched the ground, a cloud of dust flew up illuminated in the light. He could hear popping like firecrackers or gunshots coming from the site. No, it was a deeper pop. Maybe like a shotgun in the distance.

Steve eased on down the road, watching the ranch house and buildings. About a mile past the facility, FM 1495 teed into FM 1046 that went back to town. Steve turned right and drove towards town. His map showed a dirt road that turned to the right, so he took it and drove about half a mile to the top of a hill. He could overlook the ranch with binoculars easily.

Popping the trunk, he retrieved his nightvision glasses, the latest technology. Steve really enjoyed spying at night with them. Light amplification was 50,000 times and they had 8 to 20-zoom magnification.

Positioning the car so that he could look through the right window and be comfortable, Steve rolled down the window and settled in to watch the ranch. A cold night wind swept through the car, he zipped his coat. Sweeping the area from left to right he was surprised to see a pickup truck parked about two hundred yards on either side of the complex towards the fence. He adjusted the 20-power zoom and zeroed in on the truck to the right. He looked right into the cab. He jerked back. A man was watching him with binoculars!

What the hell! These guys maintain night surveillance. No wonder Tommy was caught. Well, I guess we'll just sit here and look at each other!

Panning the buildings, he picked up activity at the building on the left, so he zeroed in on it. Three men came around the corner with a fourth who looked like his hands were tied behind his back. The captor jerked him along as he stumbled. Steve zoomed in. He could see the prisoner wore a suit and the guards wore cowboy outfits, boots, hats, blue jean jackets. They put the suit man in the back of the dual cab pickup and one man got in with him, the other two got in front. One had a small bag and a rifle with him. Steve read the license plate and noted it in his mind. The truck started up, lights came on and it pulled out to the road turning right towards town.

Steve mused to himself, *That just might be Sammy Friedman. I better follow them.*

Steve swung the glasses back to the ranch house and saw more people come out of the building on the left. He zoomed in again. Five people stood quietly looking out towards the front while one pointed. One of them had a helmet on, it appeared. Three were in dark coats that hung to the ground. *Man, I sure do like these glasses. I can see the buttons on that 'ol boy's coat!*

The helmet person raised his arm and pointed in his general direction. White light leaped out in a streamer across the prairie, blinding Steve. He snatched down the glasses and tried to focus in the intense white light that seemed to extend from the people to and around him. The top of the hill lit up like a magnesium flare was hovering overhead.

Steve felt something in his head. No, it was in his mind. He clawed at his head frantically! The noise was deafening. It pulsed with his heartbeat. Panting, gasping, he clawed at the door handle to get out of the car. He found he couldn't control his muscles. His mind mercifully blanked out as he collapsed in the front seat.

Steve woke up hanging over the wheel of the car at his motel room the next morning. The sun beamed into his eyes over the roof. *What tha hell. I can't remember what happened last night. What did Tommy say?*

***

Saul got his usual 6 PM call from his trucking manager, Bo, in Marian concerning any news in town. He listened carefully to the report about the crime solving, Enhancer deal. He slammed his fist down on his desk when Bo told him about the attempted murder at the hospital.

Saul hung up the phone, screaming. "Shit, can't anybody do anything right today?"

He stormed into the kitchen, yelling. "Sheila, make me a sandwich. Chicken or something. I'm leaving."

His wife asked timidly from the door. "Saul, have you seen or heard from Sammy today? He normally is here or he calls in if he won't be home for supper."

Saul spun around, barking, waving his hand. "Sammy won't be home tonight, maybe tomorrow."

He grabbed the sandwich and napkin Sheila offered, glared at the two women, and stomped to the garage.

There, Butch met him. "Mr. Friedman, we have two men at the warehouse lab."

"Good, let's go there now.

Is that the hole they drilled in the windshield and gassed our boys, Butch?" Saul asked with curiosity.

"Yes, the car is unhurt in any other way." Butch answered carefully.

"Well, how the hell did they get in the car with the doors locked?"

Butch shrugged his shoulders. "Hell, it's a General Motors. It's one of the easiest to break into or steal. They may have used somebody's key."

"Okay, okay, let's go to the lab." Saul snarled.

Butch called three more men to the car as they drove out.

***

Following standard procedure, Butch pushed a door actuator and watched the triple door swing up. He eased the car into a large warehouse building signaling the big door to close behind them. Offices, living quarters and a lab for a variety of activities, both chemical and electronic lined the walls.

Saul looked his men over. "Ya'll stay in the office. Bring in one of the bums when I call you."

Jacob was already in the lab with a computer.

Saul looked around for Mory. "The Doc isn't here, yet, huh?" he asked bluntly.

Jacob nodded carefully. "No. Do you know how the EEG was connected to the computer, Mr. Friedman?"

Saul scowled. "I don't know anything about the setup. But I do have some tapes of their conversations. Maybe that will help."

Saul opened his briefcase retrieving several cassette tapes. He handed them to Jacob. Jacob plugged one in a tape player and listened to the conversations. He fast forwarded through blank spots and put another in the machine.

Saul glanced at the wall clock, 7:30 PM and Mory hadn't shown. Saul's scowl deepened as he paced about mumbling to himself.

Mory came in 45 minutes late with EEG equipment, leads and a recorder. He held up his hand. "Don't say it, Saul. I have to work for a living."

Jacob looked over the equipment and found he could plug the recorder into a monitor. He ran the signal through the computer to his monitor.

"I'm ready, Mr. Friedman."

Mory asked with raised eyebrows. "Who are the patients?"

Saul opened a door and called. "Butch, bring in the first one."

A rather seedy looking man came in with Butch holding his arm as if to steady him. The wash and shave did a lot to clean him up. The Salvation Army clothes fit like a scarecrow.

"This is Benny. He gets $50 for the test." Butch smiled as he gave Benny a $50 bill and went back to the office.

Mory approached Benny, sighing, nodding, trying to assume his bedside manner. "Okay, Saul, this is our man, okay?" Turning to Benny, "There is nothing to be concerned about, Benny. I'm going to attach a few signal leads to you and monitor your brain with an EEG machine. It won't hurt you. You will feel no pain. Please sit in the chair and be calm."

Benny sat down in the armchair staring apprehensively at Mory as he placed the electrode pads on his head and taped some to keep them in place. Mory smiled, patting Benny on the arm.

"Don't fret, Benny, it's all okay."

Clutching the fifty seemed to soothe him somewhat.

Mory smiled at Benny again as he turned on the EEG machine. Jacob keyed in the computer. A brain wave pattern appeared on the screen. Jacob pushed one of the pirated disks into a slot on the machine and keyed enter. A second waveform appeared in conjunction with the normal pattern.

"What's that?" Jacob asked.

"I don't know." Mory answered as he stared at it curiously.

Jacob hit the up key. The signal increased slightly.

Saul pointed to a drink can on the bench. "Get the can, Benny."

Benny laughed. "Hell man, I can't reach that with all this crap on me."

"Try anyway." Saul demanded.

Benny reached out. The can leaped into his hand. "Shit, did you see that?" Benny shouted.

He released the can and it floated in the air. Benny raised his hand and the can moved upward.

Saul shouted. "We've got it, by God! Let's try something else. Benny, try to lift that chair over there."

Benny extended his hand towards the chair, but nothing happened.

"Kick the power, Jacob." Saul ordered as he kept his eyes glued on Benny.

Jacob held the up button and watched the screen. The carrier wave became sharper and denser.

Benny's eyes sparkled as he looked at Saul, then Mory, then Jacob. "Ha, ha, I can see what you are thinking. This thing is worth a hell of a lot more money than any $50 bucks!"

Saul indicated to Jacob with his finger. "Jack it up some more."

Benny screamed slapping his head. Mory and Jacob grabbed his arms and held them to the chair.

"Don't do that, Benny. You'll tear the electrodes off."

Benny was thrashing around in the chair, yelling. "Get away from me! Get away from me!"

Saul went to the computer and held the up button. Benny screamed once and collapsed. Mory quickly checked his pulse in his neck.

"His heart stopped." Mory looked at the screen, his brainwaves were slowly declining. "Oh my lord, Saul. You killed him!"

Saul pushed the down button and the screen declined to only the EEG straight lines.

"We needed to know the upper limits, Mory." Saul stated matter of factly as he stared at Mory with no sign of emotion.

"Jacob, somehow we need a measurement of power when you push the up and down button. Got any ideas?"

Both Jacob and Mory looked at each other and then at Saul. "Do you realize you just killed a person, Saul?" Mory asked.

Saul waved his hand as if warding off a bug. "Aw hell, Butch got him off the street. He was a derelict. He'd be dead in a year at the outside. We've got one more. I'll get Butch to move this one and we can fine-tune this program on the second one."

He turned to the door and yelled for Butch.

Butch came in scanning the scene quickly. Saul motioned for him to take the body away.

"Mory, pull the damned electrodes so we can get going. We could finish this thing tonight." Saul demanded.

Mory pulled all the leads and contact pads. Butch picked up the body and walked into the large warehouse area.

Saul yelled after him. "Bring in the next one."

Mory mumbled, shaking his head. "I won't be a part of it, I won't be a part of it."

Saul laughed scornfully. "Yes you will, Mory. Look up on the wall."

Jacob and Mory looked up and saw a closed circuit TV camera aimed at them.

"Both of you are accessories to the event. It's being recorded so let's get with it." Saul demanded sarcastically.

Butch came in with a black derelict. He looked pretty good cleaned up.

"This is Ralph and here's your $50 bucks, Ralph. Sit in this chair."

Ralph panned the shop. "Where is Benny?"

Waving his hand, Butch answered casually. "Oh, he's already taken his $50 and left. He did good."

Mory went through the same procedure with him and connected the electrodes and wires. Jacob tapped in numbers this time and the carrier wave appeared.

"That's great, Jacob. We may have a handle on this thing after all." Saul applauded. "Go up two units." Saul turned to Ralph. "We're testing for telekinesis, Ralph. See if you can grab that can over there. Just extend your arm towards it." Instantly the can jumped in Ralph's hand. "That's great, Ralph. Jacob, two more." Saul ordered as he rubbed his hands and watched Ralph intently. Ralph lifted the chair and himself off the floor and hovered.

"Mr. Friedman, you really need a man like me. One hundred grand will turn the trick." Ralph offered and grinned at Saul.

"Two more, Jacob." Saul grinned. "We just might have a deal, Ralph."

Ralph closed his eyes as he floated and turned to Saul. "Mr. Friedman, that was a terrible thing you did to Benny. You know, I can see deep into your past. You are one bad dude!"

Ralph's smile disappeared. "You are very rich, Saul. I believe I'll up the ante to half a million."

Saul ignored Ralph. "Up four units, Jacob."

Jacob tried to key in the numbers, but he couldn't get his hands to the computer. They seemed to be hitting an invisible wall.

The computer clicked by itself. Ralph smiled from 5 feet off the floor. "You see, Saul, I had an OD experience on crack a while back and was DOA at the County hospital. But somehow I pulled through. I may be something like the girl in Marian, you know, Saul?" Ralph suggested as he tapped Saul on the head from above.

The chair settled to the floor. "How much you got on you right now, Saul baby?" Ralph leered at Saul.

Saul stepped back and tried to call Butch. All that came out was a whisper.

"Saul," Ralph whispered. "Gimme your green. You, Doc, gimme your green." Ralph held out his hand.

Saul sneered. "Kiss my ass. I'll unplug you."

Saul hit the floor on his face, hard. His head bounced twice more. He looked up, gagging. Blood poured from his nose and cuts on his cheekbone and eyebrow. He slowly raised himself to his hands and knees with his head hanging down, gasping through his mouth.

"Doc, are you next?" Ralph asked nonchalantly.

Mory jammed his hand in his pocket jerking his money clip out. "That's it, Ralph."

Jacob's lip quivered. "All I've got is five dollars, Ralph. Here, you can have it."

"Saul baby, come on. Stand up here. Let's see you." Ralph cooed.

Slowly, Saul floated upright landing on his feet. He stared in a daze as he wiped the blood away from his nose and mouth with his coat sleeve.

"You look awful, Saul. You better have the Doc look after you." Ralph admonished.

Saul's money clip floated out of his pocket and into Ralph's hand.

Ralph turned to the metal building wall and pointed his arm. White fire erupted from his fingers and streaked through the wall blowing a large hole into the street. Ralph reached up, stripped off the electrodes and walked out as Butch ran through the door.

Saul snapped back to the present. Holding up his hand, waving, gasping. "Wait, Butch, we need Ralph." Saul called after Ralph. "Ahhh, hey Ralph, ahhh, come back Ralph. There's a hell of a lot more money than what you got there."

Ralph smirked as he looked over his shoulder. "I'll get back to you, Saul. I have several important things I need to do first. Saul, baby, you have given me a new life!"

Blood ran into Saul's mouth making him conscious of his battered face. Pulling his handkerchief, he carefully dabbed at his nose as his eyes roved the group. "Did you see what he did? Great balls ah fire, this thing is a hell of lot more powerful than I imagined! He just pointed and blew a hole through the wall like dynamite or a cutting torch. Mory, do you see what this thing is? It is power beyond our imagination. This is fantastic! We must get Ralph back in here!

"Butch, you have to keep Ralph in sight. We have a lot more experimenting to do."

"Yes sir, Mr. Friedman." Butch acknowledged signaling his hands to follow.

Brandy nudged Butch. "Man oh man, could we use some of that stuff. Knowin 'ol Saul, we'll get it, too. We are gonna be the big dog on the street, wow!"

Mory gaped, pointing at the wall. "I don't believe it, Saul. You really were telling the truth. Here, you better let me look at your face. I'll get my bag."

Jacob's face twisted in a sour scowl. "He took my last five dollars, I'm broke."

"Forget that shit, Jacob. I'll give your money back. We have a program here that's fantastic and you're part of it! Money is going to fall out of the sky!"

THE ENHANCERS

SATURDAY DECEMBER 24TH

The morning paper was an exclusive. Huge headlines: ENHANCERS SOLVE SERIAL KILLER CRIME GIVE CHRISTMAS PRESENT TO POLICE. The story gave almost verbatim details Hartzog had gleaned from Jessica.

Police Chief Thurmond stormed into the station. "How in the hell did the paper get this story? I want an immediate staff meeting!"

Glaring at his department heads, he yelled, pointing at each one. "Who leaked the story? Who? You better tell me. When I find out, he's gonna be shit on ah shingle!"

No one said a word.

Calls were coming in from wire services and Police Departments from other towns. Chief Thurmond had to release something to the press and he had no way of getting in touch with the Enhancers. The prosecuting attorney was concerned that the evidence might be compromised in some way.

Chief Thurmond screamed. "This is a cluster fuck. Find the Enhancers!"

***

In Dallas, a late breaking story on the radio and TV created wide news. The local zoo caretakers found a man in the lion cage. Using tranquilizers, the cats were put under control. It had been a night of ecstasy for them. The ground and the lower tree bark gave a vivid picture of the romping, clawing excitement of the night. The news media and the ambulance arrived together, so the world benefited from close-up shots of the recovery. Initial shots of the shredded clothing, bloodied legs and crotch made the 7 O'clock news, but pressures forced that scene to be cut in later editions. Mt. Sinai Hospital listed him as critical in intensive care. Identity following notification of next of kin. Standard fare, but that lasted until the 8 AM release. Sammy Friedman, son of a local business tycoon followed. As usual, officials have the event under 'investigation.'

The media enjoyed another opportunity to embarrass police and bank officials. "We are baffled as to how a thief could burn a hole in an autoteller machine and rob it without being caught. In fact, the thief robbed five teller machines in the same way cutting through stainless steel paneling and not burning the money. Apparently he was able to compromise the alarm systems, because none alarmed. These stations were out in the open. No witnesses. It is under 'investigation.'"

***

Ralph Lofton woke up with a hard headache from drinking. Woozy thoughts drifted back to last night, *Wow, what a party!* He had left the warehouse and walked down the street. *What in hell is this power?*

A man was getting in his car at the curb and Ralph approached him. "Give me your car." He said casually.

The man stepped out of the way, gave Ralph the car keys and walked off. "Thank you, my man. Nice ride! Liquor store, here I come." Saul's clip paid for all of it. "I like this life style.

"Let's see what the brothers and sisters are doing." Gathering a tribe, he delivered them to his flophouse pad for serious partying. By 1 AM, all were pretty drunk and Ralph had given all his money to his friends.

Clawing his way vertical, Ralph gasped, almost puking. "Ahhh——, hey man. I'm outta money. I'll be back with some more."

Ralph cruised around town searching, spotted an ATM (autoteller machine). *That's it*, and pulled up beside it. It was no effort to burn a hole in the stainless steel cabinet and burn through the wiring to kill the alarm. That was so easy, he decided to clean out everyone he could find. After four more, he found that he couldn't burn through the steel housing anymore.

Hey man, I got to go back and see my buddy, Friedman. He returned to his flophouse and continued drinking until he passed out.

***

Gathered in the family room, Soe, Jac and the girls watched the news intently.

Soe waved his hand at the TV, snorting. "That's a classic example of what I told you the other day. The police can't keep any information secret. I'm surprised they don't have it footnoted, 'on condition of anonymity.'"

GrandJac stood, hands on hips as he watched the news with a sour sneer. "Well, you're now public, Enhancers. Make your plans. I suggest you get the computer disks from the CIA and Saul. He's been able to enhance someone in Dallas. It's just stupid to use such a tool to rob teller machines. There's no money there and the exposure is too great. I don't think Saul is stupid. This can't be his doing. His guinea pig did this, somehow."

Soe interjected, glancing at GrandJac. "Let's go to the lab. I've got to make a helmet for Carol and we do need to think this through."

Jac stayed with grandpa, indicating he would like to talk. "Yes." GrandJac sadly nodded agreement.

"Son, you are at a crossroads, and not a short term one either. If you continue your medical career, you are going to have to divorce yourself from these goings on. Secondly, you are the sole survivor to the Cochran family and it will need your attention. More and more as time goes on.

"I'll admit that I influenced you to get a MD, ME and EE degrees. There is a method to my madness and I'm not through."

GrandJac leaned forward in his chair and stared straight into Jac's eyes. "This will be the strangest demand that I place upon you, son, depending upon the outcome of near future events." GrandJac continued, holding his hands between his legs. "It may become imperative that you go in the service. The Marine Corps."

"For crap's sake, Grandpa. Why should I do that?" Jac asked startled. Jac stared at his grandfather, at the strange twist to his face. "We are not at war nor is there a need for men in the military. They are cutting back in all of the services."

"That's absolutely true, son. But I have an insight into the future that I cannot tell you about." GrandJac stared back at Jac watching the disbelief on his face.

"In about two years, your mission may come about. As I said, depending upon near time future events." GrandJac spread his hands, "Here are the alternatives. Be a doctor and get out of this Enhancer scenario. Get involved in the business and give up doctoring and Enhancers. Join the Enhancers, give up doctoring and maybe the business, depending on events to transpire. Join the Marine Corp in the next few months, give up doctoring, give up the business and give up the Enhancers."

Jac watched his last of kin and tried to read something behind the deepset eyes. "Just how much of the future can you see, Grandpaw? The other day you mentioned the white firepower. You already knew of it, didn't you?"

GrandJac spread his hands. His expressionless face said nothing.

"Well, those are poor alternatives. I want to continue to be a doctor and I want to stay involved with the Enhancers. The strangest thing is a continuing feeling of déjà vu. You may be able to see the future. Why don't you tell me what you see? I must be a part of it. Somehow, I feel I've been here before. It's very strange—, weird."

GrandJac paused, then, smiled for the first time. "Yes, that doesn't surprise me at all. Take my advice, play out the Enhancers, give up doctoring and business, short term. It doesn't make sense now, but it just might real soon. That's all I can say, son."

Jac dropped his head for a moment, then met his eye. "Grandpa, I seem to be floating in and out of this crazy deal with these déjà vu feelings. It's almost like it revolves around me. Meg comes here dead and I revive her. I call Soe and he revives her brain. Soe drops cryptic comments about me and the future, then you do the same. Carol becomes one of 'them' with my help. Now you tell me that for the future possibles, I must be a Marine. You even admit you influenced me towards engineering and medicine. You and Soe know the future about me. What is it?"

GrandJac paused again, then spoke with emphasis looking off to the side. "Get a leave of absence from MCH and follow the Enhancers. Do it today."

GrandJac patted Jac on the back as both stood. "Go to it with God speed."

Stumbling through the door, Jac mulled over the conversation.

The light at the end of the tunnel is very near came to GrandJac's mind as he stared into the next leg to the future.

***

Down cast, eyes glowering, Jac moved into the lab with his feelings on his sleeve. Carol already could read Jac's body English. She came over, pulled him down and kissed him.

"Come on hunk, get with the program. You never got your uniform. We need to get it today."

Jac hugged her, pulled her in close. He could feel her breasts pressed against him. "You are my Sweetiepie, my rock, Pixie." He whispered as he kissed her again. He paused, staring off into space. "I just had a very enlightening conversation with Grandpaw!"

Soe hunched over the workbench putting the finishing touches on Carol's helmet.

He looked up. "She's right, Jac. We can get it this morning."

Jac countered. "We better do it this morning. Shopping is going to be a mad house. This is Christmas Eve." *What tha hell, I guess it'll sort itself out——, I hope.*

The aching pain of wanting to be a part of a family, his family, welled up in him. "Since we haven't had time to think of Christmas or even be aware of it, I took it upon myself to get each of you a small present. I think of you as my family. I never had a brother or sister. I was an only child. So here, and Merry Christmas!" He handed each one a small wrapped package.

"You are absolutely right, Jac baby. I clean forgot about it. I was so enthralled with the Enhancer deals." Soe declared with a big grin. "What's the present?"

259

Paper shredded as they all tore open their gifts. "Oh, I love it," Carol screamed, "You knew what I wanted."

She waved a Snickers candy bar high in the air.

Jac admitted. "I gave it some serious thought. But what the hell, go all the way. I got it from the kitchen cabinet, gang."

Finally a little real relaxation, an easing of tensions. Jac could feel it from the big laughs.

"You see, you are my Sweetiepies!"

Carol and Meg hugged Jac and Soe shook his hand patting him on the back.

They said in a chorus, hands in the air. "Jac, we are your family and you are ours, 'One for all and all for one'"

Jac held up his hand, doing his best to control his emotions and remain analytical. "Thank you——, let me finish telling you about Grandpa's comments. He thinks this Enhancer thing is going to become a full time job. I agree with him. So I am going to get a leave of absence from MCH."

Carol and Meg studied Jac's face for a moment too long. Soe stood stonefaced, staring at Jac.

"I believe you are right." Meg finally said.

"I just picked up an unusual thought from him before you came in. 'The light at the end of the tunnel is very near.' He continues to surprise me. It is as if he has a window into the future."

"I certainly agree with you, Meg. We just had a conversation in that direction. Did you pick up the other day on GrandJac's remark about white power? I asked him and he ignored me."

Soe quickly interrupted as he turned to Meg. "You know, that poses an interesting idea, Meg. You have never indicated any future clairvoyance capabilities. Can you see into the future?"

"I can see nothing. Maybe I don't know how." Meg shrugged.

Soe waved his hand in dismissal. "A project for the future. We must address today's pressing problems."

Assuming the role of the general, Soe sat in a swivel chair and leaned back. "Let's make plans to get the disks. We know that

THE ENHANCERS

Wilson Williams at DEA headquarters in Dallas has a lab and they have the disk copies. We know that his lab tech is named Salvador. We also know that Friedman has the disks in Dallas, but we don't know where. Looks like a trip to Dallas is in order. Any ideas?" Soe asked scanning the gang.

Carol proposed. "Do we want to take Morris and Duncan as bodyguards?"

Jac interjected, as he reviewed Carol's thought. *She can cut to bone on any subject. She's sharp.* "I think we ought to go as the Enhancers. If necessary we can blank their minds. I don't think Morris and Duncan can help unless we get in a brawl. We sure don't want any shooting. Also, we want an inconspicuous car such as a pickup truck."

"Maybe change the license plates, too." Meg suggested.

"Sounds good." Soe agreed. "Let's get your outfit today and go."

Carol leaned forward. "Why don't we take Steve? He can front for us."

"Hey, that's a good idea. We'll get our buddy, Steve." Meg laughed. "Christmas Eve is a poor time." Meg remarked. "The office will probably close at noon."

Jac grinned at his family. "I don't have to go to work today. So let's go play. It's Christmas holidays!"

Carol called her parents, yelling excitedly. "I got a man!" She bragged. "Found him here in a hospital. Tell y'all about it soon. Merry Christmas, bye."

Soe called his mother, wished her a Merry Christmas and apologized for not sending a card. "I'll come see you in January."

Jac yelled. "Hey gang, let's go to the back forty and explore some of the girl's capabilities."

***

A pattern follows each Norther, it seems. Beautiful clear blue skies, crispness in the air with low humidity, maybe 55 degrees descends upon the land. The Enhancer outfits felt good absorbing the heat from the sun.

"Soe has stated that the people in Atlantis could fly." Jac pointed out. "Let's try it."

Carol, always the happy little extravert, jumped out of the truck and floated up in the air. Then turning she moved forward like Superman with her coat flapping in the wind. Suddenly Jac was flying beside her. Meg and Soe joined them flying and floating over the pastureland for hours. Up in the air to 500 feet and diving back down, it was exhilarating beyond description.

Telepathy provided an intimate form of communication far beyond words. Frankness and trust seemed to be an intimate part of telepathy. Personal feelings, fears, wants, and desires were easily understood. When they finally settled to the truck and drove to the ranch house, they were almost one person. It was an exulting and gratifying experience. Even Soe relaxed a little and let them peek into his mind on casual subjects, at least.

***

The evening news on TV indicated that Chief Thurmond was very interested in getting in contact with the Enhancers.

In an interview by the media, "I, we, ahh—, we must get in touch with the Enhancers. We have many inquiries concerning the capabilities of the Enhancers."

The local paper, The Marian Clarion, continued to milk the police scene regarding the Enhancer contributions.

The tight knit Cochran family gathered in the den after supper Christmas Eve.

Meg broached the subject again. "We really could be a factor in law enforcement. See, the little bit the world has seen in the news has whetted their appetite."

Carol blurted. "I like Morris's summation, 'When the hosses see it and want it, they'll just come and get it. Shame on anyone who resists.'"

GrandJac listened attentively to various ideas then effectively summarized all the possibilities succinctly. "We can't fight the world with four people. You must get the disks from the DEA and Friedman. The Quark wave power is just too much for the world. It can't be released!"

THE ENHANCERS

SUNDAY DECEMBER 25TH

Christmas morning was a surprise for Soe, Jac, and the girls. GrandJac and Annie had a tree, decorations, gifts and a feast for them. The many people who lived on the ranch and took care of the chores for GrandJac had a huge celebration, also. GrandJac had presents for all of them and their children. Christmas day was a very happy occasion for the Cochran clan and the troops.

Meg suggested to GrandJac. "Let Carol and I give the families a demonstration of the wave. It's public knowledge now and they deserve a first hand demo."

GrandJac smiled. "Okay, but don't get too far into the mind reading concept. I have chairs and provisions for meetings in the aircraft hangar. Use it."

Jac cautioned Soe, anticipating Soe's love for oration. "Don't overwhelm them. Just a brief summary."

***

On two pallets, Soe took a deep breath as he surveyed more than 60 people. "I'm sure all of you are aware of the Enhancers. They have remarkable mind power. I developed the concept and applied it to Meloney here, Meg, to assist her recovery from a coma. Very strange powers soon developed. This may be a peek into life during the time of Atlantis." Soe ended with a little melodrama.

Carol and Meg flew into the room and down the aisle to the front wearing long white gowns they had cut from bed sheets. While they hovered beside Soe and Jac on the pallets, Annie keyed a stereo to play a Christmas gospel song.

A 55-gallon drum of oil for the jet-plane drifted forward. Soe pointed. "One of the powers is levitation."

Jac floated to the drum top, balancing. "Telepathy is the ability to transfer thoughts or read other people's thoughts. Meg and Carol are going to take you to 'The Garden of Eden.' It will be your concept of Eden because they will stimulate your mind to develop the picture as you might imagine it."

263

Annie let the stereo play into the next gospel song. The whole assemblage had their own senses stimulated to view Eden. It was truly a beautiful world. It seemed to drift before them unspoiled and alive with animals, cool breezes, forests and seas.

The rough shod cowboys, the moms, dads and the children coalesced towards the end of five minutes into one being to experience the music, the tranquility, the peacefulness in touch with their God. It was not the making of Meg and Carol. It was the minds and feelings of everyone creating the awe-inspiring experience. When it ended, many of the people were crying for more.

GrandJac stood. "There is a greater being. You have experienced Him. He is in your mind always. You can bring Him forth at your will. Merry Christmas to all!"

THE ENHANCERS

MONDAY DECEMBER 26TH

The Great Dallas Slash and Chop Raid as Carol named it began with a simple visit to the hospital. "Albert, I need a leave of absence to get over the brawl with Eddie Broussard. Maybe a week or two."

Albert reared back in his chair, running his hands over his face twisted into a grimace. "Damn it, John. This will put a hell of burden on us. I can't believe you are suffering from anything associated with the fight."

Carol smiled sweetly as she stepped before Albert's desk. Slowly bending over to display her endowments, she whispered. "John really needs the time to take care of me, Albert. The fight and trauma have made him almost impotent. I just won't have that, you understand? He has a job to do and he will do it!"

"Uhmmm, yes, yes, I do understand. You are absolutely right, Miss, ahh—. John, you really look bad and I can see you have the tremors. Take all the time you need." Albert answered graciously.

As they left, Carol looked back at Albert. He was shaking his head, muttering to himself. "What have I agreed to now?"

***

"C'mon, Jac, we're going to the Mall and dress you properly." Carol murmured in his ear.

"What did you tell Albert at the hospital, Pixie?" Jac urged as they contemplated the mall crowd.

"Ha, ha, he believed me when I told him you were impotent, just flaccid and needed rest." She answered in a loud voice.

Jac grabbed her head and licked her in the ear. "You twerp!"

***

It turned into "elbow city" attempting to get to the counters. The after Christmas shoppers attacked ferociously. A little physical displacement and mind bending by Meg helped move the buying along quickly.

***

A stop by Steve's motel netted nothing.

265

Meg floated by the door to his room. "He's gone to eat. We'll pick him up down the road ah ways."

In the parking lot of a small diner, Meg pointed to Steve's car parked at the end.

Before a plan could be developed, Carol demanded with a set to her jaw. "I want to get Steve, that little shit."

Dressed to the gills in her complete outfit, she walked to the door. She stood there until most of the patrons saw her. As is typical of lawmen, Steve was seated in a booth facing the door eating breakfast. He had just started.

Striding purposefully down the row of booths, heels clicking raucously, she stood in front of him, legs spread apart, hands on hips, saying nothing. Shaking her finger at him, glaring, she finally caught his attention. Several people turned and looked, then stared. The whole diner complement caught the signal and watched curiously.

Steve's head snapped up. His face froze with his mouth hanging open, his eyes staring. His fork clattered to the table flipping eggs on his shirt. Carol stepped aside as he slowly slid out of the booth and stood. Steve coughed, gagged a little as he slowly shuffled down the aisle. With his mouth open and eyes slightly bugged out, he leaned forward like a zombie. A ragged breath rasped from his throat in gasps as he drooled. Approaching the register, he fished $5 out of his pocket and dropped it on the counter.

Carol's heels clicked on the floor in sharp raps, short stepping behind him as he turned and went outside.

Turning sharply, her coat flaring out like a dancer's might, she addressed the group of locals loudly. "Daddy got out of the asylum again last night. Thank God we found him before he killed any of you."

Someone spoke up. "What do you mean, kill someone?"

"Daddy's a homicidal maniac, a sociopath. He's killed everyone in the family except me. I'm all he has. I have to care for him."

One of the onlookers, an elderly man, gasped. "Good God!"

"What's with the uniform?" A boy asked, holding up his hand.

"He respects authority. I have to wear this when I whip him with the wet rope. We are a religious sect that believes in harsh, corporal punishment for sins."

Again, in a loud voice that boomed and echoed in the small diner. "SIN AND YE SHALL BE SMITTEN BY THE HAND OF GOD!"

The same onlooker gasped again. "Are you God?"

The old man seemed to rise up out of his booth and move into the aisle.

"Are you a sinner? Have you ever sinned? The hand of God shall punish thee!"

A long black rope appeared in Carol's hand and snaked down the aisle, popping and twisting. The old man snatched up his hand in front of his face, eyes staring into nothing. The crowd sat tensely, absolutely quiet.

Carol's coat swirled in a wind as she turned and left. All eyes in the café followed the black-garbed jailer to a white pickup truck. The lights blinked twice and a strange howling came from it.

Steve sat in the back seat between the girls staring straight ahead.

"To Dallas. Steve is homesick."

Jac turned from the front seat amid the laughing, "You little buggar. How do you come up with this stuff?"

"We are the 'Better Be Good Boys.' You better be good, Jac baby."

***

In a small town on the way, Jac pulled into a car dealership. Carol went inside and addressed the manager. "Please give me a temporary license plate that you issue to new cars."

A customer and a salesman looked on curiously.

The manager grimaced with a hand wave. "We issue them with cars we sell. We don't just give them out to anybody. I'll give you one if you buy a new car."

Carol assumed her demanding pose, her legs spread apart and her hands on her hips, speaking loudly. "It's for my spaceship, Mr. Manager. We're going into battle and we need to be legal."

"I understand perfectly, Mr. Vader. I'll get one immediately."

He returned with a paper plate and masking tape. "What sector of the universe are you battling?"

Carol spun on her heel. "We are just beyond the rings of Saturn. The Outworlders are very powerful and are closing rapidly. Earth is in real danger."

"Heaven sakes, what should we do?" The manager stuttered, casting about frantically.

"Dig a foxhole." Carol quipped and was gone.

The salesman and customer just stared, openmouthed.

"Far out, far out!" a teenager with the customer exclaimed."

"I've got to find my shovel." The manager said as he frantically dug behind the counter.

Carol taped the plate in the back window.

Meg informed Carol. "I've already pulled the plates off the truck."

"Great, let's get Steve home."

***"

As they rode towards Dallas, Meg introduced her idea again. "Let's talk about utilizing the Enhancers in the legal system."

Jac spoke up. "Frankly, I don't see how we can go forward from here. We can't serve all the legal departments in the country and we can't expand the Enhancers easily."

Carol's somber suggestion startled the group. "You're right. I think we need to get the disks from the DEA/CIA and Friedman and shut the Enhancers down. We are very vulnerable to being taken over by powerful groups."

She turned to Meg while looking to the front seat at Soe and Jac. "We have at our disposal some form of energy, power we don't even understand. We can assume it is tapping an unknown source that might be limitless."

Soe interrupted. "Hold on, I think we need to show the world what the Enhancers are and are capable of just in case we don't clean out the data from the CIA, in particular. The turd is already rolling with the local police department and news media. The CIA could use this force on various people and the world needs to know of its power."

"We do need our disks back as a start," Meg agreed. "And maybe you are right. The world needs a bigger picture of us."

Further discussions developed a plan with alternatives.

Soe's superficial mind watched the scenery as they drove to Dallas. *Deep down, I don't care what GrandJac thinks. I want to see what we have here. I can get the power whenever I want it. That's already been proven with Carol. These two girls are too emotional to use it logically!*

***

In Dallas, Steve directed them to the DEA offices. As the building came into view, Carol chirped. "There it is! Shining like a diamond in a goat's ass walking up hill."

Jac tousled her hair. "You're a little Texas squirt, aren't you, Sweetiepie?"

"Don't you call me squirt, Bubba. I'll reconfigure your face. I can do that now, you know."

Meg interrupted. "C'mon you guys, let's get with the program."

"Yeah, yeah, I know, get serious. But serious people don't have any fun." Carol retorted.

"Is there security, passes or anything like that, Steve"?

"Yes, you have to have a DEA security clearance pass visible and you pass through a metal detector." Steve answered stone-faced.

"Let me see your pass, Steve." Soe asked.

He pulled a wallet from his coat pocket and removed an official looking pass that fit in his breast pocket.

As they watched, a group of men left the building and walked down the steps.

Meg pointed. "There are our passes. These boys are going to lunch."

The men turned, approached the truck, pulling their passes as they came. Four of the men stepped forward and gave Jac their passes.

"Thank you." Jac acknowledged. "You're so sweet."

The men turned and left with no awareness of what they had done.

The Enhancers slipped the passes in their coat pockets and stood beside the truck. Jac had parked dead in the middle of the no parking zone in front of the building. A DEA employee had stopped at the bottom of the steps to say something to Jac. "Here, boy, watch my truck 'til I get back, you hear, boy?"

"Wal, sho nuff, sur."

Carol helped Steve out. "You've got to shape up, Steve. You look like shit on a white chicken." Carol scolded him.

He immediately straightened up and got a look of intelligence in his face.

As they climbed the steps to the door entering the lobby, Meg ordered. "Steve, take us to the computer lab."

Steve led them forward to a metal detector gate where a guard was standing surveying everyone who entered. The guard didn't seem to acknowledge them. He just stared ahead as they passed through. Apparently the machine was very sensitive. It picked up some form of metal on each of them.

"Thank ya, Rover boy." Carol slurred out.

The elevator took them to the third floor. Steve continued deeper into the complex where they turned down a hall to the left. Two men walked by and didn't even glance at them.

"Stevie, where are you going?" Carol prodded him as he shuffled along.

"Here." He pushed open a door into an electronics lab. Salvador looked up in mid mouthful of sandwich at his desk. "Yuffes, can I help you?"

The only other man present sat in a wheel chair pinned to a computer with wires to his head. Wheelchair man quickly spun around pointing his hand like a gun at Carol who led the group. White fire leaped out striking a return from Carol and Meg. The ensuing ball of fire collapsed in a vacuum causing a loud bang.

Carol stepped to the side and directed a bolt towards the computer that the man was attached to, but he anticipated it and another thunder boom crashed in the room.

Jac grabbed Soe's pants tugging him down and out of the immediate line of fire. "Let the girls handle it, we can't compete!"

Wheelchair man glared at the two girls flanking him in an apparent standoff.

Eyeing wheelchair man carefully, Meg spoke to Salvador without looking at him. "Get me the computer disks, all of them."

Salvador smiled. "Sure." He obligingly began picking the particular disks from a storage slot above the computer.

The man in the wheelchair sat with both hands on the arms, fingers locked on the chrome tubing. Raising one finger, a bolt of fire blew through Salvador's chest. Blood and tissue sprayed across the room onto a wall. The remains of Salvador collapsed in a heap of bloody clothing, twitching involuntarily.

In the instant that move took, Carol shot a blast through the leads between the computer and wheelchair man's head. He fell back gasping, his eyes rolling into the back of his head.

"Okay, we may have a moment, Soe. Get those, I'll get these." Jac snatched the disks from the desk and stuck them in a plastic carrying case that was handy. Soe pulled the disk from the computer and tapped in instructions to wipe the memory. They searched the area for more disks and found another cache in a cabinet. Apparently, Salvador had made several copies.

Meg looked at the computer. "Soe, they can still recover the data from the hard drive, I'll fix it."

She leaned on the cabinet as it crushed like an aluminum beer can.

Wandering over to the window and looking out, Steve stretched his arms above his head as if he didn't have a care in the world.

Wheelchair man began to recover, Meg swept his mind.

She spoke quickly, hissing the words. "This is Norman, an accident and NDE victim. According to him, we got all the disks."

Norman fell back in his wheelchair unconscious with his mind wiped. Meg put some thoughts in his head concerning the events as they turned to go. Carol had locked the door. It sounded like a jackhammer beating on the door as they faced their only exit.

Crouched low and to the side of any gunshots, Meg flashed a thought to the other Enhancers. We will open the door and walk out telling them we are the cleaning people. We need to get more supplies to clean up the mess. Would you look at the mess of Salvador? That bolt blew his body apart, ugh, ugh!

Jac flicked the lock and jerked the door open. Three men stumbled in with guns drawn, but quickly regained their balance. "Whoa, would you look at that!" One said pointing to Salvador. "Ya'll sure do need to get the shovel and mop. Hurry along now. Get two trash bags, now, ya hear?" They stood to one side holstering their guns as the Enhancers filed out and down the hall to the stairs. Several people stood to the side as they moved single file. They appeared to not notice.

The exit door in the stairwell entered the lobby outside the security gate. The one-way locking system snapped open as Meg quickly disarmed it. They walked into the lobby.

Several men in uniforms pointed their guns at the Enhancers, screaming. "Hit the floor, hit the floor!"

A moment later, they turned and opened the street door so that the Enhancers could walk out. The Enhancers pulled their badges and handed them to the guards.

"Thank you, we enjoyed the visit." Carol said.

One of the guards spoke up. "Good luck with the soccer game. I like your uniforms."

Carol curtseyed. "Thank you."

Jac spoke to the DEA agent guarding the truck. "Thank you, Joe Bob, for watching the truck." They scrambled in the truck and drove away, careful to obey all traffic laws.

Meg cautioned. "They will be after us quickly. We need to hide the truck for a while."

The Super Wal-Mart parking lot made an ideal hiding place.

Leaving the motor running for A/C control, Jac looked in the rear vision mirror. Turning a resigned face to his family, his team, he spoke dejectedly. "I believe we are committed to the

THE ENHANCERS

Enhancer scenario, gang. We just took part in the killing of a human being, regardless of the circumstances. We are no better than GrandJac and the Cochran/Friedman feud. I had hoped we could, or at least I could, remain above the hate, bitterness and bloodshed."

Carol touched his arm, trying to sympathize. "Jac—, you're right. It just seemed to flow from one situation to another, getting steadily worse. For my part, I feel justified in my actions. I believe I'm on the right side. I intend to take it to a conclusion. I do feel sorry for Salvador. He is, ah, was just a pawn in the game."

Soe looked out the window with little or no emotion or agreement. Meg's face and set jaw line indicated her position though she said nothing.

***

Wilson Williams, the local Director, had received a cell phone call while at lunch alerting him of the break-in. His car screamed to a halt in front of the building. Charging up the steps to the lobby where a contingent of DEA agents milled around, shouting and pointing, Williams bellowed. "Just shut up. None of you know anything. Get the surveillance camera tapes and report to the conference room, now!"

The security guard spread his hands. "They checked out perfectly. They had badges, no weapons, Sir."

Another group stated. "We met them in the hall by the lab. They were a cleaning team to clean up the blood in the lab."

Steve smiled, shrugging, "Hell, they're friends of mine. I don't understand what all the hollering is about."

Norman nodded, "I thought they were a doctor team coming to check on me."

The lobby guards spoke unanimously, "They were the DEA soccer team in their new uniforms."

Wilson pounded on the table. "Run the Goddamn video tapes. We have a dead man here."

The entire staff sat through all the tapes, some twitching, some shaking their heads in dismay. The tapes showed clearly the four people dressed in black, coats, helmets, and boots. They walked through security, into the lab led by Steve.

The lab scene was graphic, but even then it gave little info. No one could explain the white blasts. The only obvious facts were the stealing of the computer disks and Norman killing Salvador.

Wilson stared at his staff. *I can't tell them about the computer disks. It's on a need to know basis.*

"We have to call the local police. It's their jurisdiction. I'll do it."

"Hey, did anyone see them drive away? What kind of car did they have?"

One lobby guard raised his hand. "I believe they took a cab, Sir."

Williams snorted. "Bull shit, you two go out front and canvas the people on the street. Maybe someone saw them."

A report came back, "A retired man sitting in his car saw them. They were driving a white fourdoor pickup truck."

Wilson pointed to his security head, "I'm calling the Dallas police. You handle the investigation."

***

Wilson returned to his office as he considered his plight. *What to do about the disks? The Enhancers have the disks in Marian, but I sure don't want to go get them. Hmmm——, Friedman must have a copy. I'll contact him.*

Spinning around in his swivel chair, he grabbed the phone. "Jeff, is that you? How many times have I told you to identify yourself on the phone? This is Wilson. Bring your butt and two extra hands in here for a small job——, now."

Jefferson Smalley peeked in the door, "Yes Sir, Boss. Sorry 'bout that, whatcha got?"

"Jeff, I want you to find Saul Friedman. He's a local millionaire who has a copy of computer disks like the ones stolen from our office today. These disks contain a program that interacts with the brain and enables the treated subject to perform ESP capabilities. We have worked two months acquiring the data. Now they're gone.

"We need a copy of the disks very bad. Use all of your skills to negotiate with Mr. Friedman, got it?"

Jeff tilted his head and eyed Wilson, unconsciously feeling his piece. "All of them, Boss?"

Wilson grimaced as he thought of using 'muscle.' "Leave the door open for further negotiations if you don't succeed the first time, Jeff. Saul Friedman owns half of America!"

Bristol, one of Jeff's 'hands' motioned with his hand. "I believe I saw something in today's paper about a Friedman. Did you see that, Jeff?"

"We'll look. C'mon men. Wilson, I hope to have something for you tonight, Sir."

***

As they walked out of the building, Bristol grabbed a paper from a newsstand. "Here it is, front page. Let's see, Saul Friedman's son, Sam, was found in the lion den at the zoo, badly mauled."

Jeff looked at Bristol. "Mount Sinai hospital, Jeff. People don't break in lion dens if they are sane. This looks like a hit job."

Mt. Sinai Hospital's admissions clerk spoke clearly. "Mr. Friedman is to have no visitors, Mr. Smalley."

"Ma'am, we're with the DEA, a government law enforcement agency. We wish to see Mr. Friedman." Jeff put a penetrating stare on the clerk.

"I'll call his doctor, Mr. Smalley. Paging Dr. Abner, paging Dr. Abner." She paused a moment listening to her earpiece, then related the situation. "Mr. Smalley, Mr. Friedman is in room 310. You may proceed to the third floor."

Dr. Abner met them at the nurse's station. After a brief exchange of blustering and flashing credentials, Dr. Abner explained the problem.

"Mr. Friedman was found in a tree in the lion den at the local zoo early this morning. He could not get high enough to escape the lions. From the police report, one lion was able to jump or climb high enough to ravage his feet, lower legs and his genitals.

Fortunately, I assume, the caretakers arrive early. Mr. Friedman almost bled out. He is in very critical condition."

"Good lord, Doctor, that's unreal. Is his, uh, are his privates, are they, uh, going to be okay?

Dr. Abner pursed his lips looking down, "Uh, ah, no, his genitals were eviscerated."

Smalley ran a hand through his hair as he felt his crotch. "That's terrible, Doctor. How did he get in the den, initially?"

"I don't know. I haven't heard anything from the police on that subject. Mr. Friedman is under heavy sedation and cannot see anyone except family.

"The strangest thing occurred when they brought him in. He repeatedly mumbled 'When in Rome, when in Rome———.' That might be a lead. That's what I told the police."

"Thank you, Dr. Abner. You've been helpful. We will be in touch on Mr. Friedman's condition."

Turning to exit the floor, Saul Friedman stood in the hallway with his hands on his hips facing them. Scowling belligerently, "I understand you are DEA. What the hell are you doing here?"

Saul unconsciously felt his face where Dr. Abner had carefully sewed, patched and cosmetically repaired the damage done by Ralph the previous night.

Smalley gave no notice of the obvious swelling and bruises. "You are Mr. Friedman, Saul Friedman?"

"Yes." Saul answered grabbing sunglasses and gingerly placing them on his nose.

"Mr. Friedman, I'm Jeff Smalley, Special Agent with the DEA office here in Dallas. These men are working with me. I wonder if we might talk in private?"

Saul sniffed, "Well, we might. But I have only a few minutes. Come, this will do."

They moved into a small alcove in the waiting room. Jeff sat forward, clasping his hands. "Apparently Mr. Friedman, your son, Sammy was in partnership with one of our agents in Marian. They were monitoring a Dr. Etheridge, I believe. In the process, they copied two computer disks from Dr. Etheridge's lab study. The end result was that we had the disks and you had the disks. Do you still have the disks?"

Saul sat back. A brief flicker of a sneer crossed his generous lips. "You are going to have to give me more information, Mr. Smalley. Have you lost your disks?"

"Well, it's possible. Then again maybe ours are corrupted. The bottom line is, we need copies of those disks." Jefferson answered with just a little pressure in his voice.

Saul eyed Smalley as he started to feel his face again. *It looks like I may have the only copies beyond Etheridge. That's a nice touch.*

He sat up straight jutting out his jaw. "Sammy was handling that deal and he never really briefed me on the details. If he has the disks, I don't know about it. Sammy is on a long road to recovery. It may be weeks before he can even talk coherently. He is alive only by the grace of God. I'm sure when he realizes his manhood is lost, he will need psychological counseling."

Jeff looked at the set jaw, cursing. *Crap, he knows about the disks, you can bet on it.*

Jeff hunched himself forward, just a trace of sneer on his face. "Mr. Friedman, do you have any idea how or what happened to Sammy, your son?"

Saul studied Jeff with his hand hovering near his face. Contemplating the dig, "Sammy has his own business interests and friends. What he was doing is anybody's guess."

Jeff continued, relaxing. "Sammy lives with you, doesn't he? At your home on Bissonet?"

"Yes, he does."

Jeff leaned forward. "Did Sammy have some kind of altercation yesterday morning in your neighborhood?"

Saul glanced away. *I wonder how much these bastards know?*

Looking back, Saul spoke cautiously. "Could be. Do you know something about such an event?"

"Mr. Friedman, we have reason to believe that Sammy was the target of a hit. Maybe enemies that you know of————, or ought to know of."

Saul stood up with his fists clenched in the air. "You bet your sweet ass he was hit. And I'll get the bastards. You can count on it!"

Ah, finally, I found his 'hot button! "Mr. Friedman, we may be able to help you with Sammy's enemies in exchange for copies of the disks." Jeff offered quietly.

Saul sat down staring at Smalley, musing. *Can you imagine the power of the DEA on your side, doing dirty work for you? However, if I can get Ralph back and get him in control, I don't need anybody.*

Saul abruptly stood up. "Let's keep in touch. Give me your card. Here is mine. If we do get together, I want to deal with your top man." Saul demanded.

Jeff stood up, to emphasize his words. "Yes Sir, of course, Mr. Friedman. Please be aware, we can do a lot of things—, lots of things. Keep that in mind."

***

Jeff called Wilson and gave him a full report along with his surmises.

"We can't afford to wait on Friedman to call us, we need to get those disks now." Wilson ordered, a sense of urgency in his voice. "A street person saw the blackcoat gang get in a white four-door pickup with dealer tags in the window. Find it."

***

Soe looked at the sun and his watch as he panned the Enhancers. "I believe we have missed lunch. My little tummy is growling."

"Okay, Chunky. We'll just take you to What-A-Burger." Carol poked him and grinned.

Meg snapped, "Carol, are you getting myopic? Soe is not chunky. He is very muscular, probably less than 5% body fat."

Carol smiled sweetly, "Of course. He's lean like a feral hog, huh?"

Soe shook his head, trying to keep from laughing out. "You girls!"

Jac turned into the drive through lane, "Okay, okay, girls. Pull in the knives. Look here, see the Arkansas plate? You

THE ENHANCERS

know, we better get another plate. They could easily have fingered us as we drove away."

"I wiped their minds," Meg said. "They won't remember."

"How about people on the street?" Carol asked.

"That's a possibility," Soe remarked, "We better get one. Let's eat first."

Carol pulled the paper tag off the window as Jac drove back to Wal-Mart parking on the side where the employees park. As they drove down the lane, Meg unscrewed the bolts on a pickup and the plate fell on the ground. Jac made the circle. Soe stepped out grabbing the plate. Jac pulled in a parking slot. Carol hopped out and screwed the plate on the truck.

"Let's review." Soe suggested as he turned to the others. "According to Sammy, Saul keeps a gang of men around his estate and the leader is Butch. We might sweep his mind and get some information. I don't know how we will get next to Saul unless we go to the house."

***

From Sammy's memory, Jac drove to the classy neighborhood where Saul lived. Bissonet was a beautiful, quiet boulevard with trees growing in the esplanade. They drove past the gate and saw a guard in a small gatehouse at the entrance. The house sat back probably 250 yards from the gate in a beautifully manicured scene of lawn and shrubbery.

At the corner, Meg got out and walked back to the gate on the sidewalk in her black outfit. As she approached the gatehouse, she projected an image of a beautiful girl walking along in scanty clothing and high heels. She stopped at the gate and sighed, her large breasts pushing against the tight dress.

The guard stepped out. "Ma'am, can I help you?"

"Yes," she replied in a seductive voice. "My car quit and I need a phone. Do you have one, Bigboy?"

Charles, the gateman, quickly agreed. As he leered at Meg's body, "Yes, I have a phone. Come to the gatehouse."

Meg pushed in the small enclosure, rubbing against Charles. "You are so sweet. What's your name?"

"Charlie. That's what my mom calls me."

279

"Charlie, my name is Veronica. Would you please call Butch and have him come to the gate?"

Charlie thought that was a wonderful idea. He dialed the house. "Butch, I have a visitor here who needs to see you."

Butch drove down to the gate in a Lexus and got out, cautiously looking around. Meg stepped out of the gatehouse and hung on the bars to the gate, leaning over with her breasts hanging out.

"Butch, I'm Veronica. Would you come here? I'll bet you've got something I want." Butch walked to the gate and hung on the other side, looking at Veronica's large breasts and seductive body.

Butch's eyes widened and a big smile lit up his face. "Yes, I do have something you want, Veronica. When and where can we meet?"

"Butch, you know about the computer disks don't you?" Meg prompted.

"Sure do, Veronica."

That was all it took to sweep his mind. Meg turned and walked away with Charlie and Butch ogling her. They turned back to the estate for some reason and looked at the house as the pickup stopped allowing Meg to float into the cab.

Meg shared the info with the others.

"This Ralph may be a dangerous entity." Soe pointed out.

"Could be, but remember that my powers declined after a few hours." Meg indicated. "He may have transitory powers that need to be jacked up with the machine. If that is so, he could be back to the warehouse tonight for further help. As you know, Butch followed him while he robbed the autoteller machines and on to his flophouse. Butch has a team watching him now."

"Let's go to the warehouse now and get the disks. Maybe we won't run into Ralph." Jac added. "I hope we don't. We may have to kill him."

Five PM Dallas traffic did its best to impress Jac as he piloted the oversized hulk of truck.

Carol yelled and pointed. "There it is, shining like a diamond _____".

Soe interrupted. "Yeah, yeah, we know. Where in the world do you get these sayings?"

Carol giggled. "They are local Texas colloquialisms. Morris is just full of them."

"I hope we don't have to run in this crappy traffic. It'll bog down a gorilla." Jac answered as he ruffled Carol's hair.

The automatic door swung up easily with a little help from Meg. Three of Butch's men came out of the offices approaching the truck.

Carol stepped down, letting it all hang out. "Hello, I'm selling magazine subscriptions for charity. Do you take Women's World?"

The one in front, named Lefty, answered. "No, but I want to, sign me up."

"Let's go inside and I'll show you everything I've got." Carol cooed.

"Yes sir, I mean ma'am, c'mon on in!" The men crowded into the office with Carol. Soe, Jac and Meg went into the lab where the computer station was located.

Carol laughed, giggled, flounced, batted her eyes as she entertained the three men by flicking their minds to sexy women in the magazines they thought she was selling.

Soe let a gust of air blow out. "Ha, there they are." He quickly took the disks and put them in the computer one by one erasing them. Wiping the memory in the hard drive cleaned it up. Checking around, he could find no more disks.

Jac interrupted, "Let me "FIX" the computer." Unplugging the cord, he bent the tines of the connector and inserted the plug into a nearby 240-volt receptacle. Smoke billowed from the computer case. Jack jerked the plug out, straightened the tines and plugged the cord into the 120-volt receptacle. "I bet that'll get 'ol Saul smoking!

"Did you see the EEG leads and recorder? It's obvious that Saul was working here with someone like this Ralph, Butch mentioned. I believe we got it. Let's go."

Carol had over $300 on the table from the men who were going to buy her magazines.

"We have to run, Lefty. Thank you for the business." Carol grinned as she caressed his face gently, scooping up the money. Exiting through the door, into the truck and out on the street took moments.

As they were driving down the street, a black limo passed them and went through the warehouse door.

"There's our boy, Saul." Meg pointed with a giggle. "Do you think he has had a bad day? What with the lions clawing the balls off poor Sammy and now his disks are gone? Hey wait a minute. I just got some vibs from Saul. Ralph smacked him around last night cutting his nose, cheek and eyebrows. Magnanimous Saul has forgiven him if he will only come back. Ha, ha, that's another tribulation for Saul!"

Jac urged, "We better get the hell out of Dodge. Saul is going to be one angry mother ape. He will sic the hounds on us!"

***

Saul left the hospital mulling over the DEA's offer.

If you could trust the bastards, it might be a good alliance. However, I don't want anyone else to have the power. I've got to get Ralph back to the warehouse somehow and see if he's controllable. If not, I'll get another subject and continue.

Saul's blood pressure and heart rate increased as he thought of the Cochrans. *I'll get those bastards. Hell, I might use the DEA for that!*

Saul motioned to the driver. "Go home. We'll pick up Butch and get a report on where Ralph is."

Butch got in the car and began his report as they drove to the warehouse. "Ralph is sleeping off a drunk in his flophouse."

Saul looked at Butch suspiciously. "Has anything else happened during the day?"

Butch waved his hand, looking out the window. "Yeah, something weird happened at the gate this afternoon. The video camera at the gate recorded this person coming to the gate and asking to use the phone. Charlie let the person use the phone and he called me. I went to the gate and talked to him briefly and he left in a truck that came by and picked him up. I absolutely don't know what we talked about. Neither does Charlie."

Saul sat upright, eyeing Butch. "What was the person wearing?"

"He was dressed in a black leather coat, helmet, high boots and gloves. You can see him on the video, really weird."

"What kind of truck?" Saul asked quickly, a quiver of fear creeping into his voice.

"It was a fourdoor white pickup."

Saul turned, "I just saw one like that pass us on this street. It looked like it came out of our warehouse. Let's get inside and see if everything is okay!"

Upon entering, Saul looked over the area. "Has anyone been by?"

Lefty leaned back. "Yeah, a magazine saleswoman came by but that was all."

A stiff glare put Lefty down in his chair. "What is that smell? It smells like an electrical fire."

Saul quickly stepped to the video recorder and played back the last half-hour. It showed three men in black outfits enter the lab and work on the computer.

Butch pointed at the screen. "Hell, that's the same ones who were at the gate!"

Saul turned to the three men in a rage. "Didn't you see these people come in?"

Lefty's eyes widened as he stood up. "Uh, no, Boss. We didn't see anyone but this purty little salesgirl selling mag subscriptions."

Saul threw up his hands, spinning around. "Holy shit, they have already been here and stolen the disks. Get Jacob here and get Ralph here. We need to see what we've got." He walked into the lab, scanning the equipment. "Hell, there are the disks. I wonder what they were doing?"

Keying the computer, Saul found it on. He slipped one of the disks in the slot and searched for the 'explorer' button. The screen remained blank. "I think they burnt my computer! That's the smell. They burnt it!

"Those assholes didn't take the disks. They just wiped them. I'll just have to wait until Ralph and Jacob get here to see what we have, if anything. SHIT, SHIT, SHIT. "Butch, get'em here now!"

***

Jac started a review as he leaned against the door. Soe was driving. "We've shutdown both the DEA/CIA and Friedman on exploring the Quark effect, I hope. Soe, do you think they can take their experimental guinea pigs and do anything with them?" Jac leaned forward. "In our case, both Meg and Carol have some powers without the boost. We really haven't explored what they can do long term without the boost. Friedman's Ralph retained strong powers after leaving the lab but we don't know how long. It's possible that continued use of the boost might make you strong enough to operate without it over time."

Meg interrupted. "I don't think Norman is going to do anything. He doesn't even remember what was happening to him. But, he still has the power until it ebbs. If he can remember."

Soe spoke over his shoulder, "Meg, why don't you and Carol remove the headgear and let's see what happens by the time we get home?"

Jac scowled, challenging Soe. "Hey, Soe, could any computer whiz take your concept and enhance EEG brain waves?"

"That's doubtful," Soe replied, tossing his head back. "I modified my computer, wrote original programs and I manipulated the frequency and waveform to get the programs they stole. The only thing they got was the operational sequence for enhancing the comatose brain. They did not get the meat that makes it work. It took me a year of research in my computer to arrive at it. But, there's the ol' adage. 'It ain't possible until someone does it, then everyone can do it.'"

"I'm getting more jittery about this thing." Jac admitted. "Even though we supposedly canceled the disks, I think we ought to go to the police in the morning with the press and expose the concept. If others come up with it, the people will know what it is. Let's discuss it with GrandJac when we get in."

***

Jac glanced at his watch. "Dark, 8:30. Finally made it. It's a long drive. Let's eat and talk to GrandJac."

GrandJac cocked his head to one side as a quizzical smile spread across his face. Meg continued the briefing with vivid pictures in the mind. While watching the dead quiet event, Annie delivered chili and beans in a great Taco salad for a quick supper.

GrandJac spread his hands, "Maybe you cleaned them out. I sure hope so."

Soe turned to the girls. "What has happened to your strength without the booster?"

"Let's go outside and see." Meg replied.

In the back yard, Meg could still shoot a beam of white power out about 400 yards. Carol's power was significantly diminished.

"As you can see, the control diminishes rapidly without the boost. It might disappear over time without boost support. That's an interesting factor. Anyway, looks like training and continued boost will help you, Carol." Soe noted as they turned back to the house.

***

From the front porch, Morris stepped up. "There's a convoy of cars coming down FM 1495. Maybe 2 minutes out."

"Let's go see." Soe said as he turned to the girls. "Get your helmets. We may have the enemy upon us."

Morris called GrandJac on the radio and sounded the general alarm. The men assumed battle stations while the families went below to a large gym like storm shelter.

"Let's get inside." Morris ordered, as he opened the front door and looked to GrandJac for directions.

GrandJac nodded. "Go ahead. Initiate the defenses."

Steel plates slid out of the walls to cover the windows.

GrandJac told the Enhancers. "I have anticipated a raid by Friedman for years so I built this house accordingly. It is completely covered with ½" steel armor plate. Rockets and mortars cannot penetrate it. The office is below grade. So if something new comes along it will pass overhead—, I hope."

GrandJac strode across the office and checked the plates over the windows. "The men have an underground shelter for them and their families. We are completely self-sufficient here with power, water, food, and sewage. If this turns into a real war, I can call on help from the outside." He said with no explanation, just a tilt to his head. "Morris, I don't want any shooting from us unless I give the word. We are going to start out in a defensive mode."

The convoy of cars and trucks stopped at the gate. Headlights shone over the property. A big man wearing black combat gear walked to the closed gate. He looked around, found the speakerphone in a box to the side. Huge floodlights came on illuminating the gate and areas around it.

A strident voice pounded through the speakerphone inside. "This is the United States Government. We have a search warrant for your premises."

GrandJac looked at the others, grinning. "Let the games begin." Raising his voice to a handheld microphone. "Please identify yourself explicitly and hold the warrant up to the camera so that it may be read."

"My name is Wilson Williams. I am Director of the Dallas branch of the DEA. We have reason to believe you stole computer disks from my office in Dallas today and possess large quantities of drugs on your property. We have reason to believe that your people were wearing black uniforms and entered our premises illegally. We have reason to believe that your people are accessories to murder."

GrandJac ordered. "Hold the warrant steady so I can read it, Mr. Williams."

The actual search warrant language was very vague and referred only to computer disks.

GrandJac challenged. "Is this your jurisdiction? Why do you have 30 men at my gate?"

Wilson bellowed back. "Our jurisdiction takes precedence over any local law enforcement agency if we believe drugs are involved."

"Is that what you are accusing, that we have drugs?" GrandJac's sharp voice barked at Williams.

"Yes," Wilson demanded in an even louder voice. "Let me in to search your property."

GrandJac spoke quietly, intensely. "I'm calling the County Sheriff's Department to put a restraining order on you until this can be settled in court. You are way out of your jurisdiction. Your charges are ridiculous. Your search warrant says nothing about drugs, just computer disks. Hell, I have computer disks. I'll admit it."

In the glaring lights, a small man dressed in a business suit stepped forward and spoke to Wilson. "Fuck this legal shit, Wilson. Let's blow him away and search the rubble."

GrandJac snickered as he jabbed with his voice. "Hey—, that's my boy, Saul! I haven't seen you in ages, Saul. You look like shit, how do you feel?

"I was sorry to hear about Sammy. Was he playing some kind of game with the lions? Like maybe, 'When in Rome, do as the Romans do?' And right here at Christmas, too!

"He really is a stupid little prick. But in reality, he favors you. It looks like he dropped the dice and picked up a hand full of shit. Whatta ya tink, Saul baby?" GrandJac let go with a berrazz.

Saul screamed. "AAAAAAAAAAH, I'm gonna kill you with my bare hands!"

Jerking an automatic pistol out of his coat, he fired into the video camera. Then he shot the floodlight out.

GrandJac yelled. "Wilson, will you check Saul's blood pressure. He's prone to strokes. Also, push his hemorrhoids back up his ass, I can see them hanging down from here."

Saul went ballistic, shooting at the house. That initiated a complete loss of control. All the men, including the DEA men opened fire at the house. Absolute chaos. Who would believe a government agency would do such a thing? Possibly a little urging from the Enhancers to bring the confrontation to a boil? Windows, shrubs, bricks, façade trim disintegrated under a hail of bullets.

A wave from Wilson okayed an explosive charge on the gate lock. The two large gates swung in under the explosion.

The tiny spy slits in the steel panels gave a good view of something out of control.

"Okay, Meg, don't shoot anyone but blow the tires on the cars as they pull in." GrandJac ordered.

The attackers cranked up four cars, spun around, wheels squealing, darting through the gate. They formed a wall as a shooting base.

Meg stepped forward and peered through the slit. White fire streaked out and demolished the tires. Several caught fire. The cars turned to the side and formed a wall that the men crouched behind. Smoke billowed up from burning tires.

"They must have brought a hell of a supply of ammo." Jac commented as the shooting continued.

A man stepped between the cars and shouldered a rocket launcher. He paused briefly to aim and pulled the trigger. The back blast struck a pickup truck and destroyed the cab. Smoke and fire streamed from the rocket as it hurtled towards the door. Suddenly it veered upward and went over the house to explode a mile behind the house. Meg and Carol hi-fived, grinning.

Morris yelled. "This frontal attack was a ruse. There's a gang charging the back!"

Carol and Jac raced to the back of the house to see maybe ten men ducking and running towards the house in the glare of flood lights. The lead man ignited a flame-thrower spraying flaming diesel towards the house. The flame's fuel fell short and dribbled out the end of the nozzle with help from Carol.

Carol giggled. "This is fun!" The attackers fell back about 50 yards as one of the men shouldered a rocket and fired towards the house.

Carol yelled. "Alleyoop." The rocket went over the house, dove into the ditch behind the road, exploding in a large ball of fire.

Over the speakerphone, someone screamed. "They're shooting rockets at us!" Five men stood up behind the cars firing grenade launchers at the house. The shredded brick veneer fell away revealing steel plate for walls.

GrandJac muttered, "That's enough." He picked up his cellphone, dialing a number in Dallas. "We're under siege here and doing okay. Execute code 3, 30 seconds notice."

The gang at the back could be heard shooting grenades into the house. A large spotlight beamed on the house from behind the cars.

Over the speakerphone, Saul could be heard screaming. "The house has some kind of steel plate or armor. We are not doing anything to it but blowing the bricks off."

From between the cars, a lone man wearing a backpack stepped forward extending his hand. White fire streaked towards the front door slamming it with a huge bang. The large steel plate shook violently and fell in on the floor, ripped from steel tracks.

Saul was screaming. "Now we got 'em. Shoot through the door with the grenades and rockets."

Meg and Carol stepped out onto the porch pointing their hands at the assemblage. Meg growled. "I've had enough of this crap. I'm gonna kick someone's ass."

White fire sprayed out striking the cars and blowing them fifty feet in air, back across the road where they caught fire and burned like gasoline. The attackers were standing naked, silhouetted in the firelight.

The lone man again extended his hand and fire shot out towards Meg and Carol. It was met 50 yards out with fire from Meg and Carol. An ear-shattering explosion occurred as fire ballooned 300 yards into the sky creating a huge air draft. Dust and loose debris were sucked into the fireball. The attackers fell back screaming, running for their lives.

The ten men from the back charged around the house and stood gawking in awe. Holding their hands up, they tried to shield their eyes and face from the pillar of fire. "What in hell is that?"

Meg took a moment to lift them in total and throw them across the ground towards the gate as if they had jumped off a speeding train. Sprawling in the mud near the gate enabled them to scramble through to the road.

The white fire continued to balloon and wave about, but it slowly and insistently moved toward the man. In an instant, he conceded by leaping 100 yards away across the fence and into the night.

"Ten minutes? I can't believe this took no more than ten minutes." Jac stuttered looking at his watch.

Carol clapped her hands. "Here comes the cavalry!"

Coming down FM 1495 were 5 to 8 police cars with sirens blaring and lights flashing. Several cars loaded up with men, roared away from the scene and the police. The police couldn't chase them because the road was blocked with wrecked, burning cars.

Carol turned to the group in the house. "You can come out. There won't be any more shooting without death. They know it!"

Easing out onto the shattered front porch, hands on hips, they watched the spectacle.

GrandJac turned, surveying his house, "I'm real proud of it. I really think it could have taken the rocket hit."

Meg and Carol laughed. "Maybe so, but we can test it later at our convenience."

Twenty men brandishing pistols, rifles and shotguns from the sheriff's department rounded the men up and disarmed them.

GrandJac and the group walked out to talk to them.

Wilson yelled, waving a wad of papers. "I still have this warrant and I will serve it."

The lead Sheriff stepped forward and took the warrant from Wilson.

"What the hell is that awful smell?" he asked loudly with his nose crinkled. He shined his flashlight around as he looked at Wilson and his men. Wilson's face told it all.

"Kiss my naked ass, did you shit your pants?"

He shined his flashlight on the paper and turned to Wilson. "What is this supposed to be, a joke? There's nothing here but blank paper. It looks like you came over here to kill somebody with a warrant as an excuse and it's nothing but ass wipe. You sure need it now! You are going to spend the night in jail. I don't care who you claim to be!"

GrandJac finished it in his best East Texas twang. "Ya jest cain't trust them govemint people. They lies a lot."

He turned to the sheriff, "Call me if you need me for anything. Let's go catch the late news."

***

The Enhancers and GrandJac returned to the house. Six men had stood the steel door up leaning it in place.

"Looks like we got some fixin to do." GrandJac laughed.

They went into the living room flicking the TV just in time to catch the 11 o'clock news.

The lead story had the usual fanfare. Across the bottom of the screen scanned "Breaking News." In the background a house appeared to be on fire. Smoke and flames shot skyward. Standing in front of a large ornamental gate a TV announcer spoke breathlessly trying to build excitement and tension into the scene. "Just 20 minutes ago, Dallas firemen rushed to this scene on Bissonet Boulevard, the home of millionaire Saul Friedman. Already the house was ablaze." The camera panned down the street to a large box semi rig with a truck wrecker in front. "The entrance way here was blocked by that truck. The fire department could not move it. Precious minutes were lost as a truck wrecker was called in to pull it out of the way. Capt. Terry, here, said he might have been able to save the house but it's gone now, gutted."

The reporter repeated again. "The house is the residence of Saul Friedman, one of the wealthiest men in Dallas and the United States."

"Wait, we have more breaking news! Just in, the police have stated that the house was hit with rocket fire. Unknown perpetrators fired military rockets from the trailer setting the house on fire. This is arson! Police have released no further details."

GrandJac turned to the group, "We better get ready for another war. If and when Saul calls home, he will turn around and come back to see us."

Meg glared at the group, "I think that was very appropriate, GrandJac. He fully intended to destroy your house and everyone in it. He still needs some of Carol's colloquialisms, like havin 'the shit slapped outta him.'"

"Amen, Meg. We're with you." Jac answered stridently.

Morris left the room talking on his radio. GrandJac wondered out loud. "How did the men get into the back yard?"

Carol waved her hand. "Oh, they were dropped back in the far corner by helicopter."

GrandJac mused. "The DEA pulled all stops to come in here and get the Enhancer data. I find it very hard to believe this DEA man, Wilson Williams, has that much stroke. I'm going to make a few calls in the morning."

A wry smile spread across Carol's face. "Saul and his troops may be delayed a little. They're going to have to stop someplace and clean their drawers. I believe the whole crowd shit their pants when the fireball erupted."

Soe and Jac laughed. "I can believe that."

GrandJac clapped his hands. "Haw, haw, that's great!"

Jac turned to Meg and Carol. "Come on mighty wizards. Let's fix the front door."

Jac directed the girls. "There, that's it. Straighten the brackets that the rollers hang on and rehang the door on its track. Here Soe, let's reattach the air-operated cylinder. This wiring and switch will let it operate for the time being."

Several sighs announced the anticlimactic ending as they retired to the living room to discuss the future of the Enhancer phenomena.

"After seeing what their Ralph could do with some kind of booster, I'm afraid we can't let the power out. He has my earliest program. I'm three echelons beyond that now." Soe declared. "I don't know how they continue to have the computer program. I erased everything I could find at the warehouse in Dallas. I guess they had a copy of the programs stored someplace else. We have to shut down Ralph and take his toy away."

Meg commented waving her hand. "Their computer man, Jacob, had the program in his laptop. The one hanging on Ralph. There is no doubt. We have the enemy defined. As much as I hate this war, Jacob and Ralph need to be sanctioned."

Jac had waited his turn, sighing loudly, "Meg, your pacifism is leaking. But, I agree with you. Sanctions. But why do you think Jacob should go?"

Soe interrupted to expand on the sanction idea. "Jacob has seen too much of the program and how it works. He's a computer nerd and might work it out. Also, we need to sweep him for further copies of the programs he might have squirreled away."

Meg continued the theme. "I think we all agree that the Quark wave must be taken off the face of earth. It resides in disks and people. Both can be eliminated. Look at it like protection of humanity. I think it's that big."

Carol stared at each of her fellow Enhancers. "I guess we are of the same cloth. Can we be trusted with this power? Should we be sanctioned? That is such a clean, ah, clinical word to describe killing a human being."

Jac commented looking at the group. "The world is protected only by your, our moral fiber.

"Assuming we don't get Jacob and Ralph and this is released on the world, how 'bout a demo for the public and the press to let them know what is out there. At least the governing bodies will know where it's coming from when Ralph pulls something. It might calm down the DEA, also."

Meg looked away shaking her head unaware. *I can't tell him. Soe says it might skew the future. This thing must continue to track.*
Jac caught the body English. *So Meg knows something. A hell of a lot more than this is on the table. Looking over this thing tonight, it's just unbelievable! A private individual challenges the United States Government in a gun battle and has them arrested! Then he burns down a house in Dallas with military rockets, blocking access to the fire department with a stolen truck! Where is the upper limit?*

***

Saul and two cars of his men drove the back roads to escape the sheriff. An hour later, I-20 showed on a cross- road sign. On to Dallas. No one answered at home when Saul called. "That's strange, even the AM didn't pickup." No one on the garage phone either. Calling the house guard's cell-phone finally got an answer.

Herford gasped. "Is that you, Mr. Friedman? Thank God you called. I've got bad news, real bad news."

Saul settled back in his seat. "What is it?" He asked quietly.

"Your house has burned to the ground. Everyone got out okay because of the call."

"What the hell does that mean?" screamed Saul.

"The house got a call about 10 PM that they had 30 seconds to get out. Sheila pulled the alarm and everybody evacuated. Somebody pulled up to the gate in an 18-wheeler, blocked the gate and shot the guard. Just wounded him." Herford paused to get a breath. "They opened the side doors on the truck and fired 5 to 8 rockets into the house. It was terrible, Mr. Friedman. The house exploded and was totally in flames in a minute.

"They left with the keys to the truck. The fire trucks couldn't get in to fight the fire. We had to call a truck wrecker to move the rig. By that time the house was almost burned to the ground. The Fire Department couldn't save anything. I'm so sorry, Mr. Friedman."

It's incomprehensible, first Sammy, then the shop attack, then the fucking DEA, then the debacle attack on Cochran, then shitting his pants and now the house burned. That's 130 years of priceless possessions

GONE! Saul shriveled down into the seat holding his head in his hands.
I can't even begin to remember what has been lost!

Butch knew it was bad, he'd better be very careful in what he
said. "Mr. Friedman, what can I do? Do you want to continue
on to Dallas?"

Saul stifled a sob. "Ahh—, let's go to Dallas. Go home.
Ugh, this fucking car stinks!"

***

At straight up 7 o'clock in the morning, Washington time,
GrandJac called Mark Weatherby, a Deputy Director with the
CIA in Washington DC. He related the whole story to Mark,
from the janitor, the break-ins, the bugging, Theo's death, to the
firefight last night.

GrandJac asked the last question. "I have it on good
authority that the CIA is behind the DEA's activities here in
Texas. Do you know anything about it?"

Mark listened quietly. He knew of GrandJac. He had met
GrandJac personally. He knew that GrandJac had the power to
do something in Washington.

Mark clinched his fist, gritted his teeth. "I can assure you I
will get the facts and I will report back to you personally. Mr.
Cochran, thank you for bringing this to my attention."

***

Mark Weatherby went immediately to the airport and
boarded a government jet for Tyler, Texas.

Airborne, he called Wilson Williams' boss. "I will be in Tyler
in two hours. Have a helicopter on the pad with your butt in it.
We're going to Marian, Texas to get your boy Williams out of
jail."

***

Saul glanced at the clock in the car, 2:30 in the morning, then
the long driveway to his home. A fire truck stood by with a
crew tamping out the last of the fire. Nothing was recognizable.
Blackened sticks jutted upward at odd angles. Wisps of smoke
curled away in the glare of the lights from the truck. The four-
car garage survived. The paint was badly blistered, but it was
intact.

The crewchief turned to Saul. "Are you the owner, sir?"

Saul stepped forward and to one side. "Yes, I am Saul Friedman. This is my property."

"Mr. Friedman," the crewchief continued. "We have a report that this was arson, your gate guard was shot and wounded and your family was given notice to get out in time to save their lives. A witness says that the perpetrators used military shoulder mounted rockets to hit the house 7 times in a span of 20 seconds. The police and the Fire Chief would like to talk to you as soon as possible."

Saul looked the rubble over shaking his head. "Do you know where my family and staff are right now?"

"The police have them in the Grand Rice Hotel on the expressway under guard."

"Why is that?" Saul asked jutting out his chin.

"The police are concerned that they may be in danger from the perpetrators."

"I'll check in with the police in the morning. Thank you." Saul turned back to the cars and directed them to the Grand Rice Hotel.

Muttering to himself. "I've got to get a shower and some more clothes. I've got nothing but what's on my back!"

At the Rice, Saul gave his hands a free ticket. "Get a room and new clothes. Let's have breakfast at 7 am."

Obviously, they had to wake the staff to open the clothes store off the lobby. It was inadequate. A nearby store opened after the name Saul Friedman was offered.

THE ENHANCERS

TUESDAY DECEMBER 27th

Soe, Jac and the girls slept in on Tuesday. Eight AM seemed plenty early for exercises. Annie was watching and had a big farm breakfast for them when they came in from showering. Mexican taquitos with eggs, sausage, hot sauce and fresh biscuits, coffee and OJ filled the trays. They took them into the living room to watch the news.

Local news rattled the rafters about 15 DEA operatives arrested; held in jail for unknown reasons.

Soe spit out. "Look at that crap, it's time to go public. Let's hold a press conference this morning at 12:00. That will give most of the interested parties time to get their shit together."

They all agreed. "Yes, it's time."

Jac called the local paper, radio and TV stations and the police department. He suggested that they call in national news. "The conference will be held at the Courthouse steps at 12:00."

Chief Thurmond sighed. "Finally the Enhancers have contacted us and we can get some answers to our questions."

He worked with Soe to develop the details of the press conference at the Courthouse.

***

Saul got wind of the press conference on the 9 o'clock news. He gathered his crew together and headed for Marian, Texas at high speed.

Mumbling, cursing, clenching his fists, Saul formulated a plan as they sped across Texas on I-20.

"Butch, this may be our last chance to get the Enhancers. We must kill them, every one of them. There will be a large crowd so we will be able to hide. We will mingle in the crowd towards the back." Saul pointed. "Butch, you and Lefty will have rifles to shoot together. Get the van positioned back and off to a side for a clear shot. Look the area over and get situated as quickly as possible. We will move forward when the crowd goes berserk and kill any that escape the rifle fire.

"Ralph, I don't want you to do anything unless it's absolutely necessary. You are our backup."

Saul checked his 9-MM and supply of clips. "I sure hope 'ol GrandJac is there. I'm gonna shoot his liver out if I get a chance."

***

"C'mon, let's get our stuff checked out." Soe ordered as he led the gang to the shop. "Here's spare batteries. Charge 'em. Check your outfits. I'm sure we will have a war with someone."

"Let's make plans on what and how we are going to present ourselves. Let's anticipate what might happen and who might be there."

GrandJac walked in the shop and held up his hands. "I want to present a concept to you. Please hear me out. Look at the Enhancer situation, my children. It has to be short term. National media will be upon us today. The world will see power beyond anything man has imagined.

"The world is not ready for the Enhancers. You have too much power. You have physical might that you don't even comprehend. You have mental powers still unexplored. The powers in control don't and won't allow you to exist. You are a very serious threat to their continued existence.

"If you had an army of Enhancers scattered throughout the United States, throughout the civilized world and you were unified in your goals, maybe you could survive and alter the world. But, blood would run in the streets.

"The Enhancers offer an idealized world of truth or— 'you better be good.' Who shall be the judge each time a sin is committed? Who shall mete out the punishment? Who shall judge the Enhancers? Can they be corrupted?" GrandJac spread his hands and shrugged.

"The Enhancers and the power must disappear."

Meg sat back in her chair staring into space.

With a somber mood, she spoke. "I have to agree with you, GrandJac. The Enhancers are short term. We are very idealistic in a very corrupt world. Do you think this is the only solution?"

"My solution, Meg, is theory. If everyone had the power and could administer it fairly, maybe we could have a Utopian world. Do you think that is possible?"

Soe, Jac and Carol nodded agreement. "Let's go make some more plans, gang."

Jac caught Carol's eye. "Feel any strange vibes, pumpkin?"

"I sure do. It's kinda like what Grandpaw said. 'The light at the end of the tunnel is near.'"

***

Jason Brown, the Regional Director of DEA in Oklahoma City, chartered a plane when he got the call from Weatherby and flew to Tyler. A local helicopter service was more than happy to provide a machine on stand-by.

"I better call the Marian police and get the skinny on Wilson. Weatherby will be demanding all the facts ASAP."

"No sir, this is a County Sheriff's jurisdiction. You better talk to the Sheriff, sir."

"Of course. I'm flying over from Tyler. Will be there in 30 to 45 minutes. Let me talk to Wilson Williams. I need to be prepared. Can you do that, Officer?"

Jason finally got hooked up with Wilson and collected the ear-full.

"That is just unbelievable. I'll follow-up and get everybody out."

Chief Thurmond spoke crisply. "The County Sheriff's Department brought the charges. There is nothing I can do, Mr. Brown."

Jason called the Sheriff. "This is Jason Brown. I'm Regional Director of the DEA in Oklahoma City. I'm flying to Marian as we speak. It would greatly simplify the situation if you would set a bond on my men. After all, we are both in the law enforcement business. I think this charade is some kind of misunderstanding. Can you help me, Sheriff?"

"Okay, Mr. Brown. I'll have a JP set a bond. Look for something in the $500,000 range."

Jason arranged the posting of the bond for the 15 DEA men. Wilson and his men were released at 10am.

Two rented vans driven by local agents picked them up. A trip to Wal-Mart, a change of clothes and two motel rooms provided a shower and clean up facilities.

Wilson stormed out of the shower, cursing, grabbed the phone and called an outside agent to fetch a package.

"C'mon, Wallace. Let's get to the airport and pick up our fearless leaders, Jason and Weatherby."

Thirty minutes was inadequate to explain the cumulative events and the unbelievable Cochrans and Enhancers, but it had to do.

Twelve noon was fast approaching. Very short-term plans were made with the DEA team. Wilson stood on the edge of the developing crowd to receive the special package. Wallace took it and mingled with several of his men, working towards the front of the crowd. Their objective was already in place.

***

Saul worked through the crowd to third row in front. Five of his hands mingled with the crowd near-by. Ralph stood behind Saul with a backpack slung over one shoulder. Turning carefully, causally, Saul spotted the van at the back left with the side door open. Two men sat in folding chairs seemingly enjoying the preparations from the elevated position the van provided.

Wilson turned to Jason and Mark. "There's Saul's Ralph I told you about."

"Yes, thank you, I figured that was him. I've seen Mr. Friedman on several occasions."

***

The Enhancer plan required a conference with the Police Chief and a survey of the steps before the courthouse.

The ever-voracious media had already assembled, selecting a spot in front of the ropes where the city workers were setting up a restricted area. Fortunately, it was good weather. Clear and cool, maybe 50 degrees.

***

GrandJac called Morris, Duncan and two more of his "helpers" to accompany him.

"I wouldn't miss this show for all the cats in China. This is the absolute beginning of the final phase." He mumbled as he retrieved a heavy object from his office. GrandJac moved up to the front, surveyed the crowd and selected an area near the outside of the milling people.

Turning to Morris, "I want to be able to see the show and the crowd. This looks like a good spot."

***

As expected, the newsmedia had the catbird seat in front of the ropes at the foot of the steps. The rope barricade held the crowd back about 10 feet. A flat approach to the doors to the Courthouse provided a stage for the podium. At least fifteen microphones adorned the front of the podium. Wires trailed down the steps to the media. Loudspeakers stood at each side of the apron. A 48-inch TV screen stood back and to the side of the podium with a light shield over and around it.

As 12:00 noon approached, several news announcers were standing in front of the cameras giving preliminary statements and feed-ins to the Enhancer phenomena. No new information was available. They had only what the local news had published a few days ago.

***

The chiming of the Big Ben like clock in the tower initiated the action, like a movie. The local police chief and mayor walked to the podium.

Mayor Wharton spoke with the politician's suaveness, "Good Morning." "Thank you for your interest in law enforcement." The mayor started. "We have been aided by a group of people called the Enhancers. I'll turn the program over to Chief Thurmond for further details. Thank you."

He stepped aside with a wave as the Chief moved forward. "Make the most of it Thurmond. This could cinch your reelection." The mayor whispered.

"Ladies and gentlemen, I am very pleased to bring something to you that is beyond your wildest dreams. We have been the recipients of help from a group of people called the Enhancers.

"In the last few days, your local police department has been very successful in bringing to justice several criminal perpetrators with the Enhancers help. We are very grateful. I am sure further criminals will be apprehended.

301

"We know very little about the Enhancers. They have strange powers that will surely startle you. Please be patient." He turned with a wave, looking up.

From around behind the Courthouse and near the top, the Enhancers flew out into view. Four beings clothed in black flowing coats, helmets, face shields and black clothes seemed to hang unrealistically as they slowly descended. The gasp from the crowd sounded like a huge sucking of air. Cameras spun around on tripods attempting to elevate to the black beings drifting down, holding hands with coats flaring in the wind. No skin could be seen. All was covered with black garb.

One figure stepped forward to the microphones with a flowing motion upon landing. Soe's voice boomed across the rapt crowd in a resonating roll:

"Man at one time could use all of the extra sensory powers. He enjoyed the abilities of telepathy, telekinesis, clairvoyance and control of a brilliant power. His world was the land of the Gods, Atlantis.

"Atlantis is a story brought to us by Plato of Greek times. No one has ever been able to authenticate the existence of Atlantis or develop the awesome powers of that time. As the story goes, the Atlantians were involved in a war with another nation. They chose to store the awesome power of the sun that ran their world in the ground. It exploded and their island disappeared beneath the sea.

"Remarkably, this power resides today in each of you. But it remains latent. We have developed ESP through a quirk in modern day electronics. We are no different from any of you without the Enhancer tools.

"This latent power could open up a New World; a world of peace and tranquility beyond today's concepts, beyond any man's wildest dreams. It could stop much if not all of the hate, cruelty and violence that goes on everyday in our lives. It could truly create a blissful relationship among men.

"On the other hand, it could create power and control of people farther than any government or organization has ever conceived. It is the ultimate power for controlling people. It gets in your mind, the last bastion of privacy of the human being. This is very likely difficult to comprehend or even believe. But you shall see, without doubt!"

Soe's voice rose to a roar, "WE ARE THE ENHANCERS. WE SHALL USE THESE AWESOME CAPABILITIES TO BRING A NEW LEVEL OF TRUST, LOVE AND PEACE TO THE WORLD!"

Meg stepped forward and attached wire leads to a clip on her coat.

"Please watch the screen."

Hartzog turned to his buddy, Jerry, "Have you ever seen the early movies, news coverage of Hitler in 1932? I'm from the goviment, I'm here to help you," he snickered.

Chief Thurmond began a recital as the picture developed. "We have been plagued with drug runners and dope sellers for years, corrupting our children and preying on the weak."

The picture showed scene after scene of people selling drugs, fights over drugs, receiving drug shipments, the whole gamut of the drug industry. The picture was crisp and clear depicting people in all walks of life and power in private, industry and government. Even their conversations were heard.

Chief Thurmond waved his hand at the screen. "These are not contrived scenes. These are actual scenes of people committing crimes. This is evidence we can use to arrest and convict these people and stop the drug trafficking in our area."

"Here are scenes of robberies, from gas stations, convenience stores, homes, and businesses. Car thefts to industrial spying. Again, these people can and will be arrested and brought to trial.

"This Enhancer technology can shut down crime. It will not be committed because of fear of reprisal by the law. We could all become very honest citizens. We could unlock our doors and walk in the streets without fear."

Hartzog turned to Jerry, "Buddy, I'm impressed! This is everything Jessica said it was. This is gonna be one hell of a story!"

Meg disconnected the wires as the group stepped forward with Soe and Meg slightly in the forefront.

Meg held up her hand for quiet. Slowly the murmurs declined to absolute stillness. Suddenly, a beautiful music entered everyone's head and through their eyes they saw a dream place of beauty and tranquility. They felt as one with each other, completely trusting and loving. The feeling lasted about a minute. The crowd gave out a huge gasp and cry for more.

Meg spoke again. "The most startling of these powers is the awesome, brute energy available at your fingertips."

A small car drifted over the heads of the crowd and floated on the steps. It appeared to be from a wrecking yard. The cameras were all aimed at it as it floated upward over the crowd to 1000 feet in the air above all the buildings in the area. Suddenly a bolt of white light flashed from Meg and Carol's outstretched hands to the car. The car vaporized in a blinding white flash and a sonic boom. The concussion drove the air downward onto the assemblage with such force that many were shaken and stumbled. The wind swirled around the Enhancers. Their coats blew in the wind.

Meg and Soe moved two more steps forward with arms raised. Two rifle shots rang out. They fell backwards onto the concrete apron, down, unmoving.

Carol's hand pointed to the van as white fire streaked across the gap. The rifles exploded in the hands of Butch and Lefty. Shrapnel from the explosions ripped through their chests. They fell in a huge puddle of blood, jerking and kicking in their final death throes.

The crowd fell to the ground screaming and yelling. Some ran, ducking down.

A DEA man stepped up behind Ralph and shot him with a tranquilizer dart. As he crumpled, two DEA agents grabbed him by the arms moving quickly through the mass confusion.

Looking neither left nor right, Saul stepped forward pointing a 9-MM automatic at Jac and Carol who were bending over Soe and Meg.

From the left side of the frantic mob, a tall 'cowboy' in a western hat moved quickly towards Saul, leveled a Colt .45 single action revolver letting the hammer fall. Wham! White smoke belched from the ancient piece delivering a heavy lead slug into Saul's chest knocking him to the ground.

Camera crews spun frantically trying to get the wild events on tape.

Ten DEA men held guns on Saul's men. Nothing else was going to happen without death.

Bending over Saul's bleeding body, GrandJac dropped the Colt .45 on his chest. "Saul, this gun killed several of your past tribe back in the 1800's. I thought you might like it as a souvenir since yours burned last night."

Saul rose up on one elbow, gasping for a breath. "I guess we are even. Remember your wife————, Ebola! I'll see you in hell, you sorry bastard."

He fell back in a pool of blood with his eyes staring up into the blue sky.

GrandJac bent over him, roughly pulling his face towards him. "I wish Jac had killed you in 1868!"

The fearless leaders of the community, Chief Thurmond and the mayor had lunged behind the podium flat on the concrete. Peering around the flimsy wooden stand, Thurmond eyed a large pool of blood welling from the soaked black clothing of the Enhancers. The two other Enhancers knelt beside their fallen comrades shaking with sobs.

Four men dressed in western attire rushed forward with stretchers, loaded the two Enhancers, picked them up, disappearing in the confusion. Thurmond waved from the concrete ineffectually trying to get the Enhancers attention.

An army of policemen charging forward from the Courthouse provided cover for Thurmond and the mayor to rise with some dignity.

"Get control of the crowds, Sergeant, and bring the media tapes to my office for review." Thurmond barked.

Sighing heavily, speaking to no one in particular, it seemed, GrandJac stared at the inert Saul Friedman, his lifelong enemy. "Yes, you will rot in hell!"

Morris reached out to GrandJac, hesitantly. "What do you mean, GrandJac?"

"Another world, another time, Morris. Let's go."

Chaos continued to rule. People pointed, screaming, trying to tell their friends, the police, any one who would look their way about the gun battle. Others huddled talking on cellphones, waving their arms emphasizing the events even though their listeners couldn't see. Cameras continued to spin trying to capture every last bit of emotion for the jabbering commentators.

Several witnesses estimated another 20 minutes elapsed before the police were able attain a semblance of order. Of course, the news commentators continued to mouth the tragedy in the best hysterical hype they could muster.

The 1 pm news exploded onto the world with the tragedy of the Enhancers. 'Breaking news' spun across the screens shutting down regular programming. All of the videotapes had been edited, clipped, formatted and streamlined by 2 pm to cover the Marian County Courthouse Enhancer exposure and massacre with as much hysteria as could be emoted.

Specific scene clips, not necessarily in chronological order were used to capture the audience. Most networks started with the camera panning into the beautiful blue sky with white puffy clouds. Then from nowhere a small car seen on telephoto lens exploded 1000 feet above. Very popular, the descending Enhancers in black garb, floating to the ground holding hands followed. Soe's speech was clipped to the last resounding statement. The exposure of crimes was edited because it was almost incomprehensible and poorly filmed. All networks liked the crowd swaying in rhythm, holding their heads with their hands over the ears. Of course, the shooting of the four Enhancers, blood pooling on the concrete apron, the police gunning down the shooters in a spray of 123 shots, and then, the blatant gunning of Saul Friedman by Wilson Williams, DEA Director of the Dallas office.

Commentary by various scientific experts, retired military and government personnel and Dr. Alfredo Esposinza from the famed ESP Rhine Institute were used as fill-ins.

Mayor Wharton made his career with an eloquent summation speech of the world's loss of a new era of peace as he stood over the bodies of the Enhancers being carried away on stretchers. "We do not know, we will never know what we have lost here today. It could very well have been the salvation of mankind!"

***

At the ranch, GrandJac sat heavily in his chair watching the news as it repeated the story. Annie brought coffee and sat on the arm of GrandJac's big leather chair trying to console him. GrandJac patted her arm as he stared into the distance.

His thoughts drifted back to his wife's death 25 years ago and the agony she had suffered. She had died of a mysterious aliment that the doctors could not define. Excruciating pain, bleeding from multiple spots on her body, crying for deliverance haunted GrandJac to this day. It was later defined as the Ebola virus from Africa. Guilt plagued him for years because all his money and power could not help in the one ultimate crisis of his life. Five years ago, he had found Annie. He reached peace with himself through the loving care and attention she bestowed upon him.

Today, in a flicker of an eye, more tragedy struck and took his children at the apex of their young lives.

The cryptic words of the dying Saul may have finally shed light upon his wife's death. Again, Saul was the root of misery in his life. It was small solace that the evil of Saul Friedman died today by his hand.

GrandJac stood, hugged Annie as he clicked off the TV and walked out of the house. The sun across the pasture presented a beautiful sunset with the high cirrus clouds glowing red streaking towards the west. An idle thought formed, *Another Norther is coming. The end is not far away!*

GrandJac walked to the shop lab where Soe and the kids had worked. Hand on the door, one last glimpse of the glowing western sky, *Maybe I can find solace in their last work place.*

Carol jumped in his arms screaming, "Surprise, surprise!"

Stumbling back against the doorjamb, GrandJac gasped, trying to comprehend what could have happened. Effortlessly,

Stumbling back against the doorjamb, GrandJac gasped, trying to comprehend what could have happened. Effortlessly, he floated to a chair, still holding the soft squeezable Carol. Jac, Soe and Meg came forward to hug GrandJac while all laughed amid crying.

GrandJac just stood gaping. Finally as the reality sunk in, he slapped his leg. "By God, you pulled it off!" Relief swept over him as he exclaimed. "That was a fantastic performance. I really liked the Williams scene where he gunned down 'ol Saul. That's some payback for poisoning the janitor.

"The news media just ate it up. They'll chew on this for a long time. The world will know what the Enhancer power can do and they will watch for it. Maybe we will get a little respite."

Stepping away from his children, GrandJac sighed heavily and dropped his arms to his sides, "Well, what's next, kids?"

"Soe and Meg are going to disappear and Carol and I are getting married." Jac stated, standing by Carol, "And I will continue with my medical career."

GrandJac crossed his arms as he let his head drop, a gasping sigh rushed from his lips. "Dear God—, I wish you could, son, but I think you are going to have to go into the military instead. The CIA captured Ralph and carried him off with whatever gear he had. They will exploit the power somewhere, somehow. It's your destiny to go into the military."

GrandJac stared down at the floor and finally raised his head. A knowing glance at Soe, then he locked eyes with Jac.

Carol and Meg chimed in together, pleading. "We can find Ralph and disarm him, GrandJac. We can do this soon and Jac can be a doctor."

GrandJac shook his head, "You can look and search, but you won't find him or where the CIA is working. They have vast resources at their disposal and they will hide very well because they know you will try to find them. They won't fall for the TV scene of the Enhancers going down. In fact, they will try to find you and kill you. Because you are the only ones who know who and what they are and what they have."

Stepping to the bench, he placed his hands on the top. "As a matter of preparation, I have new identities for each of you, so you can disappear into the mad world out there. Jac, you should go into the military very soon under your new name. Each of you has a complete new life ahead of you and you should leave now. The details are in the folders in the house. Pick them up. Take a car here and disappear. The CIA will be snooping very soon. I had them prepared anticipating such an ending."

Meg, Carol and Jac looked at each other in stunned disbelief. GrandJac was way ahead of them in anticipating the Enhancer phenomena and the end result.

Soe nodded, looking at GrandJac. "Yes, I believe you are right."

Carol threw up her hands. "We don't even have time for a party to celebrate or anything, do we GrandJac?"

"No, you really don't," GrandJac replied. "Get your butt in gear and go!"

Carol cried out. "This is terribly anticlimactic and unfair. We have worked hard to bring the Enhancers forward to the public and try to do good."

Meg spoke after a long silence. "We were not organized, prepared or in an anticipating mode to really do a good job, thus you see the result. GrandJac warned us of the powers to be and what they would do to stifle the concept, try to steal it. We are beaten because the power behind the CIA will hunt us down and kill us. We don't have that kind of firepower. I think we should disappear and watch events closely. We may still have an opportunity to surface in a more organized team and bring the concept forward. But it's going to take a hell of a lot more planning than what we put into this attempt. I think we will need a lot more soldiers like us the next time."

GrandJac nodded absently to Meg and turned to Jac, "Son, you have two years, maybe two and a half in the military before the next move. I would love for you two to have a child to further the Cochran family chain."

Jac stared at GrandJac. "You are on some agenda that I don't have any awareness of. It's like you know the future. Can you tell me or us anything about it?"

GrandJac shook his head. "No I really can't; because it is only a possibility. I have information that is beyond anybody's imagination. But it may not come to pass. I can only prepare you as best I can. That is why you are a doctor, an engineer and soon to be a military war machine."

GrandJac spread his arms. "Tell me goodbye. You have a car in your name, money in banks and all that you need to establish yourself in a new life far from here. We will work out a contact schedule and procedure through your bank accounts in the future. Come, let us begin the journey before the CIA interferes."

Carol blurted out. "CRAP, this is depressing. We haven't won anything. We have lost the war before it began! Now we're running off into the dark and hiding!"

***

As they walked outside in the dark, Morris approached them. "We have visitors."

He motioned towards a car that had parked on the hill across from their gate. Someone was watching them with nightvision glasses.

All the disappointment and frustration of today's events poured forth in Carol's actions. She turned towards the car, lashing out with an extended arm. White fire flashed across the ground, 600 yards to the top of the hill, and lifted the car in the air several hundred feet sailing it to the ground in front of them with a crash. The operative sprawled at their feet as the door flew open.

Tommy Silva, the CIA agent from Washington DC, cowered, holding his arm up to protect himself. "Don't hurt me. Don't hurt me. They made me do it—, please."

Meg swept his brain in an instant. "He's our old buddy from the CIA with instructions to finger us for a major hit if and when we leave the property. A DEA hit team is at the edge of town fully prepared to blow us away."

Carol chirped, "That sure didn't take very long. They're on us like stink on shit. I do believe a serious ass kickin is gonna be needed to get an attitude adjustment. Meg, I'm for it, how bout you?"

Meg swirled up in the air, yelling. "Your suckin hind tit right now, Blondie."

In a blink, Carol lifted the car high in the air where it exploded in a brilliant ball of fire that could be seen for miles. Meg wiped Tommy's brain to 10 years old and blew him onto the road a mile down from the gate.

"The righteous hand of God shall smite thee." GrandJac spoke loudly with a wave of his hand.

Coats snapping in the wind, Meg and Carol lifted into the air disappearing at a high rate of speed towards town, across the fields. "Vengeance shall be mine." Carol echoed.

***

Three cars parked at the convenience store on FM 1495. They had been there for 30 minutes. The store manager watched them carefully, prepared to shoot and call the police after if they chose rob him. From the glare of the storefront lights, it appeared that several men were in each car. Some were smoking, some sitting quietly, waiting for a cue, maybe.

"This is going to be too much me, I'm calling the cops for a drive-by."

Something happened. One of the cars cranked and drove away towards the country. Curiosity forced the manager to slip the 9 MM into his belt and step outside. "Just as I thought, something is going to happen." The car drove possibly 300 yards and spun around squealing the tires, accelerating back to the store.

Hanson, the manager, pivoted into the store, grabbing the phone, dialing 911. "Here they come!" he screamed. "They're gonna shoot up the store." At 50 yards, the attacking car had all windows down and automatic weapons firing. Hanson stared in disbelief. They fired at the other two cars! Those two cars returned the fire in a hail of 9 MM slugs until the cars crashed shooting each other. They're on fire. Bring the fire department!"

Drive-bys and other gawkers from the near-by freeway parked along the farm-to-market road to see the burning bodies. Police and fire trucks, sirens screaming and lights flashing, crashed through two gawkers parked in the road. Water from the tanker truck sprayed on the red hot metal sending clouds of white steam into the air. Firemen rushed in with dry powder extinguishers trying to protect the men in the cars. Through the flames, the bodies twisted in agony much to the horror of the gawkers. But none turned away. This was a once in a lifetime thrill to tell their friends.

"I saw it! I was there! God, it was horrible! You shoulda seen the bodies twitching. They all burned to a crispy. No one got out, ugh, ugh! The fire truck rammed two cars and totaled them. Wow, what a show!"

The efficiency of the fire department was evident. In 15 minutes the police poked into the ashes, trying to find ID's, anything to explain the tragedy.

***

The trip back to the ranch was anything but a victory lap, but the big boys had come to play.

A quick preview from Carol shocked Jac. *Nine men dead, murdered by this power! It's just incomprehensible that I'm balled up in something like this. And the girl I love is the instigator. We have plunged over the edge of chaos into the age of GrandJac. Kill first, assess the damage. I have no alternative. I'm committed.*

Facing GrandJac, Soe, Jac and the 'hands,' the girls stated in unison. "In the future, we will be playing hard ball. Let's get the good-byes going and look into the future for what it might bring!"

THE QUARK EFFECT

Blackmar spins a fascinating tale of intrigue wrapped around
ESP powers acquired from electronics. If you enjoyed *The
Enhancers,* you won't want to miss the sequel that finally
exposes GrandJac's strange tale and the Déjà vu that has
gripped Jac in, *The Quark Effect.* Turn the page for excerpts
from this provocative new novel. Soon available from GEB
Publishing.

As a final word, Colonel Halley stood at ease with his hands crossed behind his back. "You have been selected as our top Marines for this mission. I have every confidence that you will carry it out to the letter. I'm proud to give you Second Lt. James Arnold Chaney as your team leader. Pack your gear and prepare to leave at 2000 hours tonight. All communications are sealed; no one is to talk to anyone. This operation is NITEOWL."

The men gathered around Jac. "Hey man, congratulations on the promotion, I'm glad you were chosen. This sounds like it's going to be fun!"

Jac was completely caught off guard, first, the promotion and team leader announcement and then the blackout. He returned to base quarters, packed his gear and suited up for full military combat.

***

First Lt. Stromberg with the quartermaster group put his team with the NITEOWLs and helped them pack their kits. He gave a lengthy briefing on the supplies in the three large crates that would drop with them.

A Lt. Caraway briefed them on the terrain and where they would be dropped. "You will be dropped on the north side of a ridge of hills out of sight and out of earshot from the camp. You will have 5 miles to trek from your camp to the weapons camp. The camp is an old military base from the 80's. It's located in a valley with low hills creating a cradle-like hollow. Heavy jungle grows down to the cleared areas and the old landing strip. You will be able to reconnoiter down through the jungle and approach close enough for good visual and audible coverage. Remember, each of you is equipped with all the latest gear, armament, communications and protection. All supplies are in the crates. They must be retrieved upon landing."

The next four hours consisted of frantic hustling, screaming and cursing getting organized, packed, and staged for 2000 hours.

The squad stood beside their gear and the three crates of supplies looking at a new type of transport. The new C-155

Vaporjet flew at 400 knots. For drop activities, huge sponsons folded out of the wings enabling it to drift at 120 knots with virtually no noise. It was a great stealth drop plane for nighttime operations.

***

Jac stepped out of the barracks for the last time. Lt. Stromberg caught his arm and pulled him into an adjoining office. The lights were off but a beam shown through the window from the staging area at the plane.

"Wait here a moment, Lt., someone to see you." Stromberg left the room.

A tall shadowy figure stepped from a dark corner and spoke softly. "Now you know what it was and is all about, Jac, my son." Jac recognized GrandJac immediately from his voice and his tall starlet shape.

Jac gasped, "What are you doing here, GrandJac?"

"I have come to tell you the rest of the story, the one you have always asked and wondered about."

Jac stuttered, "I don't think we have the time."

"I know, son," GrandJac said softly, "It really couldn't have been any other way." GrandJac was crying, tears streaming down his weather-beaten face. "Son, I couldn't change it, I did my level best. This is your chance and you will have to make it happen, you will have to stop it once and for all."

Jac was groping for his grandfather. "What in the world do you mean, Grandpa?"

He grabbed GrandJac and pulled him to him in a tight embrace against his armor.

GrandJac spoke as if the words were doom, "Take this and put it in your kit. You must guard it as if it were your life. It will tell all you need to know. One last thing, you must be last to jump. Go out with the last crate of supplies."

He turned away choking on a sob. "Please, God, be with my son." He was gone in the shadows of the buildings.

Jac stood stoned. *What an absolutely wild scene.* Thoughts tumbled through his head, *how did GrandJac get on the Base and to the building to see him? What did he mean? Why was he crying? What is the package he gave me?"*

He looked out the door and saw Lt. Stromberg waving him on. Jac ran out, up the ramp and into the huge cargo hold. He moved forward to the front of the hold past the crates where his team was strapped in. The large ramp/door was rising quickly and closing, obliterating the lights and the last view of the United States.

***

The engines whined up in rpm as the plane moved rapidly away. A dim overhead light shone down on the crates strapped to the floor and the men lined up along one side. Jac looked at his men, his team, he was proud to be leading them on their first mission. He vowed that it would be a successful one.

Jac slid his face shield down and activated his night vision spotter as he surveyed the cargo and his men. The area was illuminated in a bright yellow light as if it were daylight. Something seemed out of place; he panned down the line of soldiers and counted ten rather than nine. Jac jerked up his face gear. *What is going on, who is the last man on the row?*

Jac addressed the group, stridently. "Countdown."

Private Henderson sitting next to him, bellowed out. "Private Henderson, present and accounted for, Sir." Each soldier spoke out loudly identifying himself. The last man yelled, "Private Rubin Friedman, present and accounted for, Sir."

Jac snorted, *Where did this man come from?* He wasn't part of the team in any way in the last 4 weeks. He had never heard of him. Jac addressed him, "Private Friedman, when were you assigned to this team?"

"Sir, I was assigned 20 minutes ago, Sir."

"Where have you been for the last 4 weeks?"

"Sir, I have been here at Camp Quantico training for parachute jumping, jungle warfare, night surveillance and equipment orientation, Sir."

"Have you been briefed on our mission, Private Friedman?"

"No Sir, I haven't, Sir," Friedman bellowed.

"I will brief you on the ground, Private. We are jumping at 0300 hours into jungle in Guatemala. You will be the first out, locate the crates as they come down and communicate with us as we drop. Thorough briefing will be held after we establish base camp."

Private Friedman responded. "Yes Sir."

As the C-155 descended through 10,000 feet, Jac got the green light. He ordered all men to check their parachutes, attach their snap lines to the overhead trailing wire. He walked around the crates and checked their release mechanisms and chutes.

He announced aloud, "All systems go."

The Captain turned on the red light and started counting the altimeter readings out loud. They would jump at 1200 feet on the north side of the low hills in a natural clearing. The copilot was watching a GPS screen with coordinates and giving directions to the Captain. The Captain throttled the big vapor jets back to a whisper and the massive sponsons moved forward out of the wings creating additional lift for low speed. The boxcar settled into a long descending glideplane. An eerie high-pitched scream pealed off the extended sponsons as they caused vapor condensation leaving a white trailing plume behind the wings.

Jac looked at his watch, it was 0259 and counting, they were dead on target and time. The huge rear door and ramp had already been lowered. Jac and three men released the crate latches. They rolled easily back to the ramp.

The copilot signaled the Captain and he yelled, "Jump," over the intercom.

Private Friedman stepped out the door and felt the snap line jerk his release on his parachute. It furled past his head in an instant and billowed out in a beautiful bowl. Swinging his chute, looking up, he could see the others trailing out and the three crates with two large parachutes on each one.

2nd Lt. James Arnold Chaney gulped a breath and stepped out into oblivion as the last crate dropped away.

THE QUARK EFFECT

In one instant Jac was looking down towards the dark earth and the last crate's chutes with his night vision. The next instant he was bathed in blinding white light. Fortunately, he had his face shield down and the lens darkened in 1/30,000 of a second to protect his eyes. Even so, he was momentarily blinded as if he had negligently glanced at a welding arc.

Slowly his eyes adjusted. It was daylight, bright daylight.

It was unbelievable! *What the hell had happened?*

The last crate's chutes were still below him and he was dropping rapidly onto a grassy plain that extended to the horizon. There were no signs of the other chutes. Scanning rapidly in a circle brought no sign of his team. The radio was quiet as if off; no responses on any channel.

In the distance, he could see what looked like several old time wagons pulled by mules. There were four lined up in a square and horsemen were riding around them shooting at them. He could see the white smoke from the guns.

An idle thought drifted across his dazed mind, *That's unusual; they must be black powder guns.*